PASTU

Julia Williams has always made up stories in her head, and until recently she thought everyone else did too. She grew up in London, one of eight children, including a twin sister, and now lives in Surrey with her husband and four daughters. For more information on Julia Williams, please visit her website at www.juliawilliamsauthor.com

Visit www.AuthorTracker.co.uk for exclusive updates on Julia Williams

JULIA WILLIAMS

Pastures New

AVON

This novel is entirely a work of fiction.
The names, characters and incidents portrayed in it are
the work of the author's imagination. Any resemblance to
actual persons, living or dead, events or localities is
entirely coincidental.

AVON

A division of HarperCollins*Publishers*
77–85 Fulham Palace Road,
London W6 8JB

www.harpercollins.co.uk

A Paperback Original 2007

5

Copyright © Julia Williams 2007

Julia Williams asserts the moral right to
be identified as the author of this work

A catalogue record for this book is
available from the British Library

ISBN: 978-1-84756-008-7

Typeset in Minion by Palimpsest Book Production Limited,
Grangemouth, Stirlingshire

Printed and bound in Great Britain by
Clays Ltd, St Ives plc

Mixed Sources
Product group from well-managed
forests and other controlled sources
www.fsc.org Cert no. SW-COC-1806
© 1996 Forest Stewardship Council

FSC is a non-profit international organisation established to promote the
responsible management of the world's forests. Products carrying the FSC
label are independently certified to assure consumers that they come
from forests that are managed to meet the social, economic and
ecological needs of present and future generations.

Find out more about HarperCollins and the environment at
www.harpercollins.co.uk/green

*For Joseph Henry Moffatt and John Douglas (Roger)
Williams, for sharing their wisdom*

PART ONE
Forever Autumn

In the allotment:
Harvest the crops, dig over the soil, and prepare the ground for winter.

State of the heart:
Barren, cold, dead.

CHAPTER ONE

'There's a fire on the anti-clockwise section of the M25, just before the junction with the M1, and the traffic's backing up to junction 26, so do avoid that if you can . . .'

Hopefully that will have cleared by the time I get back, thought Amy, as Sally Traffic made way for a debate about gun crime. She'd always hated driving on the motorway, and never more so than now, when she had to do it alone.

Oh Jamie, I miss you so much . . .

The thought came unbidden and unprompted, and she blinked back the sudden tears.

This would never do.

Pull yourself together, girl, Amy admonished herself sternly, straightening her slight shoulders and gripping the steering wheel tighter. If she really was going to make this move, she had to be strong. She had to. Hold on to that thought . . .

At least it was a gloriously sunny day, and the soft undulating Essex countryside was looking its best. Field after field of sun-drenched corn. Thanks to the rotten summer, the harvest was late, but here and there bales of hay indicated that it was finally underway. And the smell of burning stubble was a reminder that summer really was drawing in. Constable country, Amy thought to herself. She wouldn't be surprised to find a haywain round the next corner.

The journey from North London had taken much longer than she had envisaged, but eventually Amy found herself driving over the little humpbacked bridge that, according to her map, marked the boundary between the Essex and Suffolk sides of the pretty market town of Nevermorewell. A feeling of excitement grew in her as she pulled the car into the picturesque high street, dwarfed by a large Norman church, and flanked on either side by tiny quaint shops with mock Tudor cladding. It was perfect. Just what she was looking for.

Amy pulled into a parking place – amazingly there were several empty ones. So different from Barnet, where she would have been driving around fruitlessly for hours before finding a spot miles away from home. That had to be a good omen.

She took a deep breath and stared at herself in the rear-view mirror. She teased out her fair curls so they didn't look quite so tangled, and put on a bit of lippy – bright red to boost her confidence. She rarely wore makeup – Jamie had always said her light natural complexion didn't need any, and now she didn't see the point. But lippy was good. Lippy was part of the mask she needed to face each day. The mask she needed right now to persuade Josh of the wisdom of this move.

It didn't help that she was so racked with guilt about it, that she wasn't one hundred per cent convinced herself.

'Right, Josh,' she smiled brightly at her five-year-old son, who was sucking his thumb and looking out of the window. 'We're here. And we're going to look at some new houses for us. Isn't that fun?'

'Is Granny coming too?' asked Josh.

'No, sweetheart,' said Amy. 'You remember, I told you. Granny's staying in her house, and we're going to have a new house. Won't that be nice?'

'Oh,' said Josh, his face puckering a little. 'But we won't see Granny very much, will we?'

'No, but she can come and visit any time she likes,' said Amy, more brightly than she felt. Damn. She thought she'd squared that with him. But then, he was very close to Mary, it was only natural he would feel the loss of her.

And she of him. Amy's stomach went into spasm as she recalled the conversation she'd had with her mother-in-law a few weeks earlier.

'So you're serious about this move then?'

As Amy was in the middle of packing up a pile of books at the time, it was hard to resist a sarcastic remark, but she bit her lip and said, 'Yes, Mary, I am.'

'What about Josh?' Mary had sniffed. 'He's not going to know anyone in the country.'

'Children are very adaptable,' Amy had snapped back. Mary had touched a nerve, as it was what Amy herself had agonised about over and over again.

'That may be so,' Mary had replied flatly, 'but it's such a long way.'

5

'I know,' Amy had said. 'And I'm sorry.'

'But that's not going to stop you, is it?' The comment had been barbed, and hit home as it was intended to. Amy had flinched, but held firm.

'No, Mary, it's not,' she'd replied, wishing beyond all measure that there was an easy way of doing this, an easy way of creating some distance from her memories.

Sighing, she got Josh out of the car, and peered down at the map the estate agents had given her. According to it, their office should be on the corner.

'Come on, Josh,' she said, taking his hand, 'it's this way.'

They were just coming up to a little cartway when Josh let go of Amy's hand.

'Hey, cool!' he said, running towards the toy shop on the other side to look at the Spiderman poster in the window.

'Josh! Come back!' shouted Amy.

At that moment a motorbike came roaring up the cartway.

'Josh!' screamed Amy.

The motorbike braked and swerved, the rider just about avoiding Josh and retaining control.

'Josh, are you okay?' Amy ran to her son and took him in her arms, trembling violently. 'You never, ever run off like that again, do you hear?'

Josh burst into tears – whether because of the telling-off or the fright he had had, Amy wasn't sure. But he was all right. She took a deep breath. That was all that mattered.

'Just what the hell did you think you were doing?'

she screamed at the rider, fear turning to fury.

'I could say the same thing about you,' spat out the rider, taking off his helmet to reveal dark hair, brown eyes and a strong, chiselled face, which would have been stern if it were not lightened by a ready smile. 'Your son ran across the road.'

'You were going too fast.' Amy's tone was accusing.

'I was doing less than twenty,' replied the rider. 'Otherwise I wouldn't have been able to stop.'

They glared at each other.

'Is your son okay?' The rider glanced at Josh, who was squirming out of Amy's grasp.

'No thanks to you,' snapped Amy.

'I'm sorry to have given you a fright,' said the rider. 'And I'm glad your son is all right, really I am. But you shouldn't let him run off like that.'

Amy couldn't speak. This stranger was right. Her moment of inattention had nearly got her son killed. She nodded mutely. Tears pricked her eyes. What if the bike had been going faster? She would have lost Josh as well as Jamie.

As if sensing her change of mood, the rider gently said, 'Look, no harm done, eh?' He squatted down next to Josh, and added, 'Hey, tiger, you make sure you hold your mum's hand really tight when you cross the road next time. You promise?'

'I promise,' mumbled Josh.

The rider got up, climbed back on his bike, and roared off up the road.

'Who was that man, Mummy?' Josh asked.

'No one,' said Amy, as she watched the departing

bike, wondering why a stranger's moment of kindness had made her feel so lonely. 'Come on,' she said, rallying herself. 'Let's go and find our new home.'

'And this is the garden . . .' The estate agent motioned Amy towards the rickety wooden door leading from the kitchen. Josh, who had been trailing behind them, immediately perked up and pushed his way forwards. Amy took a deep breath. It was still going to be a tough call selling Josh this move, and so far he had been deeply unimpressed, but a garden might just swing it. The shared patch of earth that passed for a garden in their two-bedroom flat in Barnet didn't amount to much, and Josh was desperate to have somewhere to kick a ball.

'It's stuck,' Josh said, disappointed. The door seemed to have swollen from the recent rain and was rather stiff.

'Here, let me.' The estate agent, whom Amy had silently christened Smarmy Simon, had a go. He really had to tug it, but eventually, with a rather worrying rattle, the door opened and they all trooped outside.

Amy knew she should be concerned about details like that. Jamie would have been making a list by now of all the things that were wrong with the place. But she couldn't – not with the tingling feeling of excitement that had been growing inside her as Smarmy Simon showed her round. It was a long time since she had felt that mixture of hope and anticipation.

The house was perfect. It could have been made for her and Josh. A Victorian terrace, full of character as requested. Three bedrooms, so more than enough room for the pair of them. The downstairs wasn't huge, and the bathroom was inconveniently next door to the kitchen, as was the case in all these old terraces, but it didn't matter. There were marble fireplaces, and real wood floors. The kitchen was oak throughout. It was quaint. Even the little archway that joined the house onto its neighbour was attractive. Like the rest of the house, it had charm. It was the house she and Jamie had always dreamed of.

Don't go there, she admonished herself, reciting the mantra that she had long since perfected to retain her sanity as she emerged into the sunlit garden. It was a bit overgrown, but someone had evidently tended it well in the past. Amy spotted lobelia tumbling out of a couple of cracked earthenware pots, and down one side of a whitewashed wall the honeysuckle was going wild, though beginning to look a little past its sell-by date. There were marigolds in the flowerbeds – self-sown, probably, as it didn't look as though anyone had planted bedding plants there for a while. They were nestled with wild poppies and nasturtiums. It was beautiful, and Amy longed to start work on it immediately.

'If you'll notice, at the end of the garden,' Smarmy Simon was saying, 'there's a gate that leads onto the allotments. I believe the owner still pays rent on hers, and if you were interested she probably wouldn't have any objection to you using it.'

'May I?' Amy asked, pointing at the gate.

'Oh, yes, of course,' said Smarmy Simon. 'It's open. No one bothers to lock things much around here.' His phone started to ring. 'Will you excuse me for a minute?' He answered it while waving her on down the path.

As Amy opened the gate, she had to restrain herself from letting rip to whoops of delight. Josh ran round and round in excited circles, shouting loudly. Amy tried to shush him – there didn't appear to be any other children on the allotments, and she didn't want to irritate people – but his enthusiasm was infectious. It was perfect, absolutely perfect.

From the road, she would have had no idea this was here. The allotments spread out before her, a tiny green oasis in the middle of a small but busy market town. They were alive with the sound of birdsong, and looked well cared for. Presently, being the middle of the day, they were mainly empty. She heard the sound of a mower in the distance, and was startled by the appearance of a rather hairy-looking man, dressed in black leather, who appeared to be talking to something in a bucket.

'There you are, me beauties,' he was muttering, 'have I got a treat for you.'

Passing by his plot, a ramshackle affair with gnarled fruit trees protected by netting, and strange wooden contraptions that Amy supposed were homemade compost heaps, she and Josh wandered down a wide path. This was glorious, quite glorious.

She could see another man pausing from digging up vegetables on one of the other plots. A black Labrador sat at his side, panting in the midday sun.

10

The man had obviously been exerting himself – he had taken his shirt off, and was swigging some water. There was something vaguely familiar about him. He leaned on his spade for a moment, before returning to his digging. Amy turned away.

This place, it was wonderful. When she had seen the details of the house Amy had had no idea it backed onto allotments, and it was the icing on the cake. She squinted in the sun, taking in the beauty of her surroundings. There were blackberries ripening in the late August sunshine, and beans, tomatoes and pota-toes all coming into fruition. The odd hut was dotted about, and some plots seemed to consist of fruit trees. It had been a poor summer – today was one of the few hot days they'd had – but the trees seemed laden with fruit anyway. There was a sense of abundance, and ripeness – the time for harvesting near. Amy couldn't help the catch in her throat, as she thought about how much Jamie would have loved this. Autumn had always been his favourite time of year – a golden time to catch his golden girl he had used to tease her. They had met in the autumn, nearly fourteen years ago, the early days of their courtship punctuated with long country walks crunching their way through leaf-strewn fields. If they had only been able to do this together.

Together. They would never do anything together again. A hard, familiar knot tightened in her stomach. It was nearly two years ago now, but the thought of never seeing Jamie again was still enough to take her breath away. She had promised herself she would be strong for Josh, but it took all her self-control not to

11

let out the raw pain, which she concealed so well these days. She was determined to leave all that behind her. This was a new start for her and Josh. A new beginning, a way forward to slough off the pain of the past.

She took a deep breath and stared around her once again. She and Jamie had always dreamed of decamping to the countryside and living in an old farmhouse. A memory forced its way into her mind – a snapshot of a perfect day on a long weekend, not far from here, a sunny day in late summer, much like this, visiting Amy's Auntie Grace in Aldeburgh.

Jamie strode ahead of her through fields of golden corn, with Josh on his back. The sun shone, but the air was crisp and bracing, a fresh wind coming from the sea.

'Isn't this perfect?' Jamie shouted into the wind as it whipped his hair, his eyes alight with laughter.

'We should come and live here,' Amy said from behind a camera, taking a photo to capture the moment.

'We'd need a big house,' Jamie said. 'For all of Josh's brothers and sisters.'

'And a big garden,' Amy laughed. 'With a vegetable patch.'

'And we'd have to have a dog.'

'We could keep chickens,' offered Amy.

'I'd rather have a goat,' replied Jamie with a smile.

'Now you're just being silly.' Amy punched him on the shoulder, and he grabbed her hands and pulled her to him.

'Still, it would be nice,' she said.

'Wouldn't it just,' said Jamie, kissing her. 'One day, I promise you, one day . . .'

It was the photo from that day, which she still kept beside the bed, that had made her determined to make this move. In the early days, when she had cried herself to sleep every night, she could hardly bear to look at it. But of late, she had found the picture comforting. As if he were still with her, somehow. She couldn't live the dream with Jamie, but maybe she could do it for him.

Amy had havered for months before taking the plunge. It was Auntie Grace who finally proved the catalyst. Actually a great-aunt, Auntie Grace had lived grumpily alone for many years in the depths of Suffolk. She wasn't an easy person, but Amy didn't have much family, so she had dutifully visited from time to time, though admittedly after Jamie had died, when every day had been such a trial, just getting up was difficult on some days, so the visits had tailed off. On the last occasion, a year ago, Grace had fixed her with a beady eye, and said, 'It seems tough now, you know, but it will get better. Remember my motto: Always look forward. Never back.'

Amy had taken no notice of her at the time, but when, after Grace's not unexpected demise at the age of eighty-nine several months earlier, she learned that her aunt had left her a considerable sum of money, it seemed like a sign. Jamie had died so suddenly, so young, he had left no will, and Amy had struggled to keep up with the mortgage payments ever since. Mary had been fantastic, prepared to babysit Josh at the drop of a hat, helping out so Amy didn't have to pay childcare fees for the whole week, pushing Amy to carry on with the gardening course she had started before Jamie's death, coming to the rescue when money was especially tight. Amy owed her a huge debt, both financial and emotional. Guilt flared in her chest once more at depriving Mary of Josh.

But now, fortunately, she had enough money to pay off the debts Jamie had left behind and even have some left over. Amy had finished her course, and she could actually afford to stop teaching and forge out a new career as she had always planned to do when Jamie was alive. Maybe it *was* time to look forward and not back. Living round the corner from Mary, whose grief had taken the form of a kind of suffocating blanket covering both Amy and Josh, she'd never be able to do that. Besides, she and Jamie had always talked of coming out this way. If only she could persuade Mary it was the right thing for them to do.

Apart from her brother Danny, who lived in Surrey, and Auntie Grace, Jamie and Mary had been her only family for years now. Her own mother had moved to the States when Amy was at college, and she and Danny had no idea where their father was. Amy's parents had split up when she was fourteen. Her dad had just walked out one day, and though she and Danny had tried over the years to contact him, their efforts had been in vain. They'd both given up now. Although Amy and her

14

mother Jennifer had never been close they had always stayed in touch, but Jennifer had remarried. Amy had long held the suspicion that her mum's demanding new husband, who had several children of his own, allowed her little room for her own offspring. It hadn't seemed to matter when Amy had had Jamie. He'd been all the family she needed.

Mary had been like a second mother to her – particularly since she had lost Jamie. Leaving her was going to be much harder than Amy had thought, and not just because of Josh.

Mary had made her displeasure so blatant that Amy still felt churned up about the decision she was making. What if she had got it wrong? But then again, what if she stayed and did nothing? Amy knew she was stifled where she was. She was frightened if she didn't seize this moment to make some changes in her life, she never would.

'And I'm doing it for you, Jamie,' she vowed silently. 'Josh and I will do this for you.'

Josh. A minute ago, he was playing at her side, and now he was nowhere to be seen. Where was he? Amy knew she could be neurotic about Josh, but after the fright he'd given her that morning she wasn't taking any chances. What if the hairy man she'd seen as she entered the allotments was some kind of weirdo? Then Amy heard the sound of a child yelling, followed by a dog barking. She started to run.

15

Ben was digging up spuds on the allotment. He always came here after surgery on a Friday, when he had the afternoon off. Particularly if it had been a bad morning. And today had been one hell of a morning. He had been running late for the whole of the session, and there seemed to be more than the usual number of timewasters bemoaning their lot. Sometimes he wondered if he was really cut out for this job. Doling out Prozac like Smarties and treating little old ladies' verrucas hadn't really been what he was thinking of when he'd decided to be a doctor all those years ago. And the only important thing he had had to do all day – find someone at his local Primary Care Trust prepared to give one of his MS patients a brand-new drug that was meant to work wonders – had met with a blank wall. If Ben's patient, a seventy-year-old man, had lived in Essex, there wouldn't have been a problem. But the postcode lottery of living in Suffolk meant that the patient's particular PCT weren't yet giving the drug out. Ben had had the unpleasant task of explaining the inexplicable to the poor man's wife, who kept saying, 'But Jane Merchant's husband gets it, I don't understand.' Ben didn't either. Sometimes this job made you want to weep.

Not only that, he had nearly run over a kid on the way home from work. He hadn't been going fast, and the kid had run out in front of him – but still. Inevitably, he thought about Sarah, and as a result he had been more angry with the kid's mum than he should have been. But then – there had been something about her that touched him. An air of vulnerability that had made

16

him want to protect her. He shook his head. He'd clearly been on his own too long. Perhaps Caroline was right, and he should have chucked it all in for a while and gone travelling with her.

Caroline. Despite his best intentions his thoughts still strayed back to Caroline. Enchanting, infuriating, mercurial Caroline. Why had he let himself get involved with her again? He'd known it would lead to trouble. But it had been hard letting go of the only person he'd ever really talked to about Sarah. Harder than he'd let on to anyone. It was the sympathetic way Caroline had listened when he'd first opened up to her about Sarah that blinded him to her faults in the first place. Caroline seemed to show such intuitive understanding, and when she'd cried about the day her father had left, it seemed their shared pain had given them a lasting bond. However, it hadn't taken Ben long to realise that although Caroline did genuinely believe herself to be caring and thoughtful, in reality she was too selfish and spoilt to think too hard about anyone but herself.

To a degree, Ben didn't blame her – her mother had remarried a rich banker, and while Caroline had never wanted for anything materially, her mother and step-father's lack of emotional support meant she was appallingly needy. Caroline's response, when she and Ben had split up, had been to flaunt a variety of different men in Ben's face. To his eternal shame, the ploy had worked, and when she'd announced that she was leaving, he'd found himself back at her place on more than one occasion. He always regretted it, but Caroline just had a way of getting to him.

It had been a great relief when she'd finally gone off travelling, presuming he would follow her. But Ben had just taken up a temporary contract working in practice, and after spending too long kidding himself he was going to be a surgeon he couldn't afford to lose time now if he was going to make partner in the next few years.

Ben had thought that would be the last he'd hear of Caroline, but a succession of emails meant he was fully apprised of her doings. He had received one this morning, which annoyingly had caused a reaction he really thought he'd got beyond by now.

She was working in a bar in California, having a great time. Too busy to write much, she said. *Must dash, C U!* And then a casual PS: *Attached are some photos of me and Dave behind the bar.* There were some jpeg attachments, and he opened them to see photo after photo of Caroline with a tall, brawny bloke who had a deep tan – presumably Dave Behind the Bar.

He knew why she'd sent them. It was to make him jealous. She had always flirted with other people when they'd been together. It was one of the many things about her that had made Ben realise he had to walk away. DBtB was probably nothing to Caroline, and she had only sent the picture to get a reaction. He hated himself for having it.

He dug furiously, trying to shake off unwanted images. He didn't want Caroline any more. If she were here now, she would drive him mad. The trouble was that Caroline, for all her faults, her selfishness and her ego, was also bewitching and dazzling by degrees. And pathetic as he was, he couldn't quite get her out from under his skin.

Ben vented his frustration on the ground and dug even harder, while Meg, his black Labrador, sat beside him, panting softly in the late summer heat. It was one of the hottest days of the year so far. Ben stripped off his shirt, and used it to mop his brow. He took a swig of water, and glanced, out of habit as much as anything else, towards Caroline's garden gate. How many times had he seen her emerge from there, spade in hand, wearing her old gumboots and dressed casually in jeans and T-shirt, effortlessly managing to combine a wild sensuality with an earthy practicality? It was an image that was never far from his thoughts when he came out here.

He was about to turn back to his digging again when the garden gate opened. For a moment his heart leapt – maybe? – before his head kicked in. Caroline was unpredictable, it was true, but even *she* couldn't make it back from California in under twenty-four hours. Maybe her rather useless letting agents had rented the place at last.

It wasn't her. But it *was* a woman. And an attractive one at that. Her long fair curls tumbled casually over her shoulders. She was slim and wore a plain strappy summer dress and flat sandals. She had a little boy with her. It was the woman from this morning; the woman whose son he had nearly knocked over. Perhaps they were going to move in. He shook his head. He returned to his digging and dismissed them from his mind.

About ten minutes later, he became aware of a rather

insistent and annoying buzzing sound. He turned round and suddenly he heard a shout of, 'Wheee! I'm an aeroplane!' and a small bundle came flying over, stamping on his carrots and crashing into his runner-bean frame. Meg leapt up and started barking wildly, and the bundle burst into tears.

'Bloody hell! Can't you control your son?'

Really! This kid had got in his way twice in one morning. His mother clearly had no authority.

'He's only a kid!' The woman came flying up in a fury. She knelt down and took the bundle of child into her arms, making soothing noises.

'Then I suggest you take better care of him!' Ben was still cross, but also a little embarrassed that he might have overreacted.

'And I suggest you keep your animal under control,' the woman shouted back, pointing at Meg, who was jumping up and down, still barking excitedly. 'Josh is terrified of dogs.'

'If your son hadn't been trampling over my allotment Meg wouldn't have barked at all. This isn't a playground!'

'I am aware of that,' the woman retorted in stiff tones. She looked pretty when she was cross, Ben casually thought. 'I'm sorry that my son trampled on your allotment. He was just playing.'

'Is he okay?' Ben felt guilty. The little boy couldn't be more than five.

The woman looked at him in disgust. 'He'll be fine, no thanks to your dog.'

They glared at each other angrily for a moment, Ben

furious with her for not taking the olive branch he'd offered.

''I think we've seen quite enough of each other today. It's all right, we won't trouble you any further,' she said, and walked away.

'Good!' retorted Ben, sticking his spade into the ground in disgust, watching her walk back towards Caroline's house.

Just at that moment, Harry Hartswood emerged from the garden next door, pushing a wheelbarrow containing a spade, a fork and some potato sacks. Harry's allotment was next-but-one to Ben's, and they were old friends, their friendship forged by a shared love of growing things, an interest in history and a fascination on Ben's part with Harry's plethora of war stories.

'I see you're getting a new neighbour,' said Ben, nodding towards Caroline's gate.

'So it would appear,' said Harry. 'I heard her telling the estate agent she wanted to take it. I thought she was rather pretty myself.' There was a familiar twinkle in his eye.

'She may be pretty, but she's got a foul temper. Her horrible little son has just trampled over my allotment and she had the cheek to blame me for not keeping Meg under control. So what if she comes to live here? I won't be getting to know her, that's for sure.'

21

Amy was still fuming when she reached the garden gate. If everyone was as rude as her unknown biker, then perhaps she shouldn't move in here. It was a shame, as in every other way it was perfect. As she went to open the door, an elderly man passed her pushing a wheelbarrow and smiled, which immediately made her feel better. On the other hand, it would be foolish to throw up such a good opportunity for the sake of one grumpy man, whom she could avoid quite easily. And Josh seemed to have quickly recovered from his trauma. Amy had to admit that she had perhaps over-reacted a little herself. All the worry about Mary had made her a little edgy, and she was always over-protective as far as Josh was concerned. Mary was right about that.

She and Josh made their way back up the garden path. Mary or no Mary, her mind was made up. Smarmy Simon was just coming off the phone when she walked up to him.

'Well?' he said.

'I love it,' she replied. 'When can we move in?'

CHAPTER TWO

'It's okay, it doesn't matter, really it doesn't.'

Pete's words should have been reassuring to Saffron, but somehow they weren't. She lay in the darkness, listening to his breathing and the snuffles of Ellie next to her in the baby basket, and fretted. She should be trying to sleep, but judging by the way she was leaking like an old milk cow (an unsavoury aspect to breast-feeding, which she particularly hated), Ellie was probably on the verge of waking up. Which would have put paid to any extracurricular activity anyway, even if *she* could have risen to the occasion.

Pete had been lovely about it, as usual, but she couldn't help the gnawing anxiety which ate into her after yet another aborted attempt at sex. After all, that was what had done for her and Gerry in the end. And they had managed it a lot more often after Becky and Matt were born than she and Pete had done so far.

Pete's not Gerry.

Now that was a better thought. Saffron smiled. Gerry had done her a favour really. Having dumped her for a

23

blonde floozie, Gerry had floored Saffron completely for a while. With Becky only two and Matt a baby, life had been tough. Without the amiable and supportive friendship of Pete, whose allotment bordered hers, Saffron doubted whether she would have hung on to her sanity. She had always got on well with him, but during that dark period she came to value his steadiness and depend upon his gentle humour to lighten up her day.

Saffron hadn't been looking for love. Her heart had been so shattered by Gerry's infidelity she had thought she could never trust anyone again. But one day, looking across at Pete planting his runner beans, it suddenly dawned on her that love had snuck up on her when she wasn't looking. After that, everything was simple. They moved in together and within months Pete had proposed. And when Ellie was born, Saffron's happiness was complete. And here they were. *Simple.*

Saffron sighed. Things didn't feel simple now.

She could probably count on one hand the number of times that she and Pete had made love since Ellie's arrival. Despite Gerry's taunts, being with Pete had proved to her that she wasn't frigid. But now, for the first time since they'd been together, Saffron felt they were struggling. *She* was struggling.

It wasn't that she didn't want to. It was just – well, she felt betrayed by her body. For a start, she had forgotten how much she hated breastfeeding. She resented the fact that her nipples, previously portals of pleasure, were now so engorged with milk, cracked and swollen that they resembled an ageing cow's udders. Anything less sexy she couldn't imagine.

24

And the rest of her body wasn't much better. Her stomach flopped and flapped about, lined with purple veins that seemed to have arrived from nowhere. From experience she knew they would fade in time and leave faint silver lines to go with the ones she already had from Becky and Matt. But now, she felt like a beached whale.

'It doesn't matter what you look like,' Pete had declared the first time she had tried and failed to seduce him after Ellie was born. 'You'll always be a sex goddess to me.'

But it wasn't enough. Her libido was practically non-existent. Somewhere between getting pregnant, giving birth and coping with those enormously painful stitches (sitting on shards of glass might have been marginally more comfortable), it had gone AWOL. And with the added complications of sleepless nights, an ex-husband who kept causing her childcare headaches, and a business partner who had scooted off halfway round the world, it was showing no sign of returning in the immediate future.

The snuffles in the Moses basket got louder, indicating that Ellie was getting ready for a full-scale roaring attack. Saffron got out of bed, determined to pre-empt events – at least one of them could have a good night's sleep. She picked the baby up, sorted her pillows out, and plonked Ellie on her breast. She didn't even attempt to try and read, as she used to when Becky and Matt were small. This time around she had perfected the art of breastfeeding in a semi-doze, and, despite a slight anxiety that she might drop the baby, so far it seemed to have worked.

As she sat in a state of numbed stupefaction, trying not to wince when Ellie suckled too hard, Saffron thought about how different this week was supposed to have been.

Gerry had whisked the kids off to Florida. She hadn't been too happy about it, particularly as it meant Becky missing the first week at junior school, but at least it had given her and Pete some much-needed time together. Pete had taken a week off work, and the idea was that they would relax and enjoy their new baby without the demands of the older two. But somehow it hadn't quite worked out like that.

For a start, thanks to Caroline's decision to bugger off round the world earlier in the summer, the business was in a huge mess. Saffron had been relying on Caroline to cover her for at least some of the early weeks with Ellie. As it was, because of Caroline's departure, Saffron had ended up doing some minor jobs up until a week before Ellie was born. Now, eight weeks later, she realised that clients were haemorrhaging away from them at a rate of three or four per week. Their fledgling gardening business, Green Fingers, couldn't afford to lose customers at such a rate. And given that summer should have been a time for gaining new business, Saffron was going to have her work cut out this autumn to make up the lost ground.

Bugger Caroline! she thought grumpily, quickly followed by the thought that she should have known better. When they had first met on the gardening course they had taken together three years earlier, Saffron had been dazzled by Caroline's enthusiasm and creativity.

But then, it was easy to be taken in by Caroline. She talked the talk so well. The reality, which Saffron had only realised once they became business partners, was that although Caroline was a great saleswoman, and had a genius for planning people's gardens, she was also incredibly lazy, and most of the work had fallen onto Saffron's shoulders.

And then, just when Saffron needed her the most, Caroline had decided to do her moonlit flit. Something to do with a bloke, no doubt, knowing Caroline, but she hadn't thought it necessary to furnish Saffron with the details.

So instead of lazy days in the sun with Pete and Ellie (not that there had been much sun, but still ...), Saffron had spent the week poring over figures and ringing disgruntled clients, to reassure them that yes, gardens would be weeded, hedges would be trimmed and lawns would be mowed – eventually. Pete had been a great help, going out on a couple of occasions to tackle some particularly difficult jobs in between his work as a marketing manager for a computer firm, but at best his help was a sop to the real problem. There was simply too much work for Saffron alone. Added to which, Caroline might be flaky as hell, but she had a good eye for design and the clients liked her. Her loss to the business was incalculable. And even supposing Saffron was to find a new partner who matched up, she probably didn't have the funds to pay for the help anyway.

A contented sigh indicated that Ellie had had enough. Saffron picked her up, burped her, checked her nappy and popped her back into her basket. Then she climbed back into bed and snuggled up to Pete, who cuddled reassuringly back. There would be other nights for sex. There was no point staying awake brooding on her problems – she was getting little enough sleep as it was. Maybe tomorrow everything would look different. And maybe pigs would grow wings.

'That's the lot then.' The removal man poked his head round the door, where Mary and Amy were sipping a final cup of tea, sitting on the last few boxes, which Amy was planning to shove in the back of the car. Josh was running round in circles, impersonating an aeroplane, and Amy was doing her best not to let it get under her skin. She could tell Mary was thinking the same thing.

'Right.' Amy took a deep breath and gave a bright smile. 'Well. See you in Suffolk then.'

The removal man nodded and left the room.

'Come on, Josh,' said Amy, 'we'd best get going.'

She staggered out to the car with the remaining boxes, while Mary washed the teacups up. She'd brought her own kettle and cups, as Amy had already packed hers. Amy hadn't wanted Mary to come over, but Mary had insisted. As Mary in full flow had the unstoppable force of an erupting volcano, Amy knew better than to try to dissuade her.

The trouble was, now it was finally time to go, last-minute doubts were beginning to creep in, and Amy didn't want Mary witnessing her weakness. Only this morning, Amy had folded up the sheets on her bed, packed away the photo of Jamie that always sat by her bedside, and burst into tears at the thought of leaving the flat. She remembered the first night they had moved in: Jamie mucking about, insisting he carry her over the threshold.

'But we're not married yet,' Amy had laughed.

'Doesn't matter, we're as good as,' was Jamie's response, before picking her up and swinging her through into the lounge, mock-complaining all the while that she'd put on weight.

He wouldn't be saying that now. Amy was aware of how painfully thin she had become since Jamie had died. Stick insect, he'd be calling her, if he were still here. He had welcomed the extra curves that came with Josh, but they'd all fallen away in the months since he'd gone.

And what would he make of her face? He'd always teased her about her long corkscrew curls and called her his pre-Raphaelite beauty. It was true her long fair curls could still be classed as such, but she knew there was a slightly haunted look in her face now – actually, haggard would probably be a better word for it. Would he find her beautiful any more? Amy didn't think so. She felt pale and wan; a shadow of her former self.

Amy made her way back into the flat. The empty flat. Shorn of all its homeliness. Every last vestige of her life with Jamie had been removed. She felt as though she had ripped out its soul. And, with it, hers. Oh God, what was she doing?

Amy shut the door with a decisive bang. This was no good. Mary had spent the morning making polite conversation with barely suppressed fury. If Amy lost it now, it would give her mother-in-law the perfect opportunity to say 'I told you so'.

Josh ran towards her. 'Is it time to go yet?' he said. 'I'm bored.'

'Yup, sweetheart, it is,' Amy replied. 'Have you been to the loo?'

Josh pulled a face. 'Granny made me,' he grumbled.

'Well, it's a long journey,' said Amy. 'Granny was right.'

Mary was ostentatiously clattering around in the kitchen. Her heels echoed on the bare floor. Amy was aware once again of the emptiness of the flat. Of the emptiness of Mary's life now she was taking Josh out of it.

'So, this is it.' Mary finished what she was doing and came and stood, stiffly and formally, holding out her hand. As if they meant no more to each other than polite strangers. As if they hadn't shared all that grief, all that heartache.

'Yes.' Amy swallowed. She wanted to give Mary a long hug, but the negative vibes that were bristling off Jamie's mother gave her little choice.

'Josh, come and say goodbye to the flat.'

Josh ran in and out of the bedrooms, the small lounge and the tiny kitchen diner.

'Goodbye-goodbye-goodbye,' he called, not appreciating the enormity of what he was saying before descending once more into aeroplane territory.

30

'Josh, do be quiet!' Mary snapped.

Unused to Mary telling him off, Josh stopped short and his little face puckered up with tears.

'Was that strictly necessary?' Amy couldn't help but rise to her son's defence.

'He needed to be told,' said Mary. 'You're too soft on him.'

'And you're being too hard.' Amy regretted the comment as soon as it was out. Mary was a doting granny, and without her Amy wouldn't have coped over the last two years.

'I see,' said Mary. 'I was too hard all the times I cuddled him while he cried when you went out to work. I was too hard the times I took him to the doctor when you couldn't. I'm not the one taking him away from everything he knows and loves. I wouldn't say *I* was the hard one, would you?'

Amy looked at Mary aghast. 'That's not what I meant,' she said shakily.

Mary shrugged her shoulders and turned to give Josh a cuddle. Josh had stopped crying now and started being an aeroplane again. Oh to have the resilience of a child, thought Amy in silent dismay. She couldn't leave Mary like this. For Jamie's sake, she couldn't. A sudden memory of Jamie laughing at her one day when she had been fuming about his mother's interference took her breath away.

'Come on, Ames,' he had said. 'She means well. And we're all she's got. Give her a break.'

Jamie would never have wanted this.

'Mary, I'm sorry,' said Amy. 'Please don't let's fall out.'

31

Mary said nothing and looked away. If Amy hadn't known better she could have sworn that a tear trickled down Mary's face. But Amy had never seen Mary cry. Not even at Jamie's funeral. She was the strong silent type – whatever crying she may have done over her son, she had done it alone.

'Please, Mary,' said Amy. 'For Jamie's sake. And Josh's. We've been through so much together. Don't let's spoil it.'

Mary turned around, her eyes glittering bright, her back ramrod-straight, and for the first time Amy caught a fleeting glimpse of the emotion she was struggling to contain.

'Apology accepted,' she said stiffly. 'Now, I think it's time you were both going.'

She shooed them out of the flat into the car as if the previous exchange hadn't happened.

'You will visit, won't you?' Amy said.

'Of course,' Mary replied, but there was a wariness about her. Amy doubted very much if she would come anytime soon.

'Damn.' Amy hunted around for her handbag.

'What's the matter?'

'I think I've left my handbag inside. Can you just keep an eye on Josh while I go and get it?'

She ran up the path, and opened the front door to the flat. She was eager to get off now. Hanging around was only prolonging the agony. She raced into the flat and found her bag on the kitchen worktop where she had left it. Then she paused and looked around her.

Memories crowded in. Of her and Jamie putting the

new kitchen in together; of Jamie coming home with a huge bouquet of flowers the day she told him she was pregnant; the strangeness of leaving the flat as two and coming back with Josh as a family . . . So many memories. And she was leaving them all behind. She was saying goodbye to her old life. She was saying goodbye to Jamie. A stab of guilt shot through her, and a sense of loss so overwhelming she was stunned by the force of it. Jamie was gone. It was just her and Josh now. She doubted she'd ever get used to it.

Eyes full, she turned her back on the home where she had been happy for so long, and mechanically went back to the car, saying her goodbyes while hoping that Mary couldn't detect the tears she was trying to hide. She started the car and sped off round the corner, Josh still waving and shouting goodbye till Mary was long gone. Then she allowed the silent tears to fall.

Amy closed the door behind the last removal man. It banged shut with a horrible finality. Well, she'd done it. She and Josh were on their own, properly on their own for the first time since Jamie had died – in a new town, where they knew no one.

'Can I go in the garden?' Josh had just twigged that there was more to his new home than just four walls.

'Of course,' said Amy, smiling to banish her gloomy thoughts. 'Let's get our coats and have an explore.'

Despite it being only early September, there was already an autumnal chill in the air, and the impression of summer being over was further enhanced by the smell of bonfires. The leaves weren't quite turning yellow, but it wouldn't be long. Amy shivered as she watched Josh running wild in their new garden. A pang of longing shot unexpectedly through her, and tears came to her eyes.

'Why are you crying, Mummy?' A little hand came and found hers.

'I was just thinking about how much Daddy would have liked it here,' Amy said. She had always been open with Josh about everything, despite Mary's feeling that children should be protected from too much heartache.

Josh looked at her thoughtfully.

'But if Daddy's in heaven, he can see where we are, and he'll like it too,' he replied.

'Out of the mouths of babes,' said Amy, laughing through her tears.

Josh looked at her puzzled, but Amy just smiled at him.

'It's all right, Josh, you've just managed to cheer me up. Come on, let's go and get some tea.'

The next morning, Amy wasn't feeling quite so sanguine. She had had a lousy night's sleep on her land-lady's rather lumpy double bed. Josh had had a night-mare, and ended up in bed with her. It was a while since he'd done that. When he had been very little, just after Jamie had died, he'd come in with her every night, but she had gradually weaned him off it. Maybe the move had unsettled him again. Oh lord, was she doing the right thing?

Amy had lain in bed worrying about that – and whether she had irrevocably offended Mary. She didn't want to cut the ties completely – just loosen them a little. Was that so very wrong? What would Jamie have done in her shoes? She was still learning to appreciate that one of the worst aspects of her situation was making decisions alone, and realising there was no way she could truly know what Jamie would have thought.

She turned over, determined to get some sleep, but then her mind went into overdrive about money. Her demons were back and running amok. Money. Her overriding preoccupation since Jamie's death. She had thought they were reasonably well off. She had thought they'd made adequate provision. But the idea of either of them dying had seemed so remote that they had never got round to doing the obvious stuff. It had always felt as though there would be plenty of time for that.

If only she and Jamie had got married, or written a will, as they always intended. Everything would have been so much more straightforward. But they hadn't, so the taxman had come to claim both his share of the computer business Jamie had run with his partner, Giles, and their property. Added to which, Amy hadn't appreciated how much debt the business itself was in – or how difficult it would be to sell Jamie's share of it. It had taken all this time to sort it out.

Amy had survived by carrying on teaching, until Grace's money had solved her problems. And now that she had sold the flat as well, things would be easier.

She planned to settle in before buying somewhere, but at least she could think about buying a house in Suffolk. Although maybe she should have consolidated a bit, before taking the plunge to move and start a new career. She had enough to tide her over for the next few months, and supply-teaching at schools would help . . . but would it be enough?

The thoughts swirled round in her head. Nights were always a bad time for Amy. The demons couldn't be as easily dispatched as during the day. And the suffocating blackness of her new room, with its thick velvet curtains, didn't help either. She was used to having a neon streetlight outside her window and found total darkness oppressive.

She turned on the light. Grabbing a book usually helped – something light and funny, like Terry Pratchett, was a must. Gradually the feelings of panic subsided, and her heart stopped racing at a rate of knots. She read, and eventually fell asleep, head propped against her pillow, the light still on.

Amy spent the morning unpacking. She felt as if she had been hit over the head with a brick. As usual after a bad night, her thoughts were muzzy and unfocused. She had managed to find Josh's train set and set it up in the front room, along with snacks and a pile of DVDs, just to keep him occupied while she got on with trying to create some semblance of normality.

She dug out a radio, which she switched on in the

kitchen. It was pre-tuned to Radio 2. Amy had grown up thinking Radio 2 was the preserve of sad middle-aged people far removed from the cutting edge of life, until Jamie had made her listen to it one Saturday lunchtime. 'Honestly, they play really good music on Radio 2,' he had promised her. And to Amy's surprise, he was right. Not only were the DJs highly entertaining, the music was great, and after that she and Jamie had often tuned in together. After he had died, she had listened to the radio obsessively – as if in some strange way it still linked them. She woke up to Wogan's gentle warblings, and dipped in and out all day. Radio 2 was an essential part of her now – a soundtrack to her life, now she no longer had one.

Sunday-morning love songs was on. Sometimes Amy found all the people ringing in with messages for their loved ones too painful for words, but of late she'd found it comforting to know that not everyone was as lonely as she was, and it was easy listening as she started shoving books onto shelves. As the room slowly got cleared up, and things began to fall into place, Amy started to feel better again, and she gradually felt that she was getting things under control.

'And this is for Bev Peters, who's away at uni, and missing her boyfriend Colin very much,' Steve Wright was saying, before Amy heard the first haunting bars of a familiar tune.

She paused in the middle of her new living room. She felt as if she had been punched in the stomach. That song – how many years ago was it? In the early days of their relationship, Amy had still been at teacher-training college, and they had spent a year apart. Jamie had compiled a tape of 'their' songs, which she had played endlessly, missing him so much it had hurt. Her favourite track on it had been 'Forever Autumn' – at the time it seemed to sum up the way she felt. How could she have known that her feelings then would be a pale shadow of the real thing – of what it was like knowing that she would never see Jamie again? The song could have been written for her, and seemed cruelly apposite now. It was all gone. Everything. The only good thing left was Josh. All the rest was dust.

'Anyone home?' There was a knock at the side door that led to the garden, and Amy pulled herself together. Her life might be over, but she still had Josh, and she had to make a go of this, for his sake.

A tall elderly man was standing on the doorstep bearing a pot with a geranium in it and holding a plastic bag with some shopping in. She remembered him as the man she had seen pushing the wheelbarrow on the day she had come to look round.

'Hello,' said Amy, with something like relief. In the early days she had found any social interaction excruciatingly difficult, but now, having to put on a show of politeness was a welcome distraction from her misery. 'Can I help you?'

'Good morning,' the man said. 'I'm Harry Hartswood, your neighbour. I just popped over to see if you needed anything, and to bring you this.' He proffered the geranium.

'Thanks,' said Amy, taking it. 'I'm Amy Nicolson. Can I make you a cup of tea?'

'That would be lovely, my dear,' said Harry. 'I don't suppose you have had time to get to the shops yet. I've brought a few provisions.'

'That is extremely kind of you,' said Amy, touched at his thoughtfulness. 'It's on my "to do" list. Sorry about the mess, I'm still unpacking.'

'Mummy, who is it?' Josh flew out to see what was going on, then hid behind Amy's legs when he realised it was a stranger.

'This is Mr Hartswood,' said Amy. 'He lives next door.'

'He's very old,' said Josh, peeking out from behind her.

'Josh!' Amy was scandalised, but Harry just laughed.

'Yes, I am,' he said. 'But then, you are very young. So everyone must be old to you.'

Josh looked at him quizzically for a minute, then shrugged his shoulders. 'I've got a train set,' he announced. 'Would you like to see it?'

'I'm sure Mr Hartswood doesn't want to be bothered with your train set,' began Amy, but her neighbour would hear none of it.

'That sounds wonderful, Josh, I'd love to,' he said, letting himself be led by the hand into the front room, 'and everyone calls me Harry.'

When Amy returned with the tea, she discovered the pair of them playing happily on the floor.

'I can see you're going to be a favoured guest,' she said. 'Mummy is normally too busy to play trains.'

'Ah, well, that's Mummy's prerogative,' said Harry. 'And my pleasure.'

'You're very good with him,' Amy said, watching how

39

naturally Josh played. Josh didn't warm to everyone, and it was rare for him to latch on to a stranger like this. 'Do you have grandchildren?'

'No.' Harry's smile was tinged with sadness. 'Unfortunately, my wife and I weren't able to have children.'

'I'm sorry,' said Amy.

'No need to be, my dear,' said Harry. 'We had a happy and full life together.'

Amy, who had acquired an instinct for picking up on these things since Jamie's death, asked, 'Had?'

'My wife died a few years ago,' said Harry, a shadow passing across his face.

'I'm sorry,' said Amy again, and meant it. She felt an immediate kinship with this man, stranger though he was, and yet, even though she shared his grief, it was still hard to know what to say. 'You must get very lonely.'

'Well, sometimes,' said Harry. 'But I have my army reunions, and lots of friends here. And there's a great deal of support to be found on the allotments, as I'm sure you will discover. I survive somewhat better than everyone had predicted.'

'I shall have to take lessons from you in being positive,' replied Amy. 'Jamie, my . . .' – she was going to say partner, and then paused, wondering whether Harry would approve of her unmarried status – 'Josh's dad died two and a half years ago, and this is a big move for me.'

'Oh my dear, how very sad for you,' sympathised Harry.

40

Amy felt herself dissolve into floods of tears. She couldn't do this. She just couldn't. It was a dreadful mistake. There was no way she was going to manage on her own. That song was right. Her life would always be autumn now – because Jamie wasn't there, and however much she longed for him, he never could be again.

CHAPTER THREE

Amy took a deep breath, and tried to get a grip. This was mortifying. Here she was blubbing in front of a total stranger. Luckily, once she and Harry had got chatting, Josh pronounced the conversation 'Grown up, boring', and disappeared upstairs.

'Oh I am sorry.' Harry patted Amy awkwardly on the back. 'I didn't mean to distress you.'

He proffered a hankie, which Amy accepted gratefully.

'You haven't,' said Amy. 'I'm just being silly.'

'It's not silly at all,' answered Harry, 'but quite natural.' His gentle concern brought fresh tears to Amy's eyes, but she managed a watery smile.

'I'm not usually like this,' Amy said. 'I think it's just with the move and everything . . . I suddenly feel so alone.'

'And however many friends you have, once you shut that door at night, you're on your own.' Harry nodded sympathetically. 'It is very hard, but it will get better, in time.'

'Will it? I keep thinking it's going to, but then, like now, I feel I've gone back to square one again. I feel I'm never going to stop wanting him back.'

'You probably won't.' Harry's response was simple. 'I think about my Mavis every day, but I am still alive, and although it isn't the life we had, it is the life I have now. You're still young, Amy, you have Josh. You have a lot to live for. Do you think Jamie would want you to be mourning him forever?'

'No, definitely not,' said Amy. 'But I don't know. It sounds so corny. What we had was amazing. I doubt I'll ever find it again.'

'You might not,' said Harry. 'But you must make it your business to learn to be happy again. You won't ever stop missing him, but that doesn't mean you can't smile sometimes.'

Amy felt her spirits lift a little. It was so wonderful to have someone who understood – so often people she knew were embarrassed and awkward and shied away from talking about how she was. Or they assumed that after all this time, she would be over it – like you got over the flu. Or, worse still, some of their so-called friends had dropped her altogether. It was as if she had some nasty disease that might be catching. There was even the faint suggestion from one or two girlfriends, to whom she had thought she was close, that somehow she was now likely to make a play for their husbands.

They had no idea of what was really going through her head – or, more importantly, her heart. So Amy had learned to smile and hide her pain so that no one knew it was there any longer. It was a relief to talk to

44

someone who was so refreshingly direct about it.

'You're absolutely right, of course,' said Amy. 'It's not always easy to be so positive, though.'

'No, it isn't,' said Harry. 'And believe you me, I still have my dark nights of the soul. But I just grit my teeth and try to get through them. There is always another dawn. Now, I'm afraid I really must be going, as I'm off to lunch with some friends. Please feel free to pop in at any time. I'm usually about.'

'Thanks, Harry, I might just do that,' said Amy. 'You've been very kind.'

'Ah well, I just like to be neighbourly,' said Harry. 'Mavis would have had my guts for garters if I wasn't.'

Amy laughed and saw Harry to the door, just as Josh came flying down demanding to be fed. One thing about children was their needs always had to come first. And sometimes, when life threatened to become overwhelming, that was a very good thing.

Saffron was running late, as usual. Matt and Becky were being so slow this morning, and Ellie had kept her up all night. Added to which, she had made the mistake of stopping to listen to Wogan's musings on the subject of mums driving 4x4s. She had been laughing so much she had forgotten the time. It was only Monday, and they were going to be late. Bugger, how did she always manage that?

'Kids, hurry up,' she called as she loaded Ellie into the buggy.

The trouble was that the children were still exhausted from Florida, so getting them up this morning had been a complete nightmare. She had so much on her plate at the moment, the last thing she needed was the kids being late for school.

Her other major headache – how to regain the trust of her clients and rebuild the business – was also not going away, despite her and Pete's best efforts. But he was right to point out that she couldn't do it alone, and while he was immensely supportive, he couldn't run the business for her. But who on earth was she going to find to help her out? None of her mum friends were into gardening. Perhaps she should do as Pete had suggested and advertise. Thank God, at least, for Pete. He had been so fantastic, she had to hold on to that. Gerry would have given her no encouragement at all.

What *were* the children doing? She had sent them upstairs ten minutes ago, to brush their teeth, and they had disappeared.

'Children, come downstairs NOW! We're going to be late,' Saffron yelled up the stairs, picking up assorted PE kits and book bags as she did so.

'Do you really need to shout that loud first thing?' Pete was halfway down the stairs still doing his tie. Their relationship was still new enough for Saffron's heart to skip a beat when she saw him. Pete looked gorgeous even though his hair was all mussed up and he looked half-asleep. Still adjusting to this parenting lark, he hadn't quite got to grips with sleepless nights.

'If I didn't shout, we'd never get anywhere,' said Saffron, giving him a kiss. After the misery of her marriage to Gerry, she still had to pinch herself to believe that she could have been so lucky as to have found Pete, even with the permanent weight lodged in the pit of her stomach about their lack of sex life.

As if by magic, two pairs of feet thundered down the stairs, and Becky and Matt presented themselves to her, both blaming the other for their tardiness.

'Not interested,' grumbled Saffron. 'Come on, we've got to go – *now*!' Kissing Pete goodbye again, she hauled coats on and shoved the children out of the door. If they ran, there was an outside chance they could make it.

As she approached the corner of her road, opposite the little country churchyard she cut through every day on the way to school, she spotted another pair of late-comers hurrying up the road that ran at right-angles to her own. It was a woman she didn't recognise and a little boy about Matt's age. The woman looked a bit perplexed, as if she weren't quite sure of the way.

Saffron smiled as they met at the corner to cross over – in the three years she had been walking to school with Becky she had discovered that the children didn't moan so much if they had a friend to walk with. As she had only recently managed to prise Matt from the buggy (the arrival of Ellie had been the key turning point, and four months later he was still sore about it), Saffron hoped that finding a friend on the walk to school might prove to be a help.

'Hi,' said Saffron as they waited to cross the road. 'This your first day?'

'Yup.' The stranger smiled. 'Josh and I only moved

here on Saturday. And despite poring over maps all weekend, I think I'm a bit lost.'

'Follow me,' said Saffron. 'We cut through the grave-yard every day. The school's at the bottom of the hill on the other side, about five minutes from the high street.'

'Great,' said the stranger with a grateful smile. She was pretty, thought Saffron – and also, she noted jealously, incredibly thin.

'I'm Saffron Cairns, by the way, and this is Becky and Matt. Matt's starting in Miss Burrows' class today.'

'Amy Nicolson,' said Amy. 'Josh is in Miss Burrows' class too.'

'Matt, that's nice,' said Saffron. 'Josh is going to be in your class.'

Matt and Josh both appeared completely uninterested in this stunning piece of news, although they quickly bonded by running in and out of the gravestones. Amy laughed and said, 'Oh well, I'm very pleased to meet you at any rate. I don't know a soul around here. Apart from my neighbour, Harry.'

'Harry Hartswood?' Understanding dawned in Saffron's eyes. Harry had mentioned someone had just moved in next door.

'Yes, do you know him?' Amy was surprised. In her busy street in North London no one knew anyone else much. Not one of her neighbours had called round after Jamie had died, and whenever she needed help round the house she'd always had to resort to the Yellow Pages.

'Oh yes, everyone knows Harry. He's an institution,

48

particularly on the allotments. Though I'd avoid his elderberry wine if I were you – it's lethal. You must be Caroline's new tenant.'

'If she's the Caroline whose name is plastered all over my tenancy agreements, then yes,' said Amy. 'Blimey, does everyone know everyone else round here?'

'Sure do,' said Saffron with a grin. 'Actually, I *should* know Caroline. She's my business partner. You're never more well than when you're in Nevermorewell, so they say, but it's the kind of place where if you sneeze at the top of the high street you're dying of pneumonia by the time you reach the bottom.'

'I'll bear that in mind,' said Amy, laughing, and finding to her surprise that they were nearly at the school gates.

'I'll have to love you and leave you here, I'm afraid,' said Saffron. 'Becky's starting in the Juniors today, and I've just got to find out where she needs to go. All change this year. Do you know your way round?'

'I think so. I'll be fine,' said Amy. 'It's been lovely to meet you.'

'Well I'm sure we'll catch up again,' said Saffron. 'Particularly if the boys are in the same class. Perhaps when you're more settled we can do coffee?'

'Coffee sounds great,' said Amy, and headed off with Josh. Maybe making friends around here wouldn't be so difficult, she thought.

Saturday morning found Amy playing plumbers. It had been a very busy week, and she had barely paused for breath. She had had several forays into the centre of Nevermorewell, where she had discovered a fine butcher's and baker's, a greengrocer's, a couple of take-aways, an Italian restaurant, and a few of the usual high-street shops. On her trip on Thursday, Amy had been delighted to see the whole high street was shut to traffic for the farmers' market. There were two rows of stalls running the entire length of the street, selling everything from organic veg to homemade honey. The market had been so well-attended, Amy had counted herself lucky to make it back with bags of fresh produce, a free-range chicken and some homemade bread.

Nevermorewell boasted two decent-looking pubs – the Plough at one end of the high street, and the Magpie at the other. Not that Amy had much time or inclination to go into pubs, but they might be worth investigating for Sunday lunches. According to Saffron, whom she had seen a couple of times that week on the way to school, the Magpie was quite family friendly.

Amy had also discovered the library and the town hall, where she had managed to find the number of the local education authority and register for supply teaching. Luckily she wasn't desperate, so she could afford a couple of weeks off to sort herself out. She had also signed up at the doctor's and the dentist's, which were in the same location, a smart new purpose-built building, just off the high street. All in all, despite a couple of terse conversations with Mary on the phone, and a niggling angst about Josh, who had cried every morning when leaving for school, she had been too busy so far to feel gloomy.

Her only real headache was that ever since they'd arrived in the house the bathroom tap had been dripping and driving her mad. So today, with Josh safely ensconced in front of the TV watching *Thunderbirds*, and armed with a spanner and some washers, she had decided to take the bull by the horns and reseat the taps. She had seen Jamie doing it a dozen times. It couldn't be too difficult, could it?

Apparently, it could. For a start, the taps were so corroded it took ages to unscrew them, and then when she applied the spanner to the original washer it just sheared off and pinged in the sink, promptly followed by a jet of water.

'Sod! Sod and double sod!' Amy shrieked as water spewed everywhere. She had forgotten to turn the water off at the mains.

'It's a bit wet, Mummy.' The lure of the TV was evidently not enough to prevent Josh from finding out why Mummy was standing knee-deep in water and wailing like a banshee.

'I know, darling,' said Amy between gritted teeth. 'Could you just pass me that bucket, please?'

Josh passed it to her and she placed it under the flood while she frantically looked around for something to plug up the hole. Ignoring Josh's pleas to be allowed to play with the water, she eventually found a flannel, which she stuffed down as far as it would go. It seemed to work as a temporary fix. She ran into the kitchen, and after a few false starts managed to locate the mains tap and turn the water off, and then returned to survey the damage.

The reward for her labours was one sodden bathroom, a tap to which she couldn't fit a new washer and a feeling of absolute failure.

'You should have got a plumber,' observed Josh, with all the sensitivity of a five-year-old. He was right of course, which didn't help. It was at times like this that Amy missed Jamie the most. There was only her to do the job, and she had made a hash of it. She hated feeling like a useless girl, and yet here she was acting like one. Even her five-year-old son knew it.

'We'd better go and see Harry,' she said to Josh with a rueful smile.

But Harry was out, and Amy was at a bit of a loss.

'Maybe he's on the allotments,' Amy mused. 'Shall we go and look for him, Josh?'

Josh agreed with alacrity, particularly when Amy said he could take his ball with him. They hadn't had a chance to go out there properly yet, and it would be a good excuse to go and have a look at Caroline's patch. Harry had told her that there was stuff growing on it, and that some of Caroline's friends had been trying to keep it tidy, but it needed, in his words, 'a good going over'. Amy had been resisting the siren call of the allotments ever since, as she had been too busy with essential stuff, but here was a reason to go.

As she stepped out onto the allotments, Amy gave a deep sigh of contentment. The sound of cattle lowing in the distance reminded her how far she was from the city. However alone and useless she felt, this *had* been a good decision. Josh immediately ran off, kicking his ball and whooping wildly. And the allotments were as wonderful as she remembered them; even more so at this turn of the seasons. The leaves were starting to go yellow now, and some were already falling from the trees. There was a distinct whiff of autumn in the air, several of the plots were already being dug over, and a sharp chill presaged the frosts to come.

Following Josh, Amy struggled down the path outside her garden gate, which was rather more overgrown than on her last visit, and gazed ahead of her. Harry had said Caroline's plot was across the main path that ran through the allotments and slightly to the left, which made it roughly next to the one where she had seen the bike rider. Oh lord, she hoped he wouldn't be out there. Remembering what had happened last time, she called Josh to come back to her. Much as she had disliked the man, it wouldn't do to go round upsetting the neighbours so soon.

As she approached the plot, there was a strong smell of manure. The bike rider's plot still had vegetables growing, but he was evidently getting ready to turn over the ground for the autumn. And ah, yes, the plot next door did look quite overgrown. It must be Caroline's. Though in among the weeds Amy could see plenty of potatoes, and at the far end were a couple of fruit trees, so she might get something from this year's crop.

She and Josh were just crossing the corner of the plot, when she heard a barking and something like a speeding bullet came flying towards her. That damned dog again. Josh screamed, and before she knew what was happening she was on her back in the pile of manure, with a black dog leaping all over her, licking her face.

Squinting up at the sun, in a mixture of fury and embarrassment, she saw the figure of a man.

'Down, Meg! Bad dog!' The man offered a hand towards her, saying, 'I am so, so sorry. Are you all right?'

Amy stumbled to her feet and grabbed hold of Josh. She glared at the man standing before her.

'I might have known it would be you,' she said.

CHAPTER FOUR

'I don't suppose it would help if I told you that I don't know what came over Meg. Really, she isn't usually like that.' Her biker looked suitably discomfited.

'No?' Amy tried to muster what dignity she could, excruciatingly aware that she was covered in manure and must smell terrible. 'First your wretched dog frightens my son, and then she knocks me flying into a pile of manure. She should be locked up!'

Ben bristled. 'Well, your son doesn't seem too traumatised, does he?'

Amy turned to look behind her, to discover that Josh was playing happily with Meg, who was licking his fingers.

'Pooh, Mummy, you stink,' he said.

It was no good. Irritated as she was with this man and his damned dog, it was incredibly hard to stay on your high horse when an infant had just pointed out the obvious. Amy did indeed stink. *And* there was the slight matter of how she was going to clean herself up.

'Oh God, he is so right,' she said, unable to prevent

the small grin that was forcing its way across her face.

There was an awkward pause for a moment, neither of them quite knowing what to say next, then Ben, feeling that he was being rather ungallant, asked, 'Can I do anything to help?'

'You could let her have a bath,' Josh declared. 'We've got no water. Mummy isn't a very good plumber.'

'Is that so?' Ben was grinning now too, while Amy tried to shut Josh up. Honestly. Children could really be the limit sometimes.

'Yes, well,' said Amy squirming, 'I had a small fight with the taps and the taps won. So now I've got no water.'

'Oh dear,' said Ben, trying and failing to suppress laughter.

'It's not funny,' protested Amy, in a rather feeble manner. 'I was coming out here to see if I could find my neighbour, Harry, and ask him if he knew a plumber.'

'You won't find Harry today,' said Ben, 'he's gone to one of his army reunions. Oh lord, now you've made me feel really guilty. We've only just met and already I've nearly run over your son, my dog's scared him and knocked you into my manure. Next time we meet, I'll probably burn your house down. Please, please let me make amends. Come over to mine and use my bath. And then I'll see if I can sort out your taps.'

Amy hesitated. This was a perfect stranger, after all. But if he was a friend of Harry's it probably meant he wasn't a serial killer.

56

'It's okay,' said Ben. 'You can trust me. I'm a doctor.'

'Are you, really?' Amy burst out laughing.

'Really,' said Ben with a smile. 'I work at the Riverview Practice if you don't believe me. The name's Ben Martin.'

'Okay, I believe you,' said Amy. 'I just signed up there yesterday, and I remember seeing your name. Luckily you don't appear to be my doctor. Which is probably just as well, given our recent history.'

Ben was impressed with the way she seemed to be taking this all in her stride. Despite her enjoyment of gardening, Caroline always managed to keep immaculate while doing it. He hated to think how she would have reacted if she'd ended up in a pile of manure. Not as well as this attractive stranger, that was for sure.

'It probably is,' he replied, grinning. 'And you are?'

'Amy Nicolson,' said Amy. 'Come on, Josh, Ben's going to find Mummy some clean clothes.'

Together, they followed Ben towards his house. Amy still felt an idiot but Ben's manner was so easy and open that it didn't seem to matter somehow. Perhaps her initial impression of a bad-tempered lout had been wrong.

'Bathroom's in there,' said Ben when they entered the house. 'Here, have a towel. I'll get you some clean clothes. Will Josh be okay watching TV?'

Josh was more than okay watching TV, particularly once he discovered that Ben had *Spiderman* in his DVD collection.

Ten minutes later, Amy emerged from the bathroom,

drying her hair with a towel, and wearing a rugby shirt of Ben's and some leggings he'd found, which presumably must have belonged to a previous girlfriend. She wondered idly what sort of woman was his type. Obviously a tall one if the leggings were anything to go by.

Ben gave a sharp intake of breath. He was taken aback by the sudden pull of attraction he felt for Amy. It had been a long time since he had looked at a woman other than Caroline.

'Tea?' he asked quickly, moving to the kitchen and switching on the radio, where Jonathan Ross was entertaining a female singer well known for her risqué behaviour in a way only he knew how.

'Oh, great, you like Radio 2 too,' said Amy.

'I listen to nothing else,' declared Ben. 'I'm sadly obsessed with that chap who does the allotment bit on the Jeremy Vine programme.'

'What, Terry, the Adopted Allotmenteer?' said Amy. 'He's brill, isn't he? Last time I heard him he was talking about runner beans. I couldn't believe he could make it so interesting.'

They paused and smiled shyly at one another.

'I know,' said Amy. 'I used to think Radio 2 was really old hat, but thanks to my –' Oh God, here I go again, she thought. Was there ever going to be an easy way to say 'my dead partner'? Today she couldn't face the questions, or the sympathy, so she fudged it instead. '– to Jamie – my boyfriend –'

Damn! thought Ben, she had a boyfriend. He was startled to find that bothered him.

'– I started listening and discovered they play loads of music I like. So I listen all the time now. This is probably going to sound barking but I'm on my own such a lot, I find it's like having a friend in the kitchen.' She paused, feeling that she was rambling. 'You probably have no idea what I'm even talking about.'

'Oh, I think I do,' said Ben, wondering why she was alone so much. He had heard the hesitation in her voice when she mentioned her boyfriend – maybe Jamie was off the scene. 'Lots of my patients, especially the elderly ones, say the same thing. And my surgery has such tissue-thin walls I often have the radio on in the background so that people outside my room don't hear what I'm saying. I find Radio 2 is usually inoffensive enough not to upset anyone too much.' He paused. 'So, what does Jamie do?'

Amy took a deep breath. The question had come after all. She should have just faced it dead on, rather than hedging her bets.

'Jamie's – oh, I didn't explain myself very well. Jamie died two years ago. I've moved here on my own, with my son, Josh.'

Oh God. Ben had imagined a parting of the ways, but Amy seemed too young to have faced that kind of pain. But then, age didn't always come into bereavement, as he knew himself, all too well. Cursing himself for putting his foot in it, Ben wondered what he could say, and finding nothing adequate, left it at a simple, 'I'm so sorry, I just assumed.'

'It's okay, people generally do.' Amy waved him away.

Harry evidently hadn't said anything to Ben about her, which pleased her somehow. She liked the fact that her neighbour hadn't gossiped. 'You weren't to know, and anyway, nowadays I cope pretty well.'

Amy smiled as she said this, but there was a sadness in her eyes and her demeanour became closed and wary. Ben took this as a hint to change the subject.

'Right, I don't know about you, but I have a fair bit to do today, so shall we head straight over to yours?'

'Thanks, that would be great,' said Amy, grateful that he hadn't pursued the subject of Jamie. 'Come on, Josh, time we were off.'

'Oh, but I wanted to see what happens next,' Josh protested.

'It's all right, you can see it another time,' said Amy, then paused. It seemed presumptuous to assume they would see Ben again.

'Or I could lend it to you,' said Ben quickly.

'Well – if you're sure . . .' began Amy.

'Positive,' said Ben. 'I've seen it loads of times. Come on then, this plumbing isn't going to sort itself out.'

It just showed how first impressions could be so wrong. In fact, as they ambled companionably back across the allotments, Amy reflected that it was a long, long time since she had met anyone who had put her so much at her ease.

Ben followed Amy and Josh up the garden path with a growing feeling of awkwardness. It had seemed like a good idea to suggest he mended her taps, but now he was here he began to question the wisdom of his offer. The last time he had been in this house, a couple of nights before Caroline left, she'd ended up seducing him again, despite his best intentions. After a night of lust and tangled passion, Ben had woken up and wondered just what the hell he was doing. He'd told her then that it was over, and the memory of her tears made him wince. He couldn't bear to hurt anyone, and they had been very close for a while. He still felt guilty that he had made her cry. Thankfully, no one else knew about it.

And now he was following another woman into Caroline's house. A woman he found very attractive, he had to admit. But even Amy's merits couldn't quite eclipse the vision of Caroline that hit him the minute he walked through the door. She was in every room – cooking in the kitchen, laughing in the lounge, dancing in the dining room, and – where he could hardly bear to picture her – sensual in the bedroom. Amy had already made her mark on the house, it was true – she had changed around some of the furniture, and got rid of Caroline's wind-chimes and aromatherapy candles – but the whisper of Caroline remained everywhere.

Trying to shake off the feeling of melancholy made Ben matter-of-fact, his manner brisk. It had been a big mistake coming back here. He just wanted to get the taps done and go.

'Right,' he said. 'The bathroom's through here, isn't it?'

Amy was surprised. 'You seem to know your way around pretty well,' she said.

'I'm often in and out of these houses, seeing patients,' said Ben shortly. 'All these houses have the same layout.'

Ben was aware his terseness sounded rude, but he couldn't bring himself to mention how he knew this house, or how intimately.

Amy was slightly taken aback by the change in Ben's manner. He had already found the offending taps and was starting work, but he seemed to have withdrawn into himself. She wondered whether she had upset him somehow, so decided to change the subject instead.

'Have you had an allotment long?' she asked. 'I can't wait to get out there and sort mine out.'

'Are you a gardener as well?' Ben was interested despite his resolve to get out of there as soon as possible. He had a soft spot for anyone who was prepared to discuss the merits of growing things. It wasn't Amy's fault she lived in his ex's house.

'I love gardening,' Amy replied. 'We always wanted to live in the country and grow our own vegetables. I'm dying to get onto the allotments. I just haven't had time yet. And when I'm a bit more settled I'd like to go into gardening properly. Actually, I've just finished doing a course.'

'Have you met Saffron yet?' said Ben. 'She runs her own gardening business, with Caroline, but with Caroline gone I think she might be after some help.'

'Is she?' said Amy, her eyes lighting up with interest. 'I might just get in touch then. Thanks.'

'Right, that's all done for you,' said Ben, wiping his hands on his jeans.

'Thanks so much,' said Amy. 'That was really good of you. Would you like to stay for a cup of tea?'

'No thanks,' said Ben. 'I'd better go. I've got lots to do on the allotment.'

'And I wouldn't dream of keeping a man away from his digging,' said Amy, disappointed but trying to sound cheerful.

When she smiled, Ben noticed, her eyes lit up her whole face. There was something about her that he instantly warmed to, and he realised, as he strolled back home, that it was a very pleasant feeling indeed.

'What's this I hear that you run a gardening business?'

Amy greeted Saffron as they stood outside the school gates. Ellie was asleep in the buggy, and Saffron looked quite relaxed for a change.

Saffron pulled a face.

'Well, I'm not entirely sure it merits the term business. "Disaster" might be more apt at the moment,' she said. 'How did you know?'

'I met Ben Martin on the allotments the other day,' said Amy. 'Or rather, his dog knocked me into a pile of manure. I felt like such a prat. But he was very nice about it.'

'So he should be,' said Saffron. 'That dog's a liability

63

sometimes. Mind you, I can think of worse people whose feet you could fall at. He's gorgeous. If I wasn't married already . . .'

'Does he have a girlfriend?' asked Amy.

'Not that I know of,' said Saffron, 'but I'm not one to listen to gossip, and I've been so busy this year with work and a new baby that I don't tend to know what's going on anyway. Why do you ask? Are you on the lookout?'

'As if! I was curious, that's all,' said Amy. 'So come on, tell me all about this business of yours.'

'Not much to tell, since Caroline left me in the lurch,' said Saffron.

'What's Caroline like?' Amy asked. 'Her name keeps popping up everywhere.'

Saffron grimaced. 'I'm probably not the best person to ask, as she's made my life a nightmare. We met on a gardening course in Sudbury three years back, and when we found out we lived so near to one another it seemed like a good idea to set up a business together. And at first it was great – she's good at self-promotion and got us loads of clients to begin with, plus she is really good at garden design. But out of the blue she decided she had to go travelling to find herself, just before Ellie was born, and left me to pick up the pieces.'

'Bummer,' said Amy. 'What a pain.'

'*She* can be,' said Saffron. 'I think her main problem is that her parents are loaded, so she's really spoilt and has never had to take responsibility for anything in her entire life. Plus she has a rather irritating tendency to flutter her eyelashes and get men to do her dirty work for her – she was always getting the blokes on the allotment to do her digging and stuff. She's a terrible flirt. She even tried it on with Pete once, when I was pregnant with Ellie. I was furious, I can tell you. But Pete just laughed it off, and said it was just the way she was.'

'Ouch,' said Amy.

'Ouch indeed,' said Saffron. 'Anyway, enough of her. Why did you want to know about my gardening business?'

'Well, I was just wondering if you had any openings? I'm itching to get my green fingers dirty.'

'Are you serious?'

'Absolutely,' said Amy. 'I've arranged with the school to do some supply teaching, but I need another income, and the idea was always to try and make money from gardening.'

'I could really, really use the help,' said Saffron. 'I'm drowning on my own. Though I warn you, the finances are a bit dicey at the moment, so I can't pay much.'

'That's okay,' said Amy. 'I've got a bit of a cushion to tide me over for the next few months.'

'Great,' said Saffron. 'That's such a weight off my mind.'

'Then it's a deal,' said Amy, grinning. 'When do I start?'

CHAPTER FIVE

Amy was cooking lunch for herself and Josh – or, rather, for Josh. She had a terrible habit of finishing up his leftovers, and eating on the run. She couldn't remember the last time she had made a proper meal for herself. She really ought to bring herself in hand. The radio was on, and it being Saturday she was listening to Jonathan Ross, who always made her laugh. And today he was making her laugh more than ever. For the first time in months she was feeling positive and cheerful about the future.

After Saffron had discovered her interest in gardening, she had insisted on dragging Amy back home and showing her the latest plans for Green Fingers. Saffron had nearly cleared the backlog left by Caroline, but she still had clients who were urgently demanding their gardens be tidied up for the autumn, as well as several who were after table decorations for Christmas.

'Mind you,' Saffron admitted ruefully, 'I am in something of a fix. Because although I have too much work at the moment, once I've caught up, I don't have any new clients. I've lost a lot over the summer, and, to be honest, with the baby and everything I've been too exhausted to think about marketing.'

'Have you got a website?' Amy said.

'God no,' Saffron replied. 'I'm way too computer illiterate for that.'

'Actually, it's quite easy,' Amy told her. 'It's simply a question of buying a domain name and a package from a company that's into website-building.'

'Oh right,' said Saffron, surprised. 'How do you know all this stuff?'

'You'd be amazed what you pick up teaching IT to seven-year-olds,' Amy replied vaguely. It was actually Jamie who had taught her about computing, and when he and Giles had set up in business together she'd ended up getting involved in creating their website. Neither of them had been much good with design, but Amy loved playing about with typefaces and graphics and she had been happy to help.

'Sounds great,' said Saffron. 'Got any other good ideas? Caroline was always great at that kind of stuff. I haven't got a clue.'

'Well, I could design you a leaflet if you like,' said Amy. 'And then you could do a drop with the local paper. Or leave them in shops – the local hairdressers would be a good place to start. You could offer a ten per cent discount on your first job or something. How does that sound?'

'It sounds fantastic,' said Saffron eagerly. 'You are sent from heaven to solve all my problems. I would never have thought of that on my own.'

'Aaah,' said Amy. 'I have been wanting to set up my own business for ages, so I've done a lot of planning over the years. And I've got a couple of weeks till my supply teaching starts, so I've got time at the moment.'

Before she knew it, Amy was also agreeing to go and price a job with Saffron the following Tuesday, once the kids were at school. It was just what she needed to move her life forward. She couldn't wait to get started.

So, a little later, humming to the tune playing on the radio, she was cheerfully busying herself in the kitchen when the doorbell rang. Puzzled, she went to answer it. She wasn't expecting anyone, and although Harry had taken to popping in from time to time to borrow some milk or play a game with Josh, she knew he had gone out to see friends today. She had been enjoying his avuncular concern. He was an easy person to be around, and it did Josh good to have a grand-fatherly figure about. They often spent time with Harry at the weekends, taking the odd walk, going for pub lunches. Despite her differences with Mary, Amy recognised she had lost a useful support system, and Harry was doing a good job of plugging the gap.

She opened the door, and nearly passed out.

'Mary! What a surprise!' She hoped the shock in her face wasn't too obvious. It wasn't that she didn't want to see Mary, but it would have been nice to have had some prior warning.

'Well, I was coming to visit my sister in Romford,' said Mary, in rather stiff tones, 'so I thought I'd pop in to see how you were both doing. I hope you don't mind.'

Romford to Nevermorewell was a good hour and a half. Something told Amy this wasn't a spontaneous visit.

'Mind? Of course I don't mind,' lied Amy, hoping the house wasn't too untidy. 'It's lovely to see you. Josh, look who's here!'

Josh, who had been playing with his train set in the front room, came diving out when he heard Mary's voice.

'Granneeee!' he shrieked in delight, and flung himself at her.

Amy was relieved to see the pleasure in Mary's face when she hugged her grandson. After all, it wasn't really Amy she had come to see. And whether or not Amy cared to admit it, by moving away from Mary, she had taken away from her mother-in-law all that was left of Jamie. Josh, too, seemed ecstatic to see his grandmother. Amy had been fretting that he had seemed very quiet since the move. Now, seeing him so natural with Mary, she realised he hadn't been his normal self. The old guilt welled up inside her, threatening to engulf the good feelings and bring her right back to square one. Mary's next comment didn't help much either.

'Oh, I have missed you both!' she said. 'The house seems so quiet without you. No chance that you'll change your mind, I suppose?'

'We've only just got here,' said Amy, trying to laugh it off and ignore the feelings of resentment the remark engendered.

'Granny could come and live here,' suggested Josh.

'I don't think that's going to be possible, Josh,' said Mary. She glanced at Amy, as if to say, is it?

Amy tried to ignore that comment too. The last thing she wanted right now was to have Mary round the corner again, even if she *wanted* to move out this way. And as they sat politely sipping their tea, Amy was suddenly struck by the gulf that had grown between them. It had only been a few weeks, but already she and Mary were strangers in this new environment; and yet, after Jamie's death they had seemed so close. Irritated as she was by Mary, Amy couldn't bear to lose that, and for Josh's sake it wasn't fair. So she asked suitable questions about Mary's life and filled her in on their own doings. And then Josh mentioned Ben.

'And who's Ben?' asked Mary. 'One of your little playmates?'

'Oh no,' said Josh in disgusted tones. 'Ben's well old. As old as Mummy.'

'And?' Mary looked askance at Amy.

'And what?' said Amy. 'Ben's someone I met on the allotments.'

'Yes, and Mummy borrowed his clothes and he lent me his *Spiderman* DVD when we were at his house. He's really cool.'

'I see,' said Mary testily.

No, you don't, Amy wanted to reply, but restrained herself.

'Yes, it was a bit embarrassing really,' said Amy, wondering why she felt the need to justify herself. 'I had a problem with the plumbing and then I got a bit mucky on the allotments so he lent me some clothes.

I barely know him.' She was aware she was gabbling. She was further aware that the more she gabbled, the more sceptically Mary looked at her.

'Well, I suppose it was inevitable that you would find a new man one day,' said Mary, 'but I have to say I'm surprised that you're rushing things.'

Amy blushed, immediately furious with herself for doing so. She had nothing to be embarrassed about or apologise for.

'Mary, I don't have a new man,' she said. 'He's just someone who helped me out.'

'If you say so,' said Mary.

'No, really,' said Amy. 'There is absolutely nothing going on between us, and even if there were, I don't really see that it's any of your business.'

The words were out before she could stop them, and she cursed herself when she saw the look on Mary's face. It was as though Amy had punched her in the stomach.

'Mary, I didn't mean – that came out wrong,' Amy began.

'Your meaning was perfectly clear,' said Mary. 'It's all right, I won't stay where I'm not wanted.'

'Mary!' cried Amy, but Mary didn't reply. Giving Josh a brief hug, she picked up her things, then was out of the door and gone.

'Why didn't Granny stay?' Josh wanted to know.

'She was in a bit of a hurry,' said Amy miserably. 'She'll come back another day.' She desperately hoped that was true.

'I want Granny! I want Granny!' Josh started to wail.

'Oh sweetheart, we'll see her soon.' Amy tried to cuddle Josh, but he kicked her and ran off screaming, 'I hate you! I hate it here! I want Granny!'

'Josh!' Amy was shocked. He'd never behaved like this before.

There was a twenty-minute standoff, during which Josh screamed and flung himself on the floor, before eventually retreating to hide under the table in the lounge. Amy managed to wheedle him out with the promise of chocolate – a bribe she knew she would later regret – and when he'd finally calmed down, she said, 'Come on, let's go on the allotments, the fresh air will do us both good.'

The tantrum now over, Josh seemed happy enough to come out with her, but if Amy had hoped for some kind of redemption from the allotments, it wasn't forthcoming. Mary's visit had left her feeling unsettled and miserable. It was a grey, dull day, and the smell of burning fires made her feel melancholy. The sound of leaves crunching underfoot reminded Amy that winter was on its way. Winter, and another Christmas to face without Jamie.

Several people she knew by sight nodded at her, but no one stopped for a chat. The strange man she'd seen on her first day here sidled up to her as she passed his allotment. 'It's a war zone out there,' he said, his soft Suffolk burr making a surreal contrast with the writhing bucket he thrust under her nose. It contained a wriggling mass of slugs. Amy didn't know whether to laugh or cry.

'Bastard slugs get everywhere,' he added, 'but they're

no match for old Jeremy.' He cackled in an alarming way before setting the bucket on the ground and pouring a brown liquid into it.

'Beer,' he said by way of explanation, cracking his fingers. 'Gets bastard slugs every time.'

'Right,' said Amy. 'Well, I'd best get on.'

The encounter unsettled her, and despite Josh's presence she felt desperately alone. She threw herself into her digging as a way of venting her emotion, but it was no good – seeing Mary again had pulled her back to the life she had left behind. Pictures of Jamie, which she had started to hold at bay here, in her new home, came flooding back.

Amy was on a boat. The sun was shining, and a band was playing on the quayside as the boat pulled out to sea. She could see Jamie up ahead with Josh in his arms, striding towards the outside decks. Why wasn't she with them? It didn't make sense. She was glad that Jamie was there. She had a strange feeling, as if something bad had happened to him. But of course it hadn't. There he was ahead of her. She called his name. But Jamie didn't turn round.

She hurried to follow them, calling Jamie's name again. Why couldn't he hear her? But when she got outside, he and Josh had vanished. Frantically she asked her fellow passengers if they had seen a man carrying a boy, but everyone looked at her blankly and passed on their way.

A feeling of panic was rising inside her. Something

was terribly wrong, but by now the boat was docking at a harbour, and Amy was standing on dry land again. The sun burned hot in the sky, and the band was playing an old music-hall tune, louder and louder, faster and faster. People were swirling past her, laughing and joking, having a wonderful time completely oblivious to her.

Up on the boat, she noticed flags waving, and people cheering. Where were Jamie and Josh? Then she spotted them high up on the top deck of the boat. Jamie had his back to her and was bouncing Josh in the air. She called to him again. But he didn't turn around. Why wouldn't he turn around?

Up and down. Up and down. Jamie kept throwing Josh, higher and higher. He didn't hear her shout of warning, and suddenly Josh was falling, falling out of his father's hands over the side of the boat. Amy screamed and called for help. And finally, Jamie turned to look at her. It wasn't Jamie at all, but a hideous grinning corpse. Amy screamed and screamed, but no sound came out . . .

Amy sat bolt upright in bed, sweating profusely. Her heart was beating wildly and her breathing was erratic. She turned the light on and looked at the alarm clock. It was 2 a.m. Beside her in the bed, Josh muttered and moaned. Damn. When had he come in? Amy would have taken him back to bed, but the dream had unsettled her. She felt like company tonight. And the sight of Josh lying safe next to her did a lot to dispel the awful dream picture of him falling, falling, falling. Amy shivered. The thought of losing Josh as well was too much to bear. She couldn't face trying to sleep again, so she got out a book and read until she could read no more, and the book slid out of her hands.

The morning dawned grey and miserable. Amy felt tired and listless, and Josh, seeming to pick up on her mood, was crabby and badly behaved. She let him watch *Spiderman* again while she cooked lunch, and then decided they both needed to get out of the house. In her wanderings the previous week, Amy had discovered a little park just before you hit the high street. And as Josh had gone into Spidey overdrive, attacking her at every opportunity, she also decided that it was time she gave Ben his DVD back. If they cut up through the graveyard, Ben's house was on the way back. So, putting the DVD in her pocket and making a resolute decision to try to be cheerful, Amy and Josh set off.

Ben had just come in from the allotments and was in the shower, when the doorbell rang.

Damn, who could that be? he wondered. He wasn't really in the mood for visitors. Caroline had just emailed to invite him to spend Christmas skiing with her in Colorado. *Dave behind the Bar will B there 2!* she had said. *It will b great!* He was sorely tempted by the skiing. But the idea of being used in one of Caroline's silly games really didn't appeal. He was probably on call anyway.

The doorbell rang again. It was most likely Harry, who was about the only person besides Pete who ever came to see him. Ben hadn't lived in Nevermorewell long, and his job meant he was always slightly wary about making new friends too close to home. Harry tended to pop over sometimes on Sunday evenings, often to ask him to come for a pint. Ben knew Harry was lonely, and found his war stories fascinating, so he never said no. Besides, Ben rarely went to the pub with his own dad, and going out with Harry fulfilled some deep need.

Despite his inclination to leave whoever it was out there, Ben felt he'd better answer it. He shouted, 'Hang on a sec', flung a towel around his waist and raced down the stairs to the door.

'What can I do for you today, Harry?' he was halfway through saying, when he realised it wasn't Harry.

There on the doorstep stood a very disconcerted Amy and Josh.

'Er – we'll come back another time,' said Amy, blushing. Up close and personal it was a sudden shock to discover that Ben was, well . . . sexy. She hadn't noticed before quite how firm his chest was, or how strong his arms . . . It must be all that digging.

'No, it's fine,' said Ben, thinking how pretty she looked when she blushed. 'I'll – just throw some clothes on. Why don't you make yourself at home? I'll bung the kettle on.'

'Well, if you're sure . . .' Amy sounded doubtful. 'I was just bringing the DVD back. We can come back another time.' She seemed destined to always meet this man in the most awkward of circumstances.

'Why, have you got any better offers?' he said.

Amy laughed. 'Hardly,' she replied. 'Go on then, where do you keep your teabags?'

While Amy hunted for mugs, Josh was getting bored. 'Can I go in the garden?' he asked.

'Yes, so long as you don't get into mischief,' said Amy, 'and remember, it's not our lawn so don't scuff it up.'

Two minutes later, Ben appeared just as Amy was taking two cups of tea into the lounge. Casually dressed in blue shirt and jeans, with his hair still slightly damp from the shower, Amy was totally unprepared for the effect he had on her. Maybe it was the thought of having seen that body so recently unclothed, but Amy was coming out in a cold sweat. She must have been blind not to have noticed how gorgeous he was.

His dark hair was slightly mussed up, and his brown eyes were lively and curious, while his mouth – which seemed to be shaping words that for some reason Amy wasn't hearing – his mouth was eminently kissable. Her heart beat a little faster and she felt faintly sick. She hadn't felt like this – well, since she'd met Jamie. Jamie's face shot into her head. And she felt a sudden lurch of guilt.

They reached the doorway of the lounge at the same time, and Ben stood aside to let her pass. The guilty tension she felt was churned up with a desire she couldn't repress. She felt dizzy. Then the words he was forming seemed to make sense.

'Ladies first,' he said, his smile illuminating his face.

Squeezing past him, a sudden vision hit her of being held by those arms, kissed by that mouth, pressed close to that chest. What *was* going on?

Understanding for perhaps the first time in her life

what was meant by going weak at the knees, Amy. mumbled something about tea being ready, before collapsing thankfully on the sofa.

Ben perched on a chair opposite her. There was a long silence, neither of them knowing quite what to say.

'So, did you enjoy the film?'

'Have you been on the allotments?'

They spoke simultaneously, and then laughed.

'You first,' said Ben.

'No, you,' said Amy.

'After you,' said Ben. 'I insist.'

'I was just making small talk,' said Amy, feeling faintly silly. 'But yes, we did. Well, Josh did.'

'Me too,' said Ben. 'But as it happens, I have been on the allotments.'

They sat for a moment, saying nothing and sipping their tea. After a few moments the silence between them grew in magnitude. Amy felt paralysed by the strangeness of her new feelings, and totally unable to say another word. This was ridiculous. She wasn't a teenager any more. And she had no interest in Ben. None at all.

'So what do we talk about when we run out of small talk?' asked Ben eventually.

'Ooh, I don't know,' said Amy. 'The weather?'

'Whatever turns you on,' said Ben, laughing. Then thought, damn, that was a crass thing to say.

Luckily, Amy didn't seem offended.

'We-e-ell, I can't say that the weather is a topic that really gets me going,' she said, 'but now you've made me curious. What does interest you?'

'Oh, I don't know, all sorts,' said Ben. 'Formula One.' Amy pulled a face. 'Okay, we won't talk about cars. I'm interested in health issues, which we won't discuss because that's work. I like politics, but if we think differently we might fall out. Books are usually a safe bet. Oh, and I'm also keen on local history –'

'Ah, now *there* you have found a subject close to my heart,' said Amy. 'I find local history fascinating. I had to research a lot about Barnet for school trips with Year 5. It was really interesting. The kids always laughed when I told them the origin of the phrase "a barnet" for a haircut.'

'Which is?'

'Cockney rhyming slang – Barnet Fair, hair,' said Amy.

'Right,' said Ben, laughing. 'If you're interested, I've got lots of books on Nevermorewell. They reckon there was a hamlet here as far back as Anglo-Saxon times, but the town didn't really get going till Norman times. They built on a river for obvious reasons, but in olden days it was reckoned to be a healthy sort of place to live. "You're Never More Well than when you're in Nevermorewell", is the saying around here.'

'Saffron mentioned that,' said Amy. 'I'll have to come back and borrow a few books sometime.'

They smiled at one another, pleased to have found some common ground. Amy glanced at her watch.

'Sheesh! Is that the time? I'd better get going,' she said. 'I need to sort Josh's tea out.'

'You could both eat here if you like? I can rustle up a mean stir-fry.'

'No, thanks, it's very kind of you,' Amy said, sorely tempted at the prospect of company as well as someone cooking for her, 'but he's got school tomorrow and needs an early night. I really ought to drag him in from the garden.'

They both got up and had another moment's awkwardness while they nearly fell over each other trying to negotiate round Ben's tiny table.

Amy's confusion made her slightly jumpy. Once outside, when they couldn't find Josh, she started to panic, until Ben laughed and said, 'I see you've found my prized possession.'

At the bottom of Ben's garden in the far corner was a small garage. With a gleaming black and silver motorbike in it. Amy hadn't thought about the bike since their first meeting. And there was Josh, sitting triumphantly on the seat, his legs dangling down at the sides. Amy took a deep breath. She should be over this paranoia about motorbikes. Really she should. But she wasn't. What was it with men and motorbikes? It was Jamie's obsession with his that had led to his death.

'Look Mummy, isn't it cool?' Josh said. 'Brmmm, brmm.'

It felt as though he and Ben were laughing at her. Amy screamed, 'Get off there at once!'

'It's all right,' said Ben. 'He's only playing. He won't come to any harm.'

'No it is *not* all right,' said Amy. 'Motorbikes are lethal machines used by stupid blokes whose dicks are too small. It is *so* not all right for my son to play on one. Come on, Josh, we're going home.'

She grabbed Josh and tore past Ben, hoping he wouldn't see the tears in her eyes, slamming the garden gate shut.

Ben stood watching her go, his mouth wide open. 'Now what have I done?' he said.

CHAPTER SIX

Saffron peeked left and right, making sure there was no one to watch her, before diving into Nevermorewell's answer to Ann Summers: a discreet 'lingerie' shop that sold sex toys to make your mother blush. She had the pram with her. Oh lord, how dumb was that? Did other women take their babies out to buy sexy underwear? Was it some kind of bad parenting to take your newborn into an atmosphere rife with passion; a place that boasted Licked Up Love Juice and Pump Up Your Volume Potion? What if someone had seen her? She hadn't even looked at anything yet and already paroxysms of embarrassment were screwing her up. Two cheerful French girls were chattering away, fingering lacy garments Saffron could barely look at, let alone touch, and she envied their insouciance.

'Can I help you?' Saffron nearly jumped out of her skin.

The slim, twenty-something shop assistant appeared friendly enough, but to Saffron it seemed that there was a sneer in her smile: a sneer that seemed to say,

What on earth is some fat middle-aged frump like you doing in a place like this? Who do you think you're kidding?

Who indeed? Saffron already knew this was a big mistake. But, happening to have heard a slot on the Jeremy Vine show about spicing up your sex life, she'd discovered that all she really needed to get her libido going again was to buy some sexy underwear. *'You will feel sexy, he will feel sexy, and before you know it you'll be falling all over each other,'* the cheery doctor chatting to Jeremy had promised, and heaven knows there'd been precious little of that in the Cairns household of late. So Saffron had decided that sexy underwear was a must.

After a first nervous flit into the lingerie department in M&S, where she had spotted three mums from school, Saffron had lost her nerve and nearly called it a day. But the lingerie shop was on her way home, and even the sexy underwear in M&S seemed somewhat on the chaste side. Instinctively, Saffron felt chaste wasn't what she was after.

Which was how she'd found herself feeling like a total prat in front of a sneering girl nearly young enough to be her daughter, whose waistline was invisible, although her thong was not, and who oozed sexuality from every pore. Being the age she was, she probably took it for granted. You just wait, Saffron wanted to say, one day you too will turn to blubber.

'Well?' The girl was not just sneering, but impatient. Jeez, didn't they send them on customer-care courses – *Remember, ninety-five per cent of your customers are going to be embarrassed, so do try to put them at their ease (the other five per cent will be so uninhibited you will be hiding under the table).*

'Erm – well, er, canitrythatonplease?' Saffron pointed to a busty black basque, complete with lacy bits and suspender belt. She hadn't worn anything like it in years.

'What size are you?' The girl, who was all of a size eight, looked Saffron up and down in the certain knowledge that she must be at least an eighteen.

'Er – fourteen, I think,' said Saffron. Once upon a time she would have said ten, and after Becky and Matt she had trimmed back down to size twelve. At the moment she was nearer sixteen, but she was damned if she was going to admit that to this jumped-up ten-year-old.

'Here you are.' The girl handed over the basque. 'Do you want anything else?'

'No, that will be all,' said Saffron, practically pulling the offending item out of the woman's grasp. She pushed the pram to the changing rooms, and squeezed into a cubicle. She undressed, wincing a little at the sight of her naked body. Why were changing-room mirrors always so unflattering? She blobbed and sagged in places she didn't know she had.

She placed the basque over her head, and immediately got entangled in bits of lace and ribbon. She tried to pull it off and realised to her horror it was stuck. She pulled it this way and that, just making out a vision of herself in the mirror, a big fat blob with a bright red face incarcerated in a mesh of black lace. Tugging just that bit harder, she heard a ping, and a button popped off, but it was enough to give her the leeway she needed. She pulled the basque over her head, and panting in disgust she looked at it more closely. On a second glance, she realised she could actually undo the basque at the front, so she duly popped it round her, and tried to do it up again. It was tight going round her tummy, but by the time she had got to her boobs she could barely breathe. It looked like every blobby bit of her was straining to jump out of the bloody thing. Sexy it was not.

'Are you all right in there?' the ten-year-old called. 'I can get you a size sixteen if you want.'

'Over my dead body,' muttered Saffron, before calling, 'Fine, thanks.'

Size sixteen? *Size sixteen?* She was buggered if she was going to buy size sixteen. What did it matter what she looked like anyway? Pete was only going to take the wretched thing off. Well, with any luck he was – that was unless he'd died laughing first. With the last remaining shreds of her dignity just about intact, Saffron swept out of the changing room, saying, 'I'll take it', and in a totally unwarranted spirit of bravado she grabbed two pairs of silk stockings, some Licked Up Love Juice and a bottle of Pump Up Your Volume Potion, while staring the ten-year-old out. The ten-year-old, sensing the change in temperature, sensibly demurred, and if she had been going to point out the missing button, she was quickly stilled by Saffron's icy look. Saffron grabbed the bag, and shoved it under the pram, before walking out of the shop with her head high. It was only when she rounded the corner that she glanced at the receipt. Christ, she'd spent a fortune. She just hoped Pete would think it was worth it.

'So, you've no idea what caused Amy to run off?' Harry and Ben were sitting in Harry's shed on the allotments sharing a cup of tea, staring out onto the plots, which were bathed in the cold bright light of a low winter sun. Ben had had a late surgery that morning and had sought Harry out.

'None whatsoever,' said Ben. 'One minute we were getting on like a house on fire, the next she'd run off. She seemed to be upset about Josh going on my motorbike.'

'There must be some reason,' said Harry. 'Amy doesn't strike me as the hysterical type. But she has been through a lot. Maybe there are things we don't know.'

'You might be right,' Ben conceded. 'She tore my head off the first time we met because I nearly ran Josh over on the bike.'

'Amy's very vulnerable,' said Harry. 'She could do with the support of a fine young man.'

'Harry, if I didn't know you better, I'd suspect you of matchmaking,' said Ben.

'Now would I do a thing like that?' replied Harry, his eyes twinkling. 'Mind you, now you come to mention it, you're a good-looking young chap. She's a beautiful young woman . . .'

'A beautiful young woman who is also still grieving,'

said Ben. 'I doubt very much she's even thought of me like that.'

'There's always time,' Harry reassured him.

'As I haven't heard from her since Sunday, I think it's unlikely she'll be speaking to me again in a hurry,' said Ben.

'Hmm, that is a pity,' said Harry. 'Joking aside, I do think Amy needs help. Maybe you should make the first move?'

Ben, who had been thinking exactly the same thing, but who had been too anxious about Amy's reaction if he had called round, shook his head.

'Harry, you're incorrigible,' he said. 'You're probably right. I've got to go and walk Meg before work, but I'll try and catch her later.'

'Good man,' Harry replied. 'Ah, Bill, have you got some elderberries for me?'

One of Harry's winemaking buddies was poking his nose round the door, so Ben made his excuses and left. Harry was right. Amy was vulnerable. Something had set her off like that. It wouldn't do any harm to discover what.

Amy sat on the bench in the graveyard overlooking town. It was a peaceful spot, high on the only hill in the area, and from her vantage point she could see the River Bourne gleaming brightly in the bright winter sunlight. The graveyard itself was ramshackle and meandering, with old paths winding their way between moss-stained graves. The bench she was sitting on was under an ancient yew. Amy found it restful here, so different from the sterile modern cemetery where Jamie's urn was interred in a wall, with just a simple plaque to remember him by. She wished she'd stood firm against Mary and buried Jamie somewhere like this, but like so many things she and Jamie had never discussed their preferred method of interment and Mary had insisted cremation was more practical and what Jamie would have wanted. At the time, Amy hadn't thought it mattered.

Amy had been sitting here for an hour already, but she seemed unable to move from the spot. She'd had a fairly useless start to the day. Josh's teacher had called her in to tell her that Josh didn't appear to be settling very well, and, worse still, seemed to be hitting a lot of the smaller children. Amy was shocked and upset. Josh had never behaved like that at nursery. The move must have unsettled him more than she had thought. Promising to have a word with him, Amy had gone home to start work on Saffron's leaflet, only to discover her printer had run out of ink. So now she was ostensibly on the way into town to get some more, but the need to sit still and think had become overwhelming.

So she had sat down and stared at Nevermorewell below her, wondering again if she had made the right decision to come here. Josh was unsettled. She was unsettled. Her reaction to Josh sitting on Ben's bike now seemed over-the-top and hysterical. Was she losing it completely? Meeting the first person she had even liked since Jamie's death had set her out of kilter somehow. Ben was a magnetic presence, and despite her embarrassment at the thought of seeing him again, she knew that she did want to see him again. And that inevitably created a conflict. Could she allow herself to be attracted to Ben? She'd never thought there would be anyone but Jamie. And now suddenly there was. And Jamie wasn't here . . .

Ben was walking Meg through the graveyard, as he normally did, when he stopped short. Sitting with her back to him, on the bench, below the tall yew tree that dwarfed the graveyard, was Amy. Ben paused. She might not want to see him. He should turn round and go before she noticed he was there. Then she turned to look at him, and the look pierced him so completely that it no longer mattered whether she wanted to see him. He wanted to make things right between them more badly than he had wanted anything in a long time.

'Sorry, I'm disturbing you,' he said.

'It's okay,' Amy replied. 'I was just thinking I owed you an apology.'

'What for?'

'The other day,' said Amy. 'I'm really sorry I over-reacted.'

'I suppose you did a little,' said Ben.

'A little is very kind,' said Amy. 'But I think I owe you an explanation.'

'Explain away,' said Ben, hovering awkwardly, before Amy motioned for him to sit down.

'I never told you how Jamie died, did I?' Amy said.

'No, you didn't.'

'Jamie was always keen on bikes, you see,' said Amy, dreamily remembering her first meeting with him, when he'd roared up to the pub she was sitting outside, astride a Suzuki, a vision of unrepentant bad-boy glory. She was pretty much smitten from that moment, and when the bad-boy bit turned out to be an act, it made her like him all the more. 'He'd always ridden them. The bigger the better. I used to get a buzz out of it when I was younger, but I don't know, as time went on I got more nervous about the bike, and kept hoping he would grow out of it – especially when Josh came along.'

'But he didn't?' prompted Ben.

'No, he didn't,' said Amy. 'More's the pity. If he had, he'd still be here . . .' She trailed off. Was it ever going to be easy to tell this story?

'. . . Anyway, to cut to the chase. He came off it one day. They said he died instantly, which was something of a comfort. I haven't gone near a motorbike since. And I certainly won't let Josh near one.'

'So when I let him climb on my bike . . .' began Ben.

'. . . I went off at the deep end,' finished Amy. 'Oh God, I feel such a fool. You weren't to know.'

'Don't even think about it for a second,' said Ben. 'I was cross because I thought you didn't trust me with Josh.'

'Oh God, no,' said Amy. 'Of course I do. Despite being the most neurotic mother in the universe, I do recognise it's good for him to have male role models.'

'I think you're more entitled than most to be a neurotic mum,' said Ben. 'And you're not that bad. You should see some of my patients. I've got one woman who comes in every week with her baby. So far it's had asthma, peanut allergies and a haematoma. I keep telling her the baby is fine. And still she comes.'

'That makes me feels so much better,' laughed Amy. 'I didn't want you thinking I was the madwoman on the allotments.'

'Far from it,' Ben assured her. 'You've had a rough time. I don't want to intrude, but have you ever had counselling or anything? It can help sometimes.'

Amy pulled a face.

'I did go and see someone for a while, but, well, I don't know . . . It helped to talk about Jamie. And you get to the point when you think you're boring people, so it was nice to offload on a total stranger. But then it seemed a bit pointless, after a while. No amount of talking will ever bring him back.'

She looked so sad as she said this that Ben had to resist an overwhelming urge to take her in his arms. But he knew that resist he must. It was clear Amy was a long way from getting over Jamie.

'Sorry,' Amy said. 'I shouldn't go on about it so much. Really, it's fine. And things are much better since I've been here.'

'I don't think you should be sorry about anything,' said Ben. 'Grieving isn't a finite process. And however hard you bury it, it has a habit of resurfacing. I should know.'

He paused, as if he were about to say something else, and Amy looked at him expectantly.

'Oh?' she said.

'Oh, I've seen it happen to many of my patients,' said Ben. He had been on the verge of confiding in her about Sarah, but thought better of it. Amy had enough troubles of her own. She didn't need to be burdened with his problems. 'All the clichés are true, you know: time is a great healer, things do get better. But any time you want to talk, you know where I am.'

'That's really kind of you,' said Amy. 'You don't know how much better that makes me feel.'

'My pleasure,' said Ben, smiling. 'I'd best be off now. I've got surgery in a minute.'

'Go on,' said Amy. 'We don't want to keep the good folk of Nevermorewell waiting.'

Ben laughed and, whistling to Meg, who had wandered off and was rooting about in the bushes, he left Amy sitting there. He cast a look back as he made his way out of the graveyard. She seemed so lonely and fragile. He just wished there was a way of making her happy once and for all.

Saffron was fuming. Sodding Gerry had been supposed to have the kids the previous weekend, and he had let them down again. Something to do with his mum, he said, but Saffron suspected it was more to do with her replacement in Gerry's bed – the third leggy blonde he had been with since leaving Saffron, who was definitely not the childrearing type. The net result was that Becky had sobbed herself to sleep for the previous two nights and Matt had wet the bed again – something he always did at the slightest introduction of emotional stress.

All of which had put paid to Saffron's best-laid plans in the bedroom department, which hadn't been helped by her attempt to introduce Pump Up Your Volume Potion. She had managed to spill it all over a towel, and discovering that it stained everything a rather delicate shade of pink, Saffron had ended up chucking it away. She hadn't dared try the Licked Up Love Juice. Lord alone knew what that would do.

Gerry really was the limit, and he had just rung up to say airily that he couldn't have them for the next two weekends either because of work commitments, and did she mind explaining. When she had told him he could tell them himself, he had just got cross and said that as usual she was being unreasonable. Unable to cope with his idiotic intransigence any longer, she had simply put the phone down on him. The guy was a total moron. She couldn't imagine now what she had ever seen in him.

A ring at the door heralded Amy, swiftly followed by Saffron's mum, Elizabeth (after whom Ellie was named), who had come to babysit. Elizabeth had high Gerry Alert Antennae, and promptly asked what That Man had done now. When Saffron told them both, trying to make it appear funnier than it was, they spent the next ten minutes devising ways of punishing Gerry, mostly involving his genitalia and lots of boiling oil.

As a result, when she and Amy finally left the house, Saffron was feeling much better.

'Sorry about that,' she said. 'Gerry always has that effect on me. Does your ex do the same to you?'

With a shock, Amy realised that she hadn't got round to telling Saffron the true state of affairs in her home. She had kind of been relying on Josh to do it for her. He had a tendency to announce rather matter-of-factly to perfect strangers that his daddy was in heaven with baby Jesus.

'Oh, I thought Harry or Ben might have told you,' she said. 'I don't have an ex. Jamie – that's Josh's dad – died two years ago.'

'Oh lord, I am so sorry,' said Saffron, her hand going to her mouth. 'And there's me ranting on about my little worries – I'm always putting my foot in it.'

'Please don't worry,' said Amy. 'I should have told you sooner. It's just not a very easy thing to say sometimes.'

'I'm sure it isn't,' said Saffron. 'Bloody hell, Amy. That's awful. How on earth do you cope? You always seem so incredibly together.'

'I'm better since I've been here,' said Amy. 'But there are times when I think I'll never get over it. I always felt like Jamie was my soul mate. I was only nineteen when we met. He was older – twenty-four. Neither of us had dads – mine left years ago, and his died when he was young – so it brought us together. And apart from my brother, I have no family here, so we became everything to each other. Jamie and Amy – "the rhyming couple" was what my mother-in-law always called us. I thought we'd be together forever . . .'

Saffron shivered, thinking of how she would feel if something happened to Pete. She couldn't imagine life without him. It didn't bear thinking about.

'Have you ever thought you might meet someone else?' she asked gently.

Amy shook her head. 'I really couldn't imagine it,' she said simply. 'I just can't see how anyone else would match up. Maybe I'll feel differently one day, but not now.'

'Oh Amy, that's so sad!' said Saffron. 'I wish I could do something to make it better.'

'You already have,' said Amy, taking her arm. 'You've given me a chance of a new start, and been a good friend to me already. It's all right really, I am so much better than I was even six months ago. Now come on, we have a job to do.'

'Are you sure this is a good idea?'

Ben and Harry were outside Amy's house, carrying plastic bags, flowers (Ben) and a bottle of wine (Harry). Ben felt stupidly nervous about this impromptu visit. Harry, on the other hand, had been very insistent, saying that he felt Amy needed company. Ben again had the sneaking suspicion that Harry was trying to manoeuvre him and Amy together, and he had to admit that the idea pleased him.

Amy had just put Josh to bed, and was sitting down with a glass of wine, when she heard the doorbell go.

'Hi,' said Ben as she opened the door.

'Hi,' said Amy.

'Here, have these.' Ben thrust the flowers into her hand. 'By way of apology for the other day.'

'Thanks, but really, you shouldn't have,' said Amy, a little overwhelmed.

'We've also got a surplus of stuff from our allotments,' Ben said, holding up his plastic bags. 'Would you like some marrows? I've got a surfeit, and there're only so many ways you can cook a marrow.'

'And I thought you might like to try some of my elderberry wine,' said Harry, peeking out from behind Ben.

'Be warned, it's lethal,' said Ben, laughing.

'We thought that as you can't get out much with young Josh, you might like some company,' said Harry.

'But this is too much,' protested Amy.

'Of course, if you'd rather be on your own . . .' Harry said, but the concern in his eyes spoke for itself. Sensing an ambush, and feeling that neither of them would give in without a fight, Amy let them in. She was touched by their thoughtfulness – she *was* often lonely in the evenings once Josh was in bed, particularly as the nights were starting to draw in. It would be nice to have some adults around for a change.

'Have either of you eaten?' Amy asked. 'I do a great spag bol.'

'That sounds delicious,' said Harry. 'Here, let me open the wine.'

'I hope you don't mind the invasion,' Ben said, following her into the kitchen, 'but after we talked the other day, Harry and I, well, we both figured you might be lonely sometimes.'

'Well, you figured right,' said Amy. 'Thanks for your concern.'

There was a warm glowing feeling somewhere in the pit of her stomach. She was being looked after and cosseted by these two unlikely friends. It was a long time since she had felt so cared for.

'And go easy on Harry's wine, if you don't want a sore head,' added Ben, while Amy carried glasses through to the lounge.

'Nonsense, old boy,' said Harry, who already seemed half-cut. 'Nectar of the gods, even though I say it myself.'

'There's nothing wrong with the taste,' said Ben. 'It's just the morning after that isn't so pleasant. And you know you should be careful with your blood pressure the way it is.'

'Oh, tosh,' said Harry, waving Ben away. 'You worry too much. And after all, I only have myself to please. If I overindulge it serves me right.'

The warm glow crept over the whole of Amy. Looking at the pair of them laughing and joking in her lounge was like having a breath of fresh air blowing into her life. She might never learn to love again, but Harry and Ben were both right: she could learn to live again. And a little chink of light had just wormed its way into her cold and barren heart. It was a start.

CHAPTER SEVEN

The Mamas & the Papas were crooning from Ben's car stereo as he headed up the motorway from his parents' house. The leaves were less brown than non-existent, but Mama Cass had one thing right: the sky was an irredeemably awful muted grey. The colour of which fitted his mood right now – a sort of sad and subdued melancholy that always lingered with him after a visit home.

He hated this annual pilgrimage down to his parents – the purpose of which was ostensibly to celebrate their wedding anniversary, instead of the act of commemoration and remembrance that it really was. It had been so many years that they had played out this godawful charade that Ben could scarcely remember a time when they had actually mentioned Sarah by name. It must have been a long time ago. But not mentioning her now made it worse. His father's forced jollity as he held his mother's hand and toasted another happy year of marriage, and his mother's cheery smile, couldn't quite hide the pain in their eyes. The pain that he had put there; the pain that he could never talk to them about. They had both tried so hard to eradicate the past, and yet the more they forced it away, the more it seemed to come back to haunt them.

Still, who was he to criticise? Would he have done anything differently in their place? And as his dad had said on many occasions, 'We still had you two boys, you know. You needed us too.' But Ben's brother was older, and now lived up north, busy with his own family. So it was left up to Ben, year after year, to face this increasingly hollow and empty ritual. How he wished he could cut through the flannel and talk to them about what had happened, but to do that would be to really open a can of worms. He still wasn't sure he would ever be ready for that.

Before he left for good, though, he had to perform one last ritual. His own annual act of remembrance and penance. The church of St Barnabas had been a feature of his childhood, from the days when he and Sarah had spent Sunday mornings scribbling on bits of paper at their mother's feet. As he walked through the familiar door, went to the front of the church, and sat down in a pew, memories crowded in on him. He had been nearly three, and Sarah a baby, but he could still recall with clarity the moment the vicar poured water on her head, and she had squawked loudly. He remembered too how proud he had been watching David, his senior by five years, marching down the aisle at Harvest Festival, holding the banner for the Scouts, and how he had longed for it to be his turn. But by the time his turn came, the world had changed, the church had become a place of mourning, and his memories were spoilt by the horror of Sarah's funeral, and the awful pitiful wail of anguish that had come unbidden and uncontrolled from his mother's lips, and the weird and unsettling sight of his father crying. By the time that Ben had held the banner for the Scouts, such things didn't seem to matter any more.

Ben stared up at the high altar, a welter of emotions swirling around him. Why did he put himself through this annual torture? The rest of the year he could hold all this at bay quite easily – and he didn't have to come here, his parents probably never even knew he came. But somehow, he felt he owed it to Sarah – a mark of atonement almost.

He went to light the candle he lit every year, and remade the promise he had first made all those years ago so that Sarah's death would mean something. He couldn't save her, but he could and would save others. Ben wasn't particularly religious, but this simple act of remembrance, while immensely painful, always did him good. And his heart was somewhat lighter when he emerged into the grey wintry day.

When he got back in the car, he realised he had missed the end of the song, and so he replayed it. On second hearing it didn't seem quite so gloomy – offering more hope than sadness. Caroline had emailed him again to ask if he would come out at Christmas. He thought fleetingly of Amy. It might be nice to see more of her during the holidays, but her reaction to the bike incident had only served to remind him how vulnerable she was. Did he really want to get involved? And what was he to her anyway? Nothing, probably. And what was there here for him at Christmas? His parents always went to David's and Ben tended to work through. Maybe skiing in Colorado was a good idea. Perhaps he would take Caroline up on her offer after all.

'Well, that's the lot then.' Amy sat back and looked in satisfaction at the winter table displays piled up on Saffron's kitchen table. Fronds of leaves and bits of green littered the floor, along with the odd discarded red and white chrysanthemum, a couple of bunches of red roses, several poinsettia and copious amounts of ribbon. There were two empty cans of gold paint spray heading for the bin, and one half-full can of silver paint left. It had been a good morning's work, and Amy was about to set off for the neighbouring town of Upper Langley to hand them out to the rich and pampered good ladies of the parish, who seemed to have oodles of time to visit the local nail bar, but rather less for tedious things like flower displays. Thanks to Amy's bright idea to put her leaflet into beauty salons as well as hairdressers the phone hadn't stopped ringing.

'I don't think I want to see another pine cone ever again,' said Saffron with a groan. 'Remind me, who wants this lot?'

'It's for Linda Lovelace.'

Saffron snorted. 'That's not her real name, surely?'

'No,' said Amy. 'Her real name's Linda Lowry. She's

an exotic dancer. Didn't I tell you about her? I went round to take her order and she sat me down in the middle of her lounge, complete with pole-dancing kit, and told me all about it.'

'You're joking,' said Saffron, roaring with laughter.

'Nope,' said Amy. 'She even offered me lessons. Funnily enough, I declined.'

'Oh that is sooo funny,' said Saffron. 'And there was me thinking that Upper Langley was the height of respectability. You'll be telling me next that Mary Pritchard-Jones is a high-class madam.'

'Don't even go there!' Amy shrieked with laughter. 'That image is one I want to dispel as quickly as possible.'

Mary Pritchard-Jones had come to them by way of Ben. She was one of his patients and a leading light of the district. She had happened to mention to him that she was planning a big fireworks party for her husband's clients but couldn't find anyone who did decent table decorations. Ben had put her in touch with Saffron, and that, combined with their nail-bar customers, meant they hadn't looked back since. Mary seemed to know the whole of the rich list in Upper Langley, and her gratitude apparently knew no bounds.

'Yes, we probably don't want to pursue that idea, do we.' Saffron looked around at the chaos and sighed. 'I'm really pleased about all this work, but sheesh, there's a lot to do. And I haven't even scheduled in those two old dears who wanted us to come and dig over their garden. I thought I wanted to garden for a living. I'm not so sure now. It's spoiling all my enjoyment of my

103

own garden. I am so shattered, I can barely think straight.'

'Ellie still teething then?' said Amy sympathetically. She remembered what a trial that had been with Josh.

'Is she ever,' said Saffron. 'Pete and I haven't had a good night's sleep for over a week now. It's not as if I don't want the work. But I keep looking at everything I've got to do at home too . . .' Saffron trailed off and looked at the mess around them and gave a heavy sigh.

'Don't beat yourself up,' said Amy. 'You do have three children, remember? Most people can barely cope with getting out of bed with a young baby, let alone juggling school runs and a business.'

'I should try and sleep when Ellie does, but there's always so much to do,' said Saffron. 'I feel really pathetic, but I'm just shattered all the time. It's playing havoc with my sex life too.'

'Perhaps you should go to Linda Lovelace for pole-dancing lessons then,' suggested Amy with a grin. 'Shall I give her a ring?'

'Don't you bloody dare,' said Saffron. 'I'm such a blubbery mess at the moment I'd probably break the pole.'

'You're not in the slightest bit blubbery,' said Amy. 'But if you won't let me ring her, why don't you sit with your feet up for a bit, and I'll tidy up here.'

'Would you?' Saffron shot her a look of pure gratitude.

'Here you go.' Amy appeared ten minutes later with a steaming cup of tea.

Saffron woke with a start; she must have dozed off.

104

'Thanks. You're a star,' she said. 'By the way, did I tell you about the fireworks display on the allotments?'

'No, I don't think you did,' said Amy. 'Which reminds me, I really do need to get down to mine and dig it over properly. What with one thing and another, I never seem to get round to it at the moment.'

'It's become something of an annual event. Everyone comes normally. The Coffee Club Crew serve hot drinks, while the Wine Producers lay on mulled wine – not their own, thankfully – and everyone else provides spuds they've grown themselves. Fireworks are usually supplied by the Guys, and a good time is had by all. Even Scary Slug Man comes.'

Amy had been baffled by the different groupings on the allotments at first, but now she was getting used to the weird microcosm of society that seemed to exist there. The Coffee Club Crew only appeared to frequent the allotments in the morning, and as they were all retired they started the day with croissants and coffee, hence their name. The refreshments were generally provided by Edie and Ada, who didn't appear to have allotments themselves, but as widows of previous allotmenteers seemed to assume their role in life was now to feed all the elderly men they could find. As old cronies of Mavis, Harry often found himself in their sights, and was always moaning to Amy about them clucking over him.

Then there was Scary Slug Man – the strange bearded individual Amy had seen the first time she went onto the allotments – so called because he spent most of his time devising more and more deviant ways to kill the slugs who dared trespass across his borders. Saffron had assured her he was harmless, but Amy couldn't quite get to grips with being friendly with someone who sang to slugs before dousing them in vinegar.

The Wine Producers, of whom Harry was one, produced a variety of indifferent wines from their grapes and different berries. From time to time they would hold wine-tastings, and Amy in her ignorance hadn't quite perfected the art of saying no, so she had had to sip her way through some truly disgusting offerings. Harry's efforts were often somewhat better than the others, and she had had a couple of rather merry evenings trying out his elderberry wine.

The Guys were two gay couples whose allotments bordered each other, both of which were impeccably tidy, and who, despite their constant bickering about who had the best crop, seemed utterly devoted to each other. All four, however, were keen pranksters, and Amy could well envisage what mayhem they could cause if let loose with fireworks.

'Sounds scary,' said Amy. 'When is it?'

'The Saturday after next,' said Saffron. 'Oh, and for the last couple of years a whole crowd of us have been coming back here and having drinks afterwards.'

'Well, you can count me in,' said Amy. 'And if you want a hand with anything, I'll be more than happy to help.'

'That would be great,' said Saffron. 'It should be good, so long as Gerry behaves himself.'

'What's it got to do with Gerry?'

'Nothing much, except that he's got an allotment

over the other side. But he doesn't use it most of the time. I reckon he thinks that if the allotments are ever up for redevelopment he'll have a bargaining chip for selling his house. He's a bit of a persona non grata round here, though, because he started an affair with one of the leading allotmenteers' wives when he was still married to me. They had a bust-up and the allotmenteer moved away, then Gerry and I split up, and the woman he went off with left him. And everyone had an opinion. I tell you what, I never want to be the subject of so much gossip again.'

'No, I bet you don't,' said Amy. 'So what did Gerry do last year?'

'Well, he took it into his head that he should come along with his latest squeeze, but the kids were so upset about it, they managed to persuade him it wasn't a good idea. I'm just hoping it doesn't happen again. I mean, I can't stop him coming or anything, but he always makes a scene, and it's so embarrassing. Much better all round if he doesn't come.'

'Well, hopefully he won't this year,' said Amy. 'Listen, I'd better get off with these now. Why don't you stay here and have a kip while Ellie's still asleep? I can pick the kids up, if you like.'

'That', said Saffron, 'would be absolutely wonderful.'

The following weekend, Amy decided that it really was time she went out on the allotments. So, shouldering her spade and pulling on her wellies, and insisting Josh did the same, she marched out to Caroline's allotment. It was a clear, cold day in early November, and a low winter sun dazzled her eyes as she looked in horror at the work that lay before her. Even though it was the middle of winter, the allotment was still a tangled mess of brambles and convolvulus. She barely knew where to begin.

'Can I go and play?' asked Josh, who'd just spotted Matt with Pete.

'Course you can,' said Amy, and waved at Pete, indicating that Josh was on his way up. 'Right,' she said to herself, 'time for some serious digging.'

'You need a man to help with that, dear.'

Amy looked up to see Edie looking at her sagely. Or was it Ada? They were interchangeable in her mind. Edie/Ada was heading ominously towards Harry's allotment with a flask and a huge fruit cake. Amy hoped for his sake that Harry wasn't there.

Biting back the reply that unfortunately there were no suitable men around, Amy smiled and just got on with her digging. There was one downside to the community spirit that existed here, so very different from the isolation of her London street – that it was damned nigh impossible to move without someone knowing your business.

Twenty minutes later, she was exhausted, had a pile of weeds a mile high, and had cleared less than a tenth of the allotment. Scary Slug Man had wandered up to her allotment, shaken his head, muttered something incomprehensible and then ambled away again, which hadn't inspired her with confidence. In between the weeds she had found the odd potato and she was putting them aside for later. Why on earth hadn't she done this weeks ago? The ground was beginning to get hard – there had been one or two frosts already – and she had forgotten how difficult digging was. Josh and Matt hadn't helped either, as they were playing some complicated game that involved running about and shrieking a lot, and jumping on and off the two patches of bare earth she had managed to expose. They were beginning to wear her ragged, and she wished she had thought to palm Josh off on Harry. But he was so good about helping out that she didn't like to ask him too often.

'You probably need a rotivator for that,' said a familiar voice.

Amy turned around with a smile. It was Ben – she hadn't seen much of him recently, and she realised with a jolt that she had missed him.

'I'm coming to the same conclusion myself,' said Amy. 'But it's probably too late today to hire one.'

'Mind you, you have to be careful digging round here,' Ben continued. 'There's supposed to be a Roman road running through the allotments. You wouldn't want to dig it up and ruin the archaeology.'

'Don't you know the most interesting things,' said Amy, laughing as she took a break from her digging. 'You should get *Time Team* in.'

'Now there's a thought,' said Ben. 'But sadly it's probably an apocryphal story. You look busy. Do you need a hand?'

Ben didn't want to be pushy, but he could see Amy

109

was struggling, and he was cursing himself. He had promised Caroline he would look after her allotment, and he had been quite good to begin with, but he had been so busy in the summer that he had let it go. And when Amy had moved in, he had thought it tactful to retire gracefully from the scene.

'That is really very nice of you,' said Amy. 'I seem to be permanently in your debt.'

'I can't think of anyone who I would rather owe me,' said Ben, and smiled.

Amy caught her breath for a moment. Her palms felt sweaty and her heart was hammering nineteen to the dozen – and all because Ben had smiled at her. She coloured at her stupidity, and turned her head away.

'Best get on,' she said. 'We've got a lot to do.'

Ben thought once more of his proposed trip to Colorado. Caroline had emailed again, and he was still sorely tempted. He needed some time away, some time to think. However, for some reason he had found himself prevaricating, which was unlike him.

Amy looking at him like that tugged at his heart, and, for the first time, staying in England seemed the more attractive proposition. But then Amy went on digging, and their conversation dried up. There was nothing more there than a burgeoning friendship, Ben reminded himself. For Amy it would probably always be a winter's day. And her heart might never heal. All she wanted from him was friendship, and he would be foolish if he looked – or waited – for anything else,

CHAPTER EIGHT

'It's a bit spooky going out in the dark,' said Josh, clutching Amy's hand as they negotiated their way down the muddy path that led onto the allotments. They were both wrapped up against the cold – it was a bitter night.

'Well, that's why I've got a torch,' said Amy, 'so we can scare away all those spooky things trying to frighten us.'

'Matt said ghosts come out in November,' Josh announced. 'Does that mean Daddy will come back?'

Amy knelt down next to her son. These questions always left her scrabbling, for what could she say that was not deeply inadequate? Josh hadn't asked anything like this for such a long time. He seemed a little better at school, but he was still coming in to her at night, and they frequently had tears in the morning. How could she know what was going on his head; how much the loss of his dad had affected him? Josh was so young. It tore at her heart to think of him suffering this way. But she did her best to try to stay positive and honest.

'Sweetheart, Daddy isn't a ghost.' She gave him a fierce hug. Not for the first time she felt angry that his young life had been blighted like this.

'Oh good,' Josh said seriously. 'I wouldn't like him to be a ghost. I think he'd be lonely. If he's in heaven, he's got Gramps with him.'

Amy sighed with relief. Gramps and heaven and being happy were as good an explanation as any. 'That's right, sweetie. Daddy is playing with Gramps. And you know what?'

Her son shook his head. 'No, what?'

'I'm sure they're both looking down at you and thinking what a lovely little boy you are.'

'Good,' said Josh, and then, in a manner that Amy never failed to find disconcerting, completely switched subjects. 'I want to see big fireworks. Do you think there'll be lots of bangs? Matt said last year there was a firework the size of a house.'

'Did he now,' said Amy with a laugh, wondering what other nonsense Matt the Oracle seemed to have filled Josh's head with. 'I don't think you should always pay too much attention to what Matt says.'

The fireworks display was being held at the far end of the allotments, close to the bottom of Saffron and Pete's garden. There was a flat patch of ground, near the allotment entrance, that was untended and mainly used for people to dump waste on, which the council picked up from time to time. The Guys had obviously taken the opportunity to use the current pile of waste as the basis of their bonfire, and were stoking it up with paper and bits of wood. They had even made a guy of their own, who was perched precariously on top of the fire. And they were dancing around it, whooping like schoolboys. One of them – Clive, she thought his name was – seemed to be waving a can of petrol round alarmingly wildly.

'That's not what I think it is, is it?' said Amy to Ben, who had just walked up with Harry.

'Yup, I think it is,' said Ben. 'Clive and Keith found some petrol in their garage when they moved in; they've been desperate to get rid of it ever since. Should liven things up a bit.'

'Ben! You're a doctor!' scolded Amy. 'Shouldn't you warn them to be careful?'

'I'm sure they won't do anything stupid,' said Ben. 'You should have seen the sorts of things we did when we were students. No one ever got hurt. Well, not much anyway.'

'Harry, you talk to him,' said Amy.

'I wouldn't worry about it, my dear,' said Harry. 'This happens every year, and really, despite appearances, they are careful. I like a bit of excitement myself.'

'You're both as hopeless as each other,' Amy said in disgust. 'What is it about fireworks that brings out the kid in men? It's the same with barbecues. You must have all been pyromaniacs in your previous lives.'

'Probably,' agreed Ben. 'And to prove it, I'm going right over to where the action is.'

Amy went to find Saffron, who she felt would offer a slightly more sane approach to the proceedings. Saffron was sitting by an outdoor barbecue and she and Pete were grilling sausages. Ellie was wrapped up and fast asleep in her buggy, and the other children were playing by the fence under the watchful eye of Elizabeth. Josh went quickly to join them.

'Good lord,' said Amy. 'A man not obsessed with burning things or blowing things up, but one doing the cooking!'

'Oh, is the conflagration about to start?' Pete said. 'I might be needed. And the Guys have made a guy. I have to see that go up in smoke. Here, Amy, would you mind turning the sausages for me?'

Amy raised her eyes heavenwards.

'It's a boy thing, evidently,' she said. 'Go on, off you go and join your pals, Saffron and I can cope here.'

'Amazing, isn't it?' laughed Saffron. 'Normally I wouldn't get a look-in at a barbecue, and now just because there are fireworks involved . . .'

Amy came behind the table and started to turn the sausages. She looked over to the fire, which had finally been lit. The Guys were chucking more bits on to get it burning better. Their guy was perching precariously on top of the bonfire and starting to burn. With a, 'One, two, three –' one of them, Charles, threw some of the petrol on the fire, which whooshed upwards, much to the delight of all the men and the disgust of all the women.

'Cool, Mummy!' said Josh. 'Did you see that?'

'Yes, I did,' said Amy. 'And you're to go nowhere near it.'

In no time at all the fire was blazing away. Bill and Bud, two of Harry's wine-producer chums, evidently ignoring orders, were handing out a dubious concoction that they claimed was damson wine. Amy tried some and thought it tasted of TCP, so politely chucked it in the bushes when no one was looking. Edie and Ada, armed with their flasks, were trying to persuade the wine producers they should be drinking hot chocolate instead, to no avail. Harry had joined Bill and Bud, who had started singing Elvis songs rather tunelessly. Amy and Saffron handed out hot dogs in fits of giggles, but they were relieved when, after a few more whooshes, it transpired all the petrol had been used up.

After that there was a bit of a free-for-all as the men competed as to who had the biggest rocket. By now, Amy's feet were beginning to freeze, and she was remembering why she always got fed up with fireworks.

At the sound of the first rocket, Ellie woke up and burst into tears, so Elizabeth took her inside. Two minutes later, Matt and Josh ran after her, deciding that fireworks were a little bit too scary after all. Elizabeth didn't seem to mind looking after everyone, so Amy stayed to hand out hot dogs – at least moving about a bit stopped her feet from turning to blocks of ice.

'Enjoying yourself?' In the dark, she hadn't noticed Ben approach. Her heart gave a little skip as she wondered if he'd sought her out on purpose, before she managed to get it under control and tell herself not to be so stupid. Ben was just being friendly, that was all.

'Apart from my freezing feet,' said Amy. 'And you?'

'Me too,' said Ben. 'And the company couldn't be better.'

Amy was glad he couldn't see her blushing in the dark. She was about to think of a deflecting kind of reply when she heard a commotion, from near the entrance to the allotments.

'I can come to thish fireworks party if I want to,' a slurred voice was saying loudly and aggressively. 'Where's my little girl, I've got a present for her.'

'Oh no,' said Ben. 'Griping Gerry's turned up again.'

'What? Saffron's ex?'

'The very same,' said Ben. 'He's a right pain in the arse. He pretty much ruined things for everyone last year. I'd better go and see if Pete needs a hand getting rid of him.'

'And I'll try to stop Saffron finding out,' said Amy. Saffron had already confided earlier on that she was furious with Gerry. He had promised to take Becky and Matt to Pizza Hut the previous evening for Becky's birthday and had failed to deliver, as usual. Saffron had been knocking back the lagers as she said this, and Amy had a feeling that a meeting between the two of them wouldn't be pretty.

She went back to the barbecue table, but Saffron was nowhere in sight, and someone said she had started to clear things away. Amy breathed a sigh of relief. Maybe the boys would get rid of Gerry before she came out again.

Gerry meanwhile had pushed his way through the crowd around him, and was striding up to the gate.

'Look, Gerry,' Pete was remonstrating, 'I have no problem with you seeing Becky, but you had your opportunity last night and you blew it. So why don't you do us all a favour and go home?'

'You can't stop me seeing my daughter,' said Gerry, swaying slightly. 'Just cos you've taken my leftovers doesn't mean you get to take my daughter away from me too.'

Pete lunged at Gerry, but Ben pulled him back.

'It's not worth it,' Ben said. 'Really, he's not worth it.'

Amy came up and put an arm through Pete's. 'He's right, you know he is.'

'Well, who's this top totty?' Gerry leered at her. 'Has the dozy doc found a girlfriend at last?'

'Shut it,' said Ben. 'Just go home, Gerry, you're not wanted here.'

'Whyyouall so horrible to 'im?' shrieked a blonde banshee at Gerry's side, whom Amy assumed was the latest squeeze.

'We're not being horrible to anyone,' said Ben, in patient tones. 'We just think it would be better if you left.'

'Better for who? You can't stop me seeing my daughter.' Gerry pushed his way past Ben and started marching up the garden path.

'Yes I can, and I will.'

Everyone turned to see Saffron standing blocking the pathway – a dark shadow against the light streaming from the kitchen, hands on her hips, eyes blazing.

'Why do you have to do this, Gerry? Why do you always have to ruin it for everyone?'

'I jush want to see my daughter,' said Gerry.

'No law against that, is there?' The harridan at his side was as belligerent as Gerry.

'Well, tough,' said Saffron. 'She doesn't want to see

117

you. You've let her down once too often, Gerry. It's not me stopping her seeing you. It's her. You were given the opportunity of taking her out last night, and you didn't take it, so sorry, you don't get to see her now. And if you'll excuse me, I'm about to host a party and I think it's time my guests came inside.'

'A party in *my* house,' said Gerry.

'Gerry, it's not your house any more, remember?' said Saffron. 'You left it. And you left your children. By rights I could stop you seeing them altogether, but for their sake I won't. So butt out of it before I change my mind. Come on, folks, let's all go inside. Show's over.'

With a parting glance at Gerry, Saffron stormed off up the path. Gerry looked around, and seeing everyone moving past him into the house seemed to sense there was no point carrying on. He shouted loudly after Pete, who had walked stonily past him, 'You know she'll go frigid on you, don't you?'

With that, Pete turned like a whirlwind, flew at Gerry and punched him straight on the nose. Gerry swayed for a minute before collapsing slowly and delicately in a small heap on the ground.

There was the sound of a slow handclap from the kitchen step.

'Way to go, Pete,' said Saffron, her voice dripping sarcasm. 'You turning into Neanderthal Man was *just* what I was after.'

'I only did it for her,' Pete said to Amy for about the fiftieth time. 'You understand, Amy, don't you?'

'Yes,' said Amy, squinting at the bottle of wine and discovering to her surprise it was empty. Oh dear, she was seeing double. There were *two* empty bottles in front of her. No, it was okay. She wasn't seeing things. There *were* two bottles on the table. Luckily they weren't the produce of Bud and Bill, but somehow she and Pete had managed to drink them both. She blinked and looked at the time. Bloody hell, it was nearly eleven o'clock. It had been a long evening.

Pete's punch had turned out to be lucky. It was alcohol that had caused the sudden collapse, though Pete was rather proud of the fact that he had drawn blood. After being given the once-over by Ben, who pronounced him fit enough not to go to Casualty, Gerry had mustered what was left of his dignity and retreated with the harpy.

It wasn't enough to pacify Saffron, though.

'What the hell did you have to hit him for?' she'd said angrily as everyone gathered in awkward groups in the kitchen.

'He was rude about you,' said Pete.

'Pete, I'm big enough and ugly enough to fight my own battles,' said Saffron. 'And I really don't expect you to resort to fisticuffs on my behalf.'

'I was only trying to help,' protested Pete.

'Well don't,' said Saffron. 'It's hard enough managing Gerry and the kids without you sticking your oar in.'

'That's unfair and you know it,' said Pete, getting cross himself now.

'It's bloody true,' said Saffron. At that moment the baby had started crying, and Saffron had glared momentarily at Pete before stalking off upstairs. Despite Amy's remonstrations, she'd refused to come down again. So Amy had ended up sitting in the kitchen, having her ear bent by Pete. The party had turned into a damp squib, and everyone else was leaving in dribs and drabs. She really ought to get Josh home.

'Pete, I'm sure Saffron will see sense in the morning,' said Amy. 'Do you want me to try to go up there again?'

'No, it's all right,' said Pete. 'I should probably go and explain.'

'And I should really go home,' said Amy, getting up only to discover her legs didn't work. She realised that she felt rather tipsy. Actually, more than that, she felt legless. Amy usually kept a lid on it as far as alcohol was concerned, as in the early days of her grieving she had discovered that too much wine would inevitably end in tears. But tonight, the stress of the evening had meant that she had been drinking rather a lot more than usual.

'Would you like me to walk you home?' Ben appeared solicitously at her side.

'I think you'd better,' said Amy, leaning rather heavily on the kitchen table. Everything seemed to be swimming rather a lot. It wasn't exactly an unpleasant sensation, but the floor looked rather too close for comfort.

'Whoops!' she said, from a sitting position. 'How did I get here?'

'You fell over,' said Ben, laughing. 'Come on, let me help you up.'

'I need to find Josh,' said Amy, suddenly remembering her parental duties.

'Drunk in charge of a five-year-old. And I don't even know where he is.'

'It's okay, he's right here.' Ben had found Josh dozing on the sofa in the lounge.

'I'm tired, Mummy,' wailed Josh.

'I know,' said Ben, 'I'll give you a piggy-back home.'

'Cool,' Josh replied.

Amy, meanwhile, had discovered that if she stood up slowly and held on to things really tightly the room didn't look quite as much as though it was spinning around like a merry-go-round.

'Sorry the party was well – you know,' she said to Pete.

'Not your fault,' said Pete, waving them both out. 'Everything will be okay in the morning, I expect.'

Amy weaved her way through the allotments behind Ben, her torch bobbing up and down. She could hear Josh chattering excitedly on top of Ben's shoulders – the cold air had evidently woken him up. With a pang she realised how much Josh was missing out by not having a dad.

But then again . . . the combination of cold air and drunkenness came together in a moment of absolute clarity. Maybe she should stop looking to the past. Jamie wasn't here any more. And she had no exes queering the patch. Josh did need a dad. Would it be so bad to think about looking for one for him? And, whispered a little voice in her head, would it be so bad if it were Ben?

Getting in the house proved tricky, as Amy couldn't find her key to begin with, and once she had, it seemed to have great difficulty fitting the lock. She couldn't think why. Ben had to help her in the end, and the touch of his hand across hers as he took the key from her sent a frisson of pleasure right through her. He really was rather attractive. Particularly when she tripped over him coming through the doorway. Yes, Ben had a particularly attractive back. Amy was aware in some floating part of her brain that under normal circumstances she would have felt embarrassed, but all she could do was lie in a helpless heap and giggle.

'Are you all right, Mummy?' Josh wanted to know.

'Fine,' said Amy, although the effort of saying that sent her off into peals of laughter once more.

'I think you need a coffee,' said Ben, in a manner that she could only think of as masterful.

'I think you're probably right,' said Amy, still giggling. 'Come on, Josh, we need to get you to bed.'

When she got back, Ben was already in the lounge with the coffee. He was flicking through her CD collection.

'May I?' He held up a Katie Melua CD.

'Ah, Katie Melua, top of every Radio 2 fan's playlist,' said Amy, before sinking down into the sofa.

She lay there listening to the music, which was pleasantly mellow. After the excitement of the evening it was soothing to listen to Ben's voice, which was floating somewhere above her head. Her mouth in the meantime seemed to have a mind of its own, and she was vaguely conscious that all sorts of nonsense was coming out of it. But Ben didn't seem to mind . . .

Amy woke with a start. She looked around the room and saw that it was 2 a.m. The lamp was still on, and someone had tucked a duvet round her. The front door was shut, but Ben was gone. There was a note on the table, saying, *You fell asleep, so I let myself out. Ben x.* A smile played on her lips. Yes, masterful. Masterful was definitely the right word . . .

CHAPTER NINE

'So what have you got to say for yourself?'

Saffron was sitting in bed breastfeeding when Pete eventually came up. She had spent the best part of the evening crying, and her nose would have done Rudolf proud. Achingly, she thought of the sexy lingerie she had bought, hidden in the drawer under the bed. The idea had been to put it on for Pete tonight, but somehow, she'd lost the urge. And anyway, how likely was he to want to have sex with a red-nosed blobby mess? She wasn't quite sure what had upset her most, Gerry's snipe about her being frigid (which had hit home because it was probably true), Pete's stupid reaction (which she knew she should have felt pleased about, but couldn't as she was so cross with him), or her deep-rooted fear that Pete had only hit Gerry as a gesture; that underneath it all he knew Gerry was right. His wife *was* frigid. And at the moment he would certainly have good reason to think so. In the hours between Saffron disappearing and Pete coming to bed, her anger had turned to ice in her veins. Yes, frigid was probably a very good description.

Pete looked at her in a woebegone manner. He reminded her of a rather doleful-looking King Charles spaniel, which usually would have made her soften towards him, but tonight she was too angry.

'Would sorry do?'

What more could he say? Saffron had no doubt Pete was sorry. Punching someone was so unlike him. She should forgive him, really she should, but –

'What were you thinking?' Saffron said. 'What if the children had seen you?' That was what had probably made her the angriest. All that bloody effort to keep the children okay about the split, and persuade them to accept Pete into their lives (not that they needed all that much persuading; young as they were they had already clocked how useless their dad was), and now her ex and her husband had resorted to fistfights. Where the bloody hell did they go from here?

She felt her frigidity melt, and suddenly she was crying again. Actually, bawling was a better word for it Noisy, sniffling, howling sobs came out of her. Saffron wished she could cry daintily like women did in the movies, with soft little tears trickling down her cheek, but she'd never been able to manage it. Christ, she must look such a fright.

'You'll have to go and apologise to him in the morning,' she said.

'Saff, I am not going to apologise to that twat ever,' said Pete. 'He started it. He had no right saying what he did about you. I'm sorry you're upset, but I couldn't let him stand there and insult you like that.'

'Yes, you could. Anyway, he's right, isn't he? I *am*

bloody frigid. We've hardly had sex since Ellie was born. You'll end up leaving me too.'

Pete sat down on the edge of the bed, and looked at her in dismay.

'Where the bloody hell has that come from?' he said. 'I know it's been a while, but we've got a new baby and we're both really tired. Come on, Saff, this isn't like you.'

'But that's what happened with Gerry,' wailed Saffron. 'And he left me.'

'When will you get it into your thick head that I am not Gerry?' said Pete. 'Look, if it bothers you that much, I'll go and grovel to him in the morning, okay?'

'You will?' Saffron gave him a watery smile.

'Yes. And for the record,' said Pete, as he got undressed and climbed into bed, 'Gerry was talking out of his arse. You aren't frigid. And now that baby has gone to sleep, I'm going to prove it to you.'

'What, you still want to shag a red-nosed Mrs Blobby?' Saffron said, still sniffling.

'You're not blobby, you're curvy. Curves are nice. They're sexy. You're sexy. So shut up, put that baby in her cot, and let me ravish you.'

'So you really don't think I'm frigid?'

'Of course I don't,' said Pete, kissing her firmly on the mouth. 'Now do shut up and let me show you how sexy I find you.'

Saffron shut her eyes and sighed with relief. Pete was right. Everything would be fine. If she only relaxed into things, her libido would come back of its own accord. As she cuddled up to Pete, she started to relax, and feel, if not sexy, cosy. Comfortable. And as Pete began to run his hands over her, to her relief she felt her body respond. She was making mountains out of molehills. She was married to a gorgeous man who adored her. And who right now was actually managing to turn her on. Maybe everything would be all right.

'Waa-aah-ahh.' The baby set up a deeply persistent cry.

'Ignore her,' Pete said, stroking her shoulders.

'Waa-aah-aahh! Waa-aaa-aahh!' The cry became more insistent.

No, no, *no*! Saffron was furious. Just when she had started to feel something.

The baby was wailing at full pelt now.

'I don't think she's going to stop, do you?' said Saffron miserably.

Pete rolled over, turned the light on and looked at her ruefully.

'Go on,' he said, nudging her. 'There's always tomorrow.'

'I suppose so,' said Saffron with a sigh. 'She can't still be hungry.' She picked the baby up and burped her, but Ellie still didn't seem to settle, so Saffron got out of bed and went to change her nappy. By the time she got back into bed, Pete was lying flat on his back, snoring loudly. Saffron tried to put Ellie down again but she still wouldn't go to sleep. Apparently she *could* still be hungry. Feeling decidedly cheated, Saffron clamped the baby to her breast and sat staring into the darkness.

Ben stood in his lounge, with a beer in hand, staring across the dark allotments to Amy's house. He could just make out a dim light, where he had left the lamp on for her. He smiled at the image of her curled up under the duvet he had found for her. He had known Amy was attractive, but not how funny and sexy she could be. Tonight had been like scales falling from his eyes. It had taken all his self-control to leave.

'Jamie bought that for me,' Amy had said, when she saw his choice of CD.

'Do you mind?' he'd asked.

'Not at all,' she'd replied, flopping down on the sofa, 'it's perfect for an evening like this.'

'An evening like what?' Ben had asked.

Amy had looked at him with a slightly quizzical look in her eye, and waved her arm vaguely around the room.

'An evening like this, when it's late and you've got good company.'

'I'll second that,' Ben had said, and sipped his coffee. He'd relaxed back in his chair for a moment, letting the music flow softly over him. There hadn't seemed any need to talk.

'I bet they call you the dishy doc, don't they?' Amy had said brazenly.

'I really have no idea,' he'd answered.

'I bet they do,' continued Amy, shutting her eyes and leaning back on the sofa. 'It's cos you're so masterful, I expect.'

'Masterful?' Ben had laughed. 'I hardly think so. You must have got the wrong bloke.'

'Nope, masterful's right, I'd say,' declared Amy, one eye peeping playfully open. She couldn't be – was she flirting with him? 'Why don't you sit here where it's more comfortable?'

Damn it, she *was* flirting with him. He'd found himself staring at those liquid brown eyes, wondering whether he should flirt back. Funny how he had never noticed them before.

'I just realised I'm lucky, you know,' said Amy, slurring her words ever so slightly.

Ben had been rather taken aback with this sudden change of tack, and said, 'Oh, why?'

'I don't have an ex,' she'd said. 'Look at all that crap that Saffron went through tonight. I don't have that. I'm young, free and single. I should probably start dating again.'

Ben swallowed. What was she saying? She seemed to be making it plain that she wouldn't knock him back. Should he make a move?

'Mind you,' Amy had continued, 'just because I'm single doesn't mean I haven't got baggage. There's Josh for a start – he needs a dad. I should find him a dad. But where can I find one . . .'

Her tone was teasingly playful, and she'd given Ben such a look, he'd felt as though she had stripped him bare, and exposed his innermost thoughts.

'Where indeed?' Ben had kept his voice deliberately light. This was where he should go over and put his arm around her, and . . .

Except he couldn't, of course. Amy was drunk. And there were reminders of Jamie everywhere – pictures on the wall, the presence of Josh upstairs, even the Katie Melua CD. Much as Ben would love to kiss her – and much as he felt Amy wouldn't rebuff him – he just couldn't do it.

He'd spent so long procrastinating that it had taken a while for it to dawn on him that Amy was asleep. His decision was made for him. He'd found a duvet from the spare room – he hadn't liked to go in her room – popped it over her and quietly let himself out.

He couldn't have taken advantage of her when she was vulnerable, that much was certain. It was absolutely, definitely, the right thing to do. But now, standing here, looking across to where he knew Amy was sleeping, Ben was already regretting it deeply.

'Mummeee!!' A speeding bullet landed *thump* on Amy's chest. 'Canigodownstairsandwatchtvthankyou?'

'Wha—?' Amy opened bleary eyes and looked across at the clock. Ten o'clock already? She never normally slept that late; neither did Josh. Mind you, it had been a late evening. She and Ben hadn't got back till nearly eleven, and then Ben had stayed for – actually, she had no idea how long Ben had stayed for. After waking up with the duvet wrapped round her she'd staggered up to bed. Her recollections of the latter part of the evening were hazy to say the least. Her head was thumping and her mouth was very dry. Lord, she had the hangover from hell. She couldn't remember when she'd last had one.

Well, at least she hadn't burst into tears and made a fool of herself like the last time – a few months after Jamie's death. That time she'd gone to a dinner party, which had proved agony, with all the other wives looking daggers at her expecting her to pounce on their husbands at any minute, and all the men looking awkward, not knowing what to say. Out of pure nerves she had ended up sinking the best part of two bottles of wine on her own, and weeping in the kitchen on the shoulder of someone she had once considered a friend, but who clearly had no capacity for dealing with the situation.

She had left the dinner party early, conscious of having ruined it for everyone, and sworn from that day she would stay sober. Which she had done, pretty much, up until now. And, searching the memory banks, she didn't think she'd made too much of an idiot of herself . . .

'Where's Ben?' Josh, who was doing a good impression of a bouncing bean, was leaping up and down next to her.

'Gone home,' said Amy.

'When can he come again?' said Josh. 'I like Ben. Can he be my new dad?'

New dad . . . where had she heard that before? A vague alarm bell rang in her brain.

'Don't be silly, Josh,' said Amy. 'Ben would have to marry me first.'

'Well, why doesn't he then?' said Josh.

'Because he doesn't want to,' said Amy. 'Go on, Tigger, why don't you go and turn the TV on?'

The alarm bells weren't just ringing now, they were practically pealing in her head. Suddenly the events of the previous evening came flooding back. She had come in and sat on the sofa, and flirted with Ben. She, Amy Nicolson, had flirted with a man! What on earth had she been thinking? It must have been the alcohol. It wasn't as if she fancied Ben, after all . . .

But now her cheeks flamed as she remembered telling him he was dishy, and that she was looking for a new dad for Josh. What must he think of her? And God, had she really told Ben he was masterful?

'Masterful?' said Amy out loud. 'Where the hell did that come from? It sounds like something from a trashy novel.'

She cringed under the duvet. How on earth was she ever going to face Ben again? He must think her a complete idiot. The fact that he had left her asleep showed he wasn't interested, for which she should be grateful, but she had to face it: she had really cocked up. Her only hope was that he had been drunk too. She was clutching at straws, she knew, but maybe, just maybe, his recollection of events would be even hazier than hers.

There was a ring on the doorbell. Who on earth could that be?

'Mummy,' yelled Josh. 'I think Ben's at the door.'

Amy had never flung clothes on so fast. She didn't want to compound the mistakes of last night by pitching up in her dressing gown. Her first thought was to leave the doorbell ringing, but Josh was already talking to Ben through the letterbox, so she thought better of it. Besides, she would have to face him sooner or later. Sooner got it over and done with quickly. Perhaps she should just brazen it out.

She flung open the door, bold as brass. 'Ben, what a nice surprise,' she said, in tones as bright as she could muster, but her confidence instantly deserted her. Something had subtly changed last night. This man, this *gorgeous* man (it was no use hiding it any longer), had been in her house only a few hours ago, listening to schmoozy music with her. He had seen her asleep, and found her a duvet. It took their relationship to a new sort of intimacy, and she wasn't quite sure how to proceed from here.

Ben was feeling equally awkward. Now he was here, he was beginning to wonder whether this was a good idea. Ostensibly he told himself he was just being neighbourly, and checking she was all right, but he knew he was hiding the real reason. He simply had to see her again. Last night he had glimpsed a side to Amy he hadn't seen before. A playful, vivacious side that seemed at odds with her generally serious demeanour. Damn it, she was too young to play the grieving widow forever. He wanted to be the one to tease her playful self out more. But how to proceed? And would she let him?

'Would you – er – like to come in?' Amy was conscious she couldn't leave the poor man on the doorstep, but reluctant to offer coffee, for it had too many connotations, even in the morning with her five-year-old son by her side. Come to think of it, she hadn't offered it last night, he had just assumed. (Masterful *was* the right word, no doubt about it.) And when she had let him, it had seemed quite natural to do so. He had been to her house several times, but never that late. If she hadn't been so out of practice in the dating game she would have seen trouble coming.

'I only dropped by to check you were okay,' said Ben.

'Yes, I'm fine,' said Amy. 'Bit hung over. But fine.'

'You were pretty drunk,' said Ben.

'And don't I know it,' said Amy. Oh God, this was excruciating. The best thing to do was to spit out what she had to say, if only to clear the air. She knew she liked Ben, but last night she had been drunk, today she was sober, and much as she was attracted to him, she still wasn't sure that she wanted to move on that quickly.

'I think I made a bit of a fool of myself last night,' she said, as Ben followed her into the lounge. 'It's ages since I've been that drunk, and I think I got a bit carried away.'

'Oh, I don't know, I thought you were very funny.' Ben looked at her with amusement in his eyes.

'Well, anyway, the thing is . . .' Amy felt more and more awkward. She had to admit to herself that Ben was very attractive, but catching a sight of Jamie's photo on the mantelpiece reminded her she wasn't free. Not really. 'I think I may have said some things, which I didn't mean, well, not exactly didn't mean – I like you a lot, but –'

'– you were very drunk and you still aren't over Jamie.'

'How did you know?'

'Oh, call it intuition,' said Ben. 'It's all right, really. I like you a lot, but I'm not looking for anything serious at the moment.'

'That's okay then.'

'Yes.'

'Good, I'm glad we cleared that up,' said Amy. 'Would you like a cup of tea?'

'Tea would be lovely.'

'We can still be friends?'

'Of course.'

'Good.'

There was a pause before Amy said 'good' again. She went to the kitchen to boil the kettle, and couldn't work out, as she stood looking at the garden from the kitchen window, why her overwhelming feeling was one of disappointment.

PART TWO
Lighten Up

In the allotment:
Dig over the ground, rake and prepare for new growth, plant out first crops.

State of the heart:
Tender, fresh and leaning towards the sun.

CHAPTER TEN

'Blimey, this is hard work.' Saffron paused from her digging and wiped her brow. From a reasonably mild November, the temperature had swiftly dropped. She and Amy were wrapped up well, but their breath steamed out of them, and Saffron's fingers were numb.

'Should we call it a day?' Amy looked in dismay at the small patch of earth they had dug over. The fruits of their labours hadn't yielded much, but the earth was hard as rock. A week earlier and they'd have had this flowerbed turned over in no time. The trouble was, they'd got so caught up with Christmas floral arrangements they'd run out of time. Still, Amy wasn't complaining. Business was picking up slowly, and Saffron seemed pleased with the results of Amy's suggestion to leaflet the local nail bars and hair salons. And, thanks to Caroline's continued lack of communication as far as the business was concerned, Saffron seemed to be relying on Amy more and more. Her confidence was growing as a result, and she knew – at least as far as her career was concerned – she had made the right choice to start afresh.

'I did promise Mrs Meadows we'd finish it before Christmas,' said Saffron. 'And she is one of our best clients.'

'You're a hard taskmaster and no mistake,' Amy laughed. 'Can I at least pause for a hot chocolate?'

Mrs Meadows usually kept them well-supplied with tea and biscuits, but since the weather had turned so cold Amy had taken to making up a flask of something hot to bring with her as well. Not all their clients were as accommodating as Mrs Meadows.

'Go on then, you've twisted my arm,' said Saffron, pouring them both a drink. 'By the way, I've been meaning to ask you, what are you doing for Christmas?'

'Good question,' said Amy, hugging her fleece round her. 'The last few years we've always been with Mary, but this year . . .'

That really wasn't on the cards. Since their meeting early in the autumn, Amy had only seen Mary once. She and Josh had gone to visit Mary's flat in North London in the middle of November, but things had been strained and awkward, and since then Mary was resolutely not answering calls. Amy was on the verge of giving up, except that she didn't think it would be fair on Josh, who kept clamouring to know when they could see Granny again. Anyway, Christmas at Mary's was evidently not on offer, and Amy didn't have the courage to broach the subject.

'. . . my brother and his wife have invited me,' she continued. 'They usually do, they're such loves. But I know for a fact that it's the first time in years they haven't had Sue's parents, and I think they really want a family Christmas just for them, so I'm a bit reluctant to muscle in. I expect Josh and I will just pig out in front of the telly.'

Amy tried and failed not to feel that this was a rather sad way to spend Christmas.

'You will do no such thing,' said Saffron. 'What I was going to say was, if you're free, why don't you come to us?'

'What, really? Are you sure?' Amy said. 'It seems like a huge imposition.'

'Don't be daft,' said Saffron. 'We love having lots of people at Christmas, and we can never bear the thought of anyone being on their own. So we tend to gather all the waifs and strays together under one roof.'

'Thanks!' said Amy, laughing.

'Well, you know what I mean,' said Saffron. 'Anyway, Harry's already said yes. Sometimes he goes to his cousin's at Eastbourne, but this year he's said he can't be bothered. I get the impression that he's not that keen on them. Clive and Keith are coming, and my mum, and Pete's sister – oh, and,' with a sly look at Amy, 'I'm hoping to persuade Ben to come.'

'So?'

'And won't that seal the deal?' said Saffron with a grin. Amy had mentioned the events of the bonfire night to Saffron, though she hadn't been quite transparent about her own confused feelings.

'Don't be ridiculous,' said Amy. 'Ben and I are friends. That's all.'

'Right,' said Saffron, without conviction.

'Anyway, Josh and I would love to come. Ben or no Ben. I really can't contemplate anything more grim than trying to entertain a five-year-old on my own on Christmas Day. It's been bad enough when we've been with his granny. You're always aware there's someone missing. It would be great to break that particular tradition.'

Amy sighed, and tried not to think about Christmases with Jamie, in the days before Josh was born, when he would come bowling in late from work on Christmas Eve, merry, his arms full of last-minute purchases. They used to spend the evening in the pub, before sitting up to the early hours wrapping presents for Jamie's family. Then, after champagne in bed, it had been off round to Mary's in the morning, where she would have gathered a motley crew of family members for whom she would provide a vast and very welcome turkey. Every Christmas Amy had ever spent with Jamie had been nigh on perfect. The last two had been dreadful. It would be good to do something different.

'Good, that's settled then,' said Saffron, contemplating Mrs Meadows' flowerbeds once more. 'Always supposing we manage to get this finished by then, of course!'

'So what's the problem then, Harry?'

Ben was used to Harry asking his advice on minor matters, but Harry had specifically sought him out on the allotments and Ben had the idea that something was really bothering him. They were now sitting in Harry's cosy little hut, complete with primus stove and kettle, sipping steaming cups of hot tea.

'It's probably nothing –' began Harry.

'But it's enough to worry you,' said Ben.

'Well, in a word, yes,' said Harry. 'I think I might be suffering from epilepsy.'

'Why?'

'A couple of times, I've been out on the allotments, and it's like my mind has gone blank. Not for long. Usually a couple of seconds. But a kind of blackness descends briefly, and then it's over. Do you think I could be having fits?'

'Has anything else happened?'

'Well, I did stumble into my bonfire one day, but that might be because I'd had rather too much elderberry wine.'

Ben laughed. But he was concerned.

'Harry, I really think you should check this out with your GP. You may be having something called TIAs.'

'What are they?'

'Transient Ischemic Attacks. They can pre-empt a stroke. It would be advisable to get some blood tests, and check your blood pressure. You already know it's too high. And if I were you I'd cut down on your drinking, it can't be helping.'

Harry pulled a face. 'I have so few pleasures left in life, are you even going to rob me of that one?'

'Yes,' said Ben. 'Because otherwise I can't promise how long you'll stay around for.'

Harry had a peculiar look on his face. 'Who says I want to stay around?'

'You can't mean that, surely?'

'Ben,' said Harry, 'I'm old, I'm widowed, my body can't do what it used to. I have no children or grand-children to worry about. Who is going to miss me when I'm gone?'

'Me, for a start,' said Ben. 'Who will I get advice about my runner beans from if you're not here? And you might not have a grandchild of your own, but isn't Josh becoming a good substitute?'

'True,' said Harry. 'Look, old boy, I'm not actively going to hasten my demise. So I promise to go and see my quack and get all the advice I should. All I'm saying is that, quite frankly, I'm an old dog who's had his day. We only get so much time allotted to us, and I'm more than happy to take my chances.'

'Would that all my patients were as philosophical as you,' said Ben, making a mental note that he was going to keep a closer eye on Harry in future.

'On another subject entirely,' said Harry, 'have you decided what to do about Christmas yet?'

Amy had made it clear to Ben that there was no future in any relationship with her, so he didn't quite know why he was prevaricating about going skiing. The fact that Pete had invited him for Christmas lunch, and he was hoping Amy might be there too, might have something to do with it.

'Well, I'm going to Saffron and Pete's,' announced Harry. 'Where I intend to stuff myself full of turkey, drink far too much, especially the port, and stagger drunkenly home at around six. What about you?'

'I still haven't sorted anything out yet,' said Ben. 'I was going to go home for Christmas, and Caroline's been badgering me for ages to go skiing with her –'

'But –?'

'Turns out I'm on call. One of the other partners was meant to do it, but he has some family crisis he has to deal with. And everyone else had already made plans. So it's fallen to me.'

'So will you come to Saffron's then?' said Harry.

'Don't know,' said Ben. 'Maybe. Christmas isn't really my thing. And I'm only on call for Christmas and Boxing Day. I still haven't ruled out skiing completely.'

'Amy and Josh are going,' said Harry with a sly smile.

'Are they?' Ben affected nonchalance, but felt a little leap in his heart. Maybe he should go. He wasn't very good at watching other people playing happy families, but if Amy was going things might be different. It was definitely worth thinking about . . .

'Saffron!' Pete was shouting up the stairs. 'Do you know where the pepper is?'

'Same place I always keep it,' Saffron sputtered as she danced around their bedroom, trying to pull the basque she bought around her ever-increasing tum. If anything the damned thing seemed even tighter than when she had bought it. It was Saturday night, and Gerry had the children for the night. Ellie was already down and with any luck would sleep till at least midnight. Once or twice recently Ellie had managed a whole night, but Saffron had learned not to count on it.

Pete had offered to make dinner, and Saffron had decided that tonight was the night she would practise her seduction skills and get down to business. Hence her prancing round their room like an overweight rhinoceros, trying to get lacy bits round her that seemed to be slipping from her grasp at a rate of knots.

The doorbell rang, just as Saffron's suspender had pinged off her stocking for the hundredth time.

Damn, who could that be? It was gone eight o'clock and they weren't expecting anyone.

'Can you get it?' Pete shouted. 'I can't leave the kitchen.'

Pete was an infrequent and therefore nervous cook. He had to hover over the stove even when the only thing that was happening was the potatoes were boiling. He had still been known to boil them dry.

'Coming,' shouted Saffron, throwing a dressing gown around her, before flying down the stairs to fling open the door.

'Oh, it's you,' she said flatly.

Gerry was standing at the doorstep with a very pale Matt in his arms and a disconsolate Becky by his side.

'Sorry to do this to you,' he said, 'but Matt said he wasn't feeling too good, and he wanted you. Thought it best he should be with his mum, if he was coming down with something.'

More like you don't want the inconvenience of your son throwing up on the shag-pile carpet that the blonde bimbo's imported into your house, was Saffron's silent retort.

'But we were going to watch DVDs,' moaned Becky, her disappointment visible.

'Couldn't Becky stay?' said Saffron, having gathered Matt into her arms. He did look a bit pale, and he was tired and teary. Not surprising really. His normal bedtime was six thirty.

'Well, the thing is,' said Gerry in conspiratorial tones, 'it seems I've double-booked myself. I'm supposed to be at the golf club's AGM, and I didn't really want to leave Becky with Maddy. You know she's not used to children. You know how it is.'

'Yes, Gerry, I do,' said Saffron, her voice dripping with sarcasm. She had to restrain an urge to go and fetch a saucepan from the kitchen and hit him over the head with it. Furious as she was with him, it wasn't fair to have a slanging match in front of the children.

'I'll come and fetch them tomorrow, then,' said Gerry with a bright smile.

'You do that,' said Saffron, hoping against hope that Matt would spend the whole day throwing up on Gerry's Armani suit, but knowing that she wouldn't be able to send him out if he were that ill.

She closed the door with a heavy heart. Bang went her romantic evening. By the time she'd got these two settled, there probably wouldn't be much of an evening left. Becky was notoriously bad for getting to bed when it was already late in the evening. And, having been let down by her dad – again – she would no doubt be unsettled tonight. Besides, if Matt was feeling as ill as he was beginning to look, it seemed that a full-on vomit-fest was in order. Great. Thanks for nothing, Gerry.

Half an hour later, though, she was feeling more hopeful. The children had both gone to bed quite happily, Matt with a towel under his pillow and bowl by the side of his mattress. It was almost as if they were relieved to be home.

So Saffron had gone back to fighting the forces of nature with a vengeance, and had just about managed to tease the basque around her protuberant stomach. She felt about as sexy as an elephant, and couldn't breathe, but looking at herself in the mirror she concluded that she didn't look *too* bad, and maybe, in the dark, Pete wouldn't mind . . .

'Mummy, what are you doing?'

Saffron jumped out of her skin and flung herself behind the bed.

'Nothing, darling,' she said, a hand frantically reaching on the bed for her dressing gown, which seemed not to be there, or indeed anywhere within hand's reach.

'What is it, darling?'

'I can't get to sleep,' said Becky.

'Well, go back to bed and I'll tuck you in in a minute,' said Saffron.

'Can't I come in your bed?'

'No, you can't,' said Saffron.

'Oh. I'm sure I'd sleep better in there,' said Becky.

'Well you can't,' said Saffron. 'Now hop it.'

Becky hopped it, and Saffron stood up. Bloody hell, why were all her attempts at nights of passion doomed?

148

'Mummy, why have you got that funny thing on?'

Becky was back, her little face a picture of curiosity and amusement at the strange things grown-ups do.

'Never you mind,' said Saffron, diving behind the bed once more. 'Now bed!'

'I don't think it's very pretty,' said Becky. 'You look nicer in that purple dress.'

'Right, thanks,' said Saffron. Great, fashion advice from a seven-year-old.

'You look fat in that,' was Becky's last offering before she scampered back to her room.

Saffron got up again, intending to throw some clothes on and go downstairs to join Pete for a well-earned glass of wine, when she heard a yell from Matt's room. Fearing the worst, she grabbed her dressing gown, which miraculously she suddenly spotted hanging on the edge of her bed, and ran into his room.

'Mummy, I feel sick,' he said, sitting up looking very sorry for himself.

'Oh you poor thing,' Saffron said, sitting down and giving him a hug. Maternal Instincts 1, Foxy Lady 0. There was no contest. Being a mummy triumphed over nights of passion every time.

Saffron realised her dressing gown was undone, and was just about to do it up, when Matt retched, leaned forward, and threw up everywhere – including all over Saffron. The basque was covered.

'Everything all right?' said Pete, when Saffron eventually emerged with a pile of vomit-smelling clothes and dumped them in the washing machine.

'Not really,' said Saffron. 'Matt's just thrown up everywhere.'

'Oh,' said Pete. 'I hope it hasn't put you off your dinner.'

Saffron grimaced. 'Can't say I'm all that hungry now,' she said.

'Never mind,' said Pete. 'Let's have a glass of wine and snuggle up on the sofa together, and perhaps your appetite will come back.'

Saffron smiled. Her plans for a sexy evening had backfired totally. The offending basque was now spinning in the washing machine with the rest of the laundry, and her appetite for food wasn't the only thing that was gone. But on the other hand, a couple of hours playing footsie on the sofa, provided she could switch the mummy part of her brain off, might be just what she needed . . .

CHAPTER ELEVEN

'That's the lot then.' Saffron staggered into the kitchen with three shopping bags under her arm. She dropped them by the huge pile of bags that were taking up a rather large corner of the kitchen. 'Thanks for your help with the kids.'

'No problem,' said Amy, looking up from the bags she was unpacking. 'If you've had the decency to invite me to come for Christmas dinner, the least I can do is babysit while you buy food for it. Now, are you sure you've got everything you need?'

'I think so.' Saffron looked anxiously at the mounds of bags spilling out onto the floor, before she realised that Amy was laughing at her.

'Come on, Saffron,' said Amy. 'I'm surprised there's any food left in the shops. This lot should keep us going until next Christmas.'

'You're probably right,' said Saffron. 'I just like to be well-prepared.'

'Listen, do you need me any more?' Amy asked. 'I'm doing a quick flit over to Mary's for an overnighter, so I've really got to get moving.'

'Yikes,' said Saffron. 'I thought she didn't want to see you.'

Amy pulled a face. 'I thought so too, but she rang out of the blue a couple of days ago. She's going on a cruise on Christmas Eve, and this was the only time she had. I felt like I couldn't say no. Besides, Josh will be pleased to see her.'

Amy gathered her things together, hauled Josh away from the TV, where *The Snowman* was showing for the millionth time, and they made their way across the allotments towards home.

It was a crisp, clear December day. The sun was bright, though not warm, and the allotments looked sleepy and content, as if they were just waiting for the right weather to bring them to life again. She nodded at Bill and Bud, who were leaning against Bill's hut, wearing Santa hats and sharing the contents of a hip flask.

Amy breathed a contented sigh. While she knew there would be moments over the next few days when she would miss Jamie terribly, she was conscious that this year, for the first time, she was relishing the New Year. And Josh was so thrilled about spending Christmas Day with Matt that he didn't seem too worried about not seeing Mary for the day itself.

A cold knot developed in Amy's stomach as she thought about her proposed trip. She hoped for Josh's sake they'd both be able to put their differences to one side. Knowing Mary, she would have gone to a lot of trouble to feed them, so Amy was just going to have to bite the bullet and go with it. She should go to the crematorium too. She always hated going, and was relieved that now it was too far to go regularly. But she couldn't really go all that way without paying a visit. Besides, Josh had insisted they had to go and say 'Happy Christmas' to Daddy. And she couldn't deny him that.

'Hi there.' Ben came to meet them gladly, Meg bounding up beside him with a joyous wag of the tail.

'Hi to you, too.' Amy was pleased to see him. 'There's hardly anyone out here today,' she said. 'What on earth are you doing?'

'Killing time,' Ben replied. 'I'm due back at the surgery in half an hour, so I thought I'd come over here with my digital radio and commune with my winter veg. It makes a welcome break from being sneezed over, I can tell you.'

'And did you glean anything useful?' asked Amy, laughing.

'Apart from hearing Terry's tips for how to tidy up your allotment, no,' said Ben. 'But on the other hand, Jeremy has just played "California Dreamin'", which is one of my favourite songs.'

'What are you up to over Christmas?' Amy knew Ben had been invited to Saffron's, but hadn't confirmed for definite yet.

'Not sure exactly,' said Ben. 'I was thinking about going to my brother's, but it turns out I'm on call. Which means I have to be sensible.'

Should he mention the skiing? Ben wondered. Then he dismissed it. Amy was scarcely likely to care one way or the other, and though he hadn't ruled out a last-minute deal, he probably wasn't going to go anyway.

'So you're not going to Saffron and Pete's then?' Amy couldn't help letting her disappointment show. 'It should be fun. I shall enjoy seeing Harry trying to palm his elderberry wine off on Saffron's mum.'

'I hadn't quite decided, to be honest,' said Ben. 'It depends on how much of the day I have to spend at the drop-in centre for patients who ring the after-hours service. If we're quiet I should be able to get away. But of course, I won't be drinking.'

'Bummer,' said Amy. 'I'm sure it will be fun anyway. Go on, see what you can do.'

'Well, I suppose someone needs to keep an eye on Harry,' said Ben. 'So okay, maybe I will.'

'Why does Harry need an eye kept on him?' Amy looked at Ben in sudden alarm.

'It's probably nothing,' said Ben. 'I'm a little worried about his blood pressure, that's all. I told him he needed to see his GP, but knowing Harry he probably hasn't gone.'

'Is it serious, do you think?' Amy had grown used to having Harry on her doorstep, a reassuring presence to whom she turned frequently. And although she knew in her head he was old, he always seemed so fit and healthy that it was hard to think of him as such.

'I'm really not sure,' said Ben. 'But it could be. I wish he looked after himself better. But you know what he's like. You can't make Harry do anything he doesn't want to.'

'That's true,' said Amy. 'Do you think me nagging would make any difference?'

'You never know,' said Ben. 'Two nagging is better than one, I suppose.'

They had reached Amy's gate, and they both paused.

'I'd ask you in,' said Amy, 'but I haven't got much time. I'm off to see my mother-in-law.'

'Well, see you at Saffron's, then,' said Ben.

'See you at Saffron's,' said Amy. 'I shall look forward to it.'

'Me too,' said Ben, and he waved as she went down the path.

Amy walked with a light step and smiled as she unlocked her door. For the first time since Jamie's death, she was looking forward to Christmas Day.

'Happy Christmas,' said Mary, giving Amy a formal peck on the cheek.

It was what Amy had expected, but nonetheless it stung. At least Mary shed her reserve for Josh, though, who got a huge hug and kiss, and was instantly whisked away into the lounge to be shown off to all Mary's cronies who had been roped in for the day. Amy followed her with a heavy heart. She had a feeling it was going to be a long twenty-four hours.

Mary, true to form, provided huge amounts of food. Lunch consisted of massive platefuls of roast turkey and the trimmings, followed by three kinds of pudding. At four o'clock, when Amy was still feeling full, cakes and scones appeared, followed at six o'clock with sandwiches and soup. By bedtime, Amy and Josh were stuffed.

'Would you like to tuck him in?' Amy said. 'I'll clear up if you like.'

Mary's face lit up, and Amy felt relieved that for once she had done something right.

Mary seemed much perkier when she came downstairs.

'Hasn't he grown?' she said, which automatically made Amy feel guilty, but Mary didn't pursue it, so she decided perhaps the comment wasn't really barbed after all.

They settled down to a desultory evening watching standard Christmas viewing, mainly consisting of repeats of *The Vicar of Dibley* and a *Strictly Come Dancing Christmas Special*, before Amy made her excuses and went to bed early.

By unspoken agreement, they had steered clear of controversial topics, so by the time Amy was leaving the next morning, she felt that she had got away without trouble this time.

Mary's last words to Josh caught her short, though.

'You remember what I said, sweetheart,' Mary said, giving Josh a big hug. 'You can come here any time you like.'

'Of course you can,' said Amy, thinking, *that's not terribly practical, but . . .*

Then Josh said, 'Mummy, you're not going to marry Ben, are you?'

Amy laughed and said, 'Of course not.'

'Good,' said Josh. 'Because Granny said you were.'

Mary's face looked all pinched and pink.

'Granny thinks you shouldn't, though,' Josh continued, oblivious to the effect he was having. 'And so do I.'

'Now Josh, darling,' Mary said, 'that's not exactly what I said, is it?'

'You've been discussing my love life with my son?' Amy was appalled.

'I think Josh has got the wrong end of the stick,' said Mary. 'He mentioned you marrying Ben, so I just said I didn't think it was a very good idea.'

Fighting a desire to be incredibly rude, Amy bit her lip and simply said, 'Mary, there is no question of me marrying Ben, I'm not even seeing him, for God's sake, so this whole discussion is academic. I think we should call a halt to it there.'

Mary, clearly not wishing to provoke the situation further, ignored Amy's last words, and gave Josh another big hug.

'Now, you be a good boy for Granny, and Santa will bring you lots of lovely presents.'

'Will Santa come on your cruise ship?' asked Josh, completely oblivious to everything else.

'Of course,' said Mary.

'But how will he get down the chimney?' Josh asked.

'Ah, he won't need a chimney,' said Mary. 'He'll fly in with his reindeer and land on the deck of the boat.'

'Oh good,' said Josh. 'Then you can get your presents too.'

Mary's laughing response lightened the mood, and Amy kissed her with more warmth than she felt. She didn't want to have a row with Mary just before Christmas, however cross she was.

It was only later, as she and Josh went to put flowers by Jamie's plaque, that Amy's fury returned with a vengeance. As Josh ran excitedly about – once the flowers were laid he had lost interest – Amy stared at the plaque bearing Jamie's name, and angry tears sprang to her eyes.

'Oh Jamie,' she said out loud, 'why did you have to leave me? I feel so guilty about your mum. But who I see is none of her business. Is it?'

The question hung empty before her. There was no response. What did she expect? She was talking to a plaque on a wall. Wherever Jamie was, he wasn't here. And he didn't have any answers for her. Sighing loudly, Amy called to Josh and they headed home.

'Mummy, Mummy, Father Christmas has been! And I got a Dalek! And Becky got a *Dr Who* DVD!' A jack in a box had landed on Saffron's bed, jumping up and down maniacally. It was Matt, who obviously felt that Christmas Day should start now.

Saffron rolled over and looked at the clock. Five thirty. Oh dear.

'Matt, it's not time to get up yet,' she muttered.

'But Mummy, I want to see if Santa's left any more presents downstairs.'

'Go back to bed,' mumbled Saffron.

'Nahahhh, whaaat?' snored Pete, as usual oblivious to the chaos caused by his wife's offspring.

'Matt, why don't you go into your room and play with your Dalek,' suggested Saffron, rubbing her head. Her mouth felt like sandpaper, and she regretted the half-bottle of port she had sunk with her mother before bedtime. Pete had snuck off to the pub with his mates for a pre-Christmas drink. Saffron was supposed to have gone too, but Gerry, in true How Can I Cock Up My Ex-Wife's Lifestyle fashion, had taken the kids out for dinner and got them back late. Not only that, but he had filled them up with E numbers, chocolate and fizzy drinks, so to say they were hyper was putting it mildly. And, by the looks of things, Matt hadn't quite come back down to earth. It didn't seem fair to dump two wild children on her mum, despite her generous offer of babysitting, so Saffron stayed in instead. Ellie was slightly unsettled anyway, so that wouldn't have been fair either. Pete had come back about midnight, full of bonhomie, and together they had ended up wrapping presents till 2 a.m.

'Remind me to do this earlier next year,' Saffron had said, yawning with relief when it was all done.

'You always say that,' Pete had replied. 'Come on, it's time Santa came down the chimney. And after he's done his duty, he might want a small reward.'

'Sounds like a good idea,' Saffron had grinned, snuggling up towards Pete. Little did he know that she had planned an extra Christmas present – herself wrapped up in all her sexy finery, just ready for him to unwrap.

They'd staggered upstairs to extricate stockings from bedrooms only to be met on the stairs by two

159

white-faced little waifs, looking for all the world like a pair of ghosts. 'Is he here yet?' the children had demanded, while Saffron and Pete had stared at one another in horror. Weren't they tired at all?

'No,' Saffron said. 'And he won't be unless you go straight to sleep.'

Of course, sleep being nigh on impossible on Christmas Eve when you're seven and five, Pete and Saffron had passed an uncomfortable hour dozing on the stairs until the kids finally nodded off. Any thoughts of extracurricular activity long gone, Saffron had rushed downstairs to grab presents to put into stockings, and eventually they'd staggered into bed about 3 a.m. Bloody hell, she'd had just over two hours' sleep.

Matt, following instructions, went haring off to his room screaming 'Exterminate!' at the top of his voice.

Shit. He'd wake the whole house up. Reluctantly, Saffron threw on her dressing gown and extricated him from his room with promises of chocolate and *Dr Who*. Becky, who had been quietly playing with her Bratz dolls, appeared as if by magic when she heard the immortal words *Dr Who*, and Saffron took them downstairs with their duvets. She curled up on the sofa and semi-dozed while the good doctor dispatched sundry villains. Eventually she was aware that the children were sleeping too. It was 7 a.m., so she decided she might as well put the turkey on. As she went back to bed, a cry from Ellie's cot informed her that her youngest was just about to join the party. Happy Christmas one and all, Saffron thought ruefully as she popped Ellie onto her breast. Dickens had evidently never done the baby thing then . . .

'Come in, come in,' Pete greeted Amy and Josh at the front door. 'Merry Christmas and all that. I'm really sorry but we're running a little late.'

'No problem,' said Amy, kissing him on the cheek. 'Happy Christmas. It's so good of you to have us.'

'Our pleasure,' said Pete, taking the bottle of wine that Amy had proffered. 'Saff's in the kitchen. She hasn't had much sleep and it's making her very bad-tempered.'

'Does she want a hand?' Amy asked.

'About four would be good,' replied Saffron, who had emerged from the kitchen. There was a slightly wild look in her eyes. 'I've had about two hours' sleep, dealt with total meltdown between my children, who are so tired now they'll probably crash out before lunch is served, and the bloody turkey isn't cooking. Meanwhile, my mother, who I was relying on to babysit, isn't feeling well so has taken to her bed. But otherwise it's going well. Bottoms up!' She waved a sherry glass at Amy.

'Blimey, it's a bit early, isn't it?' Amy said.

'I figured I couldn't feel much worse than I do,' said Saffron, 'so I'm topping up from last night. Hair of the dog and all that.'

'You look knackered,' said Amy.

'Tired and emotional just about sums it up,' said Saffron. 'Why did I invite so many people to lunch? Why? Why? Why? I must be mad.'

'What is there to do?'

'Only everything,' said Saffron, hiccoughing hysterically and dropping her sherry glass on the floor. 'Oh shit,' she said.

'Look,' said Amy tactfully, 'why don't you go and catch up on sleep? I'm sure Pete and I can manage here.'

'I couldn't,' said Saffron doubtfully.

'Yes, of course you could,' said Amy. 'I'd be happy to help. Go on, off you go.'

Amy's confidence drained away from her once she was in the kitchen. The only time she had cooked Christmas dinner it had been for herself and Jamie. The thought of cooking for – how many people did Saffron say were coming? It had to have been at least eight adults plus the children – was daunting to say the least.

Luckily the turkey was already on, though a quick prod demonstrated that it was anything but ready. Saffron meanwhile seemed to have made it as far as the potatoes in terms of peeling, but while they were in the pan, they weren't cooking yet. First things first. Amy turned on the potatoes, before confronting the carrots. There was a mammoth pile of sprouts looking at her, but she wasn't sure she could face them just yet. Pete seemed to have vanished off the face of the earth, the sprouts were beckoning to her alone.

'Whoever decided that sprouts were a must-have on Christmas Day?' wondered Amy aloud. 'No one eats them for the rest of the year.'

'My thoughts exactly,' said a welcome voice.

Amy looked round. Ben was standing before her.

'You made it then?' she said.

'Yup, I worked last night and this morning and someone else is covering now, so I've got until nine o'clock before I need to do my duty again,' he said. 'Do you need a hand? I'm a dab hand at sprouts, even though I loathe them.'

'That would be great,' Amy said. 'I'd better just check on the children. I dread to think of the mayhem that's going on.'

'It's okay,' said Ben. 'They were all jumping on Harry, so Pete put a video on. And Pete seems to be coping with the baby admirably. The Guys and Pete's sister have just turned up, so I offered to help you while he plays Mine Host.'

'It wouldn't go amiss,' said Amy with a grin. 'The sprouts are all yours.'

'Don't I get a Christmas kiss?' Ben murmured as he walked past.

'Of course,' Amy said, brushing her lips across his cheek, although she had a feeling that this wasn't quite what he had in mind.

They chatted companionably as they chopped veg, a Christmas carols CD that Saffron had been playing in the background.

'You look as though you've done this before,' said Amy, watching Ben expertly cross the Brussels sprouts.

'I usually end up in the kitchen at parties,' said Ben. 'Or certainly on Christmas Day. On the rare occasions I go to my brother's I often help his wife.'

'Don't you see him much?' asked Amy.

'I don't see him often,' said Ben. 'We're not a close family.'

'That's a shame,' said Amy. 'I can't imagine not being close to my brother. I wish I saw more of him. He's pretty much all I've got, apart from Josh. I speak to him and his wife all the time on the phone. I'll probably go and see them after Christmas.'

'You're lucky then,' said Ben. And a look of sadness passed across his face, but was gone again so swiftly that Amy wondered if she had imagined it. 'Oh, that was really crass,' he said. 'I'm sure, particularly today, you feel anything but lucky.'

'You know,' said Amy, as she tipped the peelings into the compost bin. 'For the first time since Jamie died, I do feel lucky. I was dreading Christmas, but this feels really restful.'

'It does, doesn't it?' said Ben, and smiled the smile that made Amy's heart dance as though one day soon it might even sing again.

Cooking with Ben felt cosy. And right. And with Josh wandering in and out occasionally, it felt almost domestic.

When they were done, the turkey still wasn't, so they looked at each other, unsure what to do next. After all, this wasn't their kitchen.

'We should go and be sociable,' said Amy.

'I still haven't had my Christmas kiss,' Ben replied playfully.

'Yes, you have,' said Amy, giving him a little punch in the ribs.

'Not what I would call a proper kiss,' Ben replied.

'Oh look, Saff's put some mistletoe up above the door.'

And suddenly, pulling her to him, he pressed his lips against hers. It was a dizzying, intoxicating moment, as she realised that not only was he kissing her, she was kissing him back, with a fierceness and a passion she had forgotten she was capable of.

There was a slight commotion in the hallway, and they pulled apart as they became aware of Saffron coming in.

'Thanks, you two,' she said, grinning. 'You've been a fantastic help.'

'Are you feeling better?' Amy was flustered, wondering if Saffron had seen anything.

'Much. Thanks so much. I can manage from now on. Go off and enjoy yourselves.'

Ben and Amy walked down the hallway towards the lounge. As Ben opened the door, he squeezed her hand.

'Happy Christmas, Amy,' he said.

'Happy Christmas, Ben,' Amy replied.

CHAPTER TWELVE

Stupid. Stupid. How could he have been so stupid?

Ben sat at the far end of the table, contemplating the remains of the turkey, and trying to pay attention to what Clive was saying to him, but he was finding concentration difficult. What on earth had possessed him to kiss Amy? She had made it perfectly clear that all she wanted from him was friendship. And he had gone and kissed her. He could kick himself. She'd barely spoken to him since and he'd spent the rest of the day avoiding her.

Everything had disintegrated into a degree of chaos. Lunch was finally served at about 4 p.m., by which time all the adults apart from him had imbibed far more than was probably good for them. The children ate very little and then retired into the lounge to watch DVDs. Harry, who was swaying rather alarmingly, followed them, ostensibly to keep an eye on them, but was now snoring rather loudly on the sofa. Elizabeth, having wanly come downstairs to eat, decided she would rather be in her own bed, so Ben had dropped her back home. He'd been glad of the excuse to get out.

And now he, Pete, Clive, Keith, and Pete's brother-in-law Steve were sitting chewing the fat and passing the port. Or at least they were passing the port. Ben was sticking to coffee and wondering when he could reasonably call it a day.

'Come on, everyone, this is supposed to be a party,' said Keith, who was a bit of a drama queen. 'We should dance.'

'Too right we should,' said Saffron, yanking a rather reluctant Amy to her feet.

'I've got two left feet,' protested Amy.

'Nobody can go wrong to Abba,' was Saffron's firm response, and soon the room was rocking to the sounds of 'Dancing Queen'. Despite her initial reluctance, Amy seemed to be enjoying herself, and she had even persuaded Kay, Pete's sister, to join in. Now, as Ben watched covertly, she was laughing and joking as she tried to follow Keith's rather wild version of the 'Macarena'. Her hair, held up in a grip, was escaping, and loose tendrils kept snaking their way down her neck. Ben longed to go over and wind them back up again.

His thoughts were in turmoil. She was so beautiful. So full of fun and life. Just seeing her this morning, so calm and capable chopping the vegetables, yet managing to exude an air of sexuality at the same time, had made him realise how much he wanted her. It had seemed natural to kiss her. And she had responded, damn it.

Watching her dancing now, teasingly trying to drag Clive and Pete out to join them, it was hard to imagine her life had been blighted by tragedy. But blighted it was.

Amy came back to sit down at the table. She was flushed and laughing.

'No more, no more!' she was saying as Keith tried to persuade her to join him again.

'Time we were off, anyway,' said Kay. 'We've got to pop in on Steve's family.'

'And we're seeing the neighbours,' Clive reminded Keith.

'What time is it?' Amy looked at her watch. 'I should really be getting Josh to bed.'

The children straggled through the door to announce that *Pirates of the Caribbean* had finished.

'Matt says I can have a sleepover,' Josh announced to Amy.

'Darling, you can't just invite yourself to stay the night,' laughed Amy. 'Saffron and Pete mightn't like it.'

'He's welcome to stay if you want,' said Saffron.

For a fleeting moment, Amy had the tempting thought that with Josh out of the way, she could perhaps snatch a moment alone with Ben, whom she had been avoiding ever since he'd kissed her in the kitchen. But she dismissed it instantly, horrified with herself for even having the thought.

'It's all right, Saffron,' she said. 'I'd rather have him with me. Thanks anyway.'

''sabout time I was off.' A rather bedraggled-looking

Harry was swaying in the doorway. He was still somewhat the worse for wear.

'Perhaps Josh and I had better see you home,' said Amy, having visions of Harry falling into someone's compost heap and dying of hypothermia in the night.

'Good idea,' said Ben. 'I'll help you.'

Saffron and Pete exchanged looks that weren't lost on Amy. She wasn't at all sure she wanted to be round Ben right now. The kiss had unsettled her. Not only had Ben taken her completely by surprise, she'd taken herself by surprise too. The force with which she had responded to Ben frightened her. And made her feel guilty. She had been both relieved and perturbed when he had spent the rest of the day avoiding her, but now they were being thrown together again. Then again, with Harry and Josh acting as chaperons, it wasn't like anything could happen.

The hall was soon full of people milling around, wishing each other a merry Christmas and kissing one another goodbye. Eventually, Amy and Ben found themselves walking down Saffron's path with Harry propped up between them, and Josh holding Amy's hand. It took all their efforts to stop Harry from falling over, and all four of them found themselves in fits of hysterics.

'What's wrong with Harry?' Josh wanted to know as Harry tripped over for the umpteenth time.

'There's nothing wrong with me,' muttered Harry. 'Don't know what all the fuss is about meself.'

He staggered to his feet and then lurched over again.

'I have a feeling this could take some time,' said Ben, in peals of laughter.

'I've a feeling you could be right,' Amy replied. And they staggered off into the dark.

'Well, I think you could call that a success,' said Pete, as he staggered back into the lounge, where Saffron was flopped on the sofa.

'Mmm. Mismanaged, dysfunctional, disastrous were words that sprang to mind,' she said. 'But I think everyone enjoyed themselves. In the end. Are the kids settled?'

'They're all out for the count,' said Pete, 'which gives us a chance for some quality time together.' He gave her a wicked grin, and Saffron smiled back.

'Doesn't it just,' she said. 'Hang on a sec. You wait here and come up in five minutes. There was something I was going to do last night, which I never got round to in the general chaos.'

Saffron scooted upstairs, and, after making sure Pete was right and everyone was asleep, ran into their bedroom, threw off her clothes, and found her sexy lingerie, where it had remained in the bottom of her drawer after her last thwarted attempt at seduction.

The bra bit of the basque seemed tighter than ever, as her breasts were filling with milk. Ellie wasn't due a feed till around midnight, so she reckoned she had an hour or so to play with. She really ought to stop breastfeeding soon, if only to restore her breasts to their former glory, but with Ellie in the next room and still waking a couple of times in the night it was so damned convenient.

Put that out of your head, Saffron admonished herself. Thinking about breastfeeding was hardly likely to make her feel horny. Whereas black lace underwear, silk stockings and the sexy lacy nightie and dressing gown Pete had bought her for Christmas were. She added a Santa's hat to complete the effect.

There was a tentative knock on the door. 'Can I come in now?'

'Be my guest,' said Saffron, arranging herself in what she hoped was a sexy manner on the bed. The alcohol she had been drinking on and off all day had emboldened her and she was beginning to think she could pull this off.

'Happy Christmas, darling,' she said. 'I thought I'd wrap myself up like a Christmas cracker, for you to pull.'

'Sounds good to me,' said Pete, pulling his clothes off with satisfying alacrity. It was working, it was finally working. Saffron was feeling sexy. She was turned on, and Pete evidently wanted her.

Pete was on the bed fumbling with her dressing gown now, and she let him undo it while she drew a lazy finger down his spine. There had been a time when his every touch sent her into paroxysms of delight, and tonight she was pleased to note that those feelings were beginning to return. Pete was kissing her now. On her mouth. Her neck. His lips were moving down her body as he gently peeled off the sexy nightie and began to caress her breasts through the basque.

Oh, this was gorgeous. It was sublime. Saffron felt like punching the air. Yee haw! When –

'What the –?' Pete pulled back clutching his eye. He had released her bulging breasts from the basque, and without warning a jet of milk had shot out. Ellie was starting to wail in the other room. It was feeding time at the zoo again.

Saffron's sexy mood evaporated as quickly as it had arrived. Bugger, bugger, bugger. She looked at Pete, who had collapsed into fits of hysterics.

'Sorry,' she said.

'Did you know they could do that?' Pete was looking semi-admiring, if a little defused.

'Nope. I just guess we have to accept that they don't belong to me any more,' said Saffron, as she flung on her dressing gown and went to get Ellie.

The baby settled quickly into a contented and happy feed, while Pete cuddled next to Saffron.

'Never mind,' he said. 'We can try again later.'

'Thanks for being so understanding,' said Saffron.

'How else would I be?' Pete was genuinely puzzled. He kissed her. 'Look, I'm really sorry but I'm knackered. Wake me up for round two when the baby's finished.'

'Round two sounds good to me,' said Saffron, knowing full well she wouldn't. Instead of feeling a sex goddess, she felt like a failure, despite Pete's reassuring words. Her body had betrayed her and she felt cheated. But she also didn't have the energy to try again. It seemed to her a normal healthy sex life was a thing of the past. Would she ever get it back? There was no help for it. Desperate times called for desperate measures.

She was going to have to make it her New Year's Resolution to rediscover her lost libido.

'Here we are, Harry,' Amy said with a grin as they finally arrived at Harry's doorstep. Harry lurched forward and nearly fell again as he fumbled for his keys.

'Can't seem to find my – you know, wotsitcalled?'

'"Key" is the word you're looking for,' Ben said drily. 'I think you'll find the spare is hidden under the flowerpot.'

'Do you know, old boy, I think you're right.' Harry swaying dangerously to retrieve the key and then couldn't seem to find the lock.

'Here, let me,' said Ben, taking the key from him.

'Thanks, old boy,' said Harry, as he staggered through the door. 'Can I offer you a nightcap before bed?'

'No, thanks,' Ben and Amy chorused, visions of being force-fed elderberry wine springing to mind.

'Right, well, I'll be seeing you,' said Harry. 'Merry Christmas.'

'Merry Christmas, Harry,' said Amy, giving him a hug and a peck on the cheek.

'Merry Christmas, Harry,' said Ben. 'And make sure you drink plenty of water.'

'You fuss too much,' said Harry, waving them away and shutting the door behind him.

'So much for us keeping an eye on him,' said Amy. 'Do you think he'll be okay?'

'I have seen him worse,' said Ben. 'But I'll give him a ring later to make sure he's all right.'

They had reached the doorstep of Amy's house. The memory of their kiss stood pregnant in the air between them.

'Mumm-eee, I'm cold,' Josh wailed.

Amy rummaged with her key in the lock, wondering whether to invite Ben in or not. Part of her wanted to pretend the kiss had never happened. But she knew she was kidding herself. It had meant something. Ben meant something. Oh, bugger it. Life was too short. There was no harm in having coffee with Ben.

'Would you like to come in?' she asked.

'Well, if you're sure,' said Ben, and everything suddenly seemed so simple.

Except that once inside the house, with Josh safely tucked up in bed, when she was sitting nervously opposite Ben holding her coffee, conscious she might spill it, she didn't know what to do next. It had been so long since she felt like this. The easy intimacy of Saffron's kitchen seemed to have deserted her. And the kiss hung between them like an albatross around their necks. Should she go to him? Should she touch him? What should she say next?

Ben clearly felt the same, as he didn't stay sitting down. He roamed the room like a caged lion, before he finally settled in the corner, leaning against a bookshelf. He picked up Josh's Action Man.

'I used to have one of these,' he said. 'I loved it.'

'Josh does too,' said Amy.

'They don't make them like they used to any more,' said Ben.

'Oh I don't know,' Amy replied, 'you should see how many versions of Action Man there are these days. SAS Action Man, Rock Climber Action Man, Underwater Action Man – for all I know they do Robocop Action Man. I can't keep up.'

'But the originals are always the best, don't you think?'

'I guess so,' said Amy. Then, 'Why are we having a conversation about Action Man?'

'What else should we talk about?' said Ben.

'I don't know.'

'Neither do I.'

There was an awkward pause.

'About this morning,' she began hesitantly.

'Yes, I'm sorry about that,' said Ben. 'I don't know what came over me.'

'Oh.' Amy was disappointed. He evidently thought he'd made a mistake.Then he looked at her, and she knew without a doubt that wasn't what he was thinking. He hadn't made a mistake, and neither had she.

She went towards him, still hesitating. But almost as if she had no will of her own, she stumbled into Ben's arms. The dizzying feeling from that morning – *was it only that morning? It seemed like a lifetime ago* – returned, and he pulled her towards him to kiss her, and –

'Mummy, what are you doing?' Josh was standing at the bottom of the stairs, with a look of horror on his face.

For the second time that day, Amy pulled away from Ben.

'I hate you. And I hate Ben!' Josh burst into tears and ran upstairs.

And after what he'd said to Mary too.

Oh my God. How could she have done this to him?

Ben stood looking awkward. 'I should go,' he said eventually.

'Yes, you should,' said Amy. 'Sorry, I've got to see to him.'

'Of course, of course,' said Ben. 'I'll let myself out.'

'I'm sorry,' said Amy. 'Josh has to come first. You do understand, don't you?'

'I'm renowned for my understanding,' said Ben, with a lightness he didn't feel. 'Merry Christmas, Amy.'

'Merry Christmas, Ben,' Amy replied, turning away, not trusting herself to speak. How could a day that had begun so right, end up going so dreadfully wrong?

CHAPTER THIRTEEN

Ben drove down the motorway towards his parents' house. His doctor's duties over, he had a few days to kill between Christmas and New Year. Given that he had blown Caroline out for skiing, that meant a long and lonely Christmas week on his own. So he had decided to pay an extended visit to his parents. His mum would be pleased. Or so he kept telling himself.

Coward, a little voice said in his head. The real reason, of course, was Amy. After Josh had seen them kissing, Ben was clearer than ever that he had overstepped the mark. The stricken look on Amy's face was enough to tell him so. Several times he had toyed with calling round, but every time he couldn't bring himself to. Seeing her would do more harm than good. Which was, of course, an easy way to justify his actions. *Coward*, the voice in his head taunted him again. And, damn it, it was right.

'Ben, how fantastic you could come after all.' His mum knew how to press all the right buttons. Now he was feeling guilty for using his parents as an escape route from facing up to Amy, as well as feeling guilty about running away in the first place. Ben bent down to kiss his mother, all five foot two of her. She seemed to shrink every time he saw her.

'Sorry it was such short notice,' said Ben. 'The on-call thing was a bit of a pain.'

'Well, you're here now,' his mum beamed widely. She was so pleased to see him. He was crap about coming. He should come more.

'How are you both?'

'Oh, fine, fine,' said his mother, bustling about making tea, while his dad just grunted from behind his paper.

Ben's heart sank. The lounge, still complete with seventies flock wallpaper, swirling brown carpet and boarded-up fireplace, hadn't changed in nearly thirty years. The artificial tree had finally been replaced by a real one, but it was slightly lopsided and shedding pine needles faster than his mother could sweep them up. The Christmas decorations, lovingly removed and scrubbed free of dust every year, looked gaudier than ever. And now there were the three of them, sitting staring at each other, not knowing what to say. Never knowing what to say. Ben thought fleetingly of the warmth and happiness in Saffron's house, and compared it with the sterility of his own. It wasn't that there was a lack of love in his home, it's just that it was fossilised, trapped in time, and stuck in that one day, all those years ago, where they were all doomed to stay forever.

He thought of Amy and his heart ached for her. She

too was trapped in a moment of pain. And so long as Josh prevented her, she would be unable to move on either. Ben had to face it. However much he wished things could be different, there was nothing he could do to change them. Either for his parents, or for Amy. It was just the way things were.

Saffron was feeling gloomy as she plonked pansies in Linda Lovelace's pots. She couldn't quite believe how disastrously Christmas had ended up. Her mum had been unable to shake off her stomach bug, so the promise of a New Year's Eve out hadn't materialised. Instead Saffron had invited several people round for drinks, but everyone was busy. That being the case, she had thought at least she and Pete could have a cosy evening watching TV in bed, but nothing much was doing there, either. Although she and Pete had managed sex a couple of times over the Christmas period, they had been desultory occasions, and Saffron had the feeling that not only was her own fire not lit, but Pete's had nearly blown out. The sight of milk spouting from her boobs was, she suspected, going to stay with them both for a long time. Perhaps she should start taking lessons from Linda Lovelace. She snorted loudly at the thought.

It was a relief that the kids had gone back to school so soon after the New Year, and she and Amy could get back to work. It gave her something else to think about.

'How much more to do?' Amy came wandering

down Linda's huge garden bearing cups of tea. She looked pale, Saffron thought. She had also been withdrawn since Christmas. This was the first time that they'd seen each other for more than five minutes. Amy had been elusive, and had cried off the New Year's Eve invite.

It was most odd. Saffron had had the distinct idea that something had been going on between Amy and Ben on Christmas Day, but nothing since then seemed to suggest it had. Ben also seemed to have disappeared off the face of the universe – or certainly the allotments – even Harry didn't know where he was. It was most unsettling.

Damn it, all this pondering wasn't going to get Linda's pansies planted.

'There's a fair amount, still,' said Saffron, waving towards one of Linda's many flowerbeds. 'There are a whole load more plants by the greenhouse.'

'I love pansies,' said Amy, as she picked up a tray of them. 'They're so sweet. I always think they look as though they have little faces, don't you?'

'You have the strangest ideas, but I see what you mean,' laughed Saffron. 'Are you okay? You look a bit peaky.'

'I'm fine,' said Amy. 'I haven't been sleeping well. Josh has been a bit upset. He missed his granny over Christmas.'

Her look brooked no further discussion, so Saffron left it alone, turning her thoughts once more to the crisis in her own love life. She was getting so desperate that perhaps taking lessons from Linda Lovelace wasn't such a stupid idea after all. She had to do something to restore not just her libido, but Pete's.

The ringing of Amy's mobile jolted her out of her thoughts. 'He was where? Doing *what*? How on earth did that happen? Right, I'll be there as soon as I can.'

'Problem?'

'That was the school,' said Amy. 'Josh escaped from the playground at lunchtime, and they've just found him down by the river. I've got to go.'

Amy rang the buzzer at the main door of the school, her heart thumping nineteen to the dozen. Such a shame schools had to have so much security these days. Even more of a shame that, for all the security, no one had kept an eye out for her son. She could get cross about that if she chose, but she was feeling so guilty about Josh that she didn't think she'd be able to bring herself to. This was all her fault. It had to be.

Josh hadn't been the same since he'd caught Amy and Ben kissing. His behaviour over the Christmas period had been abysmal. He had disobeyed her constantly, and screamed and shouted when she told him off. His tantrums were spectacular, and then when they were over he would break down into sobbing fits that lasted ages.

And now this. Amy had already been beside herself not knowing what to do, or who to turn to. She couldn't even talk to Saffron, whom she would trust with her life. How to admit to someone else that you had just screwed your kid up?

But now it looked like her choice would be made for her. No doubt Josh had told his teachers what kind of a mum he had. And they would be forming their own conclusions. No, don't be paranoid, Amy told herself. She had sat on the other side of the desk in these situations, after all, and had felt for a mother struggling through no fault of her own. Why would Josh's teachers be any different?

To her relief, Josh's teachers were so wound up about the fact that he had escaped that they weren't looking to blame poor parenting for his bolting lapse.

'We are so sorry, Mrs Nicolson,' said Miss Burrows, who had taken Amy off into an unused classroom. 'It appears that there is a gap in the fence in the playground that no one knew was there. Josh wriggled through it at the end of lunchtime play, and we only realised he was missing when we called the register. Luckily he'd told Matt what he was doing, so we were able to get him back pretty quickly.'

Amy was shaking by now at the thought of what might have happened.

'But he's okay?' she said, her voice trembling.

'Yes, thank God,' said Miss Burrows. 'He gave us all a fright, but though we found him by the river, he seemed to at least have the sense not to go near it.'

'Can I see him?'

'Of course,' said Miss Burrows. 'He's very upset, so it might be best if he went home for the afternoon.'

'Has he said why he did it?' Amy asked, feeling sure

that any minute now a hand of God was going to fall in front of her saying, It's Your Fault, Bad, Bad Mother!

'No, he hasn't breathed a word. All I could get out of him was that he wanted to go and see his granny.'

Amy sighed. 'He probably does,' she said. 'Oh God, this is all my fault. I took him away to a new place, away from all his familiar surroundings. Of course he wants to see Granny.'

'It is true that Josh has been having some trouble settling in,' said Miss Burrows. 'But I am surprised at this. I hadn't got him taped as a bolter.'

Amy laughed through her sniffles.

'It isn't like him, it's true,' she said. She couldn't face admitting that she had added to Josh's problems by kissing Ben. 'I'll have a long chat with him. It won't happen again, I promise.'

Saffron had tidied up the rest of the pots, and was heading for the kitchen door, where Linda Lovelace was on the phone. Linda nodded to Saffron to put the cups down on the side. Saffron didn't like to come in with her muddy boots, but Linda waved her inside.

'Yes, doll,' she was saying. 'I do classes on a Wednesday and Thursday evening at Legends night-club in Bairstow. Do you know it? You can try out a taster session, if you like, before booking for the whole six-week course. And you get a certificate at the end to prove you've completed it. Great! See you Wednesday then.'

She snapped her mobile phone shut. 'Hi babe, I owe you some money,' she said.

Saffron had to hide a smile. Most of her clients had to be reminded to pay up, but Linda was almost embarrassing with her largesse. Saffron suspected the woman didn't have a clue how much anything cost. She and Amy could probably get away with charging twice what they did.

'Amy gone then?' Linda delved into her Gucci handbag for some money.

'Yes, she had a problem with her son,' said Saffron.

'Shame,' Linda said, although Saffron thought she was probably just being polite.

'I was telling Amy only the last time I saw her, she should come to some of my pole-dancing classes,' continued Linda. 'Good-looking girl like her shouldn't be on her own.'

'I'm not sure pole dancing is really Amy's thing,' said Saffron.

'Oh don't be put off by the idea,' said Linda. 'It's not about exotic dancing any more. It's more about aerobic exercise. And it's a great way to lose weight. You should try it.'

Reminding herself that Linda was a client, so telling her to shove her pole-dancing classes up her rectum wouldn't quite be the thing, Saffron smiled politely instead, and said, 'Yes, perhaps I should.'

'Here, I've just printed a new leaflet,' said Linda. 'Why not take one and have a look? I've got a new course starting soon. You could come for a taster lesson if you like.'

'I'll bear that in mind,' said Saffron, suppressing a fit of the giggles, and shoving the leaflet promptly in her pocket with every intention of binning it as soon as she got out of the house. It was only when she got into the car and released the gales of laughter that had been building up inside her that she took the leaflet out, and, impelled more by curiosity than anything else, had a look.

The leaflet had an out-of-focus picture of Linda swinging round a pole in a position that looked positively dangerous, against a dark pink background that was evidently meant to be erotic.

Love-life down the tubes? Partner got the hump?
Pole dancing could be the answer to your dreams.

The first was certainly true, and who knows, before long the second might be too. Despite herself, Saffron read on. Apparently pole dancing was growing faster than any dance craze in the country. And far from it being, as Saffron had hitherto imagined, an activity indulged in by exotic dancers in seedy pubs on Sunday lunchtimes, pole dancing had apparently gone mainstream. Perhaps she should give it a go. It would probably be a laugh. She might lose some weight. And she might even rediscover her lost libido. It couldn't do any harm to try.

Amy dropped Josh's book bag by the front door and sighed. The walk home had been longer than usual.

Josh hadn't stopped crying, and no amount of molli-
fying seemed to help. He still hadn't given a reason for
his actions, and Amy felt there was no point pressing
it. Whatever it was that had tripped his wire would
probably come out eventually. She hoped. As soon as
Josh had come through the door he had run upstairs
and hidden in his bedroom.

Amy made a cup of tea and decided to leave him
for five minutes. Perhaps he would come down in his
own good time.

Once five minutes had elapsed there was still no sign
of Josh, so she went up to his room and found him
sobbing into his pillow.

'Sweetheart,' she said, feeling more helpless than at
any other point since Jamie's death, 'whatever's the
matter? Did you think Mummy was going to be cross
about you running away?'

The sobs carried on, and Amy sat down and put her
arms around him, and stroked his head.

'It doesn't matter, Josh, no one's angry, we're just
pleased you're safe,' she said. 'I'm here now.'

Josh pulled himself up from the bed and looked her
straight in the eye, with a look that pierced her heart.

'Daddy went away,' he said. 'And Granny's gone away.
What happens if you go away?'

'Josh, I'm not going anywhere,' said Amy. 'And
Granny's only gone on holiday. She'll be back soon.'

'Yes, but we don't see her any more,' said Josh,
bursting into fresh tears. 'I want to see Granny. I want
to go back home.'

'Is that why you ran away?'

'Yes,' Josh snivelled.

Amy found a hankie for his nose and held him close.

'Oh sweetheart,' said Amy. 'This is our home now.'

'No, it's not,' said Jamie.

'Yes, it is,' said Amy. 'You know, it's like in that book about the tiger, when he moves house and he realises his home has moved with him.'

'But Granny isn't here,' said Josh.

'I know,' said Amy. 'And I'm sorry about that. So when she's back from her holiday, why don't we invite her to come and stay for a while? I know it's all a bit strange here still, but you've got lots of friends. And if we go back to London you won't see Matt any more.'

'Matt and I had a fight,' said Josh.

'Aah,' said Amy. 'And what was that about?'

'Matt said I didn't have a daddy. And he's got two daddies. So then I said I did have a daddy, but he'd gone away. And he said you'd go away too and I wouldn't have a mummy.'

'Darling, I've told you, I'm not going anywhere.' Amy cuddled Josh closer, relieved that at least he was talking.

'But if you marry Ben you'd go and live in his house,' said Josh. 'And then where would I go?'

It was like an arrow through her heart. Amy felt terrible. So it was *her* fault, after all.

'Josh,' she began carefully. 'What you saw on Christmas Day was nothing. Ben kissed me to wish me happy Christmas, that's all. I'm not going to marry him. And if I did, I certainly wouldn't leave you anywhere.'

'Really?'

'Really,' Amy said, giving him a kiss. 'What would I do without you? Now why don't you dry your face, and I'll toast you some marshmallows while you watch a DVD.'

Miraculously, it was like the sun coming out.

'Great,' said Josh. 'Can I watch *Spiderman*?'

'Okay,' said Amy, thinking it ironic that he'd chosen that film, since it was Ben who had introduced it to Josh. Josh had badgered her about it so much that Father Christmas had bought him a copy. It was the first time, though, that he had asked to watch it. 'But no more running away from school, you promise?'

'I promise,' said Josh. 'Come on, Mummy, what are you waiting for?'

Amy followed her son downstairs, feeling both better and worse. Josh was clearly upset, but at least he'd been able to tell her about it, which was something. But the fact was, he had been upset because of her. It was Amy who had taken him to a new place and away from his beloved Granny. It was Amy who had kissed Ben and further unsettled her son. Had she done the right thing by coming here? The more she thought about it, the less certain she became. Maybe she should think about leaving Nevermorewell after all.

CHAPTER FOURTEEN

'Children are very resilient,' Saffron said, when Amy told her about it the next day, while they were tidying up Mrs Meadows' garden. 'Becky and Matt went through their ups and downs when Gerry first left, and you should have seen the way they behaved the first time I brought Pete round. But they got over it. Things aren't perfect – they never are – but Josh knows he's got you, and that's what really matters.'

'Thanks,' said Amy gratefully. 'Being on my own, I have no one to bounce ideas off, and it's so easy to blame yourself when things go wrong. Josh seemed happier today, so I'm hoping it's a one-off.'

'Well, you've got me and I'm sure it is,' said Saffron. 'What gave Josh the idea you'd go off with Ben?'

Amy blushed. She had been so confused about what had happened on Christmas Day, she hadn't told anyone about it.

'No idea,' she said. 'Why do you ask?'

'No reason,' said Saffron. 'I just thought you and Ben looked very cosy on Christmas Day.' She cast a sly look at Amy, who was trying, nonchalantly, to rake the leaves they hadn't got round to clearing before Christmas.

'I'm right, aren't I? When I came into the kitchen that day, you both jumped apart like frightened rabbits. Come on, tell your Auntie Saff all about it.'

Amy laughed. Saffron was hard to resist, and it felt good to get it off her chest.

'I haven't seen Ben since that day,' she said. 'So it's not as if this is a great love affair or anything. And, given how much it's upset Josh, it definitely won't be happening again.' As she said this, Amy's stomach tied into peculiar knots. Despite her protestations, the fact that she hadn't heard from Ben since Christmas had been bothering her. Sure, it made dealing with the Josh issue easier, but it also made her doubtful about Ben. Why had he kissed her? Had he been toying with her? At the time it felt like he genuinely cared, but the longer it went on, the less sure Amy was.

'I think Ben's away,' said Saffron. 'Pete said something ages ago about him going skiing.'

'Oh.' Amy felt disappointed that Ben hadn't thought to mention it to her. 'He never said.'

'I think it was some last-minute thing,' said Saffron absently, as she started to dig Mrs Meadows' flowerbed over, ready for spring planting. 'Don't look so tragic.' Amy's thoughts were plain to see. 'I doubt very much that Ben is going to find love on the ski slopes.'

'I'm not, as you put it, looking tragic,' said Amy, chucking some leaves at Saffron, before putting the rest of them in the bag. 'Even if, and it's a big if, I was interested in Ben, it's not as though I can do anything about it. We're both free agents. He can do what he likes.'

'Hmm, you sound so convincing,' said Saffron.

'Oh do shut up,' said Amy, giggling. 'Otherwise I might just be tempted to shove these leaves down your neck.'

The following Saturday morning, Amy and Josh found themselves on the allotments. There wasn't much to do at this time of year, but as this was her first year here, Amy wanted to plan her plot for the spring. She had managed to get some onion sets in at the end of November, and was pleased to see they were doing well. Her seedbeds were carefully covered over with old carpet to prevent the weeds from growing – a tip Harry had kindly passed on. A few of her raspberry canes had fallen over in the recent winds, and she'd tied them up again, but really there wasn't much to keep her busy.

Very few people seemed to be out and about. Hardly surprising, really. Though the sun was out, it was freezing, and the wind whipped through her and Josh, who had soon had enough and was demanding to go home.

'In a minute,' said Amy. 'I just want to find Harry and borrow his seed catalogues to order some pota-toes. Come on, you know it's nice and warm in his hut. And he might have a biscuit if you're lucky.'

Thus mollified, Josh put his hand in hers, and they

walked past Scary Slug Man, who was muttering his usual incantations, towards Harry's hut.

Harry came to greet them with a steaming cup of tea.

'How are you both?' he beamed. 'We haven't seen much of you down here lately.'

'We've been a bit busy,' said Amy. 'It feels like we've gone straight from Christmas into meltdown without a break.'

'I ran away from school,' said Josh proudly as he sat on Harry's comfy old sofa eating a chocolate biscuit.

Harry raised his eyebrows.

'It's nothing to be proud of,' said Amy. 'And you're not doing it again, are you?'

Josh pulled a face. 'No-o-o,' he said. 'I know, I know. It's dangerous and I could have got hurt.'

'What happened?'

Amy gave Harry a potted version of events, missing out the kiss as Josh was sitting there all ears.

'Well, young man, I hope you've learned your lesson,' said Harry.

'Of course,' said Josh indignantly. 'I've already told you.'

'And why wouldn't we believe you?' said Amy, laughing. 'Come on, we'd better get you home for some lunch. Fancy popping in for a bite, Harry?'

'I think I might,' said Harry. 'I spot Edie at four o'clock, no doubt bearing gifts of fruitcake and coffee. I need an excuse to avoid her.'

'I'm an excuse now, am I?' Amy asked in mock petulant tones. 'I like that.'

'And I can't think of a better one,' was Harry's gallant response. 'I'll just tidy up here and follow you home. I shouldn't be long.'

In fact, Harry was quicker than Amy had envisaged. She had only been in a couple of minutes when there was a knock on the door.

'Phew,' said Harry. 'That was a close one. Edie nearly got me, but I managed to escape. I swear that woman is after my body.'

'Stranger things have been known,' said Amy, laughing as she poured Harry a cup of tea.

Josh had settled down in the lounge and was playing a complicated game with his Action Man, so Amy and Harry sat chatting in the kitchen.

'Is Josh all right now?' asked Harry.

'I think so,' said Amy. 'He gave himself as much of a fright as he gave me. So I'm hoping he doesn't do it again.'

'Any idea why he did it?'

Amy paused, but Harry's ready sympathy was enough to release the floodgates and she found herself pouring out the whole story.

'It's not as though I want a relationship with anyone,' she said, 'but I feel so guilty about Josh seeing what happened. I should have thought about him more.'

'Amy, you're an attractive young woman,' said Harry. 'You can't go round wearing a hair shirt for the rest of your life. And Josh will have to get used to the idea that one day you'll find him a new dad. Give him time, I'm sure he'll come round.'

'Do you think so?'

'I know so,' said Harry. 'Trust me. I'm a wise old owl, and there isn't much about human behaviour that I haven't seen before.'

'One thing that's been puzzling me, though,' said Amy, 'is why Josh suddenly turned against Ben. He was quite happy at fireworks night. And he even said he wanted Ben for a dad. But then, before Christmas, he told his granny he didn't want me to marry Ben. And now this. It does seem a bit odd.'

'Do you want me to have a chat with him about it?' asked Harry. 'Perhaps another point of view might help.'

'Well, if you don't mind,' said Amy. 'Because I'd hate to think I've scarred him for life.'

'Now that I doubt very much,' said Harry, patting her hand. 'Any chance of another cuppa?'

Ben strode across the allotments, his spade over his shoulder. He breathed a deep sigh of relief. It was so good to be back. Thanks to a severe dose of the winter vomiting bug (no doubt picked up from some of the patients he'd seen at Christmas), his stay at his parents' had ended up prolonged till after the New Year. He had come back halfway through the week, got immersed in work and had still been feeling so wiped out from the bug he hadn't seen anyone since he'd been back.

He breathed in the fresh, crisp air. Though it had been good to spend more time than normal with his parents, it was nice to get away from his mother's endless ministrations. It was hard not to feel suffocated at home, and he felt free for the first time in a week.

He pottered about tidying up his allotment. He was only growing a few lettuces in his improvised cold frames. Harry had been watering them for him. But being here was therapeutic, and he did need to dig over the vegetable patch, ready for sowing in the spring. At least, that's the excuse he'd given himself. Really he was hoping he'd see Amy. It would be easier than going over there.

He felt bad about Amy. About the way he'd left her to deal with Josh, and then not contacted her. Ben had kidded himself she needed time on her own. But now he wasn't sure. The truth was, he hadn't known what to do. Or say. So he had done nothing. Said nothing. She had every right to be cross with him. He wished he were better at this sort of thing.

'Hello, old boy.' Harry emerged from his hut sipping coffee, which had a distinctly medicinal smell to it. 'Good trip?'

'Okay,' said Ben, trying to appear noncommittal. 'But it's good to be back. Should you really be drinking whisky at this time in the morning?'

'Oh do stop nagging. Anyone would think you'd had a bad time.'

'I've had better holidays,' admitted Ben.

'Seen Amy yet?' Harry nodded in the direction of her garden gate.

'Er, no,' said Ben.

'When you do, take it easy,' said Harry. 'Josh has been giving her a tough time, and she feels it's all her fault.'

'What kind of a hard time?' Ben felt lousier than ever.

Harry filled Ben in on Josh's attempt at running away.

'The last person she needs to see is me,' said Ben. 'I presume she told you what happened?'

'She did,' Harry replied. 'So what's your story?'

Ben shrugged his shoulders.

'I like Amy,' he said, 'more than I've liked anyone in a long time. But she's vulnerable. And she has Josh. I think it's pretty much a non-starter, don't you?'

'Oh, I don't know,' said Harry. 'Give her time. And give Josh time. I'd say all is not lost just yet.'

'Harry, you're a hopeless old romantic,' Ben told him. 'But this time, I think you're wrong.'

Fancy yourself a bit of a minx? Want a purrfect body?
Then come to Pole Kittens,
and discover the New Sexy Dance Craze.
Let us show you our moves!
Learn from the Sexperts at Pole Kittens.
All ages and abilities welcome.

'What on earth am I doing?' Saffron wondered aloud as she sat staring at her computer screen. A trawl of pole-dancing classes online had come up with a huge haul. She was amazed that there were so many classes locally, though she was amused and not surprised to discover there seemed to be more on the Essex side of the river than the Suffolk side. They ranged from the Pole Kittens she was looking at, who seemed vaguely respectable, to the Hot Vixens Luv Dancin', who most decidedly didn't, the venue their classes were held being a rather seedy pub that held stripper sessions on a Sunday lunchtime. Saffron was only privy to this information because it was one of Gerry's less salubrious habits to totter over there in his youth, when he'd had a few, and one of the many reasons why she thanked God daily for no longer being married to him.

Thinking about Gerry made her wonder again why she was even contemplating doing this. She and Pete were fine. They were jogging along quite happily together. And now that she'd stopped breastfeeding (the spouting breasts at Christmas had been A Sign, she was sure), their sex life was slowly improving.

But it wasn't what it had been. She needed a lot more to get herself going these days, and even Pete's suggestion of watching exotic videos together hadn't helped. Exhausted by the combination of motherhood and work, she found herself falling into bed most nights, with sex the last thing on her mind. Pete was forever telling her it didn't matter, he was often tired too – but suppose, just suppose, that it did matter.

Saffron sighed. She couldn't face the Vixens, and the Pole Kittens looked a bit too glamorous for her. She turned over the leaflet Linda had given her. It might be embarrassing to go to a class where you knew the teacher. But on the other hand, Linda was a laugh. For all her brashness and new money (her husband, Johnny the Brickie, had made money in the building trade, from what Saffron suspected were nefarious practices), Linda was very good-hearted. She'd mentioned the classes to Saffron again, the last time Saffron had been round (thankfully on her own – Amy had been on another job). Oh bugger it, thought Saffron, picking up the phone. What have I got to lose? My pride. My dignity. My self-respect. She looked again at the leaflet.

Weight loss guaranteed, or your money back. Damn it. It had to be worth a try.

Amy was doing the washing-up, staring aimlessly out of the window. Despite everything, she hadn't been able to stop thinking about Ben. She hadn't seen him for over two weeks and she missed him. And though she knew, for Josh's sake, there could be nothing more than friendship between them, she still hoped that they could have that at least.

The doorbell rang, and she nearly jumped out of her skin.

She went to the door and opened it.

'Ben.' Her mouth was as dry as powder.

'Amy – is it –? Can I come in?' He seemed hesitant, awkward.

'Yes, of course,' she said. 'Though I can't guarantee you'll get a great reception from Josh.'

Josh was sitting at the kitchen table, drawing. He shot Ben a dirty look, but otherwise ignored him.

'Tea?' Amy asked, thinking, why do we always offer

tea when we feel awkward? People had made her pints of the stuff when Jamie died.

'No, thanks,' said Ben. 'I'm not staying long. I just popped by to wish you a Happy New Year.'

'That's nice, isn't it, Josh?'

'Suppose,' grunted Josh, and went back to his drawing.

'What are you drawing?' Ben asked.

Josh sat up, shot him a look of pure hatred, and said, 'I'm drawing Dr Octopus. He's got you in his grips and Spidey isn't going to rescue you. So there.'

He flung the paper on the floor and ran off upstairs.

'Josh!' Amy called in horror.

'Leave him,' said Ben. 'I know why he did that, and I'm not upset.'

'I'm sorry,' said Amy. 'You see how things are.'

'I do,' said Ben, resisting the urge to stroke her cheek. 'I just wanted to come round to say I'm sorry for causing such a mess. I didn't mean to upset anyone.'

'It's okay,' Amy replied, her eyes brittle with unshed tears. 'It's not your fault. It's no one's fault.'

'But we can still be friends?'

'Of course,' said Amy. 'I'll talk to Josh again.'

'Good,' said Ben. Then, giving her a swift kiss on the cheek, he was gone.

It was only later on that Amy realised she had no idea where Ben had been. Or with whom.

CHAPTER FIFTEEN

'Hi, Mary?' Amy was on the phone as Harry poked his head round her front door. She waved him into the lounge, while continuing her conversation. 'Yes. A happy New Year to you too. How was the cruise?'

'Be with you in a minute,' she mouthed to Harry. She had rung Mary more for Josh's sake than hers, and was pleasantly surprised to discover that her call had been greeted, if not with warmth, with tepidity at least.

'Yes, we had a lovely Christmas, thanks . . . Josh has been asking after you.' Amy took a deep breath and plunged right in, 'So we were wondering, would you like to come for a weekend soon?'

Nothing like holding out an olive branch. To her surprise (and considerable relief), Mary said yes, she would love to come. They agreed to consult their respective diaries and Mary promised to ring back when she had worked out her availability.

'Phew!' said Amy as she put down the phone. 'My mother-in-law appears to have forgiven me at last.'

'Ah,' said Harry. 'I have something I was going to tell you about your mother-in-law.'

'Oh, what would that be, then?' Amy was puzzled. Harry hadn't met Mary; what could he possibly know about her that Amy hadn't already told him?

'I've been meaning to tell you,' said Harry. 'When I had that chat with Josh, it seemed to me that it was Mary who put the idea into his head that Ben wasn't to be encouraged. In fact, I'd go further and suggest she might have even given Josh the impression that you'd lose interest in him if you got married again.'

'She didn't!' Amy was shocked. 'How dare she? I've a good mind to ring her back.'

'Amy, Amy, think about it,' said Harry. 'Your mother-in-law has lost everything. She's a widow and her only son was killed. And you've taken the one person she's got left away from her. Is it any wonder she's bitter? Or that she's taking it out on you?'

Amy sighed. She ran her hands through her curls, which were falling over her shoulder, and piled them back behind her ears. Angry as she was, she had to acknowledge her own responsibility in this.

'I'm mad as hell, but you're probably right,' she said. 'I couldn't have managed in the first few months after Jamie died without Mary. She was stoical and strong when I was falling apart. She even encouraged me to keep up with my gardening course, which I'd have given up otherwise. I wouldn't be here now without her. I suppose it's inevitable she'd feel rejected.'

'People do strange things when they're grieving,' said

Harry. 'She probably didn't even think about what she was saying.'

'And she is Josh's granny, whatever my current feelings towards her are,' said Amy. 'So I'll just have to bite the bullet and not say anything. It is my fault too. I'm the one who left her behind. Do you think that was wrong of me?'

'Amy, I can't say what was wrong and what was right,' said Harry. 'Why did you decide to leave?'

'Lots of reasons,' said Amy. 'Jamie and I had always talked about coming out this way. I felt I needed a new start. And, well, with the best will in the world, I was beginning to find it utterly claustrophobic living in the shadow of Mary's constant devotion. So I didn't feel I had any choice really. I still don't.'

'Well then,' said Harry. 'That's all that matters. Everything will be well, Amy, you'll see.'

'Mum, are you sure you're okay to babysit?' Saffron was worried. Ever since Christmas her mum hadn't seemed herself. 'You still look a bit peaky.'

'I'll be fine,' said Elizabeth. 'Go on, off you go, you two. You deserve a night off.'

It was Saffron's birthday and they had planned a night out. Gerry had been supposed to have Becky and Matt, but as usual blew them out, so Elizabeth now had all three children to look after. In her current state of health, Saffron was worried it was asking too much of her mother, but on the other hand, she and Pete hadn't been out for ages, they weren't going far, and Elizabeth was very insistent.

They strolled hand in hand down the road into town. At the far end of the high street was a little Italian called Al Fresco's, although, despite the presence of patio heaters for the tables and chairs in the small courtyard outside, the January chill was enough not to tempt them there. They were ushered to a table in the corner. The restaurant had murals on the wall, and wooden tables. It was small and cosy, and they were close enough to the kitchen to hear the chef shouting orders. The waiters were friendly, the service quick, and they soon found themselves chomping their way through pasta, salads and tiramisu, topped up with lashings of red wine.

'I am so going on a diet next week,' said Saffron, pushing back her plate. She wished she had the self-control to resist puddings, but when God gave out those genes, he clearly hadn't endowed her with that one.

'You don't need to diet,' said Pete. 'Diets are bad for you.'

'I do,' said Saffron. 'I don't seem to be losing any baby weight. And if I eat any more I'm going to be putting even more on.'

Saffron was half-tempted to tell Pete about the pole-dancing class, which she had booked for the following week. But she was so embarrassed about it, she couldn't bring herself to. Besides, she wasn't sure yet if she was going to have the nerve to go. It would only take Pete to laugh at her for her to forget about the whole thing.

Pete looked her up and down.

'Well, maybe a little trimming up wouldn't go amiss. But you know I like my women cuddly. I'm always telling you that. You really should believe me, you know.'

Saffron laughed and sat back, relaxed and happy. It was true. Pete was always telling her he liked curvaceous women. She had nothing to worry about.

Saffron was still feeling happy as they wandered up the high street on their way back home.

'Have we got time for a swift one do you think?' Pete asked, checking his watch as they passed the Magpie.

'I'll just ring Mum to check,' said Saffron, 'but yes, why not. We hardly ever do this, do we?'

'Nope, and we should more often,' said Pete, pulling her to him and snogging her in the doorway of a shop.

'Stop, someone will see,' laughed Saffron.

'So?' Pete did it again.

'I feel like a teenager,' said Saffron.

'Me too,' said Pete. 'Good, isn't it? Race you?'

And, still giggling, they ran towards the pub.

The Magpie was packed and steamy, and as they walked in Saffron spotted various allotmenteers. There was a group of wine producers in the corner, and the Guys were all sitting together by the fireplace.

Saffron and Pete nodded their hellos, before heading for the bar, where they encountered Ben.

'Hi, mate,' said Pete. 'It's not like you to be out on a week night.'

Ben usually made a point of doing his drinking away from Nevermorewell, as, given the town's incapacity to keep anything secret, it invariably led to a patient telling him he'd been spotted the next day.

'I just fancied getting out for a change,' said Ben. 'And I did go to the gym first, so I feel I've earned it. Where've you two been?'

'Al Fresco's,' said Saffron. 'It's my birthday.'

'Oh, happy birthday,' said Ben, giving her a kiss. 'Can I get you both a drink?'

'Mine's a pint,' said Pete. 'Just excuse me while I powder my nose.'

Pete disappeared into the throng, while Saffron chatted to Ben.

'How's Amy?' he asked.

'She's fine,' said Saffron, carefully feeling her way, not sure how much she was supposed to know.

'And Josh?'

'Well, he hasn't done any more moonlit flits from school, if that's what you mean,' said Saffron.

'Good,' said Ben. 'I suppose Amy's filled you in on everything.'

'I don't know that there's an awful lot to fill me in on,' said Saffron, 'but I know Josh has been upset about a few things. He seems to be a bit calmer now, though. So Amy's a little more relaxed.'

'That's a relief,' said Ben. 'I've been so worried about them.'

'Have you? Amy said she'd hardly seen you.'

'Yes,' said Ben. 'The thing is, I said to Amy I wanted us to be friends, and I do, but Josh seems pretty set against me at the moment. So I thought it best if I stayed away – at least for the time being. Can you say hi to her for me though?'

'Of course,' said Saffron.

'Where's that pint, then?' Pete was back, having been accosted at the bar by a couple of workmates. The conversation turned to other things, and Amy was forgotten. It was only when they got home that it occurred to Saffron that for someone who professed just to want to be friends, Ben was showing rather a lot more interest in Amy than he might.

Ben ushered out a harassed mother of three whose children had all come down with chickenpox and looked at his day list to check his next patient. He was pleased to see Harry's name on the list. They must have squeezed him in. Good. Harry had evidently heeded his warnings and was doing something about it. Presumably he couldn't get in with Jane Warrender, his own GP and Ben's more senior colleague. Although, knowing Harry, maybe he preferred coming to a man.

His next patient was a tricky one. Angela Moorcroft, fifty-three, mother of two teenage daughters and just diagnosed with breast cancer. And despite the new ruling about Herceptin, Ben had been having a devil of a job trying to get the PCT to fund Angela's, even though they were now supposed to by law. The trouble was that all the bloody PCTs were up to their eyes in debt. It was all very well politicians making the rules, but it was much harder to make them work. Still, Angela was a feisty sort. Ben expected that she wouldn't take no lying down, and maybe she'd have more luck with the PCT than he had. It helped that her husband was wealthy, so if it came to it they could afford to take legal action, but Ben always thought of the other Angelas, the ones who didn't have money and couldn't seek recourse in the law.

Angela, as it turned out, had been expecting his news, and was more than happy to go public on the story. She barely needed his help at all. Sometimes, he really did wonder why he did this job.

When Harry came in, he cheered himself up by thinking that here at least he had made a difference.

'Okay, Harry,' he said. 'Come on, let's be looking at you.'

Having quickly established that Harry's blood pressure was too high, and prescribing medication to help, Ben also suggested that Harry go and have an angiogram to find out the state of his heart.

'What good is that going to do?' asked Harry, buttoning up his shirt.

'It will let us know the state of your arteries,' said Ben, 'and hopefully prevent you having a heart attack.'

'I think we can safely say my arteries are probably terribly furred up,' said Harry. 'And if I have a heart attack, well, so be it.'

'Now that is not the attitude, and you know it,' warned Ben. 'I'm sending you for an angiogram whether you like it or not.'

'You fuss too much, old boy,' said Harry.

'Someone's got to,' said Ben.

'Quite right too,' agreed Harry. 'And, really, I'm not ungrateful.'

'Good,' said Ben. 'So you will go to your appointment?'

'Yes, I'll go,' Harry replied. 'Otherwise I'll have Amy going on at me too.'

'Oh?'

'Well, who else do you think made me book an appointment?' said Harry. 'She hasn't stopped nagging me for weeks.'

So much for his influence, Ben smiled to himself wryly as he saw Harry out. But he was glad Amy was taking an interest in Harry too. It was like an unspoken bond between them. And for the time being it was all he could hope for.

Saffron poked her head around the corner of the door, and looked left and right. This had to be the right place. She was in a studio room, with a mirror at one end, and a series of poles protruding from the floor. She felt an absolute idiot, but was hoping that coming out to Bairstow meant she wouldn't see anyone she knew. She'd told Pete that she was going to an aerobics class. Well, it was an exercise class, so she hadn't stretched it too much.

Now she was here, she was beginning to wonder what on earth she was doing. Legends nightclub was the sort of retro eighties place she hadn't been in – well, since the eighties, when aged fifteen she and her friends had snuck their way into places like this and lied about their age. They would then spend the rest of the evening sharing a Babycham, which was all they could afford, and dancing round their handbags under the glowing disco ball to Kylie and Bros, awaiting the ritual humiliation of the slow dances, when nine times out of ten Saffron had found herself propping up the wall.

Glancing round the room and realising with a sinking heart that nearly all the women present were younger and more glamorous than her by miles, Saffron had a feeling that ritual humiliation awaited her again. Her cup of happiness was complete when a loud voice she recognised said, 'Saffron, you come to join the fun then?'

She turned round, and to her amazement saw Edie and Ada giggling their heads off like a pair of school-girls.

Oh my God. What were *they* doing here?

'We try all these classes out, you know,' said Edie. She had to be seventy if she was a day. 'We've done belly-dancing classes and all.'

'We widows have to keep ourselves available, if you know what I mean?' Ada winked conspiratorially at Saffron. The thought of two septuagenarians keeping themselves available (presumably for Harry and co.) was too much to bear, so Saffron smiled weakly and went to stand by the nearest pole.

'Hey, babe, you came,' Linda said as she joined her. 'I'm sure you'll have fun. You just wait and see.'

Linda started the class with a series of basic moves, showing them how to grip the pole and how to hook their feet around it and swing down it. She made it look effortless, but all Saffron's attempts ended in disaster. Every time she tried to swing herself onto the pole she ended up losing her grip. And she just didn't have the strength in her legs to swing round anything. She was way too unfit and blobby for this. Her hands felt sweaty and sticky, and when Linda demonstrated the more sexy moves, Saffron just felt mortified. What on earth was she doing here?

But, surprisingly, Linda was right about one thing. Despite feeling totally humiliated for the whole class, by the end of the evening Saffron was having fun. And, kind-hearted as she was, Linda couldn't have been more encouraging, though Saffron felt she was probably the least sexy pole-dancer on the planet. Even Edie and Ada seemed to get the hang of it quicker than she did.

'It's all right, babe,' Linda said at the end of the evening. 'It gets better with practice. You just wait, by the end of the course you'll be showing your moves to the rest of the class.'

'She's right, love,' said Edie. 'Do you remember how rubbish we were at belly dancing to begin with, Ada?'

'Oooh, I do, I do,' said Ada. 'But we got there in the end, didn't we, Edie?'

'We did. And so will you. Your young man will be dead proud of you.'

Pete. Cripes. She didn't want this getting back to him.

'Er. Could you do me a favour?' said Saffron. 'Pete doesn't actually know I'm here. Would you mind not telling him? It's a surprise, you see.'

213

'Ooh, get her,' said Edie. 'Do you hear that, Ada? Her young man don't even know she's here.'

'Well, you're a dark horse and no mistake,' said Ada. 'But it's okay, love, your secret's safe with us.'

'Good,' said Saffron with relief, and made her way back to the car.

Pete was sitting watching TV when she came in.

'Good class?' he asked.

'Yes, fine,' said Saffron, going to the kitchen to fix herself a stiff drink. God, she hoped this subterfuge was worth it.

CHAPTER SIXTEEN

'Mary, it's good to see you.' Amy greeted her mother-in-law at the door, and realised with a jolt that she wasn't lying. Despite having felt so cross with Mary, it *was* good to see her again. And the absence of so many weeks had worn the edge off her anger. They'd both been so busy, it had taken several weeks to arrange a convenient date for them to meet up, and it was already heading for the end of February.

Bulbs were poking up everywhere. Her first daffodils were about to flower. It was a time of new birth, regeneration, therefore a good point, she felt, to renew her fractured relationship with Josh's grandmother. And, judging by the pleasure with which Mary greeted not just Josh, but Amy too, Mary felt the same way.

If only every relationship could be renewed in such a way. As Amy walked into the kitchen to put the kettle on, she looked longingly over towards the allotments. Josh had showed no signs of forgiving Ben for what had happened on Christmas Day, so for weeks now all she had seen of Ben was the odd nod and five minutes' chat on the allotments. She was surprised by how much she missed him. And how much she wanted to see him again.

Despite her insistence to Saffron that Jamie had been the love of her life, and there was no way she could fall in love again, Amy was beginning to wonder if she quite believed that any more. She hadn't been looking for anything new, it was true, but Ben had come along and lit up her world in a way she hadn't thought possible since Jamie's death. But nothing was going to happen. Now or in the future. Because of Josh. There was nothing she could do to change that, so she should lighten up and not worry about it. In other ways her life was becoming a happier one. She should be content with that.

It helped being busy at work. Saffron was finding it difficult juggling her childcare at the moment, as her mum still didn't seem much better. On several occasions Saffron had ended up taking Ellie out with them to various clients. Although none of them minded, Ellie was getting to the stage where she wasn't content to sit in the buggy any more, and it slowed them both down as one of them would have to take turns to look after her. So Amy had offered to do the lion's share of the work till things had calmed down.

'Are you sure?' Saffron had asked anxiously. 'I don't want to take the piss.'

'It's only for a while, isn't it?' said Amy. 'Anyway, you can sit at home and plan a spring marketing campaign to bring in punters. Not that we need it.'

Word of mouth seemed to be doing them lots of

favours, and with the advent of spring they had had a flurry of new clients. Amy didn't mind as it kept her busy, was paying her a decent wage, and allowed her less time to fret about Ben.

She sighed again as she poured the tea. She would do anything for them to go back to the earlier easy companionship they'd had, when Josh had positively relished Ben's company. He needed a male figure in his life. It seemed such a shame he wouldn't let it be Ben.

'You sound like you've got the weight of the world on your shoulders,' said Mary, coming into the kitchen as Amy sighed once more.

'I'm fine.' Amy forced a smile.

'You know, my dear,' said Mary as she looked over towards the allotments, 'you don't have to be alone forever. I'm sure Jamie wouldn't want you to be.'

Amy looked at her in surprise.

'But last time I saw you, I thought –'

'Yes, well. I think I was perhaps a mite hard on you,' said Mary. 'And I think I may have said one or two things to Josh that I shouldn't have. Please forgive me. I was angry and upset that you had taken Josh away from me. And that you were apparently carrying on with someone new. It made me feel redundant.'

'Oh, Mary, you couldn't be further from the truth,' said Amy. 'The last thing I wanted to do was hurt you. And Ben is a friend, nothing more.'

'Still, a pretty young woman like you shouldn't be alone. And Josh needs a dad in his life. Are you sure there is nothing more to this friendship?'

'Positive,' said Amy, waving it away. 'He's just

217

someone on the allotments. Josh and I are quite content as we are. We don't need anyone else.'

Mary looked sceptical.

'I thought so too, after Jamie's dad died. And I've spent the best part of twenty years on my own, thinking I couldn't ever find anyone who'd match up, but now . . .'

Amy looked at her mother-in-law in surprise. Mary was actually blushing.

'Have you met someone?' Amy nearly laughed out loud. It seemed so ridiculous to think of Mary, who had always seemed to her to be resolutely single, as having a lover of some sort, but judging by the girlish way Mary was looking at her, it must be true.

'Well, let's just say there was rather a nice chap on the cruise. His name is Jim, and we did say we'd stay in touch. I haven't heard from him yet, so it will probably come to nothing, but whatever happens, meeting Jim has given me a whole new lease of life.'

'Mary, that's wonderful news,' said Amy. 'I'm so happy for you.'

'It's partly thanks to you,' said Mary. 'I was stuck in a rut too, feeling that you needed me. When you and Josh left I decided I could either sit down and feel sorry for myself, or go and get myself a life. So I got myself a life. Even if I don't see Jim again, I might do a bit more travelling. I've got a taste for it now.'

'You go for it,' said Amy, reaching over and squeezing Mary's hand and feeling truly thankful that things were working out for her.

'You know, Amy, you don't have to wear widow's

weeds for the rest of your life,' Mary said. 'Don't make the same mistakes I did.'

'I'll think about it,' said Amy, as she took their tea into the lounge, and tried to crowd out the thought that there was someone waiting for her, if only she could persuade Josh of the fact.

'Bloody Gerry!' Saffron stormed at Pete as he walked through the door. 'He promised me he could have the kids for the first week of the Easter holidays, and he's gone and blown me out once again. He is the limit.'

'Hi, darling, how was your day?' Pete came over and gave her a very pointed kiss on the cheek.

'Sorry.' Saffron gave him a rueful smile. 'I'm just so fed up with Gerry mucking me about. How was your meeting? I take it they didn't fire you?'

Pete had been called to an urgent meeting earlier in the day. There was some restructuring going on in his office, and he had mentioned there might be some redundancies.

'Nope,' said Pete. 'In fact it was the opposite. They've opened a new European office in Brussels and they want me to head up the European side of things. It means more travelling, of course, but it's also more money, bigger office. You know the kind of thing.'

'Oh Pete, that's brilliant.' Saffron forgot all her own worries for a moment. 'We'll have to do something to celebrate.'

'Do you think your mum is up for a spot of babysitting?'

'Actually, I don't think she is,' said Saffron. 'She's still sick. I've told her if she doesn't make an appointment with her GP soon, I'll take her there myself.'

'Do you think it's serious?' Pete looked alarmed. He got on well with Elizabeth and knew Saffron thought the world of her.

'I don't know,' said Saffron, 'but I am beginning to get a bit worried. And you know what she's like – she doesn't like me making a fuss. Anyway, until I know for sure she's well I'm not going to ask her to babysit for us, so unless we can find someone reliable enough to look after a baby I think any celebrating will need to be done at home.'

'Well, I'm sure we'll manage.' Pete had a twinkle in his eye. 'Once the kids are in bed, we should be able to think of one or two things to do.'

Saffron laughed. Despite still feeling more like Mrs Blobby than a lap-dancing lovely, Saffron had to admit her pole-dancing classes were having an effect on her libido. There was something about spending an hour hot and sweaty, writhing round a pole, that made her much keener to get into bed when she got home than she had felt, well, forever. It made her feel a bit like Jamie Lee Curtis. All she needed was Pete to quote Italian at her and she'd probably start ravishing him on the kitchen table. Shame he didn't know any languages . . .

'Oh, by the way,' said Pete, 'I'm afraid the first business trip is around the start of the Easter holidays – will you be able to manage on your own?'

'I managed for a good few years before you pitched up,' said Saffron, 'so I expect I'll survive. Now go and get changed while I work out a suitable menu for an impromptu celebration.'

'So long as it includes oysters,' said Pete.

'Why oysters?'

'Well-known for their aphrodisiacal qualities.' Pete's voice drifted down the stairs.

'Well, gee, we're all out of oysters,' Saffron called back, 'will fish fingers do?'

Ben knocked on Harry's door. He had tried to ring Harry from the surgery to say that the date for his angiogram had come through and to make sure that he was actually going to go and have it. He'd got no reply, so, trying to pretend that he wasn't making an excuse just to catch a glimpse of Amy, he'd decided to go round instead.

There was no reply at Harry's, but he could hear music coming from Amy's. He grinned to himself. Six p.m. Drivetime. All Request Friday – listeners rang Chris Evans all evening and asked for their favourite tracks. He could hear the faint strains of 'Born to be Wild'. He wandered over to Amy's side of the alley. Dare he knock on the door? On the window to the right of the front door, he could just make out the kitchen, where he could see Amy was dancing. She was even playing air guitar. Blimey. He hadn't had her down for a rock chick.

A spasm of longing and desire came over him. Suddenly he knew, with absolute clarity, that he couldn't let this relationship die before it had even started. He knew for certain that Amy was the woman he wanted to be with. He'd been on his own long enough. Maybe, now several weeks had gone by, Josh would be prepared to forgive him, and he and Amy could start again. There was only one way to find out. Taking a deep breath, he knocked on the door.

Amy was feeling happier than she had done for some time. The visit from Mary had been a success and she had promised to return the favour. Mary's confession had made her think. Life was about living and taking risks. And doing so involved getting hurt. Maybe she should just go for it. The sun was shining, spring was here, perhaps it was time to lighten up.

So, as Amy was cooking tea, she had cranked the radio right up, and got into the spirit of the tracks people were choosing. 'Born to be Wild' was followed by 'Soak up the Sun', which, given the mood she was in, seemed appropriate. Amy raucously joined in with Sheryl Crow's desire to soak up the sun while she still had time, much to Josh's disgust, who retired to the lounge with Matt, who had come to tea now they were friends again.

'Mummy, look at this!'

A small body slid across the hall on its knees. Josh and Matt had devised a new game to see who could slide the furthest on the wooden floorboards.

'Boys, calm down!' said Amy, pausing in her dancing as she had sudden visions of broken bones.

'Look, Mummy, look!' Josh slid even further than Matt.

'Josh, stop!'

'Oww!' Amy watched as Josh, almost in slow motion, crashed his arm right against the door. She ran forward to where he was sitting huddled up, looking a bit dazed. He stared at her in some confusion and then burst into tears. Amy was just wondering what on earth to do now when the doorbell rang. She opened it, and there on the doorstep stood Ben.

'Ben, am I glad to see you.' Amy practically man-handled him into the house.

'It's lovely to see you too –' he started.

'Can you look at Josh's hand? I think he's really hurt himself.'

Josh was sitting in the corner, holding his hand and sobbing. He flinched when Ben came near him, but Ben just knelt down and said, 'Woah, Tiger, what have you been up to then?'

'I was sliding against the door, and hurt my hand,' Josh said between sobs. He seemed to have forgotten he wasn't speaking to Ben.

'Ouch,' said Ben. 'Can I take a little look?'

Josh held out his hand, and Ben gently prodded his arm.

'Now, let's see if you can wriggle your fingers,' he said. 'I bet you can't count them at the same time.'

'I can, too,' said Josh in indignation. 'One, two, three – ow!'

'Is that where it hurts?' Ben asked, as he pressed Josh's index finger.

'Yes, and there.' Josh pointed to his wrist.

'Right, let's get a cold compress on that,' said Ben, getting to his feet. 'I'm sorry, Amy, I've got a strong suspicion that he's got a greenstick fracture. You're going to have to take him to casualty to get an x-ray. Do you want me to run you over there? I haven't got anything else on.'

'Would you?' said Amy. 'That's really good of you. I'd better ring Saffron and drop Matt home. Damn. They haven't had their tea yet.'

'Don't, whatever you do, feed him,' said Ben. 'It's highly unlikely, but he may need an operation.'

As Amy got Matt's things together, Ben expertly put Josh's arm in a sling, all the time keeping up a cheerful patter that took Josh's mind off things. Josh was clearly in a lot of pain, so Amy dosed him up with Calpol, and then they were on their way.

Luckily, Casualty wasn't that busy and they were seen quickly. It didn't take long for them to be told that yes, Josh did indeed have a greenstick fracture, and he would need to be plastered up.

'No more footie for you for a while,' said Ben.

'Oh.' Josh pulled a face, although Amy could see he was secretly beginning to enjoy the attention. He was particularly pleased by the fluorescent-orange plaster he came home with.

'I can't wait to show Matt,' he said, 'it's *so* cool.'

Ben dropped them back home, made his excuses and left. Amy was disappointed, but respected his discretion. Now that the crisis was over, Josh would no doubt remember before long that Ben was his sworn enemy.

But when she tucked him in, propping his plastered arm on a pillow, Josh gave her a hug and said, 'Mummy, you can marry Ben if you want.'

Amy burst out laughing.

'It should be my dad saying that, not my son,' she said. 'I thought you hated Ben. What's made you change your mind?'

Josh looked sheepish.

'He helped me today and made me laugh. And he was pretty cool at the hospital.'

'Yes,' said Amy, giving Josh a kiss good night, and turning out the light. 'He was, wasn't he?'

CHAPTER SEVENTEEN

'How are you, old boy?' Harry nodded at Ben, who was wheeling his barrow past Harry's hut.

Harry was sitting on a bench in the sunshine, drinking something from a flask. Unusually for him, he didn't appear to be doing any work on his allotment.

'Fine, thanks, Harry,' said Ben. 'I called in last night to let you know about the angiogram, and you weren't there.'

'Yes, yes,' said Harry. 'You don't need to fuss. I shall be going to the hospital to have it.'

'Good.'

'No doubt they'll tell me I'm old and the ticker's about to pack up,' said Harry. 'I could probably tell them that myself.'

Ben came and sat down next to him. 'And what are you doing about it?'

'Why, nothing at all, old boy,' said Harry. 'I'm eighty-five years old. It's remarkable I've lived this long, considering how much I've abused my body. I've already told you, the way I look at it, you only have so much time given you, and I've already had more than my three score years and ten, and I count myself very lucky. Which is why I plan to enjoy the time left. Look what a glorious day it is. I'm enjoying sitting in the sunshine and appreciating what I have.'

Ben laughed. Harry was right. It was a wonderful day. And the allotments were fairly bursting into life. After the inertia of winter, the sunshine had brought out an assortment of allotmenteers, who were all busy digging, sowing and pruning. Daffodils, croci and tulips were popping up everywhere and the allotments were a riot of different colours. The birds, who had been fairly silent over the winter, had returned, and along with the almost constant sound of lawnmowers was the sound of bird-song. In the corner he could make out Scary Slug Man, who, as usual, seemed to be shouting at something in a bucket. It was rare for Ben to sit down and look at his surroundings like this, he was usually too busy.

'Well, I guess we could all do that a bit more often,' said Ben.

'Privilege of age, old boy,' said Harry. 'One of the damned few, I can tell you – but having time to stop and stare is one of them. I gather you had a bit of an adventure with Amy and Josh last night.'

'Oh, you heard,' said Ben.

'Josh was very proud of his pot this morning,' said Harry. 'I had to see it before he went to school.'

'So he wasn't too traumatised, then,' said Ben.

'Not a bit of it,' said Harry. 'And I should say your standing with young Josh has gone up considerably as a result.'

'That's a relief,' said Ben.

'So now you have no reason whatsoever to put off your pursuit of the lovely Amy,' continued Harry.

'Do shut up, Harry,' Ben told him. 'Don't you ever stop meddling?'

'Nope,' said Harry with a cheerful grin, 'but that's another privilege of old age. I can be as interfering as I like and I don't give a damn. And I have no one else to meddle with but you two.'

'Well, don't meddle too much, or we might stop speaking to you,' said Ben.

'Am I at least allowed to point out that the lady in question has just emerged from her garden door?'

Ben's heart jumped. Maybe she had come to see him. He hoped so.

'Oh, and by the way, old boy,' said Harry, 'I'd rather you didn't mention this business with my ticker to Amy. She's been through enough. I wouldn't want to worry her.'

'Sure thing,' said Ben. 'But as your mate, and a GP, I really wouldn't recommend you drank whisky this early in the morning.'

'How did you know?' Harry looked crestfallen.

'Lucky guess?' said Ben, and, reclaiming his barrow, moved purposefully off to meet Amy.

'I'm not sure I can carry on like this much longer,' said Saffron to Amy as she backed down her driveway. They were off to Mrs Turner's, who was notoriously fussy.

229

Saffron had arranged a swap with another mum so she could provide Amy with some back-up.

'Your mum no better then?' Amy asked sympathetically.

'She doesn't seem to be,' said Saffron. 'The doctor thinks she picked up a bug in Morocco.'

'I can cover you some more,' said Amy, 'if that would be any help?'

'That wouldn't be fair, would it?' Saffron asked. 'You've been shouldering the burden for weeks now. No, I think the best thing is if I stop relying on Mum and get a childminder. I can probably just about afford it now.'

Saffron's phone rang, so she pulled over to answer it.

'Sorry,' she mouthed to Amy, 'it's Gerry. We need to talk about Easter.'

Within minutes it was clear the conversation was not going well.

'No, Gerry, the children can't come to you for the Easter weekend,' Saffron said in exasperation, trying to restrain herself from slamming the phone down. 'We've made other arrangements now. I can't just go changing things around to suit you.'

'Sorry about that,' Saffron said when she got off the phone. 'Bloody Gerry. He was supposed to have the kids the first week of the holidays, but blew me out. And now Pete's going to be away on business, and with Mum having been ill it's all a bit much . . .'

'Is there anything I can do?' Amy offered.

'No,' said Saffron. 'It's fine, really. You've done more

230

than enough. By the way, I've been meaning to ask, how's Josh's arm?'

'Oh, fine,' said Amy. 'He moaned about the pain for the first couple of days, but now he's proudly showing it off to all and sundry.'

'And I take it he's a little more pro Ben now?' asked Saffron.

'Sure is,' said Amy. 'Now he wants to go on the allotments all the time and follow Ben about. It's such a relief, I can tell you.'

'So you're seeing more of Ben then?'

'We've run into him a couple of times on the allotments, yes,' said Amy.

'And?'

'And nothing.'

'Nothing else?' Saffron was disappointed.

Amy laughed. 'No,' she said. 'Josh has been with us most of the time. And I know Ben is his current idol, but after everything we've been through over the last few weeks, I think it's best if we just keep things as they are. I had another meeting with Miss Burrows this week and she says Josh has settled down again. I would hate to rock the boat.'

'But don't you want something to happen?'

'To be honest, I really don't know,' said Amy. 'Before Christmas, I thought I did. I like him. He's good-looking. We get on. But . . . there's Josh to consider, and I'm in no hurry. Anyway, isn't that Mrs Turner's house?'

'Bugger, you're right,' said Saffron, performing an illegal U-turn and nearly smashing her four-wheel drive into a lamppost in the process. 'Whoops!' she said. 'That would take some explaining to Pete.'

She and Amy were still giggling when they got to Mrs Turner's doorstep. They rang on the bell and waited. And waited. They rang again. Still no reply.

'That's odd,' said Saffron. 'Are you sure it was today?'

'Positive,' Amy replied. 'I wrote it in the diary.'

After several more attempts, they gave up.

'We've still got Linda Lovelace's to do,' said Amy. 'You remember, we promised we'd replant her borders.'

'Oh, can you do that one?' asked Saffron hurriedly. 'I've got to do some paperwork.'

She hadn't had the nerve to tell Amy about her pole-dancing classes and had sworn Linda to secrecy. But there was something about having seen Linda gyrating about a pole scantily clad, and, more importantly, that Linda had seen Saffron doing the same, which made her cringe every time she went round. On Saffron's previous visit, Linda had told her she could do with a bit more pouting sensuality, which wasn't quite what Saffron was expecting to hear at nine thirty in the morning.

Saffron dropped Amy off then headed home to sort out some paperwork. The answer-phone was beeping as she came in through the door. Saffron pressed it, and heard the rather whiny voice of Mrs Turner telling them that after due consideration she had decided their quote was rather high, and she had chosen another firm to do her garden.

'Bloody cheek!' said Saffron out loud.

'She could have had the guts to be in when we called

232

and tell us herself,' Saffron grumbled to Amy when Amy returned an hour later.

'Maybe she was,' said Amy. 'Perhaps she was hiding behind the settee.'

The thought set them off giggling again, but after Amy had gone, Saffron played the message again. It didn't make sense. She had talked to Mrs Turner two days ago. Why was she suddenly turning them down?

'What are you up to on Sunday?' Amy found Ben on the allotments as she carried out a tray of seedlings ready to plant. Edie and Ada waved at her from the far side of the allotments, and she could see Harry working on his. The surroundings were a hive of activity, the sun was shining, the birds were singing, and she felt that all was right with the world.

'Hmm, I'd better consult my diary,' said Ben. 'Let me see: oh, I expect I'm already booked in at least three different places.'

'Oh, are you? Damn.' Amy looked stricken.

'No, sorry. My stupid idea of a joke. Apart from going to the gym and reading the Sunday papers, nothing much. Why?'

'I'm planning a Sunday lunch,' said Amy. 'And I wondered if you'd come. I've invited Pete and Saffron. And Harry said he'd come too. It might be a bit wild with lots of children, but it could be fun. I thought we could go for a stroll by the river afterwards if the weather's nice.'

'Sunday lunch sounds perfect,' said Ben. 'Can I bring anything?'

'Only your sweet self,' said Amy, and then blushed.

'Amy . . .' He paused and looked awkward.

Amy felt her stomach contract. She wondered what he would say. This was the first time they had been properly on their own since Josh's broken arm. There always seemed to be someone around.

'Yes?'

'I was just wondering . . . do you – could you – I don't want to rush you or anything, but maybe sometime we could go out for a drink. No strings or anything,' he blurted out. 'It's just, well, I'd like to get to know you better.'

'I'd like that too,' said Amy. 'What happened before . . .'

'. . . was too soon, and I rushed you,' said Ben. 'I know and I'm sorry. I know Josh could still be a sticking point. And I do understand about Jamie. You might never want to be with someone again, but surely that doesn't preclude you from having fun?'

'You're right, it doesn't,' said Amy, relieved that Ben seemed to understand what she needed so instinctively.

'Shall we just take things slowly and see where we end up?'

'Sounds good to me,' Amy replied. 'Thanks for understanding.'

'I'm a master at that,' said Ben with a dry grin, and before she went he brushed his lips softly against hers. Her heart caught in her throat. He was so perfect in every way, and every time she turned round he seemed to be there, just where she needed him. Just where she wanted him. The only problem was, he wasn't Jamie, and she still felt caught between her past and her future. But as she walked back in the dappling sunlight, for the first time she felt that perhaps the pull of the future could one day be stronger.

'I just don't get it,' said Saffron as Pete staggered in with the shopping a couple of days later.

'Get what?' Pete was starting to empty bags out while Saffron tidied away the remnants of tea. Ellie was gurgling happily in the high chair, and Becky and Matt were ensconced in front of the TV.

'One minute Amy and I are really busy, and getting lots of new business,' said Saffron, 'and the next we have clients cancelling all over the place. Even some of our more regular clients are beginning to make excuses and saying they don't need us. And yet no one's complained of the work we've done. I don't understand it.'

'Oh, it will probably just be a blip,' said Pete. 'I expect you'll get busier again in a week or two. Anyway, didn't you say it was going to be tricky to work in the holidays? I'm sure it will pick up after then.'

'Yes, but suppose it doesn't?' said Saffron. 'We might find ourselves with no work at all.'

'I'm sure it won't come to that,' said Pete. 'Where do the teabags go, by the way?'

Saffron rolled her eyes. 'Where they normally go,' she said.

'Which is?' Pete still looked blank, so Saffron took pity on him.

'Top left cupboard, second shelf,' she said. 'Honestly, one of these days I'll teach you to be domesticated.'

'I'm doing my best,' protested Pete.

'I know. I'm just being grouchy because of this business with work. It's almost as if someone's badmouthing us or something, but who?' She went over to pick the baby up. 'Yeuch, a smelly nappy from you is the last thing I need.'

'Now you're being silly,' said Pete. 'Who would do such a thing?'

Saffron had the sudden awful thought that maybe Linda Lovelace's neighbours had spread the word that she was a part-time hooker. But she could hardly tell Pete that. He still thought she was going to aerobics classes every Wednesday. Somehow, the longer it went on, the less able she was to tell him. Anyway, half Linda's neighbours came to her classes, so they were a fairly broad-minded bunch. But if not them, then who?

She snapped her fingers. 'Gerry, that's who! It's the sort of petty, spiteful thing he would do, just because I said he couldn't have the kids at Easter.'

'Oh, come on, Saffron, even Gerry wouldn't be that small-minded?' Pete replied. 'Surely he's got better things to do with his time?'

'You don't know Gerry like I do,' said Saffron, a grim look on her face. 'He's quite capable of anything. But you're right, he probably doesn't have time. I'm just wondering who the blonde bimbo is friendly with. I wonder if she knows anyone on Mrs Turner's street?'

'Saffron, you have no way of proving any of this,' warned Pete.

'Don't I?' said Saffron. 'You just watch me try.'

'Is everyone sure they've had enough?' Amy asked for the third time. She had hardly dared to hope what a success her lunch party had turned out to be. It had been a little cramped, it was true, but everyone had had enough to eat, and the kids had run off to play, allowing her and Saffron time for girly chat while the boys got into passionate arguments about the football. Harry had happily pottered in and out of conversations and seemed to be taking the greatest delight in blowing bubbles at Ellie.

'Amy, I am absolutely stuffed,' said Pete, finishing the last mouthful of apple crumble, and everyone chorused the same.

'How about coffee?' Amy got up to go to the kitchen, when Ben hijacked her lunch party in a most decisive manner (masterful was definitely his word, she thought again dreamily).

'I'll do it,' he said. 'You sit down.'

'I can't possibly let you,' she said. So instead the pair of them did the washing-up together, while they watched the kids playing in the garden.

'We always seem to find ourselves in the kitchen at parties,' said Amy.

'Don't we just,' said Ben, flicking her with a tea towel. 'Are we done, do you think?'

'Yup, that will do,' said Amy. 'Let's round up the troops and walk off our lunch.'

Harry got up to make his excuses and go. 'I'm not really up for walks on the downs these days,' he said, 'so I'll love you and leave you and snooze off my dinner in front of the box.'

'Not with a whisky, I hope,' said Ben.

'Oh do stop fussing,' said Harry, pottering off to the front door. 'Thank you, Amy, my dear, for a lovely meal.'

He kissed her on the cheek, and opened the door. As he turned to go, he muttered under his breath, just so Amy could hear, 'You'd do much worse than Ben, you know. I think it's time to let go, don't you?'

'Oh get away with you, you old matchmaker,' she said, pushing him out of the door.

'Just remember, Amy,' he said, 'life's really too short.'

She turned back into the house with a smile playing on her lips.

'So now you've been here a while,' said Ben, 'are you glad you came out this way?' They were on a picturesque path down by the river, and had walked past countless pretty little pink cottages. 'Suffolk pink', Ben had called it.

'Absolutely,' said Amy. 'I can't tell you how lovely it is to be out here after the hustle and bustle of the city. Just to smell this air is a joy.'

'What, even here?' Ben grinned as they meandered towards the water meadows where several cows were grazing, leaving a rather rich aroma behind them.

'Even here,' said Amy. 'And thanks to those books you lent me I'm beginning to get a feel for the place. I found it fascinating learning about the wool industry here. I had no idea.'

'Yup, it was pretty big in the eleventh century, so I believe,' said Ben. 'Which is why you get such big churches round here – they were all paid for by the wool industry.'

'I was wondering why a town this size has such a huge church in the middle of it,' Amy mused. 'It could almost be a cathedral, couldn't it?'

Pete and Saffron were up ahead. Somehow they had taken all the children between them, and while Saffron carried the baby on her back, Pete was pretending to be a cyberman and chasing the others. Which meant that Amy and Ben had been forced to walk together. Not that it was much of a hardship, thought Amy. And really, the others couldn't have been more transparent if they'd tried.

'Isn't it just perfect out here?' Amy continued. The path had broadened out now and they had left the river behind and were walking in woodland, where the children were now rushing about playing Robin Hood. The sun shone high in the sky, and though there was still a cold spring wind, the air was fresh and bright. It was a day for feeling vivid and alive. Everywhere you looked you could see people: families out walking, dog-walkers, couples holding hands, the occasional horse-rider.

Amy thought back to days like this that she had

shared with Jamie. He was no longer by her side, but Ben was. It was time to grasp that future. She took Ben's hand in hers.

'Come on,' she said. 'I know why Saffron and Pete have gone ahead. Let's give them something to talk about.'

CHAPTER EIGHTEEN

'Now, have you got everything you need?' Saffron knew she was wittering, but she couldn't help it. When Gerry had gone on business trips, she couldn't wait for him to go out of the door, but with Pete it was different. The taxi was coming for 5.30 a.m., and though Pete had said she didn't need to get up, Saffron felt she had to squeeze the most out of even these last few remaining minutes together.

It was pathetic, really. She was behaving like a schoolgirl with her first crush, but they had barely spent a night apart since they were married, and now they faced a whole week. She was dreading it, but she didn't want Pete to know how much, so was busying herself with mundane tasks to keep her mind off it. Pete was evidently getting rather irritated, as he had twice banned her from going through his suitcase again, just to make sure he had packed it properly.

'I have done this before, you know. I may be a man, but I'm not totally incapable,' said Pete. 'I can tie my own shoelaces and everything.'

'Ah, but "before" you didn't have me,' said Saffron. Then she looked contrite. 'Sorry, I'm fussing, aren't I?'

'*Yes*,' said Pete. 'However, if you feel like part of the fussing should involve stroking the back of my neck to ease the inevitable tension that has arisen out of your demented behaviour, you have my permission to do so.'

'Oh go on then,' said Saffron, and started to tickle his hair and massage his neck. Before they knew it they were rolling on the bed, giggling like a pair of school kids.

They pulled apart, and Pete looked at her. 'I'll miss you,' he said.

The look on his face sent a shiver of delight right through her. It still took her by surprise to know how much he needed her.

'Give over,' she said. 'You'll be so busy with your high-powered meetings you won't even notice I'm not there.'

'Ah, but the bed will be far too big without you,' said Pete.

'Won't it just,' Saffron agreed with feeling, and snuggled up to him again.

They broke off to the sound of a car beeping.

'That'll be the taxi, then,' said Pete.

'Yes, it will,' Saffron agreed.

'Right, best be off,' said Pete, showing no signs of moving.

'Yes, you had,' Saffron replied.

They held each other for a few seconds more, then Pete shook his head. 'No, really, I had better be off. I don't want to miss my plane.'

She followed him downstairs, and saw him to the front door. She kissed him again, and waved him off with a sinking heart, trying to tell herself that it was only a week.

It might only be a week, but the way she felt watching him go, it could have been a lifetime. Plus, it would be the first time she was going to have to manage all three kids completely solo.

'Thank the lord for helpful mothers,' she said out loud as she went to make herself a cup of tea. At least she wouldn't be totally alone.

'That's strange,' Amy frowned as she snapped her mobile phone shut.

'What's strange?' Saffron looked up from Linda Lovelace's vast flowerbed – the job had been too much for just Amy, so Saffron had reluctantly come along to help. Amy still didn't know about the pole-dancing lessons and Saffron intended to keep it that way.

'Mrs Reeves has cancelled for the second week running. You know – she was the one I went out to on my own when your mum was ill. I went over, dug over the beds, did a bit of weeding, and she asked me to come back to do her hedges. But she's just rung to say her nephew did them at the weekend and she won't be needing me again. It seems so odd. She was really keen when I first went round.'

'Not another one!' Saffron put her trowel down and stood up.

'What do you mean, not another one?'

'God, Amy, I'm sorry, I should have mentioned it

243

before, but I thought it was nothing. And then with Mum not being that great, and Pete being away, it slipped my mind . . .'

'What did?'

'The fact that we seem to be losing clients at a scarily rapid rate. Mrs Reeves isn't the first. You remember how Mrs Turner rang up to cancel? Well, I've had others too.'

'But why?' protested Amy. 'We offer a good service, at a good price. I thought the business was growing.'

'So did I,' said Saffron. 'But something odd's going on. It's as if someone's badmouthing us.'

'But who would do that?' said Amy. 'And why?'

'Oh, I've got an idea,' said Saffron, looking grim, 'but I don't know how to prove it.'

Just then Saffron's phone rang.

'Hi,' she said. 'Oh, Mum, it's you. Everything all right? *What?* Stay there. I'll be with you right away.'

'What's the matter?' Amy asked as Saffron frantically gathered her things together.

'That was Mum,' said Saffron. 'She's just thrown up blood in our bathroom. I think I need to get her to the hospital pronto.'

'That's awful,' said Amy. 'Go on, you'd better get over there straight away. I'll finish here, and I'll get the kids from school. What about Ellie? Shall I take her too?'

'It's okay, I'll take her with me.' Saffron looked distraught. 'Oh God, Amy, if Mum's really ill, what am I going to do?'

244

Later that day, Ben rang Amy's doorbell, but there was no reply. Since her lunch party, he and Amy had only seen each other a few times. It was still all very casual. He came over occasionally at the weekend and played football with Josh, and the three of them went out for walks on Sundays. He and Amy didn't get a lot of time alone, so they hadn't done much more than hold hands and have the odd kiss, but it was cosy and comfortable, and, more importantly, he was growing used to it. She was normally in at this time on a Friday. It was odd that she wasn't.

He should have tried to ring her, but he'd been busy all day and just popped in on the off-chance after work. A lazy sun was setting over the allotments, and the birds were chattering in the trees. Spring was definitely in the air. He knocked on Harry's door – maybe he'd know where Amy had gone – but there was no reply there, either. He rang her mobile but it was switched off. Damn! Now what should he do?

He glanced at his watch. It was a bit early for Pete to be back from work, but occasionally he was. Perhaps he should call round there and see if he was up for a quick pint. He could always call back on Amy afterwards. And, thinking about it, there was a strong likelihood that Amy was with Saffron anyway.

'Ben! Thank God you're here,' Amy greeted him with a kiss. A scene of total carnage met him. There were toys scattered all over the hall floor, Becky and Matt

245

were arguing loudly by the stairs, a PlayStation was beeping equally loudly in a room to the left of him, and from the depths of the house he could detect the wailing of a baby.

'Wha—? Where's Pete? And Saffron?'

'Pete's away on a business trip. Back next week. Saffron's mum was rushed to hospital yesterday morning – she's just had an emergency gall bladder operation. Saffron's with her now. So Josh and I are holding the fort and sort of camping out here for the weekend.'

'Oh, right,' said Ben. 'Is Elizabeth okay?'

'I think so,' said Amy. 'But it was a bit touch and go yesterday. Apparently she had a massive gall stone removed and lost a lot of blood. She's still in ICU. Saffron's been beside herself.'

'God, I should think so,' said Ben. 'Poor Saff. Is there anything I can do?'

'Unless you want to enter the pit of hell, no,' said Amy. 'I am *so* glad I only have one. The baby doesn't seem to want to settle. The kids just keep fighting. And I haven't even started on the dinner yet. I don't know how Saffron does it.'

'Why don't I stay for a bit and help,' said Ben. 'I've got nothing better to do.'

'Would you?' Amy shot him a grateful look. 'It's been a bit wild to be honest. I don't know how I'm going to cope for the weekend. Saffron came back really late from the hospital last night and it looks like she will again tonight.'

'No probs,' said Ben. 'Why don't you go and sort Ellie out, and I'll try and get this lot to tidy up a bit.'

'If you can manage that, I'll cook you dinner – and throw in wine,' said Amy. 'I have all the impact of a gnat.'

To Amy's surprise, not only did Ben manage to get the kids to tidy away their toys, by dint of playing a rather noisy game in which he seemed to be impersonating a lion most of the time (even Becky, who had affected to be too old to join in, couldn't help but be won over in the end), but he also took Ellie from Amy to let her cook dinner. He sat for ages, pulling silly faces and bouncing her on his knee, till by the time the food was ready, she was all smiley and cuddly, just the way babies should be.

'That was nothing short of miraculous,' Amy told him as she sat back and watched the children tuck into not-very-inspiring fish fingers and chips, but it was all she could manage to find in the freezer. Saffron evidently hadn't done the shopping this week. 'You're a natural.'

She smiled as she said this. The sight of Ben holding the baby so calmly and with such affection had given her a real insight into the kind of dad he would be. Since Jamie she had assumed there would be no other children for her, but a sudden image came into her head of her and Ben holding a baby, with Josh bouncing around at their sides. Maybe it wasn't impossible . . .

'I've had some practice, with my brother's kids,' explained Ben. 'Besides, I like babies. Ever since I did my obs and gynae bit at college. I usually volunteer for the baby clinic at the surgery. I've always wanted a family of my own.'

'Have you now?' said Amy teasingly, thinking there was undoubtedly something very sexy about a man who liked babies. Something very sexy indeed.

'Sure have,' said Ben, giving her a deeply flirtatious look, 'I just need to find the right woman . . .'

'And where do you think you'll find her?' Amy archly returned the look.

'Oh, I don't know,' Ben batted back, and in an instant they were back to Christmas Day and their ill-fated kiss.

'Matt hit me!' The moment was broken with Becky's loud noisy sobs.

'Did-*urn't*!' said Matt.

'Did too!' said Becky.

'Only because you kicked me,' said Matt.

'I hope no one is kicking or hitting anyone,' Amy reprimanded in her sternest teacher's voice. 'I want you to say sorry to each other this instant.'

'Sorry,' Becky and Matt mumbled half-heartedly to one another.

'Right, you monsters,' Amy said. 'If you help me clear the plates away, Ben might play with you while I'm putting Ellie to bed, but then it's bath and bed for the lot of you!'

Now there *was* a great idea, thought Ben, wondering if it applied to him too.

'Are you sure you don't mind staying?'

Saffron looked pale and drawn. She had come back at ten from the hospital, and joined Amy and Ben for a bite to eat and a glass of wine, before crashing out. Ben had left not long after, promising to return the next morning.

'Not at all,' said Amy. 'Come on, your mum needs you. And you needn't worry about the kids. Ben and I will take them out for a picnic or something.'

'I am so grateful,' said Saffron. 'I don't know how I'll ever be able to repay you.'

'There's no need,' said Amy. 'Come on. You've been a great friend to me since I've been here. I'm just glad I can help you back.'

Saffron left at eleven the next morning, having first rushed off to do a mad flit round Sainsbury's.

'I've just grabbed stuff off the shelves,' she said, 'but at least you've got food now.'

'Don't worry about a thing,' said Amy firmly. 'You just go and help Elizabeth get better. I'll sort this out.'

'Okay.' Saffron left reluctantly. 'The kids are going to forget who I am if this carries on,' she said. 'Bloody Gerry. If he'd had them like he was supposed to, everything would be so much easier.'

'Well he didn't,' said Amy. 'Now, go on, go.'

The sun was shining as they parked the car on the edge of a country park. It had been unseasonably warm for April, and a vast blue sky arced before them in a wonderful panorama. Green undulating fields stretched out ahead. It was the perfect place for a picnic.

The kids immediately ran off to a spot they knew

well. Amy pushed the pram, thinking how difficult it was being with a baby, as well as how nice. For the first time, she envied Saffron her second-chance family. Did she and Ben have the option of doing the same? And, more importantly, did she dare take the risk?

Once the food had all been devoured, they sat in the sunshine while the baby slept in her pram, and the three children alternated between kicking a football about, and playing hide and seek. Amy lay back on the rug looking at them all and feeling a deep contentment. She was so lucky to have what she had; despite what she had lost.

'Penny for 'em?' Ben sat back and looked at her, a gentle smile playing on his lips. Her heart lurched for a minute.

'I was just thinking how lucky I am,' she said. 'And you?'

He leaned towards her and let his lips softly touch her hair. She shut her eyes briefly, enjoying the sensation.

'I was just thinking how I'd kiss you if the kids weren't here,' said Ben. 'But I'll just have to dream about it for now.'

Amy took his hand and squeezed it. Just then Josh and Matt ran up, so Amy smiled ruefully at Ben and together they packed up their things and headed back for the car, achingly aware of each other.

'I've just got to pop home and see how Meg is,' said Ben when they got back. 'I'll take her for a walk and be back later.'

'No probs,' said Amy. 'See you later.'

'That you most certainly will,' said Ben, giving her such a look that she didn't know where to put herself. It had been a long time since anyone had looked at her like that. It was time she stopped prevaricating. Once Saffron was back on an even keel, perhaps they should take things further.

Ben let himself into the house, and was immediately pounced on by Meg.

'Down, girl!' he said. Honestly, she was a stupid mutt sometimes. Anyone would think she'd been left alone for days.

It was odd. He felt sure he had put the mortise lock on, but he must have forgotten. Picking up his post, he wandered into the lounge, and was aware that something was different. There, in the corner of the room, sat two enormous suitcases.

'What the –?' Who the hell did they belong to? He didn't think burglars usually came in through the front door complete with luggage.

He heard a creak on the stairs, and turned to see who his intruder was.

'Hello, big boy. Aren't you pleased to see me?'

Standing in the doorway, in the skimpiest dressing gown possible, was Caroline.

PART THREE
Here Comes the Summer Sun

In the allotment:
*Weed and tend the growing plants. Separate the
seedlings and grow on.*

State of the heart:
Growing stronger, reaching for the sun.

CHAPTER NINETEEN

'Caroline, what a surprise,' Ben eventually managed to stutter. Surprise? Talk about understatement of the century. It was a goddamned disaster. What the hell did she think she was doing here? As usual around Caroline, he felt a warring conflict of emotions. He was torn between an incandescent fury at the way she seemed to think she could breeze back into his life, irritation that she had made herself at home, and a guilty lurch of sudden desire, which he couldn't quite help. How on earth was he going to explain this to Amy?

'Didn't you get my emails?' Caroline pouted as she sashayed down the stairs.

'What emails?'

'The emails to say I was coming,' she said. 'I thought you were avoiding me.'

'I didn't get any emails,' Ben replied. 'I think I'd remember a little thing like being asked if I could put you up for the night.'

Although, actually, now he thought about it, he'd

been so busy recently he hadn't spent much time online. There were probably a stack of emails sitting in cyberspace waiting for him.

'Don't I get a kiss?' She had come up close to him now, and he was painfully aware of her expensive perfume, not to mention her semi-nakedness. Once it would have excited him, but now he just felt embarrassed. The lurch of desire had been replaced with a sudden picture of Amy.

Ben gave her a perfunctory kiss on the cheek, before swiftly moving away into the kitchen to make a coffee.

'What are you doing here anyway?'

'Well, that's a nice greeting,' said Caroline, putting on her patented little-girl-lost look.

'Caroline,' he said, trying to keep his temper, 'I haven't heard from you in ages, and you've just turned up in my house, where it appears you're planning to stay for the duration of your visit. I think it's a reasonable question in the circumstances.'

Caroline pouted again, then pulled her incredibly flimsy wrap ostentatiously round her. Ben tried looking in the other direction. He was often pretty dense about these things, but even he could see what her intentions were.

'Let's just say things haven't worked out exactly as I'd hoped,' she said, in a rather dramatic manner. Ben knew of old he was supposed to ask why not, but couldn't be bothered to play that little game. He contented himself with asking if she wanted tea or coffee instead.

'It's all gone horribly wrong, if you want to know.'

Caroline was undeterred by Ben's lack of interest, and the drama queen in her was evidently going to make the most of the situation.

'I'm sorry to hear that,' Ben said evenly, as he passed her a cup of tea.

Caroline took a sip, paused dramatically, and then burst into tears.

Oh lord, the tears. He had forgotten how often and frequently they came.

'It's been terrible, Ben. My visa ran out and the police came and said I shouldn't be working, and then Dave Behind the Bar chucked me out. I've had a row with my aunt, I had nowhere to go, so I came home. And I had nowhere else to come but here. You know I've let the house out.'

'What about your parents?' Ben knew the Nowhere Else to Go bit was exaggerated. Caroline had incredibly wealthy parents who doted on her. She was hardly destitute.

'They're in Florida, looking for a house to retire to. I'm all alone in the world.'

'Caroline, you know that's not true,' said Ben. 'You do exaggerate.'

Clearly this wasn't the right thing to say, as Ben was met with a glower. But she changed tack and simply said, 'Do you mind if I stay for a few days?'

'Given that you're already here,' said Ben, 'I would say it's going to be pretty hard for me to say no. But I am rather busy. I only popped in to check on Meg. If you'll excuse me, I have to go out now. I have a friend waiting for me.'

He caught a flash of anger in her eyes. Anger that the tears hadn't worked? Anger that he wasn't dropping everything for her?

'Female, by any chance?' The anger was replaced quickly with a sly knowing look.

'Yes, female,' said Ben. 'Now, I really have to go.'

He left as quickly as he could, cursing Caroline for coming, cursing himself for not having been firmer with her, and wondering just what the hell he was going to say to Amy.

Amy was in the middle of cooking tea by the time Ben returned.

'That was quick,' she said, looking up from scraping vegetable peelings into the compost bin.

'What was?' Ben seemed a bit distracted.

'You were taking Meg for a walk?' Amy flicked a tea towel at him teasingly, and he felt an instant physical response. Damn Caroline for turning up now, just as things were going so well with Amy.

'Oh, yes, well, I didn't quite get there,' said Ben, trying to work out how to explain Caroline to Amy. He'd never mentioned her before. Amy was going to find it a bit odd that Caroline should suddenly be staying with him.

'Dearie me, you seem dozy all of a sudden,' Amy said, deftly dishing out fish pie. 'Just as well I'm here to whip you into shape.'

Mentally cooling himself down at the thought, Ben

took the opportunity for a welcome distraction. 'Shall I call the kids in?' he asked.

'Good idea,' said Amy, who thankfully appeared to have forgotten all about Meg.

Ben breathed a sigh of relief. He would tell her about Caroline later, once the kids were in bed. Maybe by then he would have figured out what to say.

Amy felt troubled. She couldn't put a finger on why, but ever since Ben had returned from walking Meg – or not walking her – he somehow seemed to have retreated into himself. The earlier intimacy between them seemed to have vanished, and she found herself wondering if she had upset him in any way. At one point in the evening she had felt sure Ben had been about to tell her something, but then Matt and Becky had had a fight, and by the time it was sorted out the opportunity had gone. She would have asked him about it when the kids had gone to bed, but Saffron chose that moment to return from the hospital, and by the time they had found out how Elizabeth was – somewhat better, but still not out of the woods – and made Saffron sit and have something to eat, then put the world to rights over a bottle of wine, it had been rather late and Ben had made his excuses and left.

Sunday came and went. Ben popped in around lunchtime, while Saffron was at the hospital, but couldn't stay long, mumbling something about other commitments. If Amy hadn't known better she might have thought he was being a bit shifty, but shifty wasn't really a word she would have associated with Ben before now.

She dismissed the thought from her head. Whatever Ben was, he wasn't shifty. She was beginning to find him vital to her existence. If she were ever to trust her healing heart to anyone, it would be to him.

By the middle of the week, Elizabeth was much better, and Saffron had come back to hold the fort once more. Amy breathed a sigh of relief. It was nice to get back to her own place and a bit of peace and quiet. Lovely and all as Saffron's children were, it was a lot to take on three extra children when you only had one of your own.

There was a message on the answer-phone from the estate agent, saying that her landlady was unexpectedly back in the country and would like to view her property, so could Amy ring in the morning. Amy frowned. Saffron hadn't mentioned that Caroline was coming back to England. But then again, maybe she didn't know.

Falling into bed that night, completely exhausted, she realised that, apart from a couple of brief visits in the evening, she had barely seen Ben all week. That was odd. Too tired to even feel paranoid, Amy turned over and went to sleep. There was probably a good explanation for it. She'd ring him tomorrow and find out.

Ben had been doing his level best to spend most evenings out. Caroline was mooching around the house dramatically declaring her life to be over. DBtB had apparently got the full measure of her and hadn't been keen to go for the lifelong commitment that Caroline was seemingly after. But then again, why would he, when it was quite clear from Caroline that, lifelong commitment or not, she was still an outrageous flirt.

'It's only to make him jealous,' she said to Ben. 'But he thinks it means I don't show any commitment.'

'Hmm, I wonder why,' Ben replied, dashing off to the gym to avoid further revelations. He still hadn't said anything to Amy about Caroline. He knew he was being cowardly, but with Amy away at Saffron's he hadn't managed to run into her on the allotments in the general way of things, as he normally did. He had called in a couple of times to help out, but things were pretty fraught with the children, who were missing their mother badly, and there hadn't been much opportunity for a heart-to-heart. He thought of soliciting Harry's help, but then decided that was even more cowardly. There was no help for it, he was going to have to face Amy sometime. And better it came from him than she heard it elsewhere.

'I hope you'll find everything in order,' Amy said, as she let in her elusive landlady. She had to admit she was intrigued to meet Caroline. The woman who had broken hearts all over Nevermorewell, if the rumours were true.

She was much tartier than Amy had imagined, as it turned out. Caroline was busting out of a tight pink top and even tighter and shorter black leather miniskirt. Amy's eyes boggled at the sight of so much flesh this early on in the year, let alone the day. She sported an even tan, and her brown curly hair was held up loosely in a grip.

'I'm sure it will all be fine,' Caroline gushed. 'It's nice to meet you at last. I've heard such a lot about you.'

'You have?' Amy was surprised. She frowned. 'Who from?'

Caroline ignored her and waltzed through into the front room. 'Oh, I love what you've done with the lounge,' she purred. 'I might keep it like that.'

Amy's heart sank. She had originally taken the let on a six-month lease, which she had just renewed. At some point she was going to have to bite the bullet and buy again, but she needed a bit more time to consolidate her finances, plus she was happy in the house. It had become home for her. Renewing the lease had seemed the sensible thing to do. At the time it looked as though Caroline wasn't planning to come back for ages. Now it seemed she'd changed her mind.

'Are you planning to stay then?' Amy asked, hoping she didn't sound too desperate.

Caroline waved an airy hand. 'My plans are, shall we say, fluid at the moment. Don't worry, I'm not planning to kick you out in the foreseeable future, although now I'm back I find I'm quite enjoying being here.'

Amy breathed a sigh of relief.

'Are you staying locally, then?' she asked.

'Oh, yes,' said Caroline. 'A *very* good friend is kindly putting me up.'

'Who's that?' One of her many paramours, no doubt.

'You probably don't know him.' Caroline's insouciance was totally studied. 'I'm staying with Ben Martin.'

'You're staying with Ben?' said Amy, trying to keep her tone light, as she fiddled with the kettle in the kitchen. 'He didn't say.'

Why hadn't he said? Why? Ben had never mentioned Caroline, so why was she staying with him? Amy cast her mind back to the first time he'd come round to the house – Ben had clearly known his way about. He'd said all the houses round there were the same layout, but what if he'd been lying? Just how close had he and Caroline been? A fleeting memory of the look on Ben's face on Saturday night, when he had clearly been trying to tell her something, and she had been too busy to hear, unsettled her.

'Oh, you know Ben then?' Again, that studied insouciance. Amy felt Caroline knew damned well that she knew Ben, and was trying to gauge her reaction. Well, two could play at that game.

'You know what it's like around here,' said Amy airily. 'Everyone knows everyone else. Harry introduced us.'

'Dear old Harry,' said Caroline without a trace of affection. 'He still knocking about then, is he? I would have thought he'd have gone to the great garden in the sky by now.'

Amy looked at Caroline with growing dislike. What

on earth was Ben doing anywhere near this wretched woman?

'I expect you know that Ben and I go way back,' continued Caroline. 'We were very, *very* close, but then I decided to go and find myself. I'm a free spirit, you see, I don't like to be pinned down. Darling Ben is a bit of a stick in the mud. But I expect you've worked that out for yourself.'

Mentally thinking that pinning Caroline down and sticking darts in her would be very good therapy, Amy merely smiled sweetly and hoped that Caroline couldn't detect the churning emotions raging inside her.

'So were you and Ben an item then?' She tried to say it as casually as she could.

'Oh lord, yes.' Caroline looked coy. 'Ben's the only person I've ever considered marrying. But like I said, I'm a free spirit, me. And gorgeous and all as he is, even Ben couldn't keep me in dull old Nevermorewell. But at least I've got him to entertain me while I'm here.'

Amy opened her mouth and shut it again. She couldn't think of a thing to say.

'Well, nice and all as it has been chatting, I can't stay round here all day,' said Caroline. 'I'd best get back. Ben said he might pop back at lunchtime, and I promised I'd make him a spicy lentil stew. It's one of his favourites. You know what men are like, they never eat properly when they're on their own, do they? And he's got shockingly thin in my absence. I need to build him back up – in every way.'

Forty–love to you, thought Amy silently, as she saw Caroline out. In one fell swoop, Caroline had claimed

Ben as her own. She tried to think back to what, if anything, Saffron had told her about Ben's love life. She couldn't remember any mention of Caroline. Was it possible that Ben was one of Caroline's conquests? Suppose he was? And it had been serious? Where did that leave Amy now? Amy owed it to Ben to wait to hear his version of events, but in the light of such over-powering certainty, Amy wasn't at all sure that she was going to like what she heard.

Saffron sat down and relaxed with a welcome glass of wine. What would already have been a tough week without Pete had turned into a nightmare with her mum being ill. Without Amy and Ben she didn't know how she would have coped. Thankfully, Elizabeth continued to improve, and was hoping to come home early next week. Mindful of how much time Saffron had spent away from the children, Elizabeth was now insisting that Saffron get home early in the evening and put her feet up. 'You've done enough for your old mum,' she'd said.

So now Saffron was home, trying to relax and not worry about work. With all the turmoil going on, she hadn't managed to do much gardening, and again was grateful to Amy for holding the fort. What she'd do without her she couldn't imagine. Amy had doubled her workload this week by going out to see Saffron's clients as well as her own. The only upside to them having lost so many jobs was that at least Amy had been able to keep on top of the ones they had managed to retain. Which, given that she had been taking the children along with her, was the only silver lining to the cloud that loomed over the business.

Saffron frowned. Perhaps it was time to be a bit proactive and turn detective. She would begin by asking her remaining regulars if they knew what was going on – in fact, Linda would be a good place to start. She knew practically everyone in Nevermorewell.

Saffron lay back on the sofa watching the TV in a desultory fashion. She should go to bed really, but she was hoping Pete would phone. She couldn't wait for him to come home.

She was jolted out of her musings by a crash in the back garden. Heart beating, and wishing more than ever that Pete were here, she turned the light off and drew the lounge curtains. The security light had flooded on, and she could make out a pot that had smashed across the path. Odd. It wasn't windy. Perhaps it was a fox.

She felt a sudden clutch of fear. Or maybe it was an intruder.

Don't be silly, she admonished herself. There were very few break-ins round here. It *must* have been a fox.

She went into the kitchen and looked for a suitable instrument. *Ah, yes*, she thought, seizing the shillelagh that Pete had once insisted on buying her on a trip to Dublin, for reasons that escaped her, but for which she was now very grateful. She felt emboldened enough to unlock the kitchen door and stride down the path. Self-defence classes she had been to always suggested going on the offensive, and roaring loudly to scare away an aggressor. Feeling too self-conscious to roar, she nevertheless walked as boldly as she could down the path. The security light illuminated most of the garden, and there weren't many nooks and crannies where an attacker could hide. There was no one there.

She bent over to pick up the pieces of the pot. It was too dark to sort out properly, but at least she could clear the path. Then she stopped and stiffened. She heard a soft thud, thud, and looked to the end of the garden. The garden gate was flapping gently back and forth. Saffron swallowed hard. She was sure she had shut it earlier.

Armed with the shillelagh, she ran down the path, looking from left to right to make sure there were no Greebos lurking in the shadows. The garden was quite empty, but the gate was still open. And in the mud that marked the allotment boundary, she could see the shape of a boot. Slamming the gate shut and locking it as quickly as she could, Saffron raced back to the house, heart hammering ninety to the dozen. Someone had been in her garden. Of that she was certain.

'Couldn't the boot print have been yours?' Amy asked the next day, when Saffron related the story.

'No, I checked in the morning. It was way too big

for mine, and Pete hasn't been out on the allotments in months, so it couldn't be his.'

'Did you call the police?'

Saffron pulled a face. 'They just said it was kids mucking about.'

'They're probably right,' Amy reassured her. 'It's not like there's a lot of crime around here. It's one of the reasons I love it so much. Back in London, you always had to watch yourself. Do you want me to come and keep you company tonight?'

'That's really nice of you,' said Saffron. 'But you must be sick of the sight of my house. Besides, Pete's back tonight. I'm sure I can manage. After all, I have got my trusty shillelagh.'

'Well, if you're sure . . .'

'I am, thanks. I tell you another odd thing, though,' Saffron continued. 'I think someone's been in my shed.'

'What makes you say that?'

'I found an empty chip wrapper, and a can of beer. And I certainly didn't put them there.'

'Now that *does* sound like kids,' said Amy. 'Perhaps we ought to mention it to Harry. He can bring it up at the next allotmenteers' committee meeting. If there are kids breaking into the allotments at night, we should all be more vigilant.'

'Good idea,' said Saffron. 'I shall try not to worry about it. Come on, let's get out to Mrs Webster's. Her beds were in a shocking state last time we visited, so I hate to think what they're like now.'

Saffron was trying to be positive. There probably *was* a simple explanation for the chip paper. But along with the haemorrhaging clients, and the intruder in her garden, she was beginning to feel as if someone had it in for her.

Ben made his way up Amy's path after work. What a difference a week could bring. This time last week he had been anticipating a relaxed and enjoyable evening with her. And now, thanks to Caroline, he wasn't sure what reception he was going to get. Caroline had casually let slip that she had been over to Amy's, and equally casually mentioned that Amy now knew where she was staying.

'I do believe your little girlfriend was a teensy bit jealous,' Caroline had laughed her tinkly laugh, which was really beginning to grate on Ben's nerves.

'She's not my girlfriend, and she has no need to be jealous, given that there is nothing going on between you and me,' said Ben, resisting the urge to slap her.

'More's the pity,' Caroline said breathily, and fluttered her eyelashes at him. Time was when that would have had an effect. But not now. Ben simply ignored her, and went out to work, determining firstly to call Amy at the earliest opportunity, and secondly to get Caroline out of his house as soon as humanly possible.

He had tried calling Amy, but she seemed to be out every time he rang. It was as if she were avoiding him. And then he'd had a couple of very busy days at work, and had got home too late to pop in on her.

But he was here now, and he had to hope that she would give him the benefit of the doubt.

Ben stood on the doorstep, and when the door opened, asked, 'Can I come in?'

'Cup of tea?' She tried to keep her voice light, and hoped he wouldn't hear the tremble in it. This was ridiculous. Last week she had felt happy and relaxed with him, and was even contemplating having his babies! And now she was all over the place.

'Yes, thanks.' Ben followed her into the kitchen, where Josh was drawing a picture.

'Ben!' Josh leapt up in delight and threw his arms round Ben's legs. 'Where have you been?' he said accusingly. 'We haven't seen you for *ages.*'

Amy's heart swelled at the way her son looked at Ben. He would make such a good father. If that's what he wanted. If that was what *she* wanted.

'Sorry, mate,' said Ben, ruffling Josh's hair. 'I've been a bit busy. I'll make it up to you, I promise.'

'I owe you an apology,' Ben blurted out, as they sat down with their tea in the lounge.

'I presume you mean Caroline?' Amy said frostily.

'I had no idea she was coming. I know that sounds lame, but I honestly didn't have a clue. She sent me emails apparently, but I never got them. She pitched up last Saturday when you were helping out at Saffron's.'

'Why didn't you tell me?'

'I'm sorry, I meant to. Really I did. But it was so hectic, and there didn't seem to be a right time, somehow. And then, having not told you, it seemed to be harder to say.'

'Not that,' said Amy. 'Why didn't you tell me you used to go out with her?'

Ben looked shamefaced.

'It never seemed relevant, to be honest,' he said. 'I did see Caroline for a while last year. It was a short and very intense relationship. Then she decided to go travelling and wanted me to go with her, and when I said no, we parted company. We've stayed in touch, but that's it. At least it is on my side. To be honest, she's a drama queen and very high maintenance. And it's a real pain in the arse having her as a house guest.'

'If you say so,' said Amy, but her tone was wary.

'Amy, you have to believe me,' said Ben earnestly. 'The last person I'm interested in right now is Caroline.'

'Okay, I believe you,' said Amy, desperately wanting to, but not entirely sure she could.

'Good,' Ben replied. 'And you're not cross?'

'Nothing to be cross about,' said Amy with determined lightness. 'Although I can't say I'm impressed with your taste in women.'

Ben grimaced. 'Well, put it like this, it took me a while to realise what Caroline was really like. To be honest, I'd much rather not have her to stay. But she has nowhere to go at the moment, and we do have history. I'd feel a bit crap if I chucked her out. She's getting over a broken heart apparently. It seems a bit heartless to make her leave.'

'How long is she staying?'

'She hasn't actually said,' Ben admitted. 'But I'm hoping not too long. It doesn't have to make a difference to us, does it?'

'No, no, of course not,' said Amy with an enthusiasm she didn't feel. She would feel so much better if she knew Caroline wasn't going to stay for long. Somehow she had a feeling that Caroline wouldn't happily accept that Ben wasn't interested. Amy had a horrible feeling that she might have a fight on her hands.

'That's great,' said Ben. 'So we're back to where we were then?'

'Yes,' said Amy, wondering where exactly that might be.

CHAPTER TWENTY

'Hi, Harry, how are you doing?' Amy passed him sitting on the bench outside his hut, as she pushed her wheelbarrow, laden with tools, onto the allotments. It was a fine Saturday spring morning, and the allotments were already busy. There was a constant hum of lawnmowers and she had stopped to chat to several people before reaching Harry. There had been a time when she could come out here and barely know anyone, and now it felt as if she had a huge extended family. Even Scary Slug Man didn't spook her any more.

The sun shone clear and bright, and there was barely a cloud in the crisp, fresh blue sky. Amy felt a deep and contented sense of renewal. Ben had said he would pop over and help her start digging over her vegetable beds, ready for planting. She smiled in happy anticipation. This was just why she had moved out here. So far Amy had managed to get a few spuds and carrots in, but, despite the warm days, the evenings were still cold so she had deferred planting anything else. Harry had kindly lent her a couple of shelves in his greenhouse, and was assiduously looking after her fledgling tomatoes, kale and cauliflowers, so Amy was hoping for great things come the summer. She felt a little thrill of delight at the thought.

A shadow passed over her, as she felt the customary tug of sadness that Jamie wasn't here to share this with her. But she shook it off. The summer sun would be here soon, and she was settling happily into her new way of life. Ben would never be Jamie, but he was Ben. And she was beginning to allow herself the feelings she had resisted for so long. It felt like emerging from a dark cave into bright sunlight.

'I'm fine, my dear,' said Harry, breaking into her thoughts. 'No Josh today?'

'He's had a sleepover with Matt,' said Amy. 'Saffron kindly said she'd have him for me, to pay me back for the help I gave her when Elizabeth was ill. So I thought I'd take advantage and get over here.'

'Do you fancy a cuppa?'

'That would be lovely,' said Amy, following Harry into his hut. Harry's hut wasn't like the ramshackle huts of most of the allotmenteers, which were mainly cobbled together with old bits of wood, but a rather more solid affair, with a brick base and proper windows. Amy had been amazed at how cosy it was the first time she had visited it. Harry had a comfy old sofa, a small work surface where he kept his kettle, and several shelves that were stacked with bottles or his brewing kit, the main purpose of the shed being winemaking.

The radio was blaring out as they entered the shed.

'Isn't Jonathan Ross a bit too newfangled for you?' Amy laughed.

'Ah,' said Harry, 'my mistake. I was listening to that allotment chappie and forgot to tune it back to Classic FM. My begonias usually like a bit of Mozart.'

A familiar song was playing; the singer was urging her lover to reconsider before he took her heart. Amy shook her head. It could have been written for her and Ben. She so wanted to entrust her heart to him, but she had to be sure that he wouldn't break it. Caroline had shown no signs so far of moving on. And despite Ben's obvious attempts to keep things normal between them (him offering to help her today being one of them), Amy still felt a lingering unease about the other woman's presence.

'What do you make of Caroline?' she asked Harry.

'Ah, the divine Caroline,' said Harry. 'Adored by men and hated by women.'

'That seems a fair assessment,' laughed Amy. 'I can't say she's my cup of tea.'

'Nor mine, if it comes to it,' confided Harry.

'Harry,' Amy twisted her hair nervously, 'do you think . . . no, I'm being stupid.'

'I don't think Ben's in love with her, if that's what you're worried about,' Harry replied.

Amy looked embarrassed. Was she so easy to read?

'Not exactly – but good,' she said. 'I don't think she's right for him.'

Harry tried and failed to suppress a smile.

'I couldn't agree more. Caroline is a very determined and spoilt young lady, who is used to getting her own way. It may do her good if she doesn't for once.'

'I hope you're right,' said Amy, staring with sudden

gloom out of the window, 'because she seems to have muscled in on the act today. Ben was coming to help me on my allotment, but it looks like he's got company.'

She pointed through the window. Striding across the allotments, with Meg beside him, was Ben. And with him was Caroline.

Ben was fuming. Caroline was so good at wrong-footing him. He hadn't planned to mention going over to the allotments today, let alone seeing Amy. He was just going to get up and go. With Caroline being of the take-your-time-in-the-morning variety, he had anticipated getting away quite easily. But for once this morning she was up early. She also seemed to be a bit out of sorts. Something to do with a long, whispered phone conversation last night, presumably to DBtB. It had ended with Caroline yelling 'Don't you bloody dare', before hurling what sounded like her mobile phone across the room. Ben would have happily given anything not to listen, but the walls in his house were paper thin, and despite turning up Mark Radcliffe really loudly, he'd still caught more snippets than he cared to.

He'd pretended ignorance in the morning, but it was hard not to notice Caroline's pale face and red-rimmed eyes. He'd wondered if she'd left her face makeupless on purpose. Normally she wouldn't be seen dead without a bit of slap on. Was she making a play for sympathy? God, even Caroline wouldn't be so devious – would she?

Wondering what he had ever seen in her, Ben set about having breakfast and getting out as fast as he could. But Caroline was having none of it.

'What are you up to today?' she wanted to know with a false gaiety.

'I'm just going to the allotments to start preparing my seedbeds,' said Ben.

'Oh great,' she said. 'I'll come too. I need some fresh air to clear my head. I slept so badly last night.'

Evidently, Ben was supposed to ask why she'd slept badly, but he was determined not to, so he concentrated on buttering his toast instead.

'And I'm so dying to see what Amy's done to my allotment. I hadn't realised till Harry told me she was such a green-fingers. Aren't I lucky she rented out my house?' Again, the same tinkling little laugh. It made Ben want to throttle her, but instead he shoved his empty plate in the dishwasher and started to put his fleece on. He was damned if he was going to walk over there with her. But if she was determined to come he couldn't stop her.

'Hang on,' said Caroline, 'I'll be ready in two ticks.'

Ben cursed his parents for bringing him up to be polite to women. He would dearly have loved to walk out then and there. Would that he had been born ten years later. Any of his twenty-something male patients could have probably taught him a thing or two about shaking off the unwelcome attentions of women you don't like, but it wasn't something he would ever be comfortable with.

Caroline's two ticks developed into twenty minutes,

the slap now having to be applied for a visit to the allotments. And care had evidently been taken to wear just the right low-slung hipster jeans to accentuate her figure, and the tightest of tops to do the same to her cleavage.

'We're going over to the allotments, not to a fashion show,' he said in exasperation as she finally joined him.

'A girl should always look her best, whatever the circumstances,' said Caroline firmly. 'That's what my grandmama used to say anyway.'

'That'll explain why you never get your hands dirty,' muttered Ben as he followed her down the path. Caroline was getting to be a serious pain in the proverbial, and he didn't have a clue how he was going to get rid of her.

Saffron snuggled up to Pete. It was lovely to have him home, and the homecoming had been celebrated in exactly the right fashion. They had fallen on each other in the manner of famine-starved people. She had had no need for any sexy accoutrements at all. It had felt great to have her libido back – she hoped it wasn't going to be temporary. Maybe the pole-dancing lessons were having some effect. Linda had laughingly told her she was getting the hang of it the last time she'd been. Mind you, with the school holidays and Pete having been away, she'd not been for a couple of weeks. She cuddled up to Pete again. If things carried on like this, maybe she wouldn't need to go any more.

There had been no further intrusions either, and Pete had also been of the opinion it was kids mucking around.

'I'll put an extra padlock on just to be on the safe side,' he said. 'But it was probably a one-off. I shouldn't think we'll see anything more of them.'

Saffron put the puzzling incident from her mind, and instead was concentrating on her detective search. Linda hadn't turned anything up yet, and Pete was convinced she was being paranoid, until she triumphantly discovered that Mrs Webster had received a couple of phone calls from an unknown woman, claiming to be Saffron's assistant, who'd rung to cancel Saffron's visit. On both occasions Saffron had turned up later that day, so Mrs Webster thought the woman must have made a mistake.

'But now you mention it, dear,' she said, 'it does seem a bit odd.'

'Doesn't it just,' Saffron replied grimly. A woman ruled out Gerry then. But it didn't rule out his bit of stuff. She determined that she would confront Gerry about it next time she saw him.

Confronting Gerry, however, turned out not to be that easy. He had returned from his business trip and taken the kids out just once since, pitching up on her doorstep looking very dishevelled and taking them to Pizza Hut for the afternoon before returning them home an hour earlier than stated. Both children had made noises about Daddy smelling funny and not wanting to see him again, which had led to Saffron not following up a suggested time for their next visit with somewhat less guilt than she would have had normally. Mind you, when she had tried to ring, she only got his answer-phone, and his mobile seemed permanently switched off. It was all quite puzzling. However crap Gerry was generally, he usually managed to see the children once a fortnight.

'Time I was up,' she said. 'I'll get the kids sorted, and then I fancy doing a bit on the allotments. Are you up for a spot of babysitting?'

Pete gave her a lascivious look. 'I'm up for something,' he said, 'but not necessarily that . . .'

'Give over,' said Saffron. 'We have four children in the house, three of whom are probably about to knock our door down.'

As if on cue, Becky, Matt and Josh piled in demanding breakfast and TV simultaneously.

'Okay, you win,' said Pete. 'If I can grab a bit more shuteye, I'll let you have your moment of freedom.'

Saffron grinned as she got up and started to get dressed. Pete was a star.

'Caroline, what a nice surprise.' Amy was disgusted with herself for her insincerity, but she didn't want Ben to think she was being ungracious.

'I hope you don't mind me pitching in,' said Caroline, 'but I thought I could help, and I wanted to see how my allotment was.'

'That's very kind of you,' said Amy, thinking it was anything but. 'Here, have a fork. We're digging over that patch there. It would be enormously helpful if you could fork the earth through, and pick out any weeds.'

Amy was pleased to see Caroline looking disgusted. From what Saffron had said, she was of the Diarmuid Gavin, 'Let's Design a Fancy but Impractical Green Space' School of Gardening. Getting your hands dirty didn't figure very highly at all.

For a while they worked companionably. Ben dug furrows – Amy would have liked to, but she knew she could only work at half the speed that Ben did, so it seemed a bit more practical to do it this way – while Amy filled them with compost. To begin with, Caroline – who was clearly trying to impress Ben – seemed to fork through with enthusiasm. But after about ten minutes, she slowed right down. A further ten minutes elapsed and she had to stop altogether to attend to a broken nail. And after that she became preoccupied by a series of text messages, which evidently required an instant response.

Amy raised her eyebrows at Ben, who was resolutely digging away and ignoring Caroline's antics. He gave her a rueful smile and an apologetic shrug. When Caroline announced she was going to pop in on Harry – 'It will be so lovely to see him again,' she trilled – 'The pleasure will be all yours,' muttered Amy – Amy and Ben drew a collective sigh of relief.

'Thank God for that,' said Ben, putting his spade down and wiping his brow. 'I thought she'd never go. I'm sorry for bringing her, but she insisted.'

'It's okay,' said Amy, thrilled that Ben had found

Caroline's presence as irksome as she did. 'Does she always do so little work?'

Ben laughed. 'Yup. She had me digging this allotment over more times than I can count, and she just used to stand watching me, directing operations. And, muggins that I was, it took me a long time to realise I was being rooked.'

'Oh dear – you could say the same about me.' Amy looked up at him, shielding her eyes from the sun, which was burning quite hot now.

'Oh, I'd never think that.' Ben leaned forward and tucked a stray curl behind Amy's ear.

Her heart lurched, and she felt a sudden sensation of the world shifting on its axis. He thought more of her than of Caroline. Caroline was no threat to her. *She* was the threat to Caroline.

'You've got mud on your face,' she said. 'Here, let me clean it for you.'

She moved closer to him, and wiped the dirt off his brow. For a second they stood, staring at each other. It was as if there was no one there apart from them.

Gently, Ben brushed his lips against hers, and she found herself responding with an instant passion. The kiss went on and on, dizzyingly intoxicating. The sun shone down on them and Amy was vaguely aware of birdsong in the background. She wanted to bottle up the moment and keep it forever.

Eventually they pulled apart, laughing.

'Erm, sorry,' said Ben. 'I don't know where that came from.'

'I'm not sorry,' said Amy.

'Really?'

'Really,' Amy insisted, kissing him again to prove it. 'What about Josh?'

'Ever since you diagnosed a broken arm, you can do no wrong,' said Amy, enjoying the sensation of being held as she happily laid her head against Ben's chest. It had been so long. 'I think if I explain things to Josh, he'll be fine.' If only such moments could last. If only she could keep them safe. And never ever lose them.

They pulled apart again.

'This won't get your seedbeds dug,' said Ben.

'No, it won't.'

'Right, to work then,' Ben suggested.

'To work,' Amy agreed.

But still they stood there, unwilling to leave the moment. This precious moment when finally their feelings for each other had been laid bare. They held each other's gaze for what seemed like an eternity.

'Come on then,' said Ben eventually, reluctantly turning away. And started to dig. Amy went back to filling holes, strangely disappointed and achingly aware of the closeness of Ben to her, of his muscular body, and of how much she wanted him.

Saffron had left Pete with the kids for a while as she went out to check on her allotment. As she approached her allotment, she noticed with dismay that the fledgling broccoli plants she had put out the previous week had been squashed flat, and something had marched right across the seedbed where she had recently planted carrots and parsnips.

'Bloody foxes,' she muttered, peering at the soil to make sure that the seeds hadn't been disturbed, and trying but failing to prop up the broccoli. She went into her shed to get out a rake and spade, so she could get on with preparing a bed for her lettuces. The door wasn't properly shut.

'I must make sure Pete doesn't forget that padlock,' she muttered to herself. Then, 'Bloody hell!'

Saffron opened the door to a scene of utter carnage. Her tools were scattered everywhere and someone had piled up several hessian sacks in the corner, as though for a pillow. There were more chip papers and a pizza box in evidence, several empty cans of beer and a couple of empty bottles of wine.

It appeared that someone was camping out in Saffron's shed.

CHAPTER TWENTY-ONE

'Harry, Harry!' Saffron burst into Harry's hut, where he was politely listening to Caroline's woes about DBtB and Ben's lack of interest in her.

'Are you all right, my dear?' he asked, looking delighted to see her. It was unlike Saffron to be so flustered.

'Not really. My intruder's back, and it looks like the cheeky bugger's been camping out in my shed. Do you know if anyone else has noticed anything strange?'

'I've been asking around, since you told me about the last break-in,' said Harry. 'But no, there's been nothing. Have you rung the police?'

Saffron pulled a face. 'It's not important enough to warrant a police officer actually coming out here, apparently. They said it was probably a tramp.'

'Well, I suppose it could be . . .' Harry looked doubtful.

'Exactly, that's what I thought,' said Saffron. 'It's not as if Nevermorewell has a reputation for being cardboard city.'

'Then, if not a tramp, who?'

'The only other person I could think of was Scary Slug Man. He is a bit odd,' said Saffron.

'Oh, surely not,' Harry replied. 'Even if he were camping out on the allotments, he'd probably do it on his own, there's enough ground cover there, and he's got enough wood on it to build himself a perfectly decent shelter.'

As Scary Slug Man's allotment was overgrown with bushes and brambles, homemade compost heaps and a series of half-built sheds, it was a valid point.

'You're probably right,' said Saffron. 'But it's beginning to freak me out a little. First my intruder, now this. And I still haven't got to the bottom of why Amy and I are losing so much business. It feels as though someone has it in for me.'

'Ooh, I do love a good mystery,' said Caroline gleefully.

'Er, hello, Caroline, how's things?' said Saffron, who hadn't noticed her before. Saffron hadn't got round to calling on Caroline yet. When she'd heard her business partner was back in town she had shuddered. She didn't want to work with Caroline again, not one bit. Amy had shown just what a mug she had been before. Luckily their business arrangement had been fairly loose, so there weren't many ends to tie up. 'Well, you might not find it so entertaining if it happened to you.'

'Can I do anything to help?' Harry offered, trying to cut the tension between the two women.

'No thanks, Harry. Whoever it was has just left a big

mess, so I'll bin it and put a padlock on the shed to make sure they don't come back.'

'I'll put the word out that everyone needs to be more vigilant,' said Harry. 'If we all keep our eyes and ears open we may be able to track the intruder down between us.'

'Thanks,' said Saffron. 'It just beats me who would do such a thing.'

'There's nowt so queer as folk,' said Harry. 'I have to say, whoever it is must be pretty desperate. I can't imagine wanting to doss down out here of an evening.'

'And you really have no idea who it was?' Amy wanted to know, when she went to pick Josh up.

'Not a clue,' said Saffron.

'Are you worried?'

'Not exactly,' said Saffron. 'But it does leave a nasty taste in your mouth.'

'My money is on it being that nutty old man who hangs about in the high street, shouting abuse at people,' said Pete, walking in at that moment.

'But do you think he'd have the wherewithal to wander up here though?' Amy asked. 'He always looks as though he's about to keel over. I can't imagine that he'd survive a night in your hut.'

'Good point,' said Pete. 'But the key thing is, what, if anything, are we going to do about it?'

'We could stake out the hut,' said Amy. 'Take it in turns to see if anyone pitches up.'

'Sounds a bit drastic,' said Saffron, 'and I'm not sure if I want to spend a chilly evening on the allotments. What happens if we find him and he turns nasty?'

'Ah, then you'll need some big burly, hunky men to tackle him,' said Pete, preening.

'What, like you?' Saffron snorted.

'Thanks for the vote of confidence. If Ben, me, the Guys and Harry took turns we could probably sort out your intruder quite easily.'

'I think it might be quite an adventure,' said Amy, her eyes sparkling, the thought of spending an evening under the stars with Ben in the allotments not being without its charm.

'Oh go on then,' said Saffron. 'I suppose we've got nothing to lose.'

'You really are the bloody limit!' Caroline was shrieking into her mobile as Ben unlocked the front door. He and Amy had cleared the seedbeds, and then she had gone to get Josh. He had badly wanted to suggest going for lunch somewhere, but with Caroline still hanging about he felt sure she would have ended up tagging along somehow. She clearly wasn't going anywhere for a while, so whatever was going on between him and Amy – and from this morning's events there clearly now was something going on – was going to have to wait till Caroline had left. As long as she was around it felt like he was part of a cumbersome and unwelcome threesome.

Caroline snapped her mobile off and flounced moodily to the sofa.

'Bloody Dave,' she said.

'What's he done now?' Ben felt obliged to ask, when really he couldn't give a hoot.

'He's only insisting on coming over here to see me,' she said. 'He wants to patch things up apparently.'

'Well, that's a good thing, isn't it?' said Ben, thinking, *Come Dave, come. Take this problem off my hands.*

'No. It Is So Not a Good Thing,' scowled Caroline.

'Why not?' Ben was puzzled now. Ever since Caroline had got here all she had done was moan about the fact that DBtB had ditched her.

'Because ... because ...' she was practically panting the words, and looking at him in a distinctly seductive way. 'I've unfinished business here.'

'Oh?' Ben felt his heart sink.

'You must feel it too, Ben,' said Caroline, getting up and slowly moving towards him.

'What?' Ben backed off in alarm, hands in the air. Good God, was she about to make a play for him? Couldn't she see how things stood between him and Amy? Or maybe she couldn't. Caroline was so self-obsessed, it was probably impossible for her to imagine that anyone else might have taken her place in Ben's affections.

'The chemistry between us,' she said in a playful manner. 'Come on, Ben, I know it's not just on my side.'

'Oh, but it is, Caroline, it is.' Panic was making Ben blunter than he would have been under normal

289

circumstances. 'I'm sorry, but whatever you imagine was between us, it's over. I'm not in love with you, if I ever was. I'm in love with Amy.'

I'm in love with Amy. The words had just tumbled from his mouth and he meant every one of them. 'And I also think you should stop playing silly games with Dave and decide just what it is you want from life.'

Caroline crumpled instantly, as if he had slapped her on the cheek.

'You can't mean that,' she wailed, tears flowing freely. How did she do that? It was a real talent.

'I can and I do,' said Ben. Flight was now clearly the only option. 'So get used to it.' And so saying he turned round and fled from the house, leaving Caroline to curse her misfortune.

Amy's heart leapt when the doorbell rang and she heard Josh say, 'Mummy, it's Ben.' She had been going to ask Ben back for lunch, but they had been disturbed by Caroline and Harry coming to tell them about Saffron's break-in. And then she couldn't quite work out a way of inviting Ben and not the other two without appearing rude. So she had said nothing, gone to pick up Josh and hoped that Ben would contact her. And now he had.

'I'm not intruding, am I?' Ben followed her into the kitchen. He seemed a bit out of breath and flustered.

'What do you think?' Amy said with a grin. 'I was hoping you'd come. I hope you like pasta salad. I've made enough to feed an army. And fusspot in there –'

she indicated the lounge where Josh was trouncing monsters on the PlayStation '– has today decided that, having been his favourite, he no longer likes it.'

'Pasta salad sounds fabulous,' said Ben. 'Mind you, the way I feel at the moment, anything sounds fabulous. Especially anything cooked by you.'

Amy blushed, but she felt warm all over.

'Where's Caroline?'

'I left her at home, sobbing on the sofa because her boyfriend's ditched her and I showed no inclination to take his place.'

'Really?'

'Really.' Ben came over to her and put his arms around her. 'I told her my heart belonged to another woman.'

'Is that so?' Amy replied.

'It certainly is,' Ben said, and started kissing her.

'Caroline! What a nice surprise,' Saffron said, with more enthusiasm than she felt, as she opened the door to her one-time business partner. Ever since Caroline's return, she had acknowledged that they would inevitably have to meet up at some point to discuss business, if only to work out a way to dissolve their partnership. For a while there, Caroline had been making a healthy profit while doing sweet f.a. and swanning round the world, but since the drip, drip loss of their clients, her profits (and Saffron's too) had plummeted.

The difference was that Caroline had wealthy parents, whereas Saffron did not. And while Saffron's contribution to the family's income wasn't huge, it was welcome, and she and Pete were beginning to miss it sorely. God knows how Amy was managing. Saffron was guiltily aware that Amy might have to do some more supply teaching if this carried on, and wished more than ever that she could get to the bottom of who was badmouthing them. With all of that worry, the last thing she wanted to have to deal with was Caroline wanting to know why the business was failing so badly.

As it turned out, she needn't have worried. Caroline hadn't come to talk about business. She just needed an audience for her woes.

'Oh, Saffron,' Caroline burst into loud noisy sobs as Saffron took her through into the kitchen, 'why is my life such a mess?'

Because you thrive on it? Because you create the mess? Saffron bit her lip to prevent herself from blurting out a few home truths. Instead she put on the kettle, sat Caroline down, gave her the obligatory hug, while simultaneously sitting Ellie in her high chair, letting Pete know that he should stay out of the kitchen if he knew what was good for him, and starting the tea. Becky and Matt had both gone to a party. Caroline carried on regardless. She barely paused for breath when Saffron re-entered the room, indeed, Saffron had the sneaking suspicion that Caroline hadn't even noticed she'd gone. She'd certainly not noticed Ellie, whom she'd not yet met.

'So Dave keeps texting to say he wants to come over, and I just don't know what to do-ooo . . .' she wailed, while Saffron chopped veg. Saffron had been tuning most of it out. She was used to Caroline. When they had been in business together barely a day had gone by without some kind of crisis or other – usually to do with a man.

Most of Caroline's problems, in Saffron's view, were entirely of her own making, and the entire time Saffron had known her, she had dated one man while flirting with others, ever searching for that elusive alternative better bet. As far as Saffron was aware, no one had ever ditched her, apart from the mystery man she'd been seeing just before she went away, and the shock had been enormous. Saffron had had to deal with the fallout for days, before Caroline, in typically impulsive style, had stung her parents for large amounts of dosh and pushed off to California to 'find herself', as she put it. The real reason, Saffron had gleaned at the time, was to show her erstwhile lover what he was missing. He was meant to drop everything and follow her, but he couldn't have obliged, because the next thing she had heard via one scrappy email months ago was that Caroline had a new man in the shape of Dave Behind the Bar. From the few parts of Caroline's monologue she had bothered to listen to, it sounded like she had behaved in exactly the same manner to Dave Behind the Bar as well.

'And then there's Ben,' said Caroline.

'What about Ben?' said Saffron.

'There's unfinished business there, you know,' Caroline laughed.

'What – you and Ben?'

'Didn't I ever tell you?' Caroline said. 'He and I were together.'

'Ben was . . . what – when?'

'Before I went away,' said Caroline, 'and I can still feel the chemistry between us.'

'You can?' Saffron was astounded. As far as she was concerned Amy and Ben were rapidly becoming an item. She hadn't taped Ben for a two-timer. She shook her head. Nope, Ben was as straight as they came. This must be one of Caroline's many sad little fantasies. Saffron frowned. But would she have made that up about her and Ben? It didn't seem likely. And unless Ben had sworn Pete to secrecy, even Pete didn't know about it.

'What do you think I should do?' Caroline demanded, as if suddenly aware that her tale wasn't reaching a terribly sympathetic audience.

'Erm –' Damn! Saffron knew that whatever she said, it would be the wrong thing. She was saved by the doorbell. It was Gerry, pitching up unexpectedly to pick the kids up. He looked exhausted and incredibly dishevelled. If she hadn't been so irritated that he'd got his dates muddled again, she might have felt sorry for him.

'Gerry, the kids aren't here,' she said. 'They're both out at parties. I can drop them off to you later if you like.'

'Oh no, sweetheart.' Gerry looked decidedly shifty. 'I'm on the way somewhere myself. I just called on the off-chance.'

'Do you want to wait and see the kids?'

'I could hang around for a bit, I suppose,' said Gerry, which wasn't the response Saffron was hoping for. Reluctantly, she led him into the kitchen. With Caroline here she couldn't even grill him about the mysterious woman who had been cancelling her jobs. She paused and had a sudden and startling thought. Suppose Caroline was the mystery woman? No, that was daft. Caroline had been abroad when the calls started. And anyway, why would she sabotage her own business? Dismissing the thoughts for the time being she introduced Gerry.

'Gerry, you remember Caroline,' said Saffron.

'And how could I forget the lovely Caroline?' Gerry took her hand and held it to his lips.

'Ooh, Gerry,' Caroline batted her eyes, unable to resist the flattery, 'you don't mean that.'

'Of course I do,' said Gerry, in a manner that was evidently intended to be gallant. 'Every man around these parts mourned when the divine Caroline left us behind.'

'What are you like, Gerry?' said Caroline. 'I bet you say that to all the girls.'

By now Saffron was beginning to feel like a spare part in her own kitchen. Caroline was preening and plumping herself like a French hen, and Gerry looked as though all his Christmases had come at once. She was relieved when eventually Caroline decided it was time to go. Not only was she spared more confidences she could do without, but instead of waiting for the kids, Gerry rather unsubtly found himself in need of running an urgent errand and left several minutes later.

God, her ex-husband and her ex-business partner. Now there was a marriage made in heaven.

Wondering idly what had happened to Maddy, who hadn't been mentioned the entire time Gerry had been there, Saffron shook her head. Caroline also seemed to have shaken off her trauma about DBtB and Ben fairly quickly too. Well, good luck to them. None of it was any of her business, thankfully. And so long as they kept out of her hair, they were welcome to do as they pleased.

CHAPTER TWENTY-TWO

The Magpie was heaving, and Ben spent several minutes scanning the room before he spied Pete in the corner, with the Guys, Bill, Bud and Harry.

'I hereby call this meeting of Operation Intruder to order,' Pete said portentously over a pint of lager, as Ben sat down.

Fired up by his enthusiasm at Amy's suggestion to stake out the allotments, Pete had decided that this was reason enough to go for an impromptu drink on Monday evening.

'Funny how this meeting just *has* to take place in the pub,' had been Saffron's snorting response. She and Amy had both decided that it wasn't worth arranging for a babysitter for the sake of playing SAS games on the allotments.

'So what's the plan?' said Ben. 'Stay out in the allotments all night? I know the weather's a bit warmer, but it's still cold.'

'We'll take it in shifts,' said Pete.

'We've got a party Friday night,' said Clive. 'So we'll go first.'

'We're free around eight,' offered Bill and Bud.

'I'll do an early shift too,' said Harry. 'As it was Amy's idea, I said I'd babysit for her while she takes a turn.'

'So that's settled then,' said Pete. 'Who's for another pint?'

Just then the bar door dramatically burst open as Caroline made an entrance.

'Don't look now, but I think your lapdog has followed you,' Pete said to Ben. Ben had brought Pete up to speed with the situation with Caroline and he'd spent the last few days poking fun at Ben's predicament.

'What's she bloody doing here?' Ben had left Caroline apparently happily ensconced in front of *EastEnders*. He wearily raised a hand to greet her, but she swept right past him in a swirl of Gucci Envy and went to the far end of the bar, where, to Ben's amazement, Gerry was waiting to greet her.

'Bloody hell,' said Pete, his jaw open, 'that woman never ceases to surprise me.'

'I didn't know Maddy and Gerry had split up,' said Ben.

'I don't know that they have,' said Pete. 'I'm sure Saffron would have mentioned it.'

'That's going to make for fun in the hen coop,' said Charles, nodding in Caroline and Gerry's direction.

'Put your claws away,' said Pete. 'Whatever they get up to, it's none of our business. Now, what about that drink?'

Saffron scooted out of Legends. She felt she was finally getting the hang of this pole-dancing thing. Linda had actually complimented her on the routine she'd worked out this week. And, incredibly, Saffron was beginning to notice a difference in her shape. She wasn't exactly svelte, but certainly less blobby. It was a very good reason for still coming to the classes.

Saffron felt bad that she hadn't got round to telling Pete about them, but somehow, the longer it went on, the harder it was to say. It was a guilty pleasure she took once a week, sneaking out and pretending for an hour that instead of someone's mum, or someone's wife, she was a sexy young thing whose body still held appeal. It was stupid really. It wasn't as if Pete didn't tell her he loved her. But it felt like a long time since he'd told her she was sexy. The pole-dancing lessons were making her feel like she still had some booty to shake. But she ought to tell Pete about them. She didn't like keeping things from him. She would. Soon.

'What are you doing here?' Maddy accosted her in the foyer of the club.

'Erm, I've been out for a drink with some friends.' Bloody hell. Of all people to run into.

'That's funny,' said Maddy, 'I've just been working behind the bar. I didn't see you in there.'

Oh God. How bad could this get?

'I didn't know you worked here.' Saffron's voice came out in a squeak.

'I've just started,' said Maddy.

Gerry not keeping you in the manner to which you're accustomed? was Saffron's uncharitable thought, but she decided it was politic not to say it. Her over-whelming desire was to get the hell out of there, before Maddy put two and two together.

Maddy snapped her fingers. 'There's only one reason anyone comes in here on a Wednesday night. Don't tell me you've been coming to pole-dancing lessons?'

Saffron felt herself turn beetroot.

'Well, well,' Maddy cackled raucously. 'I didn't know you had it in you!'

'Look, do me a favour,' said Saffron, hoping she didn't sound too grovelling. 'Please don't mention this to Gerry. Pete thinks I'm at an aerobics class, and I'd rather he didn't know.'

'Oh it's all right,' Maddy said with a smile. 'Gerry's the last person I'd tell anything at the moment. Your secret's safe with me.'

'Oh God, Amy, what am I going to do?' said Saffron dramatically, as she and Amy sorted out Linda's pots. The crisis of meeting Maddy had resulted in her confessing all to Amy. Once Amy had stopped hooting with laughter, she had been doing her best to reassure Saffron that all would be well. 'Pass me those petunias, would you, they'll go nicely here, next to this freesia.'

'You never know, Maddy might not tell Gerry,' said Amy, who was arranging marigolds and pansies in another pot.

'She did say he was the last person she'd tell, and Pete did see Gerry with Caroline in the pub the other day. I'm wondering if they've split up. But I can't risk it,' said Saffron. 'So it's better if I don't go at all. Oh well, it was fun while it lasted.'

'You could tell Pete,' said Amy. 'Wouldn't he find it funny?'

'I could,' said Saffron, 'but then I'd have to tell him I've been lying to him for the last three months. And that wouldn't be very funny at all.'

'Why didn't you just tell him to start with?'

'Why? Why? Why? That's what I keep asking myself,' said Saffron. 'What do you think, these pink busy lizzies, or some more purple petunias?'

'Petunias, definitely,' said Amy. 'And you haven't answered my question.'

'Well, to begin with, I was too embarrassed. Then after I'd finished the first course, I don't know, I got hooked. And after that I had this mad idea I'd work out a routine for him and surprise him on his birthday. And now, it's gone on so long I just don't know *how* to tell him. So I think it's probably better to draw a line under this episode and forget about it.'

'If you say so,' said Amy. 'But I still think you should tell him.'

'Anyway, listen to me wittering on,' said Saffron. 'How are things with you and Ben?'

'Good, I think,' said Amy. 'Well, they would be if I ever got to spend any time with him alone. If I go round there Caroline is always hanging about, and if he comes to me she'll suddenly turn up like a bad penny. It's making me a bit twitchy. Ben says it's all over between them, but she is living in his house, and she is very pretty.'

Saffron thought briefly about what Caroline had said to her. Should she tell Amy? But then again, Caroline had been spotted in the pub with Gerry. It was probably nonsense anyway. There was no need to upset Amy, not when things were going well for her at last.

'I'm sure Ben can see through that,' said Saffron. 'Anyway, Pete reckons she was all over Gerry in the pub on Monday.'

'Caroline and Gerry?' Amy fell about laughing. 'Oh dear, what is Maddy going to say about that?'

'I don't know and I don't care,' said Saffron.

'Talking of Maddy, did you get anything out of her about the phone calls?'

'To be honest, I was so embarrassed, all I could think of was to get out of there as fast as possible,' admitted Saffron. 'It didn't even cross my mind.'

'I tell you what, though.' Amy looked thoughtful. 'It might be quite handy that she works at Legends. Do you think Linda would be up for a spot of sleuthing?'

'I think Linda would think that was a hoot,' said Saffron, getting up. 'I'll go and ask her now.'

Linda seemed to find the idea of being an undercover agent hilarious.

'What do you want me to do, exactly?' she asked.

'I don't know really,' said Saffron. 'Just get friendly

with her, I suppose, and see if she lets slip anything useful.'

'It'll be a laugh, doll,' she said. 'I'll go into the bar after my Wednesday class and get chatting to her. See what I can find out.'

'That would be great,' said Saffron. 'I'm sure she's the one stirring up trouble. I can't think who else it would be.'

'You leave it with your Auntie Linda,' said Linda. 'Are you sure you're going to give up coming to my lessons? It seems a shame. You were just getting the hang of it.'

'I'm sure,' said Saffron. 'I'm so busy it's been quite hard fitting it in, anyway. It's probably better I stop now.'

'Oh well,' said Linda. 'If you ever want to come back, you know where I am.'

'I'll bear it in mind,' Saffron replied.

'Do you actually imagine you're going to catch anyone?' said Saffron dubiously as she packed Pete a flask of hot tea.

'Oh ye of little faith,' said Pete. 'You know I'm just dying to prove myself your hero.'

'You know you are anyway,' Saffron laughed.

Although there had been no further signs of entry, it had been decided to stake out Saffron's shed on Friday night. The weather had turned warmer, and there was a general consensus that it could be a laugh.

The Guys claimed to have some rockets left over

from Guy Fawkes Night, and were threatening to shoot them at whoever came near the place, but thankfully Ben and Pete had put the kibosh on that.

'So who else is going?' Saffron wanted to know. She had no intention of doing any staking-out herself – far too cold and muddy – but she was touched that people had rallied round.

'The Guys said they'd do the early stint, so they're there now, and then Harry said he'd do a turn. Bud and Bill are, and so's Ben.'

'So I really don't need to come,' said Saffron with relief.

'No need at all, fair wench,' said Pete with a grin, 'this is Man's Work.'

'Oh give over,' said Saffron, hitting him with a tea towel. 'You probably won't find anyone anyway.'

'Probably not,' said Pete, 'but you have to allow us boys to release our inner SAS man somehow.'

Saffron waved him down the path, laughing. Though she was still unnerved about the idea of someone camping in their shed, the thought of all the men she knew going all Ray Mears on her was highly amusing.

'Have you seen anything yet?' Pete crept up the path to the allotment opposite his and Saffron's, where the Guys were lying prostrate on the floor, peering through some night-vision binoculars.

'Nope, nothing,' said Keith. 'Here, you can have a look.'

'Nice kit,' said Pete as he focused on his shed. The Guys were right, there was nothing to see.

'Clive's got a mate in the army,' said Keith, 'and he asked if we wanted them.'

'Whatever do you need night-vision goggles for?' Pete asked. The Guys leered at each other, and started muttering about war games and pretending to be SAS soldiers. 'On second thoughts, I don't think I want to know.'

'Hello, old boy, any luck?' Harry popped up beside the hedge Pete was crouched behind.

'Not yet,' said Pete. 'I had no idea surveillance was so boring. Who'd be a policeman?'

'You should try standing guard on an ammunitions dump on a winter's night,' said Harry. 'This is nothing.'

'Point taken,' said Pete. 'Another beer, anyone?'

They all sat in silence for a while longer, jumping at every rustle and straining to see if there were any movements coming from the shed.

'This is turning into a right rave-up,' giggled Keith.

'Hardly,' said Ben, who'd followed behind Harry. He flopped down next to Pete.

'Do you fancy a beer? Saffron packed tons of supplies.'

'Beer sounds good to me,' said Ben, leaning back and staring at the shed. 'Do you honestly think we'll find your intruder?'

'Probably not,' said Pete, 'but it's a bit of a laugh, isn't it?'

'Not for us it isn't,' said Keith. 'Our butts are beginning to freeze off. We've done our bit, and now we're off to a party.'

'Well, thanks, guys, for coming,' said Pete.

'Don't mention it,' said Keith, giving Pete a leery look. 'Sure you don't want to join us? There'll be lots of hunky SAS types there.'

'No I do not,' said Pete. 'Off you go before you ruin my reputation.'

'That was the idea, darling, that was the idea.'

An hour later, everyone was getting restless. Apart from one false alarm when a fox knocked open the shed door, there was nothing to see.

Another half an hour elapsed, and still nothing had happened.

'If nothing happens in the next hour, I think we should call it a day,' said Pete.

A rustling in the bushes and muttering on the path got them momentarily interested, but it was only Bill and Bud come to relieve Harry, who'd announced he'd had enough.

'I'll come with you and fetch Amy so you can babysit,' said Ben.

Minutes later, as Ben and Amy walked down the path, they were both aware of the peculiar intimacy that darkness brings.

'I'm sorry things have been so difficult this week,' said Ben. 'Caroline's incredibly hard to shake off.'

'Well, so long as nothing's going on between you,' said Amy, only half joking.

'Amy, you know there isn't.' Ben was serious and grabbed her hand. 'The only woman I'm interested in is you.'

'You're sure?' Amy wanted to believe it, but despite Ben's protestations, she couldn't help the niggling little doubt that kept intruding into her thoughts.

'Absolutely,' said Ben, and stooped to kiss her. Then he paused.

'Shh!'

'What?'

'That.' There was a rustle in the bushes behind them.

Ben whispered, 'It might be our intruder. Let's get back to the others, and see if he follows us.'

They went swiftly up the path, and ducked in behind the bushes where the others were.

Ben pointed silently to the path behind them.

They sat still for a few moments, the tension unbearable. Then, when Amy was about to think they had got it wrong, there was some more rustling and some giggles coming from the bushes next to Saffron's shed.

'One, two, three, go!' Pete and Ben shot out from their hiding places and pounced into the bushes. There was a muffled shout of 'Oi, le'go!' and a moment of confusion when bodies, legs and feet seemed to be tripping over each other.

'What the –?' Ben stood up and burst out laughing. Then Pete did the same.

Emerging awkwardly from a passionate embrace were Caroline and Gerry.

CHAPTER TWENTY-THREE

'So what did they say?' Saffron wanted to know, when the vigilantes returned to base to report on proceedings. After discovering the illicit lovers, Operation Intruder was abandoned by mutual agreement. Any trespasser would be unlikely to come within a mile of the place now.

'They were totally brazen about it,' said Pete. 'At least Caroline was. Gerry looked a bit sheepish.'

'If he hasn't split up with Maddy, he's got good reason to be,' said Amy. 'I can't see that going down too well, can you?'

'True,' said Saffron, mentally relishing the picture of Gerry being hauled over the coals by his harpy of a girlfriend.

'Shame we didn't find your intruder,' said Ben, who was sitting down next to Amy. 'Do you want us to come back tomorrow?'

'Ooh, I'm not sure if I can take the excitement,' said Saffron. 'Perhaps we should wait and see if anything more happens. You lot came back like a pack of marauding elephants. I should think anyone planning to sleep in our shed again will have probably got the hint by now. I doubt very much whether they'll be back.'

'Shame,' said Bill. 'I haven't had so much fun in ages.'

'Sorry we didn't catch whoever it was,' said Amy. 'But it was worth it to see the look on Gerry's face when Ben sat on him.'

'Intruder or no intruder, I wouldn't have missed *that* for the world,' agreed Pete.

'So *now* do you believe me?' Ben wanted to know as he walked Amy home later that evening. They were holding hands tentatively. It was the first moment they'd had alone since the discovery of Caroline and Gerry in the bushes.

'Okay,' said Amy. 'I accept that nothing is going on between you and Caroline. But you can't blame me for being anxious. You weren't exactly straight with me about her. And she is very attractive.'

'I know, and I'm sorry about that,' said Ben. 'The relationship I had with Caroline could hardly have been described as deep. She wasn't here. I didn't think it was important.'

'Oh, right,' said Amy. 'Does that mean the next girl you go out with will get told that I'm not important too?'

They had reached Amy's garden gate. Ben grabbed her and pulled her close.

'I don't want there to be a next woman. I just want you. What I had with Caroline means nothing. You are more important to me than any other woman I've ever met. You have to believe me.'

'I want to.' Amy's reply was soft. 'But I'm scared. You're the first person I've had feelings for since Jamie. It's like a door opening up, and I have to choose whether to go through it or not.'

'Go through it, Amy,' Ben insisted.

'I'm not sure,' Amy replied, eyeing him warily. 'I might never be sure.'

'It's worth the risk,' urged Ben. 'I won't let you down.'

'I hope not,' said Amy, 'but I'm not ready for this yet.'

She kissed him swiftly on the cheek, and pulled away from him, rapidly walking up her garden path. Ben stood watching her go. He had been so sure they were getting closer. If it hadn't been for Caroline coming back, they would be much closer. Damn it. She always put a spanner in the works.

'So what's the verdict, old boy?' Harry was sitting in Ben's surgery the next morning. The results of his angiogram were back, and they didn't make for comfortable reading.

'I think you know the answer to that one,' said Ben. 'I'm sorry to have to tell you, Harry, but your arteries are not in great shape. You're going to have to start looking after yourself a bit better, otherwise you're running the risk of a serious heart attack.'

Harry looked decidedly grumpy. 'So I expect you're going to tell me to cut back on my drinking.'

'You know I am,' said Ben.

'Do you mean I can't even have the odd drop of whisky?' protested Harry. 'For medicinal purposes?'

'I think you'll find the medicinal properties of whisky tend to be negated in direct proportion to the quantities drunk,' said Ben. 'The odd drop is fine, but a bottle a day isn't.'

Harry pulled a face. 'Now that's a bit harsh, old boy. I don't think even I drink a whole bottle a day.'

'However much you drink,' continued Ben, 'it's too much. So you need to cut back. And it's not just the booze. You need to watch what you eat too. Which means no more fry-ups. I know how much you like them.'

Harry pulled another face.

'Well you're a barrel of laughs and no mistake,' he said. 'I won't have any pleasures left in life at this rate.'

'And cake,' added Ben. 'I know Edie and Ada keep you in supplies.'

'Now you're talking,' said Harry. 'At last I have a reason to refuse them. I can say it's for my health. Ben, old boy, maybe there are some benefits to this healthy-lifestyle malarkey after all.'

'Did you have any joy?' Saffron was round at Linda's again, having just spent a morning tying honeysuckles to trellises, and preparing a bed for Linda's sweet peas. Amy had taken a much-needed supply-teaching job for the day. Saffron felt terrible about it, although Amy had firmly told her not to be so daft. But it was becoming a real worry. Their supply of work was drying up rapidly. Without Linda, Mrs Meadows and Mrs Taylor they were in danger of having no business at all.

'Cup of tea, babe?' Linda asked as Saffron took off her boots and gingerly stepped over to the sink to wash her hands. She always felt so filthy dirty in this pristine, gleaming Nigella kind of kitchen, but Linda never seemed to mind.

'Sorry, doll, I didn't get a lot,' said Linda. 'I went into the bar on Wednesday and she wasn't there, but I did see her on Thursday. She wasn't very chatty, but said she had got the job because she needed the money.'

'I'm surprised about that,' said Saffron. 'Maddy's barely worked since Gerry's been with her. She spends all his income in nail bars and on beauty treatments.'

'Now that is one thing I have found out,' said Linda. 'They're not getting on at all well. She thinks he's cheating on her.'

'She's right about that,' said Saffron. 'Gerry seems to have taken up with Caroline. I'd love to be a fly on the wall when Maddy finds that out.'

'Amy, how nice to see you.' Caroline accosted Amy in the high street, where she was killing a bit of time between school finishing and Josh's football lesson starting by doing some shopping. She had a splitting headache from having taught a class of eight-year-olds that day. It was odd. She'd been working in schools for years before she started the gardening work, but now it seemed a hostile environment, dry and dusty; and she had yearned to be outside the whole day.

'Hi Caroline, how are you?' said Amy, wishing she were anywhere but here. Caroline was the last person she wanted to see.

'And this must be little Josh,' Caroline cooed, 'I've heard so much about you.'

'Oh,' said Josh, not at all impressed. 'Mummy, can I have a Spiderman comic, please?'

'Not today, sweetheart, we're in a bit of a rush,' said Amy, though it wasn't strictly true.

'I'm just off to buy Ben's dinner,' said Caroline. 'You know how he likes his curries. I thought I'd surprise him tonight.'

'That's nice,' she said between gritted teeth.

Caroline patted Amy on the arm. 'You don't mind me borrowing your boyfriend for a while, do you? Only I get so lonely without my Dave to keep me warm, and Ben and I go back *such* a long way.'

'He's not exactly my boyfriend,' said Amy, aware that Josh was right beside her. She hadn't yet plucked up the courage to talk to Josh about what was going on between her and Ben, mainly because she wasn't quite sure herself. One day her heart told her to do one thing; the next her head told her quite the opposite.

'Now, Amy.' Caroline suddenly took a big sisterly

314

tone. 'You mustn't let Ben do to you what he did to me. You must pin him down, and make sure he looks after you properly.'

'What do you mean?' Amy's voice didn't sound right to her.

'Oh, just that he never really knows what he wants. He was like that with me. One minute we were practically engaged, and the next he wasn't interested. And then when I came back, there he was again, wanting to start all over. I know I shouldn't have, but you know what he's like. He's pretty irresistible, isn't he?'

'Yes,' whispered Amy in horror. 'He is.'

Ben came in from work on Friday feeling thoroughly gloomy. He dumped his briefcase on the kitchen table and gave Meg a cuddle. Today had not been a good day. One of his elderly patients had died, and another, an eighty-year-old man with Alzheimer's, had just gone into a home to the distress of his older wife, who was riddled with arthritis and would find it difficult to get in to visit him. It had been Ben's turn to do the baby clinic, which, despite his enjoyment of the babies, always ended up giving him a headache. He had an ongoing, underlying anxiety about Harry, and for some reason Amy had been avoiding his calls all week. He was exhausted and just wanted to crash out.

'Ben, I'm so glad you're home.' Caroline swept in dramatically. 'I've had *such* an awful day.'

'Me too.' Ben's response was deliberately short and

terse, but Caroline didn't seem to notice.

'I can't get hold of Dave,' she wailed. 'Normally he rings me or emails me every day, but I haven't heard from him at all this week. His mobile isn't working, and there's an answer-phone message at his flat. Suppose something's happened to him?'

Ben refrained from saying that, considering Caroline had spent the best part of the last fortnight playing tonsil tennis with Gerry, it seemed a bit rich to think she actually cared what happened to Dave. Instead, he said, 'I expect he'll turn up.' He poured himself a can of lager, took off his tie and pointedly went into the lounge and collapsed on the sofa in front of the TV.

Caroline followed him.

'But what do you think I should do?' she asked. 'I'm really worried about him.'

'Caroline,' said Ben in exasperation. 'If you care so much, what are you doing with Gerry?'

'Gerry?' Caroline looked blank for a moment. 'Oh, I dumped Gerry. He was just a bit of fun.' She pouted. 'I was cheering myself up because you turned me down.'

Ben groaned. 'Caroline, don't start.' He switched off the television and made for the stairs. 'I'm going to get changed and then I'm going out,' he said.

'Where to?' Caroline demanded.

'Anywhere but here,' said Ben.

Half an hour later, Ben was knocking on Amy's door.

'Ben, hi.' Amy looked a bit flustered.

'Do you mind if I come in?' Ben asked.

'Of course I don't mind,' said Amy, who didn't appear all that pleased to see him.

'You've been ignoring my calls,' said Ben, as he sat down in the kitchen.

'Sorry,' said Amy. 'I know it sounds feeble, but I have been busy.'

'Too right it sounds feeble,' said Ben. 'So does that mean you were ignoring my calls, or that you really were too busy to answer them?'

'A bit of both,' said Amy. 'I'm sorry, Ben, I just needed some time to get my head round things. Caroline told me you were practically engaged and –'

'She said what?' yelled Ben.

Then, suddenly, there was a crash of some kind followed by muffled cursing. It was coming from the direction of the allotments.

'What was that?' Amy stood up and went to the kitchen window.

'Shit, do you think Saffron's intruder is back?'

'Wait there,' said Ben, opening the back door and grabbing a garden fork that was leaning against a wall.

'Don't be daft,' said Amy. 'There's safety in numbers. I'm coming too.'

A wild figure burst up the garden path. 'Ben, help me!' It was Caroline, looking unusually unkempt and sobbing hysterically. She threw her arms around Ben. 'I think someone's just been trying to break into your house. And I think they tried to follow me here. I've got a stalker!'

'What?' Ben replied. He let go of Caroline and

advanced slowly towards the garden gate, holding his fork aloft. Amy and Caroline followed behind him.

Amy's garden gate was swinging in the light summer breeze. There was a rustling sound, followed by a cough. Ben pulled back the gate, ready to pounce on the intruder.

A big burly bloke wearing a backpack stood by the garden gate.

'Hello mate,' he said in a distinctive Aussie accent. 'I'm looking for Caroline. I thought she came in here.'

Caroline looked at the man, in a state of shock. 'Dave,' she gasped. 'What are you doing here?'

CHAPTER TWENTY-FOUR

'This is Dave,' Caroline said rather unnecessarily.

'Well, this is a bonza welcome,' said Dave. 'Do your friends normally wave garden forks at people?'

'Sorry,' said Ben, 'case of mistaken identity. We were expecting an intruder, and thought you were them.'

'I was just coming to find Caroline,' said Dave. 'And now it seems I have.'

Caroline was looking shell-shocked. Amy almost felt sorry for her.

'You came,' Caroline whispered.

'Well I told you I would,' said Dave. 'We need to sort things out, Caz, once and for all.'

Ben coughed and looked at his feet.

'Preferably without an audience,' added Dave.

'Right, yes, of course.'

Ben coughed again, and held out his hand. 'I'm Ben,' he said. 'Caroline's staying with me.'

Dave disdained the proffered hand. 'Ah, the love rat,' he said coolly. 'Caroline's told me all about you.' He turned to look at Amy. 'I'd watch this one if I were you.'

Ben looked stunned and opened his mouth to say something, but Caroline forestalled him.

'Oh Dave, don't be such a gorilla. There's no need to be jealous of Ben any more, is there, Ben?' And, so saying, she leaned forward, putting a hand on Ben's chest and brushing his cheek with the slightest of kisses, leaving Ben looking even more stunned.

Amy stood there fuming. Had they all forgotten she was there?

'Amy, let's go back inside,' said Ben. 'I think these two have some catching up to do. Dave, you're welcome to crash at mine. Caroline's got keys. I'll see you both later.'

Amy followed Ben down the path, churning up inside. Why had Dave told her Ben was a love rat? And why did Caroline's simple kiss make her feel so jealous? Before Caroline's return Amy had begun to feel she was entrusting her heart to Ben more and more. She was on the threshold of something new, and as she'd said to Ben, she would need to decide either to go through the door that was opening up before her, or stay where she was. Earlier in the week she had been on the verge of telling Ben she was prepared to make a move, but since Caroline's revelations she didn't know where she stood with Ben any more.

Ben arrived home just after midnight. He had gone back to Amy's with a heavy heart. He had tried to laugh off Dave's comments about him being a love rat, but he could tell Amy didn't quite believe him. They had ended up spending a perfunctory evening in front of the telly watching Jonathan Ross, then he had left. And something Amy had said as he left made him feel even more lousy.

'Take care with my heart,' she whispered as she kissed him softly good night. 'It's still very fragile.'

'I know,' he'd whispered back, kissing her on the top of her head. 'I know.'

And it was that fragility that worried him. Caroline had caused him nothing but trouble since she'd got here. And he felt that Amy wasn't up to being a pawn in one of Caroline's games. Nor did he want her to be. If he wasn't careful, Caroline could ruin it all for him before it even started.

As he turned the key in the lock he was greeted by the sound of Caroline's sobbing.

Great. Just what he needed.

'Oh, Be-e-en,' she wailed. 'He's gone. I've lost him.'

'Who – Dave?' said Ben. 'Why, what happened?'

'Well, we came back here,' said Caroline. 'And at first it was fine. We had a bit of a kiss and a cuddle, and I thought maybe I was wrong to go. And then, just as things were getting interesting, he had to ruin it.'

'How?' Despite himself, Ben was intrigued.

'He only asked me to marry him,' said Caroline dramatically.

'But isn't that what you wanted?' Ben was perplexed. Despite her flirtation with Gerry, Caroline had spent the best part of the previous few weeks moaning about Dave, and now he was here she was pushing him away.

Women were a mystery to him, they really were.

'Nooo. Yesss. I don't know,' said Caroline. 'I do want him. But not all that marriage malarkey. It's way too much commitment. I mean, suppose he's not The One. Then what do I do?'

'Caroline,' Ben laughed, 'you can't go through life thinking that the next person you meet might be better than the one you're with. You have to make a choice sometime.'

'Yes, well,' Caroline looked at him, tears streaming down her face, 'we all know why I'm not good at commitment.' And Ben did know. It was the reason they had got together in the first place. Their common experience of early grief, forming a bond that Ben had mistaken for much more.

'Caroline,' he said gently, 'lots of people lose a parent when they're young. You can't use that as an excuse forever. And it's not as though you were so unhappy growing up, is it? I mean, you get on okay with your stepdad, don't you?'

'My dad left me,' Caroline practically howled. 'I was six years old, and he walked out one day and he never came back. He didn't leave a note. We never heard from him again. Why would he do that? How could he do that? And how can I ever trust a man again?'

Ben sat down next to her. 'Oh Caroline, because you have to. If you're to live your life well, you have to learn to trust again.' He put his arm around her, and gave her a hug. 'Come on, you're not usually like this. And this Dave bloke, well, he thinks enough of you to travel halfway round the world for you. I think that's worth risking your heart, don't you?'

Caroline looked at him, and for a moment he was back there with her, in the early days of their relationship. He gently wiped the tears from her eyes. When she was vulnerable like this, she made him care, even though he didn't want to.

'You know there's only one man I know worth risking my heart for.'

A look passed between them. Ben thought of Amy, lost and lonely on the other side of the allotments, waiting and wondering. She, too, thought it was worth risking her heart for him. How had he ended up in such a mess?

'I'm not,' said Ben. 'I'm sorry, whether she wants me or not, I'm in love with Amy. But Dave *does* love you. And I think, whatever you say, you love him too. Go to him. Give him a chance.'

'What chance can he have, when you're here?' Caroline persisted.

'Every chance,' said Ben, more firmly than he felt. 'You have to give him that chance. I think he deserves it, don't you?'

'So what's going on with Caroline and Dave now, do we know?' Saffron greeted Amy as they made their way down Mrs Wallace's path. Mrs Wallace was another of their few regulars left, and today they were pruning some of her bushes and tidying up her bedding plants.

'I have no idea,' said Amy. She looked miserable. 'I've barely seen Ben since Friday. And when I do he's distant and standoffish. I hate myself for doing it, but I can't stop thinking about the things Dave and Caroline said.'

'Oh I'm sure he's wrong,' said Saffron. 'He's just jealous of Ben, I expect. And you know what a flirt Caroline is. She's probably used Ben to wind Dave up.'

'I hope you're right,' said Amy. 'But he didn't tell me that he and Caroline had been together before she went away. Maybe he's been lying to me.'

'Amy, I'm sure he hasn't,' said Saffron. 'Maybe he just didn't know how to tell you.' She tried and failed to suppress the thought that perhaps Amy was right. Although she knew Ben was decent and honourable, he and Caroline did have history. And he wouldn't be the first to get swept away by Caroline's charms. Saffron shook her head: there was no point even thinking this, and certainly no point telling Amy.

Mrs Wallace came down the path to greet them.

'I wasn't expecting you today,' she said, looking puzzled.

Amy and Saffron looked at each other in alarm. Not again.

'Sorry,' said Saffron, wondering if she'd made a mistake, but knowing she hadn't, 'I had you down in my diary for today, have I made a mistake?'

'Oh, no,' said Mrs Wallace, 'it was right. But that nice lady from your office popped round, and said that you wouldn't be coming today after all.'

'*What* nice lady?' Saffron's hackles were up.

'The fair-haired one.' Mrs Wallace peered shortsightedly at Amy. 'Not your friend here, the other one.'

'Let me guess,' said Saffron grimly, 'she was about five foot four, rather well endowed, done up to the nines, with platinum-blonde hair, blue eyes, too much foundation and sharply polished nails?'

'Yes, that's her,' said Mrs Wallace. 'She apologised profusely and said you'd ring me.'

'I bet she did,' muttered Saffron to Amy. 'Well at least I've got my proof. It has to be Maddy badmouthing us. The description fits her to a T.'

'What are you going to do?'

'Don't know yet,' said Saffron, 'but for now I think we need to reclaim our client, don't you?'

Turning back to Mrs Wallace, she said, 'I'm so sorry, I think there's been a mistake. My colleague can be a bit enthusiastic sometimes. She must have got her dates muddled. It's next week we can't make. But as we're here, we might as well do something, mightn't we?'

'Right,' said Saffron as they drove away from Mrs Wallace's house a couple of hours later, 'how about a spot of Maddy-bashing? We've still got time before the school run.'

'You're not going to do anything stupid, are you?' Amy suddenly had visions of a girly cat fight in the street, and herself, Saffron and Maddy all behind bars.

'No, of course not,' said Saffron, 'but we *are* going to pay her a little visit, to find out just exactly what she's up to.'

'Won't she be at work?'

Saffron snorted. 'Work? You have to be joking. Someone like Maddy only exists to take men for a ride. In this case the lucky chap happens to be Gerry, so I don't feel too sorry for him. He works his rocks off, while she stays at home playing the trophy wife, and being a lady who lunches.' Saffron frowned. 'Well at least she used to. I have no idea what she's doing working behind a bar. Still, I don't expect she has to work *too* hard for her living.'

'Nice life if you can have it,' said Amy. Then she looked at Saffron and grinned, 'Nah, I think I'd be bored witless.'

'Me too,' said Saffron laughing. 'Ah, here we are.'

She pulled into a road where scores of brand-new executive houses, all looking like they'd come out of a real-estate magazine, were crammed together in the smallest space possible. But they were all detached, which no doubt made them highly desirable.

'Blimey, their gardens must be the size of handker-chiefs,' said Amy. 'We wouldn't get much work around here.'

'Oh, I don't know,' said Saffron, 'they might need help with their flower arranging.'

She drove up to a house that was exactly like the rest, except that it looked so sparkly and neat it was more like a show house than a real home.

Saffron got out of the car and marched to the front door, which she banged on vigorously.

There was a slight pause before the door was opened, and Maddy stood nonchalantly before them.

326

'He's not here,' she said, and started to close the door. 'As *you* should know.'

'It's not Gerry I'm looking for,' said Saffron, expertly putting her foot in the doorway and preventing Maddy from shutting the door. 'It's you.'

'Oh?'

'Come on, Maddy, I think you know why I'm here,' said Saffron.

'No, not really,' drawled Maddy, examining her nails with some enthusiasm.

'Well, let me enlighten you. Do the names Mrs Wallace, Mrs Matthews, Mr Price . . .' Saffron reeled off a list of their clients '. . . mean anything to you?'

'Can't say they do,' said Maddy.

'Well, that's funny,' said Saffron, 'because they all know you.'

For a moment Maddy's calm exterior was slightly ruffled.

'They do?'

'Yup,' said Saffron. 'Because you've been ringing them and either cancelling jobs on us, or you've been badmouthing us. And it's got to stop.'

'You've got no proof it was me,' Maddy said with supreme confidence.

'Oh yes we do,' said Amy, stepping out from behind Saffron. 'Mrs Wallace gave us a perfect description of you.'

'Besides,' said Saffron, clutching a sheaf of paper she had taken out of her bag, 'we have evidence of your mobile phone having been used to make the calls.'

The colour drained from Maddy's face.

'So what if it's me,' she blustered. 'What are you going to do about it?'

'Sue you for loss of earnings,' said Saffron promptly.

'You wouldn't,' said Maddy.

'Just try me,' said Saffron. 'I'd built up a nice business over the last couple of years, and in the last few months you've done your best to ruin it. You bet your life I'm going to sue. So you'd better get Gerry to get out his chequebook sharpish.'

'He's not here,' said Maddy, a look of panic crossing her face.

'So you said,' said Saffron. 'Luckily it's not Gerry we're interested in.' She smiled sweetly at Maddy, who was beginning to resemble a fish very much out of water, she was opening and shutting her mouth so often.

'But – you can't sue me,' said Maddy. 'I don't own anything.'

'You own this,' said Saffron.

'It's Gerry's.' The look of panic on Maddy's face nearly made Saffron feel sorry for her. Nearly, but not quite.

'So you're going to stop making nuisance phone calls and ring up all these people and say that you've made a terrible mistake, aren't you?'

Maddy looked truculent, as Saffron held out a list of all their clients.

'Why should I, when you've been sleeping with my boyfriend?'

'Maddy, I haven't been near your boyfriend,' said Saffron. 'I wouldn't touch him with a bargepole. So are you going to make these calls?'

'And if I don't?'

'Well, we'll just have to send those photos of you that Mrs Wallace took to the Serious Fraud Squad,' said Amy, 'and let them take it from there.'

Maddy gulped.

'All right,' she said sulkily, taking Saffron's list, 'I'll do it.'

'Good girl,' said Saffron, 'you know it makes sense.'

And she and Amy left, wiping tears from their eyes.

They were still laughing as they drove home.

'Photos? What photos?' Saffron said. 'I nearly died when you said that.'

'I was on a roll,' admitted Amy. 'It just sort of came out. But what about your list of numbers called from her mobile? Where did you get that from?'

'It's my phone bill,' giggled Saffron. 'I was going to pay it today and forgot. Did you see the look on her face? It was priceless.'

'It was,' agreed Amy. 'Thanks for the laugh, I needed that today.'

The route back from Maddy's house wasn't one they normally took, and they found themselves driving past a local motel. There were several cars parked in the forecourt. And one motorbike.

'Hang on a minute,' said Amy, with a sudden lurch of anxiety, 'isn't that Ben's bike?'

Saffron slowed down. 'Don't be silly,' she said, 'what would Ben be doing out here –?' She broke off. Caroline and Ben were walking out of the motel, both carrying crash helmets and talking very intimately. They paused as they reached the bike, and Ben gave Caroline a hug. And a kiss.

Amy went white.

'Maybe there's a rational explanation,' began Saffron.

'Like what?' asked Amy. 'We both know what we saw.'

Saffron had to acknowledge the truth of what Amy was saying.

'So what are you going to do about it?'

'I don't know,' said Amy, as the motorbike roared off. 'But follow that bike and let's find out.'

CHAPTER TWENTY-FIVE

Ben drew up outside his house. Caroline got off the back of his bike, took her helmet off, and shook out her hair.

'Thanks for that,' she drawled.

'Sorry it wasn't much help,' Ben said. 'Look, I've really got to get back now. Will you be okay?'

'I'm a big girl, Ben,' Caroline said, 'I'll be fine. Go on, off you go.'

She pecked him on the cheek, and he roared off.

At that moment a car raced up the road, and came to a sudden stop outside Ben's house. Saffron and a very angry-looking Amy got out.

'Where is he?' Amy demanded.

'Who?' Caroline did her best to look puzzled.

'Father Christmas!' snapped Amy. 'Ben, of course.'

'He's just gone back to work,' said Caroline. 'Why? Did you want him?'

'Oh.' Amy was slightly deflated. She'd been all set for a row with Ben and he wasn't there. 'When will he be back?'

'I'm not sure,' said Caroline, 'I know he was planning a late surgery.'

'Where's your Australian boyfriend?'

'I have no idea,' said Caroline. 'We had a row.'

'I'm sorry,' said Amy, not meaning it.

'That's all right,' said Caroline with a little tinkly laugh. 'Ben's been taking care of me.'

Amy felt the bile rising in her throat. 'What do you mean?'

'Well let's just say we've been renewing our acquaintance.'

Amy wanted the ground to swallow her up. 'What about me?' she whispered. 'I thought he cared about me.'

Caroline smiled the sweet gracious smile of the victor. 'Well I'm sure he didn't mean to upset you, but Ben made a mistake about me – and it's taken a while, but now he's realised it. And so should you. Shall I tell him you called?'

'Yes,' said Amy, 'and you can tell him I never want to see him again. You're welcome to him.'

Ben came in absolutely shattered. It had been a mad idea to take two hours off at lunchtime to help Caroline look for Dave. For all Ben knew, Dave was back in America already, but somehow he doubted it. He'd come all the way over from California to find her. Ben had a hunch that Dave wasn't going to give up without a fight, and he certainly hoped so. Though he felt sorry for

Caroline, he was also fed up with having her in the house, and fed up that she kept getting in the way of him and Amy. He was conscious that things were a little tense with Amy now. If he weren't feeling so knackered he'd go round tonight, but he could do with an early night. The previous weekend had been largely spent sitting up till 2 a.m. listening to Caroline's woes. Although there had been a fair amount about his woes too. Caroline was the only person he had ever told about Sarah, and he had forgotten how good it was to sit and discuss it with someone. Usually he kept his pain so well hidden away, no one would even know it was there. But Caroline had probed that particular vulnerable spot and he had confided in her more than he had ever confided in anyone else. It meant that there was still a connection between them, despite his feelings for Amy. He just hoped he could make Amy understand that.

He walked through the door to the smell of curry. Candles were lit, the lights were on low, and the table was set for two. Presumably Caroline had found Dave and was preparing to make it up to him. Ben sighed; that meant either an early night curled up listening to Mark Radcliffe, or going over to Amy's where he was uncertain of the reception he was going to get.

'I'll get out of your hair, shall I?' Ben said, as Caroline came out of the kitchen door. He had to admit she looked ravishing. Her hair was piled up high on her head, and loose curls trickled down her neck. She was wearing a strappy yellow summer dress, and silver high-heeled sandals. She looked gorgeous. She was holding a glass of wine and proffered one.

'Where are you going, silly?' she said. 'This is for you, by way of saying thank you. I know how you like your curry.'

'Actually, Caroline,' said Ben, pushing the glass away, 'I've never liked curry. It was one of the many things that wasn't right about our relationship, that you liked curry and I didn't.'

'Oh,' said Caroline, pouting, 'I thought it was your favourite.'

'Well, you thought wrong,' said Ben. 'Look, it's not that I'm ungrateful, but all of this – you shouldn't have –'

'Oh but I should,' she positively purred at him.

'What about Dave?'

'What about him?' Caroline looked slightly annoyed.

'Well, considering I spent the best part of my lunchtime today driving you around to look for him, I was rather assuming this was all for his benefit. I don't quite know what you're playing at, but I don't want to be part of it, all right?'

Just then the doorbell rang. Ben went to answer it. Dave was standing on the doorstep, with a bunch of flowers.

'Is Caz in?'

'Yes, come in,' said Ben with great relief.

'Caroline,' said Dave, 'I don't know what you're up to with your silly games to try and make me jealous. But let's get one thing straight here. I love you, despite all that crap, and I want to live with you for the rest of our lives. But if you don't want me, then I am going back to California tomorrow, with or without you. I

334

am not going to say it again. You have to choose between me and the love rat here. But after tomorrow there won't be a choice. The flight's at 12.30 p.m., from Terminal Three. That's all I have to say.'

He turned and left the house, leaving Caroline and Ben stunned.

'So, Caroline,' said Ben, 'now what are you going to do?'

'Are you all right, Amy?' Harry looked concerned as he came through her front door, bearing elderberry wine.

Amy smiled a pale smile. She knew she was looking wiped. After she and Saffron had demolished all the chocolate in her cupboard, and dissected every detail of Ben's actions, they had realised they were late for the school pickup. Amy had then rushed off to get Josh to his swimming lesson, and not being able to face either cooking or coming home, she had taken him to McDonald's. Josh seemed to sense her tension and had been so naughty she had opted to takeaway rather than eat in. Trying to keep up a cheerful outlook in front of a five-year-old who was playing up had been hard work, but luckily, she thought grimly to herself, she had had plenty of practice.

It was only once Josh was settled into bed that she had given full vent to her frustrations. Ben was two-timing her with Caroline, that much seemed perfectly clear. She supposed it was inevitable that his old feelings for Caroline should have resurfaced, given how she still felt about Jamie. What if the tables were reversed and Jamie were to walk through that door now? Could she choose between them?

Angrily she wiped away a tear. That was never going to happen, so the question was irrelevant. Ben hadn't lost Caroline in the way she had lost Jamie, he had rejected her. But now it looked like he was welcoming her back. And there was precious little that Amy could do about it . . .

'I'm not very good company tonight, Harry,' Amy said, as she followed him into the lounge.

'And why is that?'

'Oh Harry,' Amy burst out, 'I'm so miserable,' and she told him the whole story.

'But you don't actually know if they were staying in the motel, do you?' Harry pointed out.

'That's what Saffron said,' admitted Amy. 'But why else would they be there?'

'Who knows,' said Harry, 'but if they'd wanted to be at it, they've had plenty of opportunity. They've been living in the same house for weeks.'

'That is true, I suppose,' said Amy. 'I just can't see why they were there. It looked odd. And he did hug her.'

'Ben's a chivalrous chap,' said Harry. 'Perhaps she was upset?'

'Perhaps,' said Amy. 'It's just that – oh, I don't know, I feel such a fool. For so long I thought I couldn't find anyone to replace Jamie, and then I met Ben, and felt maybe I could. But it doesn't matter how much I want it to be right, it just feels like it's all going wrong. I've been through so much, I can't take any more.'

She looked up at Harry, the tears in her eyes half-formed. 'Does that make any kind of sense to you?'

'Oh, yes, my dear, oh yes, it does,' Harry said. 'I could never have replaced Mavis because Mavis was my everything, and I'm too old to start again. But you, you're young and you shouldn't be alone. Ben won't let you down, I'm sure of that.' He patted her on the arm. 'Why don't you go and see him tomorrow? I'm sure it's a misunderstanding, and you'll clear it up in no time.'

'You're probably right,' said Amy.

'I usually am,' Harry replied. 'Now, are we going to have a drop of this wine or not?'

Ben breathed a sigh of relief as he came down to find Caroline's suitcases in the hall. Thank God for that. He had made it as clear as he possibly could that there was no future here with him. 'But that's no reason to go running after Dave if you don't love him,' he had also warned Caroline.

'Actually,' Caroline had the grace to look a little shamefaced, 'I think I do love him. I just wasn't sure he loved me. Everything's so fickle when you're travelling. And then he started to get serious and I got cold feet, so I bolted –'

'And came back here?' guessed Ben.

'Sorry, I didn't know where else to come,' said Caroline. 'I'm sorry if I've stuffed up things for you and Amy.'

'Well, I hope it's salvageable,' said Ben, 'just so long as you get on that damned plane.'

'Oh I will, I will,' said Caroline. 'It was hearing Dave say all that stuff last night about how he wanted to spend the rest of his life with me. No one's ever said that sort of thing to me before, not even you.'

'Good, keep hold of him,' said Ben. 'I'll run you to the station if you like.'

'No, I think you've done enough,' Caroline replied.

So now she was finally off. Ben breathed a sigh of relief. He cast a look across the allotments towards Amy's house. Would she still be waiting? He could only try and find out.

The doorbell rang. That would be the taxi. He started to take Caroline's bags outside. The sooner he helped her, the sooner she was gone . . .

Amy made her way back from dropping Josh off at school, feeling very nervous. After a sleepless night, she had decided the only thing she could do was to confront Ben with what she had seen. Maybe Harry was right and there was some other explanation. At the very least, she owed it to Ben to find out.

So, heart pounding away, and feeling sick as a parrot, she made her way to Ben's house. She knew he'd be in as he didn't have a surgery on Wednesday mornings.

As Amy approached his house, she saw two things. A taxi was waiting, engine running, and two people were standing outside talking to one another. Ben and Caroline.

Her heart leapt. Was Caroline leaving? She hurried down the road determined to find out more. She was about to call out gladly to Ben, who hadn't seen her, when Caroline threw her arms around Ben and kissed him full on the lips.

'Thanks for everything, Ben,' she gushed. 'I love you.'

She got in the cab and blew kisses at him as she drove away.

Ben turned to see Amy standing behind him.

Amy couldn't believe the barefaced cheek of him.

'It's all right,' she managed to say, 'I'm not going to make a scene. I had given you the benefit of the doubt, but I saw everything, Ben. Dave was right, you are a love rat.'

'You've got it all wrong –' Ben began.

'Don't try to deny it,' said Amy bitterly. 'I'm not an idiot. Finally, I've got it right. I was wrong to trust you. And I was wrong to let myself fall in love with you. I should have stayed with my memories of Jamie, they can't hurt me any more than you have.'

'But Amy –'

'I don't want to hear it,' she said. 'In fact, I never want to see you, ever again.'

She turned and fled, leaving Ben open-mouthed behind her.

CHAPTER TWENTY-SIX

'Amy, my dear, how would you and Josh fancy a little holiday?'

Amy sat at the kitchen table, phone in one hand, fiddling awkwardly with her hair as she stared out of the window. Mary sounded horribly cheerful. It was a glorious summer day, but she had never felt less sunny in her life. She hadn't seen Ben for weeks, and it felt like all the light had gone out of her heart.

'That would be lovely,' Amy said, with more enthusiasm than she felt. She couldn't care less about a holiday, not now. But Josh could do with getting away. And he would be happy to see Mary again. Besides, he kept complaining that they hadn't seen Ben for ages, and she was finding it difficult to come up with any more excuses. Telling him they were going on holiday with Granny would be a welcome distraction.

'Wonderful,' said Mary. 'Menorca is meant to be good for young families, how does that sound?'

Thinking that anywhere would be better than staying

in Nevermorewell for the summer, Amy said, 'Menorca sounds great. I'll look forward to it.'

'When does Josh break up from school?'

'I don't know,' said Amy, 'I'll just check.'

She stood up and walked to her noticeboard, flicking through bits of paper about swimming, football, Beavers. Crikey! How did one child generate so much paperwork? As she did so, a leaflet dropped to the floor. It was for Framlingham Castle. Ben had given it to her weeks ago; knowing she liked visiting castles, he had promised to take her and Josh for the day. Amy's heart contracted a little. That would never happen now. Damn Ben for making her feel like this. And Caroline for ruining everything. She picked up the leaflet and stared hard at it before turning back to searching for Josh's holiday dates. Aah, there they were.

'He finishes on the twenty-third of July,' said Amy. 'I wouldn't want to go the minute school ends, but any time from the following week will be fine.'

'Brilliant,' said Mary, 'I'll book something and ring you back with the dates.'

'I'll look forward to it,' Amy told her. She put the phone down and sighed. Then she picked up the leaflet for the castle again, scrumpled it up and put it in the bin.

'I think our intruder's back,' said Saffron.

'Why?' Pete looked up distracted from his laptop as Saffron came marching in from the garden. She was grimy, soaking wet, and covered in mud – a result of a sudden and unexpected summer shower.

'Just the usual – there were chip papers in the shed again, and it looks as though somebody has been making a bed out of our potato sacks.'

'Well, whoever it is, they haven't done us any harm, have they?'

'No, I suppose not,' said Saffron. 'It just makes me feel uneasy, that's all.'

They hadn't seen hide nor hair of their intruder for weeks, and Saffron had convinced herself that it had been a tramp who'd gone on to pastures new, but now she wasn't so sure. She had also discounted Scary Slug Man in the end, as he had apparently been spotted in his local with a new woman whom he had shacked up with. It had seemed unlikely at first, but several people had told her it was true, so she had reluctantly crossed him off her list of suspects.

'I wish you weren't going away next week,' she moaned.

'Me too,' said Pete, 'but we both knew it would be like this with my promotion. And you have to admit, the extra money is nice.'

Saffron wandered off upstairs to clean herself up. She hoped Pete was right about their intruder. As she pulled the curtains in their bedroom, she looked out across the allotments. Usually they felt like a haven to her, and the thought of anyone doing anything to harm her was almost laughable. But since their mysterious visitor had been on the scene, she hadn't felt quite so sanguine.

She wished that at least they had uncovered the identity of their unwelcome guest by now. Maybe she should get Amy to come and crash out while Pete wasn't there. Amy was still moping about after Ben, maybe she could use the break from her usual routine.

'What are you, woman or mouse?' she chided herself, drawing the curtains firmly together. The intruder on the allotments was probably nobody, and certainly shouldn't be causing her sleepless nights. Pete was right, whoever it was hadn't hurt them so far, so why should that change now?

Ben pushed his barrow, replete with plastic cans full of water, onto the allotments, sweating profusely. It was only ten o'clock but already it was baking hot, heralding more sun to come. With a hosepipe ban already in force, the allotmenteers were having to become more and more resourceful about how they collected their rainwater. Ben had several waterbutts on his allotment, and a couple in the garden. He was thinking of copying Harry's intricate system, which involved pitching several waterbutts at different levels, flowing on one from the other. Ben laughed at himself. If this water shortage went on any longer he was going to become completely obsessed. As it was, he had a couple of empty plastic petrol cans, which held several litres, and had taken to filling them up and staggering out onto the allotments with them. But it was hard work. He stopped and wiped his head for a minute.

Though the recent rain had filled the waterbutts up again, the ground was so damned dry that as soon as some sunshine got on it all the water evaporated. But he couldn't risk leaving his precious water there without using it, because people were becoming very sneaky, and it had been known for the less scrupulous allotmenteers to do water raids. The situation was getting ridiculous. Added to which, according to Harry, who was there most days, there were people who were defying the ban, and coming along in the middle of the day to use their sprinklers. Harry had nearly come to blows with Scary Slug Man, who kept filling waterbutts up with his hose in order to drown a family of slugs who had attacked his cabbages.

Harry. Ben frowned. The last couple of times Ben had seen him, Harry had seemed a little forgetful, and he was certainly getting shorter of breath of late. And Ben was certain he was getting TIAs. But Harry refused point blank to get himself checked out again, and short of dragging him into the surgery Ben didn't know quite what else to do. Besides, as Harry had put it to him frequently, 'What are you going to tell me that I don't already know?' Which, Ben had to admit, was probably true.

He half-hoped that Harry wasn't out on the allotments. It would give Ben the excuse of checking he was all right, and maybe, just maybe, he would run into Amy. There was no sign of her here, although the stuff they had planted together was looking well-tended, so she must be coming out at times she knew he wouldn't be there.

Ben hadn't spoken to Amy in weeks. He had tried at the beginning, but Amy had rebuffed him at every turn. So he had given up in despair. There was no point persisting in knocking at a door that was permanently shut. Damn, bloody Caroline. If she hadn't come back when she had, he and Amy might have been together by now.

'Penny for them?' Harry wandered over from his allotment with a bag of produce. 'I seem to have had a run on courgettes, do you fancy some?'

'I'll swap you them for my lettuce. It's about to go to seed at any minute. Seems a shame to waste it.'

'Fancy a drink?'

'A bit early, isn't it, Harry? Even for you?' Ben laughed.

'I meant a brew,' said Harry. 'It's a bit hot for me out here today, so I got here early and was about to pack up.'

'Oh, go on then,' said Ben, grateful to have an opportunity to rest for moment.

Harry had flung the doors of his hut open, and his two easy chairs were sitting outside it. He made the tea and brought it out to Ben.

'This is the life,' said Ben. 'I shouldn't have sat down. I probably won't be able to get up again.'

'What, at your age? You should be raring to go,' Harry told him. 'Leave it to us old boys to sit in the sun.'

'You're not so old,' said Ben.

'You know I am,' Harry replied. 'And, to be honest, I'm getting pretty tired of all this.'

Ben shifted uneasily in his seat. He sometimes had

these kinds of conversations with his patients, but it didn't feel right having it with Harry.

'Don't be daft,' he said. 'You've got years left on the clock.'

'Ben, you and I both know that's not true. As Terry Wogan likes to put it, I've only got so many beats left in this old ticker, and I can't go on forever. But the thing is – well, to put it bluntly, old boy, I haven't got anyone much to leave what little worldly wealth I have. But I'd really like you to take over my allotment, if they'll let you. I know you'd look after it. Keep it nice in memory of me and Mavis.'

'But –'

'But nothing.'

'Harry, I wasn't expecting –'

'I know you weren't. But can you promise me something?'

'Of course,' said Ben, 'anything.'

'You will look after her, won't you?' Harry nodded towards Amy's house. 'She needs you more than she realises. And she shouldn't be alone.'

'I would if she'd let me,' said Ben.

'She'll come round, my boy,' said Harry, 'you see if she doesn't. You two are meant to be together. In fact I would stake my life on it.'

'You don't want to go doing that,' joked Ben, 'you don't know where it will lead. Thanks for the tea, but I really had better get on.'

He made his way back to his own allotment. Life here without Harry didn't bear thinking about. He glanced over at Amy's house again. He wondered if she had any idea how little time Harry might have left. It was going to break her heart if Harry died. He just hoped that when it happened she'd let him pick up the pieces.

Saffron settled down with a well-deserved glass of wine. The children were in bed, thankfully – as usual when Pete was away, they were playing up more than normal. This hadn't been helped by the fact that they had seen even less of Gerry of late. Since the debacle with Maddy, Saffron had found Gerry to be incredibly elusive. He would turn up intermittently to take the children out, very often at times they hadn't agreed, or, worse still, forget all about arrangements he had made, and letting them down. She had tried to confront him with this on one or two occasions, but he wasn't to be pinned down and she had given up. Reluctant to tell the children that their dad was a useless waste of space (there was plenty of time for them to work that out when they were older) she had simply stopped bothering to ring him. Had it been anyone but Gerry, she might have been worried about him – on the few occasions she had seen him recently he'd had a wild, slightly unkempt look, most un-Gerry-like. If she had cared she might have concluded that since the Caroline debacle, he and the bimbo were on the way out. But she didn't care, not really. Not now she had Pete. She would be so glad when he got home.

Suddenly her peace was disturbed by a loud crash outside.

'Shit!' Saffron spluttered. 'What was that?'

She ran to the back door, leaving the lights off, and stared down the garden, where the security light was beaming brightly onto a figure who lay groaning on the floor underneath one of her patio pots.

Grabbing the shillelagh again, Saffron flung open the back door. 'Stay right where you are!' she said. 'I'm calling the police.'

'Don't, please don't,' the figure replied.

'Oh bugger.' Saffron put the shillelagh down and stared at the sheepish form beneath her. 'Gerry, just what the hell do you think you're doing?' she said.

CHAPTER TWENTY-SEVEN

'I can explain everything,' said Gerry.

'You'd better come in,' Saffron told him, thinking it was the last thing she wanted, but Gerry had a nasty graze on his leg from where the pot had broken and a piece had scraped it.

'Sit down,' she said, 'I'll get something to patch up the war wound.'

Ten minutes later, Saffron found herself in the bizarre position of kneeling at her ex-husband's feet while she cleaned up what turned out to be a surface scratch. Although he was wearing a suit, he had no tie, and looked, well – grubby. He also appeared to have been drinking.

'So, are you going to tell me what's going on?'

'Erm, well, I don't – hmph, it's, well, erm –' Gerry managed to look both abashed and brazen at the same time.

'Come on, Gerry, spit it out,' said Saffron. 'It's not like you to go all shy and retiring on me.'

'ThethingisyouseewellitsMaddythebitchandthe-businessisintroubleandIvenowheretogoand –'

'Woah, slow down, I missed most of that – what about Maddy?'

'The thing is . . .' Gerry paused for dramatic effect, and Saffron smelt the alcohol on his breath. 'She's kicked me out.'

'Well, if you will go round two-timing people, what do you expect?' Saffron was impatient with Gerry, but nonetheless staggered. Gerry never got dumped. He always did the dumping. It was a rare bimbo who got one over him. What with the business sabotage as well, Saffron's estimation of Maddy rose a few notches. She turned on the kettle. 'I think you could use a coffee,' she said. 'So Maddy's ditched you?'

'Yes, and now I have nowhere to stay, and the business is suffering, and I think I might be about to go under.'

Saffron, who had been trying to repress her giggles at the pathetic figure before her, stopped short.

'What? Really under?'

'Yes,' said Gerry. His usual swagger had disappeared and for the first time he looked genuinely vulnerable. 'It started when I lost a couple of big clients. I had been relying on their money, and bought some new stock upfront. I made a mistake, the stock hasn't shifted, and now I owe thousands to my creditors.'

Saffron felt seriously alarmed now. Unreliable father he might be, but Gerry had always been good at paying maintenance. Even though Pete's job was paying better now, every penny they had was accounted for. Losing Gerry's money for the children would make a big hole.

She tuned back in to Gerry and suddenly realised what he was saying.

'– so I've nowhere to live, it looks like my business is down the pan, we're going to lose the house, even if Maddy has me back.'

'Gerry,' said Saffron, 'where did you say you'd been staying?'

'I didn't.' A slightly panicked look crossed his face.

'You sneaky bugger! You've been staying in our shed.'

'It's only temporary,' pleaded Gerry, 'till I sort myself out.'

'Why can't you go to a hotel like normal people?'

'I didn't want anyone to know she'd chucked me out,' said Gerry. 'And several of the sales reps I deal with stay in the motel in town.'

'What about friends?' Saffron looked at him and shook her head. 'No, I forgot. You don't do friends, do you? You simply have business acquaintances.'

'I'm sorry, Saffron.' Gerry did seem genuinely apologetic. 'I tried not to make a mess. And it's probably temporary. She'll probably let me back home again in time.'

'What? This has happened before?' Comprehension dawned on Saffron. That was presumably why the intruder had disappeared for a few weeks. Gerry had just gone home. 'So go on then, go and make it up to her.'

'I'm not sure that it will be so easy,' Gerry said.

'Look, Gerry, I know you find them hard to say but most women respond pretty well to two little words, "I'm sorry", and a bunch of flowers. It's worth a shot, isn't it? You can't carry on like this.'

'The trouble is,' said Gerry, 'she's jealous.'

'Well, you should have learned by now to behave yourself,' said Saffron, who was getting irritated now. 'You should have left Caroline well alone.'

'Oh, it's not Caroline,' said Gerry.

'Who then?'

'The thing is, Saffron, Maddy's incredibly jealous of you.'

Ben paused as he walked up Harry's path. He had come to return some cutters he'd borrowed earlier. Strictly speaking, he didn't need to bring them back tonight, but he knew that Amy was going away soon, and he half-hoped that this way he could run into her by accident.

Harry wasn't in, and in the semi-twilight Amy's house looked forbidding. Or maybe that was just his imagination – it appeared forbidding because he wasn't sure of the welcome he was going to get.

Just then her door opened, and there she stood on the doorstep, framed against the light, two empty milk bottles in hand, looking as lovely as she had ever looked.

'Oh.' Amy gripped the milk bottles tightly. 'I was just taking the milk bottles out,' she said.

'I was just taking Harry's cutters back,' Ben told her, waving them about, as if that made his story stand up more.

'So I see,' said Amy. 'Harry's out.'

'Yes,' said Ben. Every fibre of his being was screaming

at him to take her into his arms and sod the consequences, but Amy just stood there, not moving, not giving him any sign.

'Well I'll be off then,' said Ben.

'Okay.'

'Harry tells me you're going away,' said Ben.

'Yes.'

Ben paused. 'Have a nice holiday,' he said.

'I will,' Amy replied.

'I'll be away myself when you get back,' he told her.

'Oh,' she said, interested despite herself. 'How long for?'

'A couple of weeks.'

A whole month. It would be a whole month before he saw her again.

'Are you going anywhere nice?' asked Amy.

'I'm going on a walking holiday in France with some university mates,' he said. 'And you?'

'Menorca,' said Amy. 'With Mary.'

'That will be nice.'

'Yes.'

'Well. Bye then,' Ben said, unwilling to leave.

'Bye.'

He lingered a moment. Then, unable to bear it any longer, he said, 'Amy, we can't go on like this. *I* can't go on like this. Please, if there's going to be nothing between us, can we at least be friends?'

'Is there nothing between us?' Amy's voice came out in a whisper.

'You tell me,' said Ben, and looked at her. 'Not if you don't want there to be.'

'Ben, if I knew what I wanted, life would be so much simpler,' said Amy. 'But I don't know if I can trust you. And if I can't trust you, I can't risk being hurt. I've been through too much, and so has Josh.'

'Don't use Josh as an excuse,' said Ben. 'That's not fair.'

'Isn't it?' Amy asked. 'You know what happened when we got too close before. I know Josh likes you, but I need to protect him too.'

'Amy, you've got it so wrong,' said Ben. 'It's protecting you both that I want to do more than anything.'

'Then why didn't you tell me about Caroline?'

Ben looked puzzled. 'But I explained that,' he said.

'You never told me that you seduced her before she went away the first time,' Amy chided him.

'Oh, that,' said Ben.

'Yes, that.'

'Amy, look, I'm sorry. I probably should have said. But the thing was, I knew I'd made a mistake the minute I got involved with Caroline again. And I'm not proud of the way I dumped her. I didn't tell you because it was irrelevant. Since I met you, you're the only woman I can think about.'

'Am I? I wish I could believe that,' said Amy.

'Believe it,' said Ben. He stared at her, willing her to listen to him, but she turned her head away.

'I want to,' she whispered.

'Well, you should because it's true,' said Ben. 'All I want is to make you happy. But I can't if you won't let me. And if I want more from you than you want to give, please say you'll be friends, at least.'

Amy nodded, barely trusting herself to speak.

'Good,' said Ben. 'I hope you both have a great holiday.'

'Thanks.'

He stepped swiftly towards her, and gave her the briefest of kisses on her cheek. 'When you're ready, I'll be here,' he said, and with that he was gone.

'Ah there you are, old boy.' Harry greeted Ben as he wandered down to the allotments after work. He was pushing a wheelbarrow with a fork in it.

'Hi Harry, how are you?' said Ben. 'I came to bring your cutters back the other night, but you were out.'

'Yes, Amy mentioned it.'

'When did you see Amy? I thought she was on holiday.'

'She is, but she popped in with her spare keys before she left,' said Harry.

'How did she seem?'

'A little stressed, but I'm sure a holiday will do her good. You wait and see, old boy, everything will be fine when she gets back,' Harry told him. 'I'm having trouble digging up my spuds. This damned breathlessness don't you know. You wouldn't mind giving me a hand, would you, old boy?'

'Of course not,' said Ben.

He followed Harry with a lighter heart than he had had of late. After what Amy had said to him at their last meeting, he felt he was no further forward, but maybe, just maybe, Harry was the key to unlocking Amy's reluctant heart. He hoped so, because the last few weeks without her had been torture. And he wasn't sure he could go on without her any more.

PART FOUR
Fix You

On the allotment:
Preparing the ground for the new season. Sowing, and growing things under cloches.

State of the heart:
Preparing to love again.

CHAPTER TWENTY-EIGHT

'Does he have to make that dreadful noise?' Pete came down to breakfast looking rather grumpy.

'Sorry,' Saffron looked apologetic. 'I forgot that Gerry likes to sing in the bath on a Saturday morning.'

'Singing? Is that what you call it?' said Pete. 'I would have called it caterwauling myself.'

They paused as Gerry segued into a rather loud and tuneless rendition of 'Wonderful Tonight'.

'You're not wrong,' sighed Saffron. 'And I might have known he'd go for cheese. It could be worse. When I was married to him it was "Paranoid" done five beats too slow, using my tennis racquet as a prop. Now that was a sight to behold.'

'You almost sound as if you miss it.' Pete's tone was accusing. God, when had Pete started to be accusatory? Saffron realised with dismay that more and more of late her exchanges with Pete had been confrontational.

'Pete! How can you say that?' Saffron knew her response sounded screechy and sharp. But the tension of having Gerry in the house was unbearable. He flirted with her at every opportunity when he thought Pete was looking, and now he was singing Eric Clapton. They'd danced to 'Wonderful Tonight' at their wedding – at the time Saffron had thought it was hopelessly romantic, but now she found it embarrassing. Gerry must have known she'd remember. The only thing that was bothering her now was had she ever told Pete that?

'Because it's true. Gerry says jump and you jump. I feel like a stranger in my own house half the time. And now he's even singing the song you danced to at your wedding. Jeez, Saffron, who is it you're married to? Remind me again. Because I used to think it was me.'

'Now you're being ridiculous. Anyone would think you were jealous.'

'Now who's being ridiculous? Why on earth would I be jealous of sad, sappy Gerry who can't hold down a job or a decent relationship?'

'Precisely. Because he is sad and sappy and I have no interest in him at all. In fact, you should feel sorry for him.'

Pete snorted. 'I cannot feel remotely sorry for someone who lets the good things in his life slip away with the ease that Gerry does. And neither, for the record, am I jealous of him.'

'Well, good,' said Saffron, glaring at him.

'Good.' Pete glared back.

'Morning, peeps.' Gerry breezed in wafting an overwhelming stench of Lynx across the room. 'What are we up to this morning?'

'*We* are not up to anything,' said Pete. 'But *I* am about to go to Wickes to buy an extra waterbutt.'

'What, now?' It was only nine o'clock, and Saffron and the children were still not dressed.

'Yes, now,' said Pete.

'What, you trust me with your missus?' Gerry said with a lascivious leer.

'Piss off, Gerry,' Pete replied, and marched out of the room, shooting a furious glance at Saffron.

'Was it something I said?' Gerry spoke in mock plaintive tones.

'Oh shut up,' said Saffron, 'do shut up.' And she noisily began to clear the breakfast things away with a bang. Damn bloody Gerry. He ruined everything.

Amy took a deep breath and looked around at the allotments. It was good to be back. It was nearly a year since she had first seen this place and so much had happened in that time. Over the course of her holiday, thanks to Mary, who had insisted she have a proper break and taken Josh off on her own several times, Amy had sat on several sun-drenched beaches, and lazed by the hotel pool, all the while doing some serious thinking. She had come to the conclusion that she was using the memory of Jamie as an excuse to stop her meeting anyone new. To stop her being hurt. If it wasn't too late, she had decided that she would give Ben another chance. Life was too short not to grab the chance of happiness when it came. She of all people knew that.

Josh had gone to play with Matt, so she had come

down here on her own. It being Saturday, she hoped that Ben would be on his allotment. He should be due back from his holidays by now. But there was no sign of him. She sighed, and wandered down to inspect her crops. She'd lost a lot of her lettuce – either to the weather or snails by the looks of things, but it seemed as though she would get plenty of runner beans and spuds. Someone had clearly been watering the allotment for her while she was away. In her state of mental turmoil before she went, she had forgotten to ask Harry to do it for her. But, bless him, it looked as though he had done it anyway.

Amy walked towards Harry's allotment to thank him. He was sitting outside his shed in the warm August sunshine. Odd that he wasn't doing anything. Harry rarely sat still.

'Amy, my dear,' said Harry. 'How nice to see you. Did you have a good holiday?'

'Yes, thanks,' said Amy. 'It was lovely. I've called in a couple of times, but you've been out. How are you?'

'Not too bad,' said Harry. 'No Josh today?'

'Playing with Matt,' explained Amy. 'Are you sure you're okay?'

Harry didn't look okay. He was pale and a little breathless, but he waved away her concern. 'I'm fine,' he said. 'Now, tell me about your trip.'

'Thanks for watering my allotment, by the way,' said Amy.

'Oh, that wasn't me,' said Harry. 'It was Ben. He's done it every day religiously.'

'Ben watered it for me?' Amy's heart skipped a beat.

Despite their conversation, despite her refusal to see him, he had still come up and watered her allotment.

'Harry, are you sure you're all right?' The colour had drained from his face, and he was sweating profusely.

'Think – probably – it's my heart,' Harry said. 'Need aspirin. Top pocket. Jacket, in the shed.'

Amy raced into the shed and grabbed the aspirin with shaking hands.

'Need. One. In mouth.' Harry's voice seemed fainter, but he took the aspirin offered and crunched it up in his mouth, then with a short sigh he tipped forward and slid off the bench.

'Harry!' screamed Amy. 'Harry!'

Ben and Meg were on their way down to the allotments when he heard the screams. They raced towards the sound of the commotion, which seemed to be coming from behind Harry's shed.

'Amy!' said Ben. 'What happened?'

Amy was crouched over Harry, slapping his face and calling his name.

'I can't get a response. I can't get a response.'

'Here, let me,' said Ben, expertly tipping Harry's head back and checking the airway was clear, before starting CPR. 'Right, you need to ring for an ambulance while I try to get his heart started. Have you got a mobile on you?'

Amy shook her head.

'Mine's in my car – the keys are in my back pocket.'

Amy took the keys and hurried off, leaving Ben kneeling over Harry, counting the number of compressions he was doing. She was shaking like a leaf, but it took her moments to find the phone. She rang 999 and gave them directions to the allotment gates, which she opened to allow them access.

'Are they coming?' Ben barely looked up, so intent was he on what he was doing. 'Come on, Harry. Come on.'

'Yes,' said Amy, watching as Ben worked steadily away on Harry's heart. There still didn't seem to be any response. At the back of her head she half-remembered something she'd once read about most heart-attack victims being lost because of the lack of a defibrilator.

'How long did the ambulance say they'd be?' asked Ben, who was beginning to flag, the physical exertion of what he was doing taking its toll.

'Ten minutes,' said Amy. 'This is hopeless. We've lost him.'

'Not if I have anything to do with it,' said Ben. He carried on with renewed efforts. To begin with nothing happened, but then Harry gave a sudden spasm, and finally he started to cough.

'Harry, can you hear me?'

Harry groaned slightly.

'You've had a heart attack. The ambulance is going to take you to hospital.'

As if on cue, the ambulance arrived, and soon the paramedics had taken over and assessed the situation before taking Harry away.

One of them turned to Ben. 'Well done, mate,' he said. 'I think you just saved that old boy's life.'

Ben sat back on the bench and put his head in his hands.

'Thank God,' he said. 'Thank God.'

'Coffee?'

Amy looked up to see Ben standing before her holding a plastic cup.

'Not very strong, I'm afraid,' said Ben, 'but it's the best I can do for now.'

'It's warm and it's wet,' said Amy. 'It will do.'

'Has anyone said anything?'

'Not yet,' said Amy. 'How long do you think we'll be hanging round here?'

'How long have you got?'

'Will he be okay?'

Ben ran his hands through his hair. He'd been dreading answering this question ever since they'd got there.

'Honest answer? I don't know. I've been expecting something like this for some time. But you know Harry, he's a tough old stick.'

'I don't think I could bear it if – you know.' Amy's eyes filled with tears. Ben took her hand and held it in his. To his delight, although hating himself for feeling so in these ghastly circumstances, Amy didn't push it away.

'He's not going to die,' said Ben. 'Otherwise it's a

total waste of my time resuscitating him, and Harry knows how I hate time-wasters.'

Amy smiled a watery smile, and squeezed his hand tight.

After what seemed like hours, a doctor in a white overall came over towards them. He rubbed his eyes, and looked exhausted.

'Doctor Cloughton,' he said, extending a hand.

'Doctor Ben Martin, GP at Riverview Practice.' Ben shook the hand. 'We've corresponded, but never met before. How's Harry?'

'Good to meet you,' said Dr Cloughton. 'Well it seems your friend Harry is made of tougher stuff than most of my patients. He has had a heart attack, but a relatively mild one. He's been lucky. We've made him comfortable and we're about to get him up to the ward.'

'Can we see him?' Amy wanted to know.

'Five minutes,' said Dr Cloughton.

Harry was sitting up in bed when they got there, looking pale, tired and rather grumpy.

'Well, you gave us a nasty shock and no mistake,' said Ben.

'Next time, don't bring me back,' said Harry.

'There's gratitude,' laughed Ben.

'Ben, I am quite serious,' said Harry. 'If it happens again I want it noted that I don't want to be resuscitated.'

Amy and Ben exchanged anxious glances.

'You can't mean that,' said Ben.

'You know I can,' said Harry. 'I'd have been quite happy to go.'

'Never mind you,' Amy joshed Harry as best she could, trying to control the turmoil inside her. 'What about us?'

Harry looked at her, as if remembering her presence. 'Don't take any notice of me,' he said, 'I'm feeling a bit grouchy.'

'Can we get you anything?' Ben asked. 'I can pop home and find you some PJs if you like.'

'Thanks, old boy,' said Harry. 'I'm pretty filthy. I was scrabbling in the mud before all of this.'

'How are you feeling now?' Amy asked. Although Harry looked a bit better than when she'd first seen him at the allotments, and seemed pretty compos mentis, the sight of him turning so pale and keeling over was going to stay with her for a long time. Thank God Josh hadn't been with her.

'I've felt better,' said Harry. 'I mainly feel tired, if you must know.'

A nurse came bustling in and said, 'Right, Harry, we've found a bed for you, so we'll get you up to the ward now and make you comfortable.'

Taking that as their cue to go, Amy and Ben left, promising to return later with clothes and toiletries.

'Is there anyone you want us to ring?' Amy asked as they left, but Harry just shook his head.

'Apart from my cousin, you two are the nearest thing I've got to family now,' he said. 'Although if you bring my address book back, I'll let you know who to call from the regiment. We've a reunion coming up and I think I might have to miss it.'

'You okay?' asked Ben, as he followed Amy out to the car.

'So-so,' said Amy. 'Actually, I feel a bit shaky.'

'Me too,' said Ben.

'You saved Harry's life,' Amy stated, and swallowed hard.

'It's my job,' said Ben. 'Come on, let's get you home.'

'Yes, I had better get back,' said Amy. 'Josh will be wondering where I am, and I promised I'd tell Saffron the minute we had some news.'

They climbed into Ben's car. Then, as if it were the most natural thing in the world, Ben came with Amy to pick up Josh, and they went together to Harry's to sort out his things. Josh needed to get to bed so Ben went back to the hospital on his own.

'I'll have tea ready for you when you get back if you'd like,' said Amy.

'I would like,' said Ben. 'I would like that very much.'

And he left, leaving Amy to struggle with a whole range of emotions – worry about Harry warring with anxiety about Ben, and muddled up in there the hugest feeling of relief that she and Ben were talking again. It felt like she'd come home.

CHAPTER TWENTY-NINE

'How are you doing, Harry?'

Amy sat down beside Harry's bed, and flashed him what she hoped was a cheerful smile. She didn't feel cheerful. On her last visit Harry had been grumpy beyond belief, and she was beginning to feel worn ragged by the constant hospital visits, which were squeezed in between work, school pickups and trying to sort Harry's house out. The first time she and Ben had gone round they'd both been shocked. Harry had always kept things neat and tidy, and yet now his home had an air of neglect about it, as if somehow he'd given up caring. By unspoken agreement, she and Ben had taken over both the house and Harry's allotment; Amy doing the bulk of house-cleaning, and Ben in charge of allotment duties. It meant they had seen precious little of each other, but at least they were speaking again.

Amy shoved the thought of Ben from her mind – now was not the time to be thinking about him in that way. Maybe when Harry was better, she and Ben would have time for each other. But for now there were more important things to consider.

'Much better today, thank you,' said Harry. 'But I can't wait to get out of this place, I can tell you.'

'Have the doctors said when you can come home?' Harry appeared to be recovering well, but the fact that he lived alone was proving a stumbling block. He looked terribly frail and Amy couldn't imagine how he was going to cope when he did get back home. Thanks to Ben, she had got in touch with social services, who were trying to set up some kind of care package to enable him to stay in his own house. They had muttered about old people's homes, but Amy had put her foot down. Harry had no family who could help, and she knew he would hate to lose his independence.

'I'm only next door,' she had argued with the patronising social worker who insisted on calling Harry 'dear' all the time, and speaking about him as if he wasn't there. 'I can keep an eye on him. The last thing he wants is to be in a home.'

'I don't know yet,' said Harry, 'but the head honcho's coming round later on, and yesterday he seemed to think it wouldn't be too long.'

'That's wonderful,' said Amy. 'Josh and I can't wait for you to come home.'

'And I can't wait to get shot of this place either,' said Harry.

'So Harry's back this week?' Saffron asked, as she pushed her wheelbarrow down Mrs Turner's side passage.

'Yes, all being well,' said Amy. She was exhausted. Ever since Harry had been given the green light to leave hospital, she'd been racing around trying to sort everything out for him. Luckily, Josh had now gone back to school, so her days were freeing up, but it had been a tiring couple of weeks.

'I must say, it's nice to be doing something normal,' said Amy, as they got to work raking and weeding.

'You look knackered. Are you okay?' asked Saffron.

'I'm fine.'

'Well, don't overdo it.'

'Leave it, Saffron,' said Amy, more snappily than she'd intended. Ben had been on about her overdoing things yesterday as well. 'Everything is okay.'

'It's been pretty tough on you recently,' said Saffron. 'I'm sorry I haven't been more help.'

'Don't be daft,' Amy told her. 'You've got enough to do with the kids and Pete, it's been fine.'

'And don't forget Gerry,' said Saffron with a grimace.

'As if I could,' Amy replied. 'No sign of him moving out then?'

'Doesn't look like it,' Saffron told her. 'We keep making hints, but he has the hide of a rhinoceros and they fall on deaf ears.'

'You'll just have to tell him,' insisted Amy.

'It's not as easy as that.'

'Oh?'

'This is going to sound ridiculous, but, well, I feel sorry for him.'

'You are joking?' Amy tried to hold back the laughter. It felt good to laugh. She'd found precious few moments to do so in recent weeks.

'Why would I be joking?'

'Hell-oooo. Earth to Saffron here. This is Gerry we are talking about. The reprobate who left you with two small children and has been a thorn in your side ever since.'

'Yes, yes, I know all that,' said Saffron. 'The thing is, Gerry's changed. I mean, he's still really annoying. And he sings very much out of tune in the bath – but well, here he is pushing forty, he's lost his girlfriend, his house and his business is going down the pan. The man I married had so many dreams and they've all turned to dust. So, yes, I do feel sorry for him. At least he's trying quite hard with the kids now, so it's better for them.'

'Blimey,' said Amy. 'I really never thought I'd hear you say that. Sounds like you're quite taken with him.'

'As if!' said Saffron. 'Mind you, Pete seems to have got it into his head that Gerry fancies me. Which is clearly ridiculous. So the way things are, it will be much better if we can persuade Gerry to move on.'

'With the way things are, I think it probably would,' said Amy. 'You don't want Pete being jealous.'

'Too late, he already is,' said Saffron with a rueful smile. 'Not that he has any reason to be,' she added hastily. 'Anyway, enough about me. How are you and the gorgeous doctor getting on? Better, I hope?'

'Much better,' said Amy, 'but we're just friends.

Nothing more. Now doesn't seem the time to progress things further.'

'But –?'

'When the right time comes, you'll be the first to know,' said Amy with a grin.

She was still grinning when she got home. Normally she had a quick shower after work, but today there was time to have a bath before the school run. She lay back, luxuriating in the warm soapy bubbles, enjoying the freedom of ten minutes entirely to herself. For once, she also allowed herself a few moments of daydreaming. She thought back to what her Auntie Grace had said about going forward and not back. It was time she did exactly that and started living her life again, to the full. She had resisted the pull of attraction to Ben from the beginning. But no longer. She was going to resist him no longer. When Harry was better, and everything was more settled, she would go with the flow and see where it took her. She had a feeling she was going to enjoy the journey . . .

Saffron was feeling out of sorts. She couldn't put her finger on it exactly. It was partly seeing Harry the way he was. She had insisted Amy take a break from hospital duties and had popped in to see Harry, and she was shocked by his appearance. Harry was one of those fixtures on the allotments who didn't ever change, but now he had. He was grumpier than he used to be, fretful about not getting onto his allotment – though

Amy and Ben were spending all their spare time making sure it was kept going – and more forgetful. Saffron wasn't stupid. She knew that Harry was very weak, and chances were he wasn't going to be around much longer. The thought depressed her. Things wouldn't be the same without him.

But it wasn't just Harry's illness that was niggling her. It was her home situation. She had tried to ignore it as best she could, but despite joking that Gerry had the hots for her, she was beginning to suspect he really did. He seemed to show no interest in making up with Maddy, who had apparently put the house on the market without him anyway, added to which he was still making no attempt to move on. Saffron had stopped hinting and started making direct comments, but she was always met with this little-boy-lost/puppy-dog look, which made her feel slightly helpless.

'But I've nowhere to go,' Gerry would say rather pathetically.

'Well, find somewhere,' Saffron would respond in exasperation.

'You know my money situation is tight . . .'

'Gerry, don't even go there. We haven't any spare cash, and if we had, do you think Pete would be keen to lend it to you?'

Saffron sighed – Pete was another problem. He was saying less and less. And spending more and more time out of the house. And where their love life had been picking up, it seemed to have slipped away again. Pete was always too tired. He kept blaming the job, but, for the first time since she had known him, Pete didn't make her feel attractive any more. In fact she was beginning to think he was losing interest. Even the suggestion of watching one of his films hadn't worked. And now he'd gone away on business for a couple of nights, and she was left alone with Gerry.

'Don't do anything I wouldn't,' Pete had said as he left, giving her a perfunctory kiss on the cheek. It was the kind of thing he often said, but this time it felt, to Saffron, laden with meaning – as if somehow he were expecting her to do something wrong. Or perhaps she was just chasing shadows. Perhaps . . .

Was it only a few months ago they had lain on the bed not wishing to say goodbye as Pete had headed off on his first business trip? And now he could barely bear to kiss her, as if his leaving were of no consequence whatsoever. Saffron shivered. The weather was turning autumnal, there was a chill wind in the air, and somewhere deep down inside she felt she was losing Pete.

'Easy now.' Ben helped Harry out of the car and into the house, where Amy, Saffron, the children and the Guys were waiting to greet him.

Although it was a hot day, Harry was wearing a big overcoat. Never a big man, he had lost weight in hospital, and it hung off him now. As Amy came out to greet them, she and Ben exchanged glances. Harry looked incredibly frail, and for the first time since Amy had known him, he seemed old. How was he going to manage on his own?

'No need to stand on ceremony,' Harry muttered as people rose to greet him. Amy smiled as she put on the kettle. Harry being grumpy at least meant he was still with them. Several times in hospital he had seemed to be totally uninterested in anything. A reaction – even a grumpy reaction – was at least an indication that he wasn't quite ready to throw the towel in. Amy shivered. She didn't want to think about what would happen if the worst came to the worst. But she had to face facts. Harry was eighty-five. Up until now a very fit and able eighty-five, but would he really be able to pull through? Don't even go there, she muttered to herself. In the short time she had known him, Harry had become indispensable to her, the father she had never had, and the grandfather Josh was missing. The thought of him not being around was unthinkable.

'Penny for 'em.' Ben came into the kitchen and lightly touched her on the shoulder.

'Just thinking dark thoughts,' said Amy, as she started to pour out the tea.

'Oh you don't want to be doing that,' said Ben, with a grin that made her feel weak all over. 'You don't know where it will end.'

'You're probably right. Here, do you want to help me taking these out?'

'No problem.' Ben deftly picked up a tray with several cups on it, and disappeared back in the lounge, while Amy swiftly unloaded the contents of several cake boxes and packets of biscuits onto some plates.

'Anything else I can do?' Ben was back.

'We always seem to find ourselves in the kitchen at parties, don't we?' Amy commented.

'I can't think of anywhere I'd rather be,' said Ben.

'Flattery will get you everywhere.'

'I was rather hoping it might,' Ben told her.

'But it won't get these plates passed round,' said Amy. 'Do you think it's okay for Harry to eat cake? I did try and find low-fat ones.'

'Everything in moderation, as my mum always says,' said Ben, picking up the plates.

'Ben – do you think –?' Amy paused. Perhaps Ben was right and she should leave her dark thoughts hidden well away.

'What?'

'Do you think Harry is going to be okay?'

Ben put the plates down and went over to Amy and wrapped his arms around her. 'Honestly?' he said. 'I'd be lying if I said he would.'

'Oh.' Amy's voice sounded unnatural to her. She had known that Ben wouldn't try to flannel her. 'I was hoping you'd say there'd be a miracle, and Harry will make a full recovery.'

Ben looked at her. 'Maybe if he was younger that would be the case. But Harry is old, and his body is beginning to pack up. He knows it. And we know it. He might pull round from this, as he is very strong, but sooner or later he won't get better. That's just the way it is.' He kissed the top of her head softly. 'But hey, let's not worry about things before they happen, eh? Harry's a tough cookie. He might well surprise us all yet.'

Amy gave him a wan smile. 'I hope you're right,' she said.

'So do I,' Ben agreed. 'Now, come on, I say it's time you left the kitchen and joined the party.'

But afterwards, when everyone had gone home and he'd stayed behind to check things through with the carers and make sure Amy got a break for once, Ben wasn't so sure. Harry seemed weak, the party having taken a lot out of him.

'I'm too old,' he grumbled to Ben, as the carers tucked him up in bed. 'I've lived too long, you know. I shan't be sorry to go.'

'We will be,' was Ben's firm response. 'So do shut up and concentrate on getting better.'

Harry half-glared at him over the bedcovers. 'If you are ever unfortunate enough to reach this grand old age, you'll understand.'

Ben laughed. 'That's more like it,' he said. 'Now, is there anything else you need?'

'I'm fine, old boy,' said Harry. 'Everyone makes too much fuss.'

'I'll see you tomorrow, then,' said Ben, heading for the door.

'There is one thing you can do for me,' Harry announced suddenly.

'Oh, what's that?' Ben turned, expecting a demand for a whisky, then in the half-light he caught Harry smiling a secretive smile.

'Whatever happens, make sure you do the right thing by Amy,' said Harry. 'I'd like to die knowing you two are getting hitched.'

'Harry, you're worse than an old woman,' said Ben, and let himself out laughing.

'Gerry, you're home early,' said Saffron. She wasn't at all sure she could say that with pleasure, but she supposed any adult company was better than none.

'I've got something to celebrate, sweetheart,' said Gerry, waving a bottle of champagne at her. 'I thought we could sit down to a takeaway and share this together, just the two of us. It will be like the good old days.'

'Apart from the fact that we are no longer married, you're staying at my and my new husband's house, and we both think it's time you moved out, yes, it is just like the good old days,' said Saffron.

'Oh.' Gerry looked deflated. She wished he wouldn't do that. For so many years he had had the power to hurt her, and now the tables had turned and she wasn't altogether sure that she liked having this ability to pull the wind out from under his sails so easily. It made her feel uneasy to have him so dependent on her.

'What are we celebrating anyway?' she changed the subject.

'You remember that contract I had?'

'What, the one for the product no one wanted?'

'The very same.'

'What about it?' Saffron asked.

'Well, turns out the company I'm dealing with aren't interested. But their parent company is. And they have offices worldwide. So, my darling, my money worries are over. It's official: this time next year I'm going to be a millionaire.'

'Watch out, Del Boy,' said Saffron, laughing despite herself. 'Don't run ahead of yourself. Wait till you've signed on the dotted line.'

'A-ha, but I have, and they're giving me the first instalment right away. So I can buy that bitch out and go back home.'

'Thank the lord,' muttered Saffron to herself, saying aloud, 'Well, that's great news. And yes, it is worth celebrating. Help me put the kids to bed and we'll open the bubbly when I get back downstairs.'

It felt strange tucking Matt and Becky in with Gerry around. Strange but weirdly comfortable. The children seemed to like it too. Particularly when Gerry actually read Matt a story. Saffron was staggered. Gerry never read them stories. She had a sudden wistful thought – *this is how it could have been* – before a squawk from Ellie reminded her that this was how it was now. And even a reformed Gerry was no match for Pete.

After a companionable curry, with the champers finished, Saffron opened a bottle of red wine. While she knew without a doubt that there was no way she would ever go back to Gerry, she felt relieved that for the first time since they had split up, they were at least getting on reasonably well. It could only be better for the children to see their parents happier in each other's company. Just so long as he realised that there was nothing on her side but friendship . . .

A few glasses later, and Saffron was feeling not just

content, but soppily happy that she and Gerry were getting on so admirably.

'Cheers,' she said, clinking her glass at him. 'To us and our children.'

'To us.' Gerry paused, then added, 'This is cosy, isn't it?'

Saffron sat up rubbing her head. Somehow they had migrated to the sofa. And Gerry had put 'Lady in Red' on. Lordy-lord. Alarm bells started ringing furiously through the alcohol-induced fug.

'Gerry,' she began, 'I don't think we'd better get too comfortable . . .'

'I've been a bloody fool, you know,' said Gerry. 'I should never have let you go.'

'Well, you did, and I forgive you, and it's history.' The alarm bells were reaching ear-splitting proportions.

'Saffron, I think I still love you.' Gerry leaned across her.

Saffron leaned back in some alarm. 'No, no you don't.'

And then he kissed her.

Saffron pushed him away. 'Just what the hell do you think you're doing?' she said, gasping in horror.

'I could say the very same thing.' Pete stood framed in the doorway. 'But I think it's quite obvious, don't you?'

CHAPTER THIRTY

Amy turned her key in the door at Harry's house. She and Saffron were taking turns to pop in on him. The carers would come in the morning to get him up, and in the evening to put him to bed. He was exceptionally grumpy about the whole thing. 'It's come to something, hasn't it, when I can't even shave myself,' he would grumble, but it was very clear to everyone, despite his moans, that he couldn't really manage alone. Sometimes when Amy came in, he was confused and didn't know who she was, and he spent more and more of his time dozing in his chair. Ben was beginning to make noises about Harry going into a home.

'Oh, Ben, you don't really think that will happen, do you?' Amy had been horrified the first time he'd mentioned it. 'He'd hate it.'

'I know he would,' Ben had replied, 'but he's not really coping. And you can't keep popping round indefinitely.'

'I'll pop round for as long as he needs me,' she'd declared.

'Amy, you're wearing yourself out, you can't go on like this.'

'Leave it, Ben,' Amy had snapped, and then regretted it.

She sighed. She'd had that conversation several weeks ago, and hadn't anticipated what the sheer strain of looking after Harry would have involved. She was tired all the time, tetchy with Josh, distracted when she was working, tense with Ben. But she couldn't envisage doing anything else. Harry had been there for her from the moment she had met him, and she wasn't going to let him down now.

'Harry, it's me,' she called. 'Do you fancy a cup of tea?'

There was no reply. Mind you, he could be a bit deaf sometimes, and she could hear the TV blaring away.

Amy pushed the lounge door open. Harry was sitting in his favourite chair, his back to her. He mustn't have heard her.

'Harry? Are you awake? It's me, Amy.'

Still no reply. A solid clutch of fear crawled over her.

'Harry,' she said again, in some alarm.

She moved towards the chair and shook him. He didn't move, and his skin felt cold to the touch. An icy dread washed right through her. His face was pallid, a strange ivory-yellow colour.

Harry was dead. The thought hit her like a thunderbolt. The only dead body she had ever seen was Jamie's, and that had been in the morgue, and quite different, but she knew instantly that Harry had gone.

Not wanting to believe it, she shook him. 'Harry,

Harry,' she said more urgently. But there was no response. Frantically, Amy looked for a pulse, but she was all fingers and thumbs, and she couldn't find one. Was it because there wasn't one there? Or because she was missing it in her panic? After several minutes she forced herself to calm down. There was no pulse, and she wasn't going to find one. Because Harry was dead. And nothing she could do could bring him back.

Mechanically she phoned for an ambulance. Then she phoned Ben. She sat down opposite Harry, cradling the receiver. There was nothing more to be done.

She was still sitting in the same position when Ben found her. He quickly checked Harry over, and then shook his head.

'Amy, I'm sorry,' he said, softly kissing her on the head, and taking her hand in his. She appreciated the gesture, a moment of kindness, a connection with the physical world as her emotional world fell apart.

For the second time in her life, she had lost someone she held dear, and suddenly all the feelings she had tried to control for the last few years were pouring out of her like a dam. She started to cry, whether for Harry or Jamie she didn't know. All she knew was that the sense of loss and desolation was overwhelming, and although Ben held her close to him, he couldn't help her at all.

'Amy, I came as soon as I heard.' Saffron puffed up the path, the children in tow. The news of Harry's death was spreading like wildfire round the allotments. It was a lousy end to a lousy week. Despite Gerry's apology, and her denials, Pete had barely spoken to her for days. Even Gerry had worked out that his presence was an intrusion and had moved into the motel.

'I really am sorry, sweetheart,' he'd said as he left. 'I got a bit carried away. Hope I haven't put the cat among the pigeons.'

Saffron had retorted angrily that she was not *his* 'sweetheart' and shoved him away. It was too little too late. Had he shown an ounce of sensitivity when they were married, perhaps they might still be together. But that would have meant no Pete and no Ellie. And, thanks to Gerry's newfound sensitivity, she might not have Pete any more. Bugger him. He always had to balls things up.

In a way, thinking about Harry was a welcome distraction from her own misery. Here was a real crisis, and not one of her own making. And within minutes of getting into Amy's house, Saffron could see she was in a bad way.

Amy sat at the kitchen table, with red eyes, staring blankly at the wall. She barely seemed to notice when Saffron offered her a cup of tea. Tears kept dripping down her cheeks, slow, silent tears that somehow seemed more dreadful than the noisy kind Saffron always managed to produce.

'I don't know how you do it,' said Saffron, shoving a cup of tea and a plate of biscuits at her friend.

'Do what?'

'Cry without looking a mess. I always look like a

'demented cow when I've been crying,' said Saffron.

Amy smiled wanly, but appeared not to really be listening. Her eyes were listless and dull, and she fiddled with her cup without drinking anything.

'I'm not hungry,' she said, pushing the biscuits away.

'You must eat,' said Saffron. 'Come on, Harry would hate to see you like this.'

'I know,' Amy sighed. 'I'm sorry I'm not very good company at the moment. I know Harry was old, and I hadn't known him for that long, but he was so good to me, and now he's gone. I never knew my real dad, and Harry's been like the dad I never had, and the granddad Josh didn't have. I don't know how we're going to cope without him.'

'Oh, Amy, I feel it too,' said Saffron. 'We're all going to miss him.'

'I know,' said Amy. 'You probably think I'm over-reacting.'

'I have no idea,' said Saffron. 'I've never lost anyone before, but I guess you take it the way you take it. The allotments won't be the same without him.'

'No, they won't,' said Amy.

'Did Ben get my message about having the wake at ours?'

'Yes, thanks,' said Amy with a shiver. 'I can't believe this time next week we'll be burying him.'

Saffron looked at her friend with some alarm. She looked so desolate.

'And if there's anything else I can do . . .?'

'Thanks,' said Amy. 'But you can't do anything really. I need to face this down myself. I just feel so out of kilter. As if someone has knocked me sideways. I know I seem to be having an over-the-top reaction, but it's brought everything back about Jamie. Why do the people we love have to leave us?'

Her eyes were brittle and bright with unshed tears. And there was a bitterness and vehemence in her voice that Saffron had never heard before.

'That's the million-dollar question, isn't it?' Saffron agreed. 'I guess we can only ever fall back on clichés, to have loved and lost, and all that.'

'The way I feel right now,' said Amy, 'I don't buy that at all. If you never love, you never lose. To have loved and lost is the worst, the very worst thing of all.'

'How's Amy taken things?'

Ben and Pete were in the Magpie having a consolatory drink with one another, though quite who was consoling who was another matter.

'Not well,' said Ben. 'It's hit her much harder than I thought it would.'

'Well, we'll all miss him,' said Pete.

'Sure will,' said Ben gloomily, staring into his pint. 'So come on then, what's been going on with you and Saffron? Surely it can't be that bad?'

Pete had made noises on the phone that Gerry had been causing trouble, but hadn't furnished Ben with the details.

'So you think Saffron and Gerry have been having an affair?' Ben looked dubious. 'What does Saffron say?'

'Well, she denies it,' said Pete, 'but of course she would.'

'Oh come on,' said Ben, 'this is Gerry we're talking about. Saffron's got more sense. Anyway, look at the mess Caroline got me in with Amy. Amy didn't believe me either. I think you should give Saffron the benefit of the doubt.'

'I would,' said Pete, 'but there is something else. A few months ago, Saffron started going to aerobics classes on a Wednesday evening. She said she was going to the leisure centre and I didn't think anything of it. But the more I thought about it, the more she seemed cagey about it. So I rang up and checked. And do you know what? They don't run aerobics classes on a Wednesday.'

'Maybe you got it wrong and she did a different class,' suggested Ben.

'All there is on Wednesday evenings is boxercise classes and circuit training, neither of which are Saffron's thing,' said Pete. 'Besides, she suddenly stopped going, for no reason. You've got to admit it, Ben. It looks suspicious.'

'Well, I'm sure there's a simple explanation,' said Ben. 'Come on, drink up. I've got to go. I've a busy day tomorrow.'

As they were leaving the pub, the door was pushed open and Maddy barged her way in.

'Oh, it's you,' she practically spat in Pete's ear. 'I'm surprised you dare to leave your missus on her own.'

'I don't know what you mean.' Pete's response was stiff and formal.

'You're wet behind the ears then,' said Maddy. 'I know

Gerry's been cheating on me, and I know who with.'

'Prove it,' said Pete. 'Saffron would never do that to me.'

Maddy looked at him slyly. 'And I bet you think she doesn't lie to you either,' she said, 'but I know for a fact she does.'

'What do you mean?'

'Ask her what she does on Wednesday evenings,' was the response.

'What?' Pete looked like a kid who'd just had his bag of sweets stolen.

'Ignore her,' said Ben, pulling Pete away. 'Ignore her, she's just trying to cause trouble. Come on, time we went home.'

The day of Harry's funeral was chilly and windy. Amy felt sick as she stood in the church and watched the few remnants of Harry's family, a cousin and a couple of nieces and nephews, follow the coffin down the aisle. She felt hollow inside. For a moment she did a double take and she was back at Jamie's funeral, experiencing that racking, devastating sense of loss all over again. Ben stood beside her, silent and grave. He squeezed her hand tightly, and she could see he was doing his best to rein in his own emotions.

Amy's mind went blank as they sang the first hymn – 'To Be a Pilgrim', Harry's favourite – and after she wobbled on the first line she stopped singing altogether. Instead she fixed her gaze on the stained-glass window at the back of the church, as if by staring hard at it she could make this nightmare go away, make herself believe that Harry wasn't in that coffin, that Jamie wasn't dead, and rid herself of the feeling that everything she loved eventually turned to dust.

The vicar spoke generally about Harry's life – Harry not having been much of a churchgoer. He wasn't well-known in the parish, but Mavis had been, so it seemed that lots of her friends were there too. The church was packed with allotmenteers – most of whom looked uncomfortable in their Sunday best – along with Harry's few remaining friends from his army days, and the numerous people he chatted to on his strolls around and about the town. At least they hadn't come to a sad, lonely affair, Amy thought, as she heard the vicar say they were celebrating a life. She knew that was the way she should look at it too, but she couldn't: her sense of loss was too extreme. And while she knew from bitter experience how selfishly lonely grief could be, she also knew she couldn't do a damned thing to stop the way she was feeling. Harry's best friend, a rather shaky old chap by the name of Gordon, got up and, in the true-grit spirit of a whole generation, made a beautiful speech about Harry, with humour and warmth, so for a moment Amy was able to forget her misery and remember the reasons why she had loved Harry, and relish the friendship they had shared. But it wasn't enough to stop the tug at her heart as the coffin left the church, or the painful reminder of the last time she had followed a coffin out of a church.

Ben walked beside her, holding her hand. He had

been a rock and such a support these last few days. All she had to do was succumb to her feelings and she knew they would be happy together. But in the face of such pain and heartache, was it really worth the risk? It would only be a matter of time before he left her too.

Throughout the service, Ben held Amy's hand tight. He was conscious at times that she was crying, and wished he could do something to ease her pain. At least she was letting him in. If one good thing could come out of Harry's illness and death, it had to be this. That he and Amy would finally be together. It was what Harry would have wanted. Ben managed a faint smile as he remembered their last conversation, just over two weeks ago. Harry had been terribly weak but quite sure of one thing. 'You just make an honest woman of her,' Harry had admonished – strange how his voice still rang clear in Ben's head as if he was sitting right there.

He felt sick to the pit of his stomach knowing that he and Harry would never share a brew together on the allotments again, even while the rational side of his brain told him that it was for the best, that Harry had been ready to go. It was hard to feel rational in these circumstances, though. And harder still to sit in a church mourning the loss of a friend, and not remember that first loss. The one he never spoke of. The one that had changed his whole life. Sarah.

How little he let himself remember her. How hard

he tried to shove the pain away. But it was always there, simmering away under the surface. Losing Sarah had made him want to become a doctor. And now here he was, having saved Harry, but only in the short term. Not the same, a determined voice in his head said. Not the same. Harry had been living on borrowed time, and he'd been ready to go.

As Ben and Amy walked out of the church to the waiting cars, which would go on to the crematorium, Amy's grief overcame her, and he held her helplessly as she sobbed in his arms. Some good had to come out of this. It had to. And as they walked to the car, he felt in his pocket for the box nestling there. Maybe today wasn't the right day – but somehow he felt it was. Harry's death was sad but not a tragedy. And it had made Ben determined that he wasn't going to sit around wasting his life waiting for the things he wanted to come to him. It was time to grasp the nettle and live life to the full. He turned the box over again. He just hoped he got the right answer.

CHAPTER THIRTY-ONE

Saffron had a headache. She had been up since six with Ellie, and had gone to bed too late drinking red wine alone for the third evening in succession. Pete had come in late, barely spoken to her and gone straight to bed. There hadn't been time to talk this morning either, as they had both been busy sorting out the house in readiness for the funeral guests. Although Amy had wanted to host the wake, there really wasn't room in her house, and so Saffron had offered straight away. Besides, she thought, Amy didn't need that kind of hassle right now.

Pete had taken the kids to school while Saffron had rushed around hoovering frantically and sorting out vol-au-vents, sandwiches and cakes. Amy and Ben had arrived at nine thirty, bringing extra cups and more chairs, as Saffron was a bit short. It had all been incredibly frantic, which was good in a way as no one had too much time to dwell on the funeral, which was not until midday.

But it wasn't so good for communicating with her husband. Saffron stared out into the garden, where Pete was in animated conversation with the Guys, while she absent-mindedly put the kettle back on. He had barely spoken to her this morning. In fact, he had been downright avoiding her. What was she going to do?

'Have you seen Amy?' Ben wandered into the kitchen where Saffron was washing up cups and saucers and making yet more tea for the good ladies of the Nevermorewell WI who had descended pack-like on the funeral, ready to dissect every aspect of Harry's life. They were presumably Mavis's friends, so probably felt entitled. They also seemed to have made it their life's work to drink her house dry of tea.

'She offered to go and pick the kids up from school, and as Ellie was asleep I said yes,' said Saffron.

'Oh,' said Ben, looking a little deflated. 'I'd have gone with her, if I'd known.'

'I think she wanted a bit of time to herself,' Saffron told him. 'You know how hard she's taken this.'

'I know,' said Ben. 'We all have. The allotments just aren't going to be the same without Harry.'

'They're not, are they?' said Saffron. 'Are you okay? I know how close you were.'

'I will be,' said Ben. 'It helps knowing that if he'd lived his quality of life would have just got worse and worse. And I know he was ready to go. The trouble is, I never really thought of him as old. Stupid, really.'

'No, it's not stupid at all,' said Saffron. 'Age shouldn't matter when we love people. It's the relationship we have with them that counts. I think that's why Amy's taken it so hard.'

'I think I might have just the thing to cheer her up.'

'Oh?' Saffron looked at him questioningly.

'Well, I was going to keep it a secret,' said Ben, 'but seeing as it's you . . .'

He felt in his pocket and produced a little box, which he opened with a flourish, to reveal a simple diamond ring.

'Oh Ben, that's wonderful,' said Saffron. 'But do you think today is the right day?'

'I absolutely think today is the right day,' said Ben. 'Harry wanted her to be happy. And his dying has made me realise you have to go out and grab happiness when and where you can. It makes perfect sense.'

Saffron looked a little doubtful. 'Ben, I don't want to put the kibosh on this, but do you think perhaps it might be better to give Amy more time? She might not see it the same way you do.'

'She might not,' said Ben, picking up a cloth and drying some cups, 'but I'm sure I can persuade her. And you must promise you won't say a thing.'

Amy came back up through the allotments with the children. Finding the atmosphere in Saffron's house oppressive, she had been glad of something else to do. Mind you, when she'd got to school and seen the look on Josh's face as Matt informed him that Harry was now officially In Heaven and wouldn't ever talk to them again, she rather thought she'd got the short straw. Josh's lip had wobbled for a moment until a sudden thought struck him. 'Does that mean Harry's with Daddy?'

'Yes,' said Amy, blinking back the tears.

'That's okay then,' said Josh. 'Daddy will have someone new to talk to now.'

And then he was fine, racing home with Matt, while Becky walked sedately by Amy's side and told her about her day in mind-numbingly boring detail, for which Amy was immensely grateful.

The wake was in full swing when they got back. Pete was at the end of the garden with Bill and Bud.

'What's that you're drinking?' Amy inspected the contents of Pete's glass, which looked a rather muddy shade of purple.

'Elderberry wine,' said Pete with a slight slur. 'It's delicious. And very, very good for you. Here, have some.'

'Perhaps not quite in the quantities you're drinking it,' said Amy. 'I think I'll pass, if you don't mind. Where's Saffron?'

'God knows,' said Pete with a noncommittal shrug, and he turned back to the allotmenteers with relish. That was odd, frowned Amy. Pete wasn't normally like that. She knew it had been tricky for Saffron and Pete with Gerry being there, but she hadn't thought their problems were serious. Until now. She had been so wrapped up in her own misery, she hadn't asked Saffron how things were at home. She just hoped that Gerry hadn't been causing more trouble.

'Is the kettle on?' Amy asked, as she finally made it into the kitchen, having been detained by some of Harry's army pals. They were a lovely bunch and full of great stories about Harry. It was incredible hearing the things they'd got up to. There was so much she hadn't known about him.

'What, they don't want *more* tea, surely?' Saffron asked, looking at Amy's laden tray. 'I don't think we have enough cups.'

'Well, the good ladies of Nevermorewell's WI appear to be able to drink for England,' said Amy with a smile – the first she had managed all day, Saffron was pleased to note. 'There's more stuff in there, by the way.'

'Who are all these people anyway?' asked Saffron as they walked back into the conservatory to collect more cups, to find a veritable horde of elderly ladies who were waxing lyrical about Harry's drinking and it being a shame he was gone, but at least he was with Mavis now.

'Well, apart from Edie and Ada, I presume the rest of them are Mavis's friends,' said Amy. 'I wonder who Edie and Ada will give their cakes to now.'

'Whereas, *they* are presumably Harry's mates.' Saffron nodded over to the corner of the lounge where three elderly gentlemen seemed to be getting rather well acquainted with a bottle of whisky.

'How did you guess?' laughed Amy. 'They're his army chums. The chap in the corner – see the one wearing the medals – he's really interesting. Harry saved his life once, apparently. He was wounded and Harry pulled him to safety, despite being under fire himself. And Harry never once said.'

'But that was Harry all over, though, wasn't it?' said Saffron. 'He wasn't the sort to brag about his bravery.'

'No, he wasn't,' said Amy. 'They just don't make them like that any more, do they?'

She looked wistfully at Harry's friends. They had been terribly affected in church. Their presence served to accentuate Harry's absence somehow.

She shook her head and went back into the kitchen. Making tea and giving out sandwiches gave her something to do and stopped her dwelling too much on her misery.

'Is everything okay between you and Pete?' Amy asked as they filled the dishwasher together and then put everything left into the sink to save time.

'Not really,' said Saffron miserably. 'Why do you ask?'

'He seems to be getting rather drunk on elderberry wine out there,' Amy informed her.

'Great, that's all I need,' sighed Saffron.

'So?' prompted Amy.

'So . . . Oh God, I never told you, what with Harry and everything,' said Saffron. 'Pete came home and found Gerry trying to snog me.'

'Oh bugger,' said Amy.

'Oh bugger indeed,' Saffron agreed. 'The trouble is, Gerry was drunk, and so was I, and though I didn't think I'd led him on, and I told him to piss off as soon as I knew what he was up to, Pete doesn't believe me.'

'He'll come round,' said Amy. 'Surely he'll see it wasn't your fault.'

'Will he?' Saffron asked doubtfully. 'We've barely

talked since, and he keeps coming home late. It's like he can hardly bear to spend any time with me.'

'It'll work out, I'm sure,' Amy reassured her, giving her friend a hug. 'You poor thing, you should have said.'

'I thought you had enough on your plate,' Saffron told her.

'Oh now I feel really guilty,' said Amy. 'Sorry I've been a bit out of it with Harry and everything.'

'It's okay, I understand.' Saffron squeezed her hand. 'That's why I didn't say anything. Do you feel any better?'

'Not sure yet,' said Amy. 'Better in some ways – I was dreading the funeral, and at least that's over – and worse in others. When everyone's gone, then I have to get used to Harry not being around. And I just can't bear to think about it.'

'Well at least you've got Ben to lean on,' said Saffron. 'Surely that will help?'

Amy shrugged and said, 'Maybe.'

'Oh come on,' said Saffron, 'he's wonderful, you know he is.'

'He is,' said Amy. 'And I know how lucky I am . . .'

'Why do I feel there's a "but" here somewhere?' Saffron said.

'But – you're probably going to think this stupid,' said Amy. 'I love Ben, I really do love him, in a way I never thought possible after Jamie. But I can't shift this feeling that everything I touch turns to dust. Everyone I ever love leaves me – my mum, Jamie, Harry. And I can't bear it to happen again. So I'm going to tell him today that we can't see each other any more.'

'But you can't!' Saffron's voice came out in a squeak.

'Don't try to stop me, Saffron,' said Amy. 'I know it probably seems irrational to you. It *is* irrational. But I can't let myself be hurt again. From now on it's just going to be Josh and me.'

Ben sat on the bench on Harry's allotment feeling nervous. Despite his confident words to Saffron, he wasn't at all sure what Amy's reaction was going to be. Sitting here, he could almost hear Harry's voice chuckling, saying, 'Come on, old boy, time to do the decent thing.'

He was going to miss Harry. They all were. He had been a sure and certain presence on the allotments, as changeless as the seasons, as permanent as the trees. And now he was gone. Not for the first time, Ben wondered what happened when you died. Where did you go? He liked to think that there was some kind of life after death – otherwise what had happened to Sarah was just too unbearable to cope with, but what that life was like, how people actually *were* – that was beyond him.

Even when he'd seen people dying as part of his work, he was no closer to understanding what death meant. It was life's great mystery, he supposed. And all the more reason for making sure that he wasted no more of his own life, waiting fruitlessly for the girl he loved to come to him. It was time he went out and got her. He took the ring out from his pocket once more. He turned it over and over in his hands.

In a minute he was going to go back to Saffron's, get her to babysit Josh, and invite Amy out for dinner, where he would propose. He sat staring over the allotments. It was getting cold and he noticed dark clouds were beginning to form on the horizon. He should go in soon and take the plunge. He just needed a few more moments to pluck up the courage to do so. She was going to say yes. She had to say yes. He couldn't bear to think of her saying no.

CHAPTER THIRTY-TWO

'Have you seen Ben?' Saffron was urgently trying to find him to tell him that project Diamond Ring was *so* not a good idea today, but no one seemed to know where he was. He'd helped her with the washing-up before Amy had come back and then gone off to talk to some of Harry's friends. But he hadn't been seen for about an hour. She had to get to him and stop him proposing to Amy. Maybe in a while Amy would think differently, but today was just too soon.

'I think he said he was going on to Harry's allot-ment,' said one of the Guys, as Saffron asked for the millionth time. 'I don't know why.'

'I do,' thought Saffron grimly. Damn him, why did he have to decide to be so bloody pigheadedly romantic now?

She hurried down the garden path, meaning to go straight out onto the allotments, when Pete stopped her.

'Well, hello there, wifey,' he said drunkenly. Good lord, he was really very drunk. How on earth had that happened so quickly? Pete liked a drink certainly, but he normally would have stayed sober on an occasion like today.

'Not now, Pete,' she said, 'I'm in a bit of a hurry. I want to get to the allotments.'

'Oh, you want to go to the allotments, do you? Why, has lover boy decided to go and live in our shed again?'

'Don't be stupid, Pete, you know he's staying in a hotel.'

'Oh I'm stupid now, am I? Yes, that's about right. I am bloody stupid. So stupid I didn't realise that my wife was making a cuckold of me with her ex right under my nose.'

He had raised his voice now, and Bill and Bud tittered nervously, not sure if Pete was joking or not.

'Pete, this is neither the time nor the place,' hissed Saffron.

'Oh isn't it?' said Pete, grabbing her arm and holding it tightly. 'You humiliated me, so I'm going to humiliate you. Ladies and gentlemen, meet my wife. My lovely, charming, cheating wife.'

'Let go of my arm, you prat,' said Saffron.

'So what exactly were you up to on Wednesday evenings?' said Pete. 'You tell me that.'

Saffron went white. Bloody hell, he'd put two and two together and made ten.

'Not what you think I was doing,' said Saffron slowly.

'So you have been lying to me,' said Pete. 'Maddy was right.'

'What the bloody hell has Maddy got to do with it?'

'She told me you were cheating on me and she was right.'

'I have never and would never cheat on you in my whole life,' said Saffron. 'I can explain about Wednesdays later, but right now I need to get to the allotments to find Ben to make sure he doesn't make a fool out of himself by proposing to Amy, as I think she's about to ditch him.'

'Too late,' said Bill, 'I saw Amy go out on the allotments five minutes ago.'

'Oh bugger,' said Saffron, and walked away. There was nothing more she could do. Amy and Ben had to work this out for themselves.

Amy shivered a little. It was a grey November day and the evenings were beginning to turn colder now. The trouble was, she wasn't sure what she wanted. Finally admitting to Saffron something she had known for months now, but not dared to say – that she did love Ben – had come as something of a surprise. She realised she had been kidding herself, hiding behind this notion that she could only fall in love once.

Lightning did apparently strike twice – and how. And that was the trouble. She had fallen in love again, and she of all people knew that love wasn't enough. It always ended, and someone always got hurt. She couldn't risk it, not again. Losing Jamie had been the worst thing she had ever had to cope with. Losing Harry had made her remember the full agony of it. She

409

couldn't bear it if something were to happen to Ben too. The best way – the only way – to protect herself was to get out now before she went in any deeper.

She had to explain to Ben that she couldn't see him any more. The sooner she said it, the better. Since Harry had been ill, they had slipped into an easy intimacy, which could so quickly become something more. She didn't want to lead Ben on – it would be fairer to nip things in the bud now. Once it was done, it was done, and they could both get on with their lives again. *A life without Ben?* a little voice treacherously whispered in her head. *Is that what you really want?*

Isn't that just cowardly? The little voice was most insidious, and most annoyingly right. She knew it was right. She was running away rather than allowing herself to become vulnerable again. But she couldn't face opening herself up to any more hurt. Not again.

'Were you looking for Ben?' One of the Guys was coming up the garden path in search of a refill.

'Yes, have you seen him?'

'I saw him wandering over to the allotments about twenty minutes ago,' he said. 'You might find him over there.'

'Thanks,' said Amy and, grabbing a cardigan to wrap over her thin shirt, she marched down the garden path. She wasn't looking forward to what she had to do. But it was now or never. If she was going to leave Ben, the sooner she did it, the better.

410

Saffron went inside fuming. She was cross with Pete, sick at heart with worry about her marriage, furious with Gerry for the mess he had created, missing Harry in a way she had never thought possible, and somewhere deep down inside she had a gnawing anxiety that she should have interfered and told Ben to hold off on his proposal.

She went into the lounge, automatically picking up cups and plates, and wondering grouchily whether anyone was going to offer to help her do the washing-up, when Edie and Ada said, 'Come on, dear, let us help you. You've been working so hard all day.'

Saffron groaned inwardly. She'd scarcely seen them since their embarrassing encounter at her first pole-dancing class. They were the last people she would have asked to help her, but she was beginning to feel like a rather resentful skivvy, so instead she said gratefully, 'Thanks very much.'

'It's a sad day, isn't it, dear?' Edie asked.

'It is,' said Saffron, thinking mechanically that she must have been saying the same thing all day long.

'In the midst of life we are in death,' intoned Edie solemnly.

'Too true, Edie, too true,' said Ada. 'Which is why we should make the most of things while we're here, eh, Saffron?' She winked at Saffron, who blushed.

'You still going to them classes?' Edie wanted to know.

'Er, not any more,' said Saffron.

'Shame,' said Edie. 'Young girl like you, needs to be keeping her man happy, if you know what I mean?'

'Ooh, Edie, you are a one,' Ada shrieked raucously. 'I say, isn't she a one?'

'Yes, isn't she?' said Saffron with heavy sarcasm.

'Mind you,' Ada switched back to solemn mode, 'Harry's better off where he is. He wasn't coping very well on his own. The house was in a shocking state. I don't know what Mavis would have said.'

'Ah, but he's with Mavis now,' added Edie comfortably, as she washed a cup up, 'and that's all for the best really, isn't it? He wasn't the same man at all after she went, was he?'

'You're not wrong there, Edie,' said Ada, shaking her head sadly, while plunging her hands enthusiastically into the soapy water. 'But he had a good send-off, didn't he?'

'That he did, Ada, and you can't say fairer than that.'

Sensing her presence was no longer required, and that they could keep up the headshaking pronouncements for rather a long time, Saffron checked on the children before chucking a coat on and heading for the allotments. The gnawing feeling of anxiety had resurfaced with a vengeance. It had been a lousy day and she was beginning to have a very bad feeling about the way it was going to end. People were drifting in from the allotments and making noises about going home. Saffron took the opportunity to slip silently away – let Pete deal with their guests, he'd done very little to help all day.

Dark clouds loured over the allotments. A wind was getting up and the clouds were scudding across the sky. Saffron shivered, there was an ominous feeling in the air. She ran as fast as she could through the allotments. It was probably too late but she couldn't help herself. She had a feeling she knew where Amy and Ben might be, but, getting up towards Harry's hut, she could see Ben and Amy facing each other in the pouring rain. She was too far away to hear what they were saying, but the body language didn't look good. It looked as though she'd got there too late.

'Amy, I was just going to come and find you.' Ben was taken by surprise. He had been sitting out here so long he hadn't realised how late it was. It had suddenly got much darker and it looked like rain. He shivered. When did it get so cold?

'Ben – we need to talk.' Amy didn't seem relaxed to him. She looked tense and unhappy. He so badly wanted to make her happy, to take that tension away. He had never wanted anything so much in the world. From the very day he had first seen her, he had wanted to make her smile again, and stop her being so sad. If only she would let him.

'Yes, we do,' said Ben. 'I can't wait any longer. You must know how I feel about you.'

'Ben – don't, please don't.' Amy looked aghast. This was not going to plan at all.

'Amy, you must know I love you. And I think you love me. Please,' he grabbed her hand, 'hear me out. I can't live without you any longer. Harry's death has made me realise – life's too short. I'm not good at all this stuff, but

Amy, I want to do this properly.' Ben stood up and, still holding her hand, got down on one knee. The rain was coming down now and if she hadn't been so horrified, Amy might have laughed, he looked so ridiculous kneeling there in the mud. But she couldn't laugh, not now. He was about to propose and she was going to break his heart. This wasn't the way it was supposed to be.

'Amy, will you marry me?' He held out a little box. He didn't have to tell her what was inside.

Amy stood rigid. Whatever she had been expecting she hadn't anticipated this.

'Aren't you going to look at it?'

Amy opened the box, and took out the ring. It was beautiful. A single diamond in a ring made of twisted white gold. It was the most beautiful ring she had ever seen.

A cold wind was whipping up across the allotments. She stood in silence for a long time. Rain had started heavily, and was now coming down in sheets. Amy was soaking wet and her hair was blowing in the wind. She looked ethereal, otherworldly, like a creature who didn't belong to him. Ben knew in a sickening flash what her answer was going to be.

'Ben, I'm so sorry.' The words came out in a whispered sob. 'I can't do this. I just can't marry you.'

'But why?' Ben knew it was useless asking, but he had to know.

'Because I've had my heart broken before and I can't bear for it to happen again. Everyone I've ever loved ends up leaving me. My dad left. Jamie died. Harry died. I'm sorry, Ben, I just can't do it.'

'So that's it?' A sudden anger had overtaken Ben. If she was to be his, she was worth fighting for. 'That's your answer? Amy, life is about getting hurt. Everyone gets hurt sometimes. You can't hide yourself away from love forever, and bury yourself in the sand pretending it doesn't exist. I know you feel the same way. How can you let something this good go?'

'I just can't.' The look on her face tore at his heart. 'You don't know what it's like to lose someone. After Jamie died, my whole world collapsed. I never ever want to feel like that again.'

'You're not the only one who's lost someone, Amy,' said Ben, the anger resurfacing. 'You don't have the monopoly on grief.'

'I never said I did,' Amy was stung to respond. 'But you've never lost someone you love. You can't know what it's like.'

'Haven't I?' Ben spat out. 'How do you know I haven't?'

'You never said – I just assumed –'

'Well don't!' said Ben. 'Don't assume things you have no idea about.'

'Who – what happened?'

Ben put his head in his hands and looked up at her, and Amy saw, in his eyes, a mirror of her own pain.

'I had a sister, once,' said Ben, very slowly. 'Her name was Sarah and she was three years younger than me. When she was born I thought she was the loveliest thing I had ever seen. We used to muck about together – you know, how kids do. And sometimes she was my annoying little sister. But I loved her. And I looked out

415

for her, and she looked up to me. And then –' His voice cracked, and Amy heard the raw, naked pain. She had never seen Ben like this.

'How did she die?'

'She drowned. She was five years old, and I was eight. And she drowned. And I couldn't save her.'

'Oh Ben.' Amy came and knelt in the mud with him, and held him close to her, as the rain beat down upon them. She could feel his heart thumping next to hers. 'You were only a child, it wasn't your fault.'

'But you don't understand,' Ben whispered. 'I was meant to look after her. I was her big brother. I was supposed to protect her.'

'What happened?'

'We'd gone for a family picnic in the park, and she wanted to come fishing for newts with me. But I wanted to play with my friends so I told her to go away. But she followed me anyway. And then –' He took a deep breath.

'Then –?' Amy prompted gently.

'Then, I felt bad about leaving her behind, so I went to look for her. But she wasn't where I left her. So I went back to the pond, and there she was – floating in it. I jumped in and tried to get her out, but I couldn't reach her, and I got tangled in the pond weed. And then my dad was there, shouting at me, and pulling Sarah out and doing mouth-to-mouth. While I sat there watching her die, knowing it was all my fault. And my parents never knew.'

'Do they know now?'

'I can't tell them that,' said Ben. 'How do you think they'd feel knowing I killed their daughter?'

'Ben, it was an accident, surely they'd see that.'

'Maybe,' said Ben, 'but I've never found the courage.'

There was a silence, the only sound the pounding of the rain on Harry's shed roof. Then Ben stood up, still holding on to Amy.

'So you see, I know all about pain and suffering and loss. And I still carry on. The reason I'm a doctor is because of Sarah. It's my fault she died, and I couldn't save her, but I can try to save others. And though I live with the pain every day of my life, I still would choose to live my life to the full, and risk being hurt again. You have to choose life, Amy. To do anything else is to condemn yourself to the dark and a life that's only half-lived. You have to choose to live, Amy. Please.'

Amy stood torn between what he had said: her heart caught by the pleading in his voice, and her fear of allowing herself to love again. Slowly she pulled herself away from him.

'I'm sorry, Ben, I want to, but I just can't.' Her voice was a strangled whisper. She thrust the ring back in his hand. He snatched it from her, and threw it into the middle of Harry's allotment.

'Don't,' said Amy.

'Why not?' snarled Ben, his face suffused with the anger and hurt she had put there. Not knowing what else to do, Amy stumbled away, tears pouring down her face. The rain was coming down now in fast and sharp needles, and the wind was whipping across the allotments.

The wind howled even louder, and the rain came down harder. Letting out a great howl of rage, Ben punched his fist into the side of Harry's shed. Harry was gone. And now, so was Amy. And he doubted he was ever going to get her back. He'd lost her, and this time it was for good.

CHAPTER THIRTY-THREE

Saffron rolled over in bed, and woke up with a start. Pete still wasn't there. That meant he hadn't come home last night. By the time she had come in from the allotments the previous day, everyone had been leaving, and shortly after he had gone to the pub. She had assumed he would be back later, but then Amy had come in from the allotments, soaking wet and in a terrible state.

'What happened?' Saffron had been shocked at the state of her friend, who was pale and sodden.

'I've made such a mess of things,' Amy had told her, and collapsed sobbing into Saffron's arms.

'Don't you think you both need to calm down a bit?' said Saffron, once Amy had filled her in on Ben's proposal. 'I told Ben today wasn't a good day to propose –' Amy shot her a startled glance, and Saffron shrugged her shoulders '– the poor lamb was excited, he had to tell someone. I did try to warn him off, but by the time I got out there it was too late.'

'It wouldn't have made any difference,' said Amy. 'I would still have said no.'

'Don't you think you'll change your mind in a few months? Things might not seem so bad then?'

'I don't know,' said Amy, wearily. 'I can't see it at the moment. I don't think it's fair to string Ben along, do you?'

'No, I don't suppose so,' Saffron replied. She'd sighed, and thought about Pete and how she would feel if she lost him. Then she'd shivered. Suddenly it seemed much more likely that's what would happen.

'Where's Pete, by the way?' Amy asked, as if reading Saffron's mind.

'Pub,' Saffron replied, and then to her horror she burst into tears.

'Oh God,' said Amy, 'just look at us. We're a right pair, aren't we?'

'Sorry,' sniffed Saffron, 'it's been a long day, and it feels like I'm losing Pete, and I just don't know what to do.'

Ben had got back to his darkened house immediately from the debacle at the allotment. He couldn't face going to Saffron's for the rest of the wake. In fact, he wasn't sure he could even face living round here any more. Not without Amy. Not without Harry to put him right about life, the universe and everything. Perhaps it was time to move on.

Meg came up, wagging her tail and licking him all over enthusiastically.

'Down, girl,' he said, giving her a hug. At least he

still had a dog who loved him. He went into the kitchen and got some dog food out to feed her. He stared across the darkening allotments, where the storm was still raging in full swing. Amy was out there somewhere, and she was lost to him. There was no way he could continue living so close and not being with her. It was too much to bear. On Monday he would start making enquiries about working at other surgeries.

He turned on the radio – a Coldplay concert was in progress. Great, just miserable enough for his mood. He poured himself a can of beer, intending to sit there and wallow in his misery. And then a song came on with lyrics that were so painfully, unbearably close to the way he felt that he could stand it no longer. He had wanted to fix her, he had wanted to make things better, but he had left her standing in the rain, tears streaming down her face, unable to help.

This was no sodding good at all. He switched off the radio, patted Meg on the head, and headed for the Magpie. Drowning his sorrows looked like the only option he had.

It was gone nine p.m. and the pub was heaving by the time he got there. Ben realised to his surprise it was gone nine o'clock. Where had the last few hours gone? He was in such a blur of misery he had lost half an evening.

He jostled his way to the bar and eventually got served by a pretty young barmaid. A pretty young barmaid who wasn't Amy. It was no good pretending he could get over her and look at other women, because he didn't want other women. He just wanted Amy. He sipped his beer, scanning the pub for anyone he knew, and then spotted Pete in the corner with a group of the allotmenteers. Pete seemed well plastered. Ben frowned. Pete had presumably carried on drinking because of the funeral, but it was unusual for him to be out this late on a Friday.

'Hi,' said Ben, wandering over to them. After a general chat about Harry and how much he would be missed, Ben squeezed in next to Pete. 'Managed to wangle a late-night pass from Saffron then?' he asked.

'I do what I want,' said Pete defiantly. 'I'm not tied to her apron strings.'

'I wasn't suggesting you were,' said Ben, rather taken aback with the aggressiveness of the response. He and Pete had been mates for years, and he'd never seen him like this.

'Well, good,' said Pete, with a drunkenly determined growl.

'I don't mean to pry, but is everything okay?' Ben asked.

'I need another pint.' Pete didn't appear to have heard the question.

'Don't you think you've had enough?'

'If I want a pint I'll bloody well have one!'

'Woah!' Ben held his hands up. 'Here, let me get it for you.' It was so busy at the bar he had visions of Pete spilling it over half the punters in the pub, and in the mood he was in, Ben could see things turning ugly.

'I've a good mind to go round to Gerry's right now,' Pete announced abruptly when Ben got back.

'You don't know where he lives,' said Ben.

'I do,' said Pete, 'he's staying at the motel on the other side of town.'

'I really don't think that's a good idea, do you?'

'I shall march right up there and have it out with him,' said Pete. 'In fact, I think I will challenge him to a duel. Fancy being my second?'

'Yeah, right,' said Ben. 'You know, there is an easy way to sort this out.'

'How's that?' Pete asked.

'You could talk to Saffron.'

'So she can lie to me again?' asked Pete. 'No thanks.'

'Pete!' Ben was exasperated. 'There may be a perfectly simple explanation for all this. From what I've seen, Saffron can barely give Gerry the time of day. Maybe he pounced on her and she fought him off?'

'I know what I saw,' said Pete sulkily, lifting his pint to his lips. He missed and half of his pint ended up on the table, the floor and over his shirt.

'Come on, let's get you home,' said Ben.

'I'm not going home,' Pete replied moodily. 'I want another drink.'

'And I think you've had enough, mate,' said Ben.

'Don't tell me when I've had enough.' Pete lurched off his chair, and swung a drunken punch at Ben. He missed but tottered forwards, hit the bar, and slid slowly down to the floor.

'You've had enough,' said Ben, 'and I *am* taking you home.'

In the end, Amy and Josh had stayed the night at Saffron's and the women sat up till very late mulling over their respective dilemmas. It was gone midnight when they went to bed, Amy going first, completely exhausted by the events of the day. Saffron had drawn the curtains, and left the bolt off the door. Despite several calls to his mobile, which was switched off, Pete hadn't responded. Saffron nearly rang Ben to ask if the men were together, but she couldn't face the questions about Amy. So she too went to bed, where, worn out with worry, she had eventually fallen asleep to the sound of falling rain on the roof. She woke once at 4 a.m., and Pete still wasn't back. She rang his mobile again, and from the irate drunken response worked out that he was with Ben drinking whisky. At least she knew he wasn't in a gutter somewhere. She turned over and tried to go to sleep, but lay awake for a long time, wide-eyed and terrified. Pete was going to leave her. She knew it. And there seemed to be nothing she could do.

Ben woke up on his sofa with a stinking head and a dry mouth. He squinted at the table where an empty bottle of whisky was looking accusingly at him. Everything after about midnight, when he and Pete had drunkenly decided that women were the bane of their existence and they were going to pursue a policy of celibacy and denial for the rest of their natural lives, was a bit of a blur. He had tried to persuade Pete to go home, but having apparently forgotten all about the punch he'd tried to throw Ben's way, Pete had gone into 'you're my best mate' mode. Ben had vague memories of Pete saying, 'We have to stick together, mate, through thick and thin. At the end of the day, when the chips are down –' Ben winced a little here – even in his hung-over haze – at the number of clichés Pete had managed to produce in one short sentence '– it's only your mates you can trust.'

The trouble with only trusting your mates was it tended to lead to appalling hangovers. Ben sat up and rubbed his head. Had all that really happened with Amy yesterday? He wanted to turn the clock back and undo everything they had said to each other.

A muffled snore from the other corner of the room alerted him to the fact that Pete was asleep in a chair. Ben had vague memories of trying to persuade him to phone Saffron, but Pete had been having none of it. Ben sighed. He had thought Saffron and Pete were one of those perfect marriages, they had seemed so right for each other. But then again, maybe there was no such thing as a perfect marriage.

Ben got up gingerly – his head really was thumping – and went to the kitchen to make some coffee. By the time he returned, Pete was awake.

'Do I look as grim as I feel?' he asked.

Scanning his beer-soaked shirt, half-open since he'd taken his tie off sometime the previous evening, and his decent trousers muddy from where he had fallen over several times in the allotments, then moving up to his pale face, complete with bloodshot eyes and wild hair, Ben laughed and said, 'Grimmer. But I probably look the same.'

'Remind me never ever to drink elderberry wine again,' said Pete.

'You're the agent of your own misfortune,' said Ben, 'and I have no sympathy.'

'It wasn't my fault,' protested Pete. 'The Wine Producers were practically forcing it down my neck.'

'Hmm,' said Ben, 'I didn't see you saying no.'

There was a pause while they sipped their coffee.

'So are you going to ring Saffron and tell her where you are?' Ben asked. 'She'll be worried about you.'

'Worried about me?' said Pete. 'Somehow I doubt it.'

'Don't you think you may be overreacting just a little bit?' Ben suggested. 'You still don't know her side of the story.'

'No, and I don't want to,' said Pete, a stubborn look setting in. Ben knew that look of old, although he hadn't seen it since they were teenagers. It was a bad sign it was here now.

'Well I think you should ring her,' said Ben. 'I would.'

As if on cue, Pete's mobile rang.

'Hi Saffron. Yes, I am still at Ben's. When am I coming home? When I feel like it.'

Pete snapped the phone shut and slammed it angrily down on the table.

'Don't say another word,' he said. 'Don't you say another bloody word.'

Saffron stood open-mouthed in her kitchen.

'He's not coming back,' she said, the words not sounding right coming from her lips.

'What do you mean?' Amy replied.

'I asked him when he was coming home, and he said, when he felt like it. And when I asked him what he meant, he put the phone down on me.'

'Maybe he's bluffing?'

'I don't think so,' said Saffron. 'Pete can be very determined when he puts his mind to it. And he's the most stubborn cuss I know. If he's decided he's not coming back, he just won't.'

'Well, if he won't come to you, you'll have to go to him,' said Amy. 'I'll hold the fort here with the kids. You go over to Ben's and sort this out.'

'Amy, are you sure?'

'Of course I'm sure,' said Amy. 'I know my love life is a disaster, but there's no need for yours to be too.'

Saffron pulled her coat on, and, heart in her mouth, made her way across the allotments. It was another grey and miserable day and the rain had made the paths muddy and slippery.

She got to Ben's house horribly quickly. She wasn't even sure what she was going to say, but she had to let Pete know how she felt about him, and how wrong he was about everything.

Ben answered the door, ushered her into the lounge and discreetly disappeared upstairs to have a shower.

'You look like shit.' The words were out of Saffron's mouth before she had thought them through. Engage brain before mouth, girl, she admonished herself.

'You don't look so hot yourself,' said Pete. He looked grumpy and dishevelled, but still her heart lurched at the sight of him.

'This is silly, Pete,' said Saffron. 'Come home, we need you.'

'Not as much as Gerry, apparently,' said Pete, with a stiffness that she didn't recognise.

'Pete, you've got it all wrong,' Saffron told him. 'Gerry pounced on me and I told him to bugger off. I do not want Gerry back, I just want you.'

'How do I know you're not lying to me?' Pete demanded. 'I was away for two days, and anything could have happened. Besides, Maddy as good as told me you were having an affair.'

'So you believe her more than me?'

'Can you honestly tell me you haven't lied to me about anything?'

A guilty look crossed Saffron's face. 'No, but –'

'So you have lied to me.'

'Not about Gerry,' said Saffron. 'Honestly, nothing happened. Nothing at all.'

'I don't believe you,' Pete replied.

'Then there's no point in carrying on this conversation any more, is there?' said Saffron. 'If we can't trust one another, our marriage is meaningless.'

'If you say so.' Again, she saw the stiffness in Pete and his fixed, rigid stare, looking past her.

'I didn't,' said Saffron in exasperation. 'You did, by

428

not believing me. But I'm not going to demean myself by begging. You know where I am if you want me.'

She turned and walked out of the door, slamming it really hard. Bloody men! Why did they have to be so dense? It was only when she was halfway home that she stopped and took a deep breath. What if Pete took her literally? What if he never came home again?

CHAPTER THIRTY-FOUR

'I've got a proposition for you,' said Ben as he walked in from work one evening a few weeks after Harry's funeral. He tried not to wince as he saw the state of his bachelor pad. Since Pete had been crashing out in his small spare room, the house not only felt incredibly crowded, but had also taken on that distinctive squalor of two lads living together. Ben couldn't help but be seduced by it. Having another bloke about the place somehow immediately transported them back into a kind of *Men Behaving Badly* state, the like of which he hadn't experienced since his student days. In fact, it was probably watching repeats of *Men Behaving Badly* till the early hours which was partly responsible.

There were empty cans of lager sitting on the coffee table from the previous night, along with takeaway wrappings. Ben liked cooking normally, but somehow with Pete in the house he hadn't been getting into the kitchen much. Instead they had been repairing to the pub after work, moaning about the state of their love lives, and then coming back around 9 p.m. Realising that, once again, it was too late to cook, they would ring up Mrs Lee Wong for a Chinese, or the Nevermorewell Bar 'n' Grill for a curry. A night at the gym was long overdue.

'What's that then?' Pete was in the kitchen, already raiding the fridge. 'We're nearly out of lager,' he said.

'Now there's a surprise,' Ben replied. 'No thanks.' He waved Pete's offer away. 'I want to go to the gym tonight and get an early night. I'm knackered.'

'So what's the deal?' Pete asked, sipping his can of lager. He hadn't shaved for about a week and was beginning to resemble a younger Captain Ahab.

'The deal is that I'm leaving.'

'You're wha-at?'

'Well, not for good. The practice needs to save some money, and I was on a short-term contract. I've got a bit of dosh in the bank. First off, I'm going to see my parents. And then I'm going travelling for a bit. I've got nothing to keep me here. I thought I'd rent the house out while I'm away.'

'But what about me?' Pete looked comically woe-begone.

'If you will insist on this stupid standoff with Saffron –' Pete was refusing to see Saffron till she apologised for accusing him of not trusting her; Saffron was refusing to apologise for 'nothing', as she put it, so the situation was at an impasse '– then you are of course welcome to stay here as long as you like. However, as your best mate, my advice to you is to stop being a prat and go home where you belong.'

'Oh, right,' said Pete. 'Well, as Saffron is probably

likely to take the shillelagh to me if I go home, I think I'll pass on that one.'

Ben laughed. A vision of Saffron as an axe-wielding Boudicca type was all too probable.

'I still think you're being a prat,' he said, 'but it's your funeral.'

'Does Amy know you're going?' Pete asked.

'No,' said Ben shortly. 'I only decided for certain today. And it's not going to make any difference, is it? She's made her feelings *quite* plain.'

'Don't you think you're being a bit pig-headed?'

Amy paused from digging Mrs Amos's frosted flowerbeds. Her steamy breath showed sharp and clear against the cold wintry sun. Even though it was hot work, she still felt chilled to the bone. She had done ever since the news had filtered through that Ben was leaving. She hadn't seen him since Harry's funeral, over a month ago now, and he was going away. And he hadn't told her.

'Er, pot calling kettle black,' said Saffron, pulling up some unsavoury-looking roots. 'God, we should have done this earlier. How the hell did we get so behind?'

'Ooh, I don't know,' said Amy, 'was it because I've been busy looking after the elderly, breaking my heart and generally ruining my life, while you've deliberately sought out single-mum status?'

'I have not deliberately become a single mum,' said Saffron grumpily. 'It isn't my fault that Pete won't come

433

home. I want him back. The kids want him back.'

'Well, tell him!' said Amy in exasperation.

'What, like you're going to tell Ben that you've made a terrible mistake, and you will marry him after all?'

Amy didn't respond.

'Didn't think so. The trouble is, it's not as simple as all that. Pete doesn't trust me. I've told him till I'm blue in the face that there's nothing between me and Gerry and he doesn't believe me. What hope has our marriage got if he doesn't trust me?'

'Then we'll just have to find a way of making him believe you, won't we?' said Amy. 'Come on, I'm sure there must be a way.'

'Hmm, was that a pig flying past?' asked Saffron. 'Thought not. Go on, give me that spade. I need to vent my fury on Mrs Amos's brambles.'

Amy thought about what Saffron had said as she put Josh to bed that night. Josh was in a foul mood and had thrown his dinner on the floor at teatime, something he hadn't done since he was a toddler, when Amy had been in the first throes of her grief over Jamie. Not only that, he had kicked her when she had tried to bath him. She had somehow managed to restrain herself from smacking him by dint of going into another room, counting to ten and screaming very loudly, but it had been a close run thing.

Amy wasn't against smacking per se, but ever since she had been alone with Josh she had been frightened that if she lost her rag with him too roundly, she would have no one but herself to apply the brakes, so a 'no smacking' rule had seemed sensible. Josh rarely pushed her that far normally, so it was a shock to even find herself in this position. And the trouble was, she knew exactly why he was behaving like this.

'When is Ben coming to see us again?' Josh asked as she tucked him into bed.

'Oh darling, I told you,' said Amy, 'Ben isn't going to come around any more.'

'But I thought he liked me,' said Josh.

A wave of guilt rushed over Amy. What was she doing to all of them? She had been so caught up with misery about Harry it had seemed like the right thing to do. She had been so certain. It was only now that she wasn't so sure.

'Of course he does,' said Amy. 'It's just Mummy and Ben have had a silly grown-up row, so Ben's a bit cross with Mummy.'

'So it's not my fault?' said Josh.

'No, darling, it's not your fault.' She kissed Josh softly on the head. 'It's mine, all mine.'

'You should tell Ben you're sorry,' said Josh sleepily.

'I should, shouldn't I?' Amy agreed. But as Saffron had said to her, if only life were that simple.

And that's when it came to her in a flash. She might not be able to get Ben back, but there was a very, very easy way to get Saffron and Pete together. She just needed Gerry to play ball.

Ben had dragged Pete to the gym. The deterioration into which they had so swiftly fallen had alarmed him so much that he'd decided they both needed taking in hand. It was either that or slit their wrists over yet another Chinese takeaway. As he completed a hard-burn workout on the treadmill, Ben concluded it had been the right thing to do. Pete was looking knackered and red in the face, it was true, but even he admitted to feeling better for it as they worked their way through the weights.

'Don't I know you?' A gorgeous tall blonde came slinking up towards them.

Pete's eyes nearly popped out of his head.

'Put your tongue away, it's rude,' whispered Ben.

'I don't think so,' said Pete, 'but I'm sure that can be amended.'

'Oooh, get you. Oh, I know you, babe.' The blonde clicked her fingers. 'You're Saffron's husband, you dropped her off at mine once.'

'And you are?'

'I'm Linda Lowry. Saffron does my garden,' said the blonde. She gave Pete a sly look. 'Has she given you your birthday present yet?'

Pete looked baffled. 'What birthday present?'

'Oh,' said Linda doubtfully, 'perhaps she's saving it for Christmas.'

'What is she saving for Christmas?'

Linda looked at Pete, as if weighing him up.

'The routine she was working so hard on for you.'

'Routine, what routine?'

'The pole-dancing one she'd devised as your birthday

present,' said Linda. 'She used to come to lessons with me, don't tell me she never told you?'

'Er, actually, Saffron and I aren't together any more,' said Pete.

'Bloody hell,' Linda replied. 'Me and my big mouth. I've really put my foot in it now, haven't I?'

'What else am I going to find out about my wife?' Pete said plaintively to the world. 'She's been having an affair with her ex-husband, she's been taking pole-dancing lessons. Next thing I know she'll turn out to be the town tart.'

'Don't you think you're exaggerating a tad?' asked Ben.

'No, I bloody don't,' said Pete. 'Sod this health lark, I'm off down the pub.'

'Bugger,' Ben muttered to himself. 'That was just where I didn't want us to end up tonight.'

Ben thought about Pete and Saffron as he was out on his allotment tidying things up for the winter, and making sure nothing too drastic needed doing in his absence. After discovering the pole-dancing lessons, Pete seemed more adamant than ever that he didn't want to get back with Saffron. As far as he was concerned, she'd been lying to him for months, and he couldn't trust her any more. Ben was still sure there was a reasonable explanation for everything. It all seemed so unlike Saffron, but Pete wasn't hearing any of it. There was nothing Ben could do to make him change his mind. He just hoped that eventually Pete would see sense.

When Ben finished his own allotment, he went over to Harry's plot. It looked lonely and neglected. He felt guilty. He should have come out here and sorted things out for Harry's sake. But with one thing and another he had hardly been here in weeks. And now he was leaving.

He had his radio tuned in to Radio 2 for old time's sake. Jeremy Vine was on talking about Christmas, and a famous chef was wittering on about roast potatoes. Ben thought fleetingly to last Christmas Day – the first time he had kissed Amy. He was going to spend Christmas this year with his family, for the first time in a long time. He felt he owed it to them. Telling Amy about Sarah had made him realise how little he did for his own family, and for how long he had been running away from his own pain. His parents deserved a bit more from him than he usually gave. It was his guilt about Sarah that prevented him going back. Perhaps it was time he faced up to it and told them what he'd done.

Several days after Christmas he was jetting off to the Far East. He had heard about a medical charity that was helping people still affected by the tsunami, and offered his services for three months. There was nothing for him here, he might as well go and do some good somewhere else.

But all it would take for him to drop everything was for Amy to come out onto the allotments looking for him. All he needed to hear was that she had changed her mind, and he would let go of his plans in an instant.

While he was digging on Harry's allotment he had carefully been looking for the engagement ring that he had so carelessly thrown away in his rage. But however hard he looked, he simply couldn't find it. It was gone. Lost forever. It seemed like a horrible, gloomy sign that Amy was lost to him also. He stared towards her house, willing her to come down the path. Willing her to come and find him. Willing her to change her mind.

But she didn't come. Ben finished what he was doing. He tidied up his tools and put them back in his barrow, turned off Jeremy Vine, who was in mid-chat with Terry about frost improving the flavour of your parsnips and sprouts, and wandered sadly up the path back to his house.

He wouldn't be back again. Not for a long time.

CHAPTER THIRTY-FIVE

'Babe, I'm so sorry,' Linda said to Saffron having confessed her faux pas at the gym the minute Saffron and Amy had pitched up to work on her garden. 'I haven't seen you for such a long time, and I had no idea you hadn't told Pete about the classes.'

'It's not your fault,' said Saffron. 'We'd cocked things up pretty well on our own.'

'I wish there was something I could do to help,' Linda said.

'Well, I do have a plan,' said Amy, 'but Saffron thinks it won't work.'

'It's not that exactly,' protested Saffron, 'it's just that –'

'You think it won't work,' Amy repeated.

'So what did you have in mind?'

Amy outlined her idea and Linda burst out laughing. 'It's worth a shot,' she said. 'And I have another idea, that I guarantee won't fail even if Amy's does.'

'What's that then?'

'I'm going to help you work out a routine that can't fail to seduce Pete,' said Linda.

'What, now?'

'Yes, now,' Linda insisted. 'Come on. I've got a studio in the basement.'

'You are joking,' said Saffron, aware that as usual she was covered in mud.

'Nope,' Linda replied. 'There's no time like the present. Come on. I'll devise you the hottest routine you can ever imagine, and have that husband of yours gagging for more.'

'Go on, Saffron,' urged Amy. 'What have you got to lose?'

Amy checked her map for the hundredth time to check she was at the right place. According to Saffron, Gerry was still living out of a bag in a motel far enough out of town that he wouldn't be spotted by the sales reps he bought from.

'He apparently has standards to maintain.' Saffron had rolled her eyes when she said this. She had still been doubtful that Amy's plan would work, and Amy, carried along with sheer bravado, had pooh-poohed her. But now she was here, Amy wasn't quite sure either. Figuring out a way of bringing Saffron and Pete back together had given her something to think about, something else to focus on other than the big gaping hole left by Ben's departure.

He hadn't even come to say goodbye. That had hurt, much more than Amy thought possible. Amy knew she had no right to feel bad about that – after all, she was the one who had rejected his proposal – but she did. Christmas had passed in a hazy blur of misery. Ben hadn't even sent her a card, and she couldn't send him one. She didn't even know where he was – Saffron wasn't communicating sufficiently with Pete to find out details.

Every night she went to bed and listened to Mark Radcliffe, wondering if Ben was listening too. It was the only connection they had left. And every night she cried her eyes out. And all of a sudden all her nonsense about not wanting to get hurt again seemed just that – nonsense. She had given Ben up to save herself from pain and yet she was hurting – and badly. And now there was no way she could get Ben back.

At least if she could see Gerry, she might be able to sort out Saffron's love life. Then one of them had a chance of being happy.

Amy went up to the reception desk feeling ever so slightly nervous.

'Do you have a Gerry Handford staying here?' she asked.

'Oh yes, room seven,' said the receptionist.

'Great,' said Amy. 'Can I leave a message?'

'He's in the hotel now,' smiled the receptionist. 'I've just sent another friend of his up. Do you want to join them?'

'Er, not particularly,' Amy was about to say, when she suddenly thought, the sly old dog. He's at it again. He presumably had a woman with him. Perfect evidence to produce for Pete that Saffron wasn't seeing Gerry.

Feeling slightly bolder, Amy went down the corridor to room seven. She fingered the tape recorder in her pocket.

She felt slightly stupid carrying it, but figured if she could get Gerry to confess all on tape then maybe Pete could be persuaded to believe Saffron was telling the truth.

When she came to room seven the door was slightly ajar. A sound of muffled giggling came from within. She knocked and nothing happened. The giggling continued. Oh lord, was she about to catch Gerry in flagrante? Not a pleasant prospect.

Eventually she heard a female voice say, 'I think there was a knock at the door.'

'Excellent, that will be the champagne,' Gerry's voice pronounced sonorously. 'Enter!'

Amy entered, and immediately wished she hadn't. Gerry and Maddy were entangled in a lustful embrace, the thin sheets of the hotel bed barely covering the parts that no one else would want to reach.

'Bloody hell!' said Gerry.

'Oh my God!' shrieked Maddy, covering herself up. 'What's she doing here?'

'Sorry,' said Amy, backing off, 'but the door was open.'

'Only because we were expecting room service!' said Gerry.

Dismissing the thought that she would never in a million years indulge in an afternoon of passion with the door ajar, and invite the hotel staff into her room, Amy got down to business.

'Look, I'll keep this brief. I'm here for one reason and one reason only. Because of Gerry being a total dipstick, Saffron and Pete have separated. Pete doesn't believe that you and Saffron aren't having an affair, so I want you to put the record straight.'

Maddy shot Gerry a furious look. 'You bloody idiot! You said nothing happened.'

'Nothing did really,' pleaded Gerry. 'I got a bit carried away. I was missing you, my sweet.' He put on a sickeningly pathetic puppy-dog look, which would have made Amy want to hit him, but Maddy went all gooey-eyed back.

'Ah, sweetums, and I missed you too.' She pecked him on the cheek and turned to Amy. 'You can tell that pathetic excuse of a former wife that we are not only back together, but we're getting married –' she flashed an ostentatious rock at Amy '– and going to have babies.'

'Oh, er, right,' said Amy. 'Perhaps, Gerry, you might like to let Pete know this?'

Gerry looked sheepish. 'You wouldn't mind telling him, sweetheart, would you? Might sound better coming from you. Whatever happened with Saffron was a ghastly mistake. Don't know what came over me. Midlife crisis or something. Maddy and I couldn't be happier, could we, poppet?'

'Ah, Gewwy, you are so cute,' said Maddy, and kissed him roundly on the lips.

As Amy had pressed record the moment she walked in, she felt she had more than enough evidence to produce for Pete. So she slid silently out of the room – if nothing else Gerry and Maddy had given her the best laugh she'd had in ages.

'So you see, it was all Gerry's fault,' Amy was saying to Pete. She had made an excuse to leave Josh with Saffron, and then gone round to Ben's house. It was weird coming here, knowing that Ben wasn't here. Part of her hadn't wanted to come at all.

Pete was surprised to see her. 'If you're fishing for news about Ben,' he had warned straight away, 'I've nothing to tell you.'

'I haven't come about Ben,' said Amy, 'it's you I need to see.' And she'd poured out the whole story about going to see Gerry, and played the tape. Pete had listened to it in silence.

'But what about the pole dancing?' said Pete. 'Are you going to tell me that's not true either?'

'No,' said Amy, thinking back to the very steamy routine that Linda had worked out for Saffron. The three of them had laughed their heads off while Saffron had tried to perfect her technique. 'Saffron did go to pole-dancing lessons. But she only did it for you. She was worried that she was letting you down in, er, the bedroom department, and wanted to surprise you. Then Maddy saw her there one night, so she stopped going. She wanted to tell you, but she didn't know how.'

Pete sat still for a moment, then he said, 'I've really made a mess of things, haven't I? Saffron's right. We need to be able to trust each other, and I didn't trust her. How can I persuade her to forgive me?'

'Ooh, I don't know,' said Amy, 'but I should think chocolates, champagne and flowers might help . . .'

Pete looked so desolate she had to laugh.

'Pete, you pillock! Saffron's just waiting for you to

446

say the word. Your trouble is you're too damned stubborn. You both are. In fact it's like dealing with a pair of five-year-olds. I could bang your silly heads together.'

'Unlike you and Ben, of course, who are both being incredibly mature,' Pete shot back.

'Yes, well, maybe I was a bit hasty,' admitted Amy.

'Why don't you email him?' said Pete.

'It's a bit tricky to email someone when you don't have their email address,' Amy replied. 'Funnily enough, Ben didn't give it to me.'

'I've got it somewhere,' said Pete. He looked round the lounge, which was piled high with paper, 'but it, er, might take me some time to find it.'

'You can give it to me later, or, better still, tell Saffron when you see her.'

Pete looked like a terrified rabbit.

'What? Suppose she doesn't want to see me?'

'Take it from me,' said Amy, 'she'll want to see you. So how about I send Saffron round here on some pretext, and you take it from there?'

'But she might not want to talk to me.' Pete still looked panicked.

'Well, knowing Saffron she'll have the shillelagh on you first, but hey, aren't rows supposed to be the precursor to great sex?'

'I wouldn't know,' said Pete.

'Go on, give it a try,' urged Amy. 'After all, what do you have to lose?'

447

Ben lay on his narrow bed in the Thai hospital, thinking about home. He was using the listen-again facility on his laptop to hear Mark Radcliffe. Despite his unhappiness over Amy, he had really enjoyed his stay out here. It felt good to make a difference to people who really had stuff to worry about. But his contract was up soon, and another doctor was coming to take his place. It was time he moved on. Perhaps it was even time he thought about going home.

Home. His heart lurched at the thought. Home meant Amy, and without her he had nothing to keep him there. Pete had hinted in his last email that Amy seemed to be softening her stance, but Ben still hadn't dared to contact her, just in case it wasn't true. But he had to get back at some point. He was an executor for Harry's will, and one of Harry's dearest wishes was to have his ashes scattered on the allotments on Mavis's birthday in March. It was already nearly the end of February. Ben couldn't dally here forever.

And he should go and see his parents again. Going to see them before Christmas had been one of the best moves he'd made in a long time. Confiding in Amy had made him see how stupid it was not talking to his parents about Sarah. So finally he'd plucked up courage to speak to them. It had been a cathartic if painful experience, and the relief on discovering his parents had never blamed him for Sarah's death was overwhelming.

'Why on earth would you think we blamed you?' his mother had said. 'You were a child. You weren't responsible. If anything we blamed ourselves. Oh Ben, all this time and you thought it was your fault! I'm so, so sorry.'

He could have kicked himself for all those wasted years trying to protect them, when they had been trying to protect him. When he got back home, he was going to make sure he saw more of them.

He thought again about Amy. He didn't have her email address. Perhaps he should get it off Pete. Then he heard Mark Radcliffe mention his Crucial Three – as usual it was a fiendish conundrum linking three songs in a weirdly lateral way. Ben wondered if Amy was still listening to the show. Then he smiled. If she was, he had the perfect way of letting her know he still cared.

Saffron stood nervously outside Ben's house. It had taken Amy a good hour to persuade her that this was a good idea, but when Amy had played the tape and told her that Pete had heard it, her heart had lifted. Maybe Pete would believe her now. It still didn't take away the hurt of him not trusting her, but it was a start. And while she had kidded herself over the last couple of months that she was better off without him, she knew in her heart of hearts that it wasn't true. Christmas had been utterly miserable – her mum had tried her best, but Saffron and the kids had missed Pete horribly and they'd ended up coming home early. And as Christmas had worn away into a cold and grey January, and then on to February, and Pete was still not showing any sign of coming round, Saffron had begun to wonder if this time she'd blown it for good.

But Amy thought not. And that gave her some hope. Having put the kids through the heartbreak of one divorce, Saffron didn't want them to have to go through another. She turned over the CD in her pocket nervously, wondering if she was going to have the nerve to use it, then took a deep breath and rang the doorbell. It was now or never. Time to see whether there was anything left to salvage from her marriage.

Pete came to the door looking awkward. God, he was so gorgeous. It hit her straight between the eyes. What had she been doing all these months? Sure there were plenty of fish in the sea, but to let this particular one go would be madness.

They stood for a few moments not saying anything.

'Are you going to invite me in then, or do I have to stay here all night?'

'Oh, sorry, yes, do come in.' Pete seemed stiff and formal. Oh dear.

'I see you tidied up for me,' said Saffron, trying not to wince as she walked through the lounge. Left to his own devices, Pete had evidently degenerated into the very worst excesses of his youth. Oh dear, oh dear.

'I thought you'd come to see me, not criticise my housekeeping,' Pete bristled. Damn. She'd said the wrong thing.

'J – o – k – e,' said Saffron, 'you do remember those?'

'Yes, you usually make them at my expense.'

'Woah,' said Saffron, 'who rattled your cage?'

'Nobody rattled my cage, as you put it, I just didn't find your joke funny.'

'Oh bloody hell, Pete, where's your sense of humour?'

Saffron could feel her hackles rising. Bugger, this wasn't going to plan at all.

'I clearly don't have one.' Pete glared at her, and Saffron glared back.

'I was coming round here to have a sensible conversation,' said Saffron, 'but as you aren't in the mood, I'll just go home instead. Ring me when you're ready to grow up.'

She turned and made for the door, when Pete said, 'No, don't, please.'

There was a plaintiveness to his voice that arrested her, and when she turned and saw the pleading look in his eyes, she melted. All the weeks of misery and loneliness vanished in an instant. He wanted and needed her. And she wanted and needed him.

'All right, you silly old bugger. Just sit down and shut up. Where's Ben's CD player?'

'Over there, why?'

'You'll see,' said Saffron, frantically looking round for anything that might resemble a pole, and spying Ben's hat stand. She drew the curtains, turned on a lamp, put the CD player on and said, 'I'm really sorry I lied to you about the pole-dancing thing, but I hope this makes up for it.'

She felt stupidly self-conscious. What had seemed like a good idea in Linda's basement now seemed ridiculous in the middle of the day, but in for a penny, in for a pound.

Abba started pounding out, and to the dulcet tones of Frida and Agnetha belting out their need for a man after midnight, Saffron started gyrating up and down the pole. Linda had showed her how to bend her legs up and down in a way that when Linda did it had looked sexy and provocative, but Saffron had always felt it made her look like a prat. But from Pete's wolf whistle, it didn't seem as though he minded.

Saffron was getting into her stride now; she remembered that she was supposed to touch herself suggestively with her free hand, while trailing the rest of her body round the hat stand. In a grand ambitious finale, forgetting that the pole wasn't attached to the ground, she leapt up and attempted to straddle it. She and the pole went tits up, and Pete fell about laughing.

'That wasn't quite how it was supposed to go,' said Saffron, nursing her head.

'I can see that,' said Pete, tears streaming down his face.

'It wasn't that funny,' said Saffron.

'Oh yes, it was,' Pete replied. 'But it was also incredibly sexy. Come here, you idiot.'

Saffron went over to him and put her arms around him. 'Okay, if you repeat after me: I'm really sorry and I promise always to trust you.'

'I'm really sorry and I promise always to trust you.'

'And I'm sorry too,' said Saffron. 'I've been pigheaded.'

'Yup,' said Pete, kissing her soundly on the mouth, 'you have.'

'You're not supposed to agree with me,' said Saffron, resurfacing from a passionate kiss.

'J – o – k – e,' said Pete, whose hands were rapidly

beginning to work down her body and remove items of clothing.

'If you think we're having a bonk in this pigsty, you've got another think coming –' began Saffron.

'Oh really,' said Pete, fingers gently teasing her nipples, 'I wouldn't be so sure about that.'

'Oh bugger,' Saffron replied, as he lowered her onto the sofa (expertly removing an empty can of lager as he did so), 'I do hate it when you're right.'

CHAPTER THIRTY-SIX

'Amy, I'm so glad you could come.' Mary greeted Amy and Josh with open arms. Amy was pleased to see her. After all the turbulence of recent months it was nice and restful to be back here. Mary's house had always exuded a sense of calm.

'Granneeee!' Josh rushed in and threw his arms around Mary, who looked suitably gratified.

'Hello darling,' she said. 'It's lovely to see you. If you just wait a minute, I may have a treat for you.'

Josh looked questioningly at Amy, who nodded laughing. 'Go on then,' she said. 'It's not every day we get to have lunch with Granny.'

'I hope you don't mind,' said Mary, 'but I've invited a friend.'

'Not at all,' said Amy, 'I always like meeting your friends. What's her name?'

Mary looked slightly coy. And, lordy-lord, she was blushing.

'It's not a male friend by any chance?' Amy asked,

laughing. 'Well you're a dark horse and no mistake. Go on, give me the lowdown.'

'His name is Jim and we met last year on that cruise I went on. I think I mentioned him before. We got pretty close and I thought he might be interested in seeing me again, but I never heard from him afterwards. I have to confess I was a little disappointed, but I was determined it wasn't going to stop me making the most of my life. But then a few months ago, Jim turned up on my doorstep out of the blue. It turned out he'd lost my address and then spent the next six months checking out all the Mary Browns in the phone directory till eventually he found me. And the rest, as they say, is history.'

Mary looked positively pink and girly as she said this. Amy couldn't help laughing.

'Well, I think that's wonderful,' she said. 'I thought you were settled on being a widow for the rest of your life.'

Mary shrugged. 'I had just assumed that I would be, I suppose,' she said. 'Jamie's dad died when I was in my late thirties, and I was so heartbroken I never felt I could replace him. Then, when I wasn't grieving any longer, I just assumed no one would be interested in a crotchety old woman like me.'

'Oh Mary, you're not crotchety,' said Amy. 'In fact, you're not even very old. I'm glad you've found Jim, and I can't wait to meet him.'

Jim turned out to be a very lively sixty-year-old – Mary referred to him as her toyboy – who still worked out and was also a keen gardener. There was more than a little hint of Harry about him, and both Amy and Josh instantly made friends.

As they were leaving, Mary gave Amy a heartfelt hug, and said, 'You won't make the same mistake I did, will you?'

Amy stiffened slightly. 'I don't know what you mean,' she said.

'Oh darling, it's obvious how unhappy you are. Josh told me all about Ben,' said Mary. 'You're still young and attractive. You deserve to be happy. Don't let your feelings for Jamie stop you. I'm sure he would have understood.'

'I'll bear it in mind,' said Amy, blinking back the tears. 'If I knew where Ben was it would help.'

Saffron came downstairs feeling a self-satisfied after-sex glow. Since Pete had come home they had been at it like bunny rabbits. Pete was already downstairs getting the children's breakfast, and had insisted she stay in bed a little longer.

She grinned at him, and was rewarded with a long, lazy, 'later' kind of look. She couldn't believe how happy she was, or how close she and Pete had come to losing each other. She shivered. It was corny to think it, but a love like theirs didn't come along every day of the week. She had been incredibly foolish to put their relationship to the test like that – if it hadn't been for Amy she might have lost Pete altogether.

'Have you emailed Ben about Harry's ashes yet?' she asked.

Amy had been round the previous day and told them

that Harry's friends on the allotments had planned a little ceremony according to his wishes, on Mavis's birthday, which was in two weeks. He wanted it at sunset, and had asked a friend from his regiment to play the Last Post.

'Lord, there won't be a dry eye on the allotments,' Saffron had said when Amy told her, 'that always gets me.'

'Me too,' Amy had agreed, 'I am so not looking forward to it, but it's what Harry wanted.' She'd paused, and then said, 'So can you let Ben know – I presume he'll want to come.'

'I thought I gave you his email address,' Pete had asked.

'You did,' said Amy, looking shamefaced. 'I haven't had the nerve to send him an email. If he'd wanted to get in touch, he would have by now.'

Saffron and Pete had exchanged glances – Ben and Amy were even more stubborn than they were.

'It's time we did something about them, don't you think?' Saffron had said once Amy was gone.

'Look, just because we've got ourselves sorted doesn't mean we should interfere in other people's love lives,' Pete protested.

'Oh doesn't it?' Saffron asked. 'If it wasn't for Amy, you would still be living in squalor at Ben's. I think we owe her, don't you?'

So Pete had promised to send Ben an email, which miraculously he had apparently done – Saffron had always had to nag him about that kind of thing.

After breakfast, Pete repaired to the study to check his emails.

'Hey, come and look at this,' he called to Saffron. 'I think perhaps you were right.'

To: peteandsaff@bt.internet.com
From: benmgp@hotmail.com
Subject: Harry's Ashes
Hi Guys,

> *Hold your horses. Don't do anything without me. I'm on my way.*
> *Ben*
> *PS Tell Amy I said hi.*

Amy lay in bed, listening to Mark Radcliffe. She had done the same thing pretty much every night since Ben had been away. In a stupid way she felt as though they were still connected through the show.

As she was dozing off she heard Mark say, 'Now it's time for the Crucial Three. Tonight's songs have been sent in by Ben Martin, a doctor who's out in Thailand. If you can work out the connection, just email me and let me know.'

Amy sat bolt upright in bed as Debbie Harry started to sing '(I'm Always Touched by Your) Presence, Dear'. What on earth was Ben up to? Was he really sending her a message?

His next choice, 'What Do I Get?' by the Buzzcocks, had her completely baffled until Mark Radcliffe mentioned it came from the album *Another Music in a Different Kitchen*. By now, Amy was beginning to see

459

where this was heading, but the Bauhaus song 'She's in Parties' clinched it.

Amy raced to her computer and sent the fastest email she'd ever written. God, she hoped no one else had got it too.

'Well, I don't think we've had a Crucial Three discovered in such a record time,' Mark Radcliffe was saying, 'but Amy Nicolson in Nevermorewell, Suffolk, you're absolutely right, the connection is "You'll Always Find Me in the Kitchen at Parties".'

Amy went to sleep for the first time in months with a smile on her face.

On the other side of the world, a few hours later, Ben woke up, and did the same.

The sun was dipping low on the horizon as a steady trickle of people made their way onto the allotments. Amy walked nervously out of her door, holding Josh's hand. Ben was back. Saffron had told her. He had arrived late the previous evening and Amy hadn't had the nerve to contact him. In the cold light of day a game on a radio show didn't seem much of a love letter. She had read too much into it. He probably wasn't thinking about her at all.

Saying hello to various allotmenteers of her acquaintance, Amy hurried over to where Saffron and Pete were standing solemnly by Harry's hut. One of Harry's army friends was holding a bugle. Where was Ben? She craned her neck to look for him.

'It's all right, he's on his way,' whispered Saffron. 'He said he had one or two things to sort out.'

And then there he was, striding up the path with Meg, looking fit and bronzed, and, well – amazing. Amy's heart did a sudden leap, in fact it leapt so high she had the weirdest sensation it was jumping straight up her throat and choking her. Ben looked fabulous. He glanced over at her, and she smiled shyly back at him. She was pleased to see her smile acknowledged with a grin. Maybe all was not lost.

Ben cleared his throat. 'Hello everyone,' he said. 'And thanks so much for coming. As you all know, today is Mavis's birthday. And it was Harry's dearest wish for his ashes to be scattered today on the allotments in memory of her. I have very strict instructions that no one is to cry, we are all to be happy for what Harry told me was a long and happy life, and then we are to proceed as swiftly as possible to Saffron and Pete's gaff. I think they've still got a supply of Harry's elderberry wine, if anyone's interested.' A ripple of amused laughter went round the crowd.

'Typical of Harry not to want a fuss,' Bud muttered behind Amy.

'However, I am going to break ranks a little,' continued Ben, 'because I think the fact that so many of us have come out today to remember Harry reflects how much of an impact he made on so many of our lives, and though we are sad he is gone, none of us can be sorry that we knew him –' he paused and looked at Amy, a deep penetrating look that made her blush and turn away '– and I for one take great comfort from

461

that. Also, I know Harry himself was very grateful for his life, and for the time he had allotted to him. So many of his young friends died in the war, and many times Harry told me how lucky he was. So with that in mind, I thought the following verse appropriate:

'They shall grow not old, as we that are left grow old:
Age shall not weary them, nor the years condemn.
At the going down of the sun and in the morning
We will remember them.'

Ben's last words died away to a sombre but rich silence, while everyone took a moment to reflect on Harry's life. Then Ben carefully passed the urn holding Harry's ashes round, and everyone took a handful, before scattering them over Harry's allotment.

Amy wiped away tears, but they were glad tears – Harry was gone and she still missed him badly, but she knew now that he and Ben were right. Everyone had a time allotted to them, and Harry had had longer than most. There would always be a gap in her life from where he had gone, and another where Jamie should have been. But sometimes someone can step into a gap.

Harry's friend took out his bugle and played the mournful, haunting Last Post. Everyone stood in silence as the sun dipped down below the horizon, and the last ashes of Harry blew away, scattered now in peace in the place he loved the best.

Then, one by one, they slowly walked away, up the path towards Saffron and Pete's swapping anecdotes about Harry, their friend, their neighbour, gone, but never forgotten.

'Have you talked to Ben yet?' Saffron asked Amy. The kitchen was heaving, and she, Amy and Pete had been flat out handing drinks and food around. Amy had only had time to say a brief hello to Ben and nothing else, and hadn't seen him since. She had hoped he would come and find her in the kitchen – it felt appropriate – but there was no sign of him. It was hard not to feel the disappointment. Perhaps she had got the look wrong, read too much into it. Maybe he was avoiding her so he didn't have to tell her that he was no longer interested.

'Nope,' said Amy. 'If he wants me, he knows where I am.'

'That attitude will get you nowhere, my girl,' said Saffron. 'Now go out there and find him.'

'But I can't leave you with all of this –' Amy started to protest.

'Oh, you so can,' said Saffron. 'So hop it!'

Saffron could be very forceful at times, so Amy hopped it.

She went out into the lounge and scanned around for any sight of Ben, but he was nowhere to be seen.

Then two little tornadoes came racing up to her, practically knocking her over.

'Ben – said – to give you –' said one tornado (Matt).

'– this,' continued the second tornado (Josh). 'We've

463

been looking for you everywhere,' he complained.

'Sorry, sweetheart, I've been helping Saffron,' said Amy, her heart suddenly lightening. Ben had written her a note. Then again, she had a sudden panic – she didn't know what it said. Taking a deep breath, she opened the note with trembling hands.

> Dear Amy,
>   I hope I'm right and you haven't totally given up on me. If I am, come and find me on Harry's allotment. I have a surprise for you.
>   Love Ben xx
>   PS I never gave up on you.

Her heart singing now, Amy read and reread the note to make sure she hadn't misinterpreted it. She hadn't. Ben was still interested. And he was waiting for her on the allotments.

She ran to the kitchen and quickly filled Saffron in. 'Way to go, girl!' said Saffron. 'What are you waiting for?'

'What about Josh?'

Saffron gave her a look. 'Josh will be fine here with me. Now, go on, go.'

Needing no more encouragement, Amy sped outside. The last glow of the sun was casting a rosy light on the allotments, which were just springing to life again after the drab dreariness of winter.

As she approached Harry's allotment, she noticed some dancing lights – Fireflies? Hardly in Nevermorewell – but as she got nearer, she realised what they were. Someone – Ben? – had lit candles all the way up the path to Harry's hut, to lead her there. He'd also trailed fairy lights along the trellis that marked the path. It looked quite magical.

Amy took a deep breath, her heart hammering at a rate of knots, and walked slowly towards Harry's hut. As she did so, she noticed something glimmering in the candlelight. She bent down, and there, curled on the edge of a leaf, was the engagement ring Ben had been going to give her. She picked it up, and walked towards Harry's hut, which was ablaze with candle-light.

The hut was transformed. Ben had placed candles everywhere, and the smell of freshly cut roses greeted her. And there he was, standing to meet her, looking as uncertain as she felt. They stood for a moment saying nothing, till Ben said, 'You worked it out then?'

'Always in the kitchen at parties,' said Amy, smiling. 'The Buzzcocks track threw me a bit, but I got there in the end.'

'I wasn't sure you'd come.'

'I wasn't sure you wanted me to.'

'Oh, I wanted you to,' said Ben, and suddenly Amy was stumbling into his arms, tears streaming down her face. How could she have been so stupid as to let him go? How?

'I'm sorry,' she said, 'I'm so sorry.'

'It's okay,' Ben told her, 'everything's okay now.'

And then they kissed, a long, slow, passionate kiss to herald the many more to come. Gently he led her by the hand into Harry's hut, and sat her down on the old comfy sofa that Harry had always kept there, but which was now covered with a throw and scattered with cushions.

'Amy,' he said, going down on one knee. 'I cocked it up last time, and I haven't had time to get you another ring, but will you marry me?'

'I think you might need this,' said Amy, laughing now through her tears, and she held out the ring.

'Where? How?' Ben was laughing too.

'You'll never believe it, but I found it on a leaf,' said Amy.

'That's unbelievable,' Ben replied, and kissed her again. 'So do I get an answer or what?'

'Yes,' said Amy. 'You were right and I was wrong. I've been so miserable without you. I can't go through life not taking risks and keeping myself wrapped in cotton wool. So, I'm not going to any more. I choose to live. And I choose to live with you.'

Ben wrapped her up in his arms and held her tight.

'You have no idea how much I have dreamed that you would change your mind. You know, from the very first moment I saw you, and realised how vulnerable you were, all I wanted to do was fix you, and heal the hurt in your eyes.'

'And you have.' Amy smiled up at him, feeling content and safe and happy.

'Good,' said Ben. 'I wasn't sure whether we'd be able to have this or not, but now we can.'

He held out a glass of champagne and they silently toasted one another.

'Oh, and there's one last thing,' said Ben, leading her

by the hand out to the allotments again. 'Stay there.'

Picking up a box, he walked into the middle of Harry's allotment, where he had cleared a space.

'I meant to use these at Saffron's last fireworks party, but forgot all about them. I hope they still work.' He knelt down and lit the box of fireworks, and then raced back to Amy.

And together they watched as the fireworks set the allotments alight. The last rays of the sun finally dipped over the horizon, and they stayed together as their happiness was written in the sky.

'To Harry,' said Ben, raising his glass. 'Do you know, if it wasn't incredibly fanciful, I could almost think I just heard him laughing.'

'Me too,' said Amy, raising her glass. 'Here's to us.'

'And life,' said Ben. 'Let's toast life in all its strange and painful glory.'

'To life,' said Amy, as the last firework faded and fell to earth. Wherever Jamie was, she had a feeling he would be pleased.

ACKNOWLEDGEMENTS

So many people have helped me on the road to publication, it is quite hard to know where to begin.

Firstly, I would like to thank the Romantic Novelists' Association for having given me so much support and help over the last nine years. I am hesitant to name names in case I forget anyone but I would especially like to thank Katie Fforde for endless support and encouragement, Jenny Haddon for frequent and sound good advice, Eileen Ramsay for wit and humour and Susan Hicks for sharing my love of rock music. Thanks go, too, to Penny Jordan and Rosie Milne for their helpful critiques when this book was at an early stage, and to Sue Moorcroft for giving me such a positive report for the NWS scheme.

Thanks are due, too, to Anne Finnis and David Fickling for so much encouragement and help.

I would also like to thank Kate Boydell, Joanna Clark and Penny Jordan for their insights into widowhood.

For advice about various points of detail during the writing of the book, I'd like to thank Caroline Praed and Catherine Wheeler for checking medical facts, Tracey Kells and Jane Hunnable for gardening advice, Gaynor Kent for telling me about teaching, and Indira Hann, Jeannette Groark and Paula Moffatt for helping me with legal points.

I owe a huge debt of gratitude to Hilary Johnson who gave me the confidence to keep going at a point when I might nearly have given up, and to Kate Mills who showed me a way to open up my writing.

I am immensely grateful to my long-suffering and patient agent, Dot Lumley, who has had such faith in me over the years.

And to Maxine Hitchcock, editor extraordinaire, Keshini Naidoo, Caroline Ridding and the rest of the Avon team I extend my huge thanks.

I would also like to thank all the Radio 2 DJs who regularly brighten my day by being my friends in the kitchen, in particular Jeremy Vine whose programme frequently gives me food for thought, and the inestimable Terry Walton from the Official Allotment who has taught me such a lot about growing vegetables.

I also would like to thank my wonderful brother-in-law, Chris Coles, for coming up with such a fiendish Crucial Three!

470

Finally, I have to say thank you to: John, Joanna, Paula, Lucy, Ginia, Hugh and Tom for being the best siblings one could hope for outside of an episode of *The Waltons*, and to my amazing mother, Ann Moffatt (who beats Ma Walton hands down), for teaching me to believe in myself.

To my wonderful mother-in-law, Rosemarie Williams, many thanks for reading and liking the book!

Without walking my children Katie, Alex, Christine and Steph to school every day, there wouldn't have been a plot, although without them I might have written the book a bit sooner! Thank you for making my life so – er – interesting.

And for Dave. Thanks probably aren't enough. But you know what I mean.

Read on for an exclusive extract of
Julia Williams' new novel,
to be published in 2008

PART ONE
The First Cut

CHAPTER ONE

'Remind me what I'm doing here again?' Emily Henderson stared into the mirror with a frown as she applied some lippy.

'Because there's free booze, we get to meet famous people and it's a laugh,' Marion, her breezy, confident friend, assured her. 'Come on, you know you'll enjoy it.'

'Oh, right,' said Emily, staring at herself critically. God, she was a mess. Her normally sleek dark bob was uncharacteristically unkempt, and she had dark circles round her pale blue eyes. She was looking gaunt. And tired. Even Mum had commented on it last time she went home. No wonder, with so many late nights since Christmas. Working hard and playing hard. It was one way of not thinking about things, she supposed.

'Besides,' added Marion, with characteristic thoughtlessness, 'you've been miserable as sin for the last few weeks. You need cheering up.'

And why would that be, I wonder? Emily thought to herself as she followed her out to the trendy bar, jammed full of Z-listers and other acolytes eager to buy copies of Jasmine Symonds' autobiography, *Jasmine: My Story So Far*. All Marion cared about, with her endless entrees into celebrity functions, launch parties, tickets for the Brits and the like, was hanging out with famous people. As if some of that shiny stuff would rub off on her. It was only a matter of time before she appeared on some crap reality TV programme. Emily could never get used to how star-struck Marion could be.

'Hey look,' Marion dug Emily in the ribs as they picked up their free glass of dubious Chardonnay from a bored-looking waiter. Crackers, the trendy bar much beloved of the celebrity set (or zedlebrities as Marion had taken to calling them. Mind you, her sarcasm didn't stop her wanting to join their ranks), was heaving.

'What?' Emily had a headache and was really wishing she hadn't agreed to come. The thought of Jasmine writing anything was risible, let alone such an impossibly thick volume for someone who was a mere twenty-two years old.

'There's Tits Up Tony,' said Marion. 'They must have made it up again.'

As Tits Up Tony, Jasmine's erstwhile boyfriend, went over to kiss Jasmine, a small, dumpy, rather bovine creature, full on the mouth, the fact that they had indeed made up was plain for all to see. Emily hadn't even realised they'd split up.

'Unless they're just snogging for the cameras,' said Emily, bored.

'Ooh, yes, you could be right,' Marion's beady little eyes lit up with excitement. How she got so titillated by all this stuff was beyond Emily. 'Word on the street is that ever since Tits Up Tony got ditched from his club, Jasmine's been looking for ways to get rid.'

'That's a bit rich, isn't it?' laughed Emily. 'For someone whose sole claim to fame is being the first person in *Love Shack* ever to have performed live fellatio on TV, she's hardly famous for her own merits. At least Tony has talent.'

'Hmm, tell that to his team mates,' said Marion. 'Wasn't it his *lack* of talent that caused them to go crashing out of the FA Cup?' (Tits Up Tony had earned his moniker by scoring an own goal in last year's FA Cup final, thereby earning the never- to- be-forgotten *Sun* headline, IT'S ALL GONE TITS UP FOR TONY!)

'Well, I feel sorry for him,' said Emily. 'I mean, what has Jasmine got that is so wonderful?'

They watched as Jasmine scrawled her illegible signature across the front of an adoring fan's book.

'Ooh, Jasmine, I want to be just like you,' the girl, a spotty fifteen-year-old, gushed.

'Jeez, there's an ambition,' said Emily.

'I dunno,' said Marion. 'Jasmine's just signed a mega deal with cosmetic dental chain *Smile, Please!*' (Marion's PR firm represented Jasmine so she knew these things). 'And if that works out, who knows? According to *OK!* magazine, her aim is to be the face of L'Oreal.'

'Jasmine?' Emily snorted into her glass. 'I didn't know they were planning to put heifers in their ads.'

'Ok,' admitted Marion, 'her looks are more bovine then elfin, but you've got to admit, those teeth... now they do look fantastic.'

They watched as Jasmine flashed her brilliant smile at another sappy group of fans.

'Well, I think without the smile she wouldn't be the face of anything,' replied Emily. 'God, the world's gone mad!'

'Maybe so,' said Marion, 'but it sure as hell beats going to work for a living. If I had a chance to appear on *Love Shack*, I'd do just what she's done.'

'I'm sure you would,' answered Emily. 'Listen, I'm knackered, I think I'm going to call it a day.'

'Don't you want to come to Macy's?' Marion looked disappointed.

'Not tonight,' said Emily, 'I've got an early start tomorrow.'

Despite Marion's efforts to make her change her mind, Emily refused to back down. Once she would have done. Once the thought of a night out on the tiles would have appealed but recently, even as a means to drown her sorrows, a wild night was losing its appeal.

Indeed, as she sat on the train, making the long journey home, watching London fleeing from her in the dark, Emily realised that she was finally beginning to think of Thurfield as a refuge and safe haven from the nightmarish world she seemed to be trapped in. Her friend Katie had been telling her for years she needed to get out of her job. Maybe Katie was right.

Her mobile bleeped and she saw a message from Callum. She'd tried to ring him earlier and his mobile had been switched off.

Where r u babe? Hope yr hot & waiting fr me.

In yr dreams, she texted back. God, she hoped he wasn't drunk. Or high. She leaned against the window and stared into the dark as the countryside flitted past her. How was it that her life had ended up such a mess?

'I don't know how you do it,' Mark Davies laughed at his flatmate as Rob bustled into the kitchen to provide drinks for his latest conquest. 'Here you are, thirty-five, plump, those famous curly locks receding faster then the tide, and still you pull them. I can't think what's sadder – the thought of you practising the waltz, or the stupidity of the women prepared to fall for your lines.'

Mark had been on his way to bed, but Rob couldn't resist showing off his prize, an over made-up girl whom Rob had picked up at his ballroom dancing class.

'Well, you either have it or you haven't, mate,' Rob winked knowingly.

'Mind you,' continued Mark, loading the last of the dirty plates into the dishwasher. Living with Rob was like revisiting their student days, only more depressing. 'It's always been a mystery how you do it. I've never known what women see in you.'

'It's my natural manly charm,' said Rob.

'Yeah, right,' snorted Mark. Rob's mop of unruly curly hair and cute grin seemed to be what got the girls hooked, but his love 'em and leave 'em habits should have been enough for them to run a mile. But somehow it never was. Presumably each and every one of his hapless victims thought they would be the one to change him. And of course they never were.

'You should watch and learn from a master,' continued Rob.

'You know there's only one woman for me,' said Mark.

'Yes, and Sam is just about to have you back. Not,' said Rob.

Mark pulled a face.

'I'm going to bed,' he said. 'Don't do anything I wouldn't.'

'Now that I *can* guarantee,' smirked Rob.

As Mark climbed into bed minutes later, he could hear the telltale sounds of Rob getting his rocks off. Great, that was all he needed. Mark sighed and played Whitesnake on his iPod, turning it up loud. Heavy metal always made him think of Sam, the most unlikely head-banger in the world. Mark lay in the dark trying to drown out thoughts of Sam. Pictures of Sam. Wishing things had turned out differently.

How the hell had he ended up here? Thirty-five, a single dad, living in a three-bedroomed flat with his best friend from uni? While undoubtedly there were advantages in rediscovering a bachelor lifestyle after so many years of domestic bliss (not having anyone nagging about leaving the toilet seat up was a real plus), they didn't outweigh the disadvantages, or the vast gaping chasm that Sam had left behind when she dumped him unceremoniously for Kevin. And to add to the ignominy, he'd been left for a lawyer.

What the bloody hell does Kevin have that I don't? Mark spoke aloud into the darkness. It wasn't the first time he'd asked that question and it wouldn't be the last.

'You never listen to a word I say,' had been Sam's constant refrain during their marriage.

'That's not true,' Mark had protested on more than one occasion. He had listened. Only too well. He'd always been putty in Sam's hands. Ever since the first night he'd seen her, at his first-year dental ball: a tiny blonde vision in a red strapless dress, strutting her funky stuff to Motörhead of all things. He was smitten in an instant and knew, not just that he wanted to take her home with him, but after she'd amazingly said yes to his offer of a dance, that he wanted to spend the rest of his life with her.

And at first it seemed that was the way things were meant to be. Although at Sam's insistence, children came along sooner then he'd planned, but he wouldn't be without Gemma and Beth now. And if sometimes he had chafed at the rather tight leash Sam had put on him, in the main he had been perfectly content.

So it had been a shock to hear that she wasn't. That for Sam, Mark had become a waste of space, a hopeless individual who'd apparently let her and the girls down on a daily basis. And now, here he was, sixteen years after he first set eyes on Sam, alone in bed in his brand-new bachelor pad. This wasn't how it was meant to be.

*　　*　　*

Emily let herself into her dormitory flat with a sigh. It was gone midnight, she had an early start tomorrow and with the way the trains had been lately, she was going to need to be up at the crack of dawn. One of the disadvantages of not living in London. Marion still didn't get why Emily had moved so far out, into the sticks, as she put it.

'I like it,' Emily constantly said. 'It's cheaper than London and I get to have hills.' Emily's flat nestled at the foothills of the South Downs. They were soft, undulating hills compared to the more dramatic Pembrokeshire coastline of home, but they were hills nonetheless. Besides, Katie had moved here first and persuaded her it was worth leaving London for the sight of green fields every morning. Mind you, that was before Katie had gone all 'desperate housewife'. Now she frequently referred to Thurfield as a fishbowl, and Emily got the impression that her friend missed the bright city lights.

There was laughter coming from the lounge. Loud, raucous laughter – the sound of lads mucking about. Oh, God. Callum had done it again. Decided to bring his mates back to hers. She only hoped they weren't shoving white stuff up their noses. He hadn't done it in her home yet, but she couldn't be sure he wouldn't. Callum liked to live dangerously.

Which of course was part of the original appeal. She still had to pinch herself that someone as hot as Callum was interested in her, the original wallflower. Emily's teenage years had been punctuated by watching her friends cop off with all the good-looking guys, while she, knowing her place as a plain Jane, was left with the dorks. So when Marion introduced her to Callum at a PR bash and he showed an interest in her – Emily Four-Eyes (an epithet from youth which she could never quite shake off despite having worn contacts for years) Henderson – she was unable to resist. Even though she knew he was spinning lines. Even though he spelled trouble with every single one of them. There was something about Callum which was just that – irresistible.

Which is how he came into her life. And somehow remained there, never progressing beyond the Occasional Screw label Emily had given him from their early days of courtship. If courtship was what it could be called. Callum had never met her parents. Nor she his. They didn't even see each other on a weekly basis. He had yet to remember a birthday or Valentine's, although he was always charmingly apologetic every time he forgot. And it was difficult not to respond to the dozen red roses that would appear like magic.

Their relationship, such as it was, consisted of Callum calling up occasionally and Emily falling gratefully at his feet, ridiculously pleased by the occasional pearl he dropped before her. Christ, she was pathetic. She knew he was no good for her. Not long term. And not now, when her body clock was beginning to tick rather too loudly for comfort. While in her wildest fantasies she imagined how Callum would react joyfully if she told him she was pregnant, Emily was far too much of a realist not to know this was a pipe dream. And the more she tried to conjure up pictures in her head of Callum holding a baby à la Athena man, the less she was able to envisage it. She had to face it – she wanted a suitable dad, and Callum wasn't it.

Reluctantly, she pushed open the lounge door to find Callum with his two side-kicks, Jez and Danny, roaring with laughter at – jeez, what were they watching? Emily didn't like to stare, but it seemed to involve animals and naked people. Lots of naked people. It was compelling in an utterly gross kind of way. Someone had spilt beer over one of the cream sofa cushions. There was a fuggy smell of smoke in the air. Smoke with a very definite scent. Shit, he wouldn't have, would he?

'Hey, babe,' said Callum, drawing on a spliff. Apparently he would.

Callum always said Emily was over-anxious about his pot-smoking, but she was a lawyer. She knew dope was the least of Callum's vices but she squared it with herself that if he wasn't taking drugs in her house, then what he did in his own wasn't her business.

'Callum, what the fuck are you up to?' Emily was furious. It was late. They'd trashed her lounge and the three of them were giggling inanely at her. She didn't have the energy for this.

'Just brought Jez and Danny back for a quick drink,' said Callum. 'I didn't think you'd mind.'

'Well, I do,' said Emily shortly, ignoring Jez and Danny's muffled giggles and snorts of, 'Get her!'

'Right, you two, out,' she yelled.

'Don't be such a spoilsport.' Callum turned his smile on her. That devastating smile that usually worked so well. But not tonight. Tonight she'd had enough.

'Callum, I've had a long day, I've got an early start, and I need my beauty sleep,' protested Emily.

'Too right you do,' sniggered Jez, who was immediately stopped dead with an icy look.

'Just go, will you,' said Emily tiredly. 'All of you. I need to go to bed.'

'Me too,' said Callum.

'Alone,' said Emily. 'I'll call you all a cab and you can just piss off home. I've warned you, Callum. I cannot have you smoking dope in my flat.'

'You know your problem, babe,' said Callum as he eventually swaggered out of the door. 'You take things too seriously.'

'And you don't take them seriously enough,' said Emily. 'Now go, before–'

'Before what? You change your mind and say I can stay?' He was like a puppy begging for a treat. It was hard to remind herself why she was angry with him, but for once Emily wasn't in the mood for giving in.

'No, I might say something I'd regret. Now go on, get out of here,' she said, practically pushing him out of the door before she weakened.

She slammed it behind her and heard the main door of the apartment block bang shut with a final clang.

Dammit! She was not going to go on like this with Callum taking advantage of her. She was going to take control of her life and start making some changes.

Emily walked slowly into the lounge and stared in dismay at the chaos in front of her. She was too tired to deal with it now, she'd sort it out in the morning.

Take control of her life? She couldn't even take control of her lounge.

CHAPTER TWO

'Mark, you have to take the girls in for me.' Mark had been shaving on Monday morning when the doorbell rang and he found Sam and the kids at the front door.

'But I'll be late for work,' Mark protested. Why the hell did Sam always do this to him?

'And so will I. My boss has called an urgent meeting and I have to get up to town.' Sam worked up in town for an American-based cosmetic surgery company called Smile, Please! It was a far cry from her humble beginnings as a dental nurse, but presumably the pay and perks were what she'd been after all along. The downside, as far as Mark was concerned, was that as he worked locally, she felt the school run was his God-given duty.

'Besides,' as she frequently told him, 'you owe me. I stayed at home all those years with the kids. Now it's my turn.'

Quite why it being 'my turn' meant she could behave like a selfish prima donna, Mark hadn't yet worked out, but knowing she could get arsy about access if he complained too much, he went along with it.

'Remind me again why Gemma needs a lift?' Mark asked. 'I used to cycle to school at her age.' Gemma, at thirteen, was more than capable of getting to school under her own steam. Her school was at the other end of town from Beth's which meant a round trip of half an hour. There was no way he was going to make it to work on time.

'We're not in the Dark Ages now, Dad,' muttered Gemma from underneath her dark spiky fringe.

Sam gave him a withering look.

'Gemma's right,' she said. 'You do live in the past. Things are different now. It's not safe for kids to cycle. Or walk. There all sorts of weirdoes about. She just wouldn't be safe on her own.'

And it's nothing to do with you worrying that Gemma can't be trusted to actually go into school, is it? Mark thought to himself. Sam would never admit it, but Gemma was probably the candidate for the kid most likely to bunk off school, but she was also very clear that she had no intention of going to prison. Taking her in every day meant Sam knew Gemma actually got there.

Sam dashed off in a flurry of citrus perfume and self-importance while Mark went to finish shaving and ring Diana, his wonderfully efficient area manager, to say he'd be late. Then he bundled the kids into the car and drove as quickly as possible to Gemma's school.

He watched her going in (if Gemma did bunk off, he didn't want Sam accusing him of negligence), shoulders hunched, head down, bag slung loosely over her shoulder, presenting a glowering miserable presence, as befitted a child of the emo generation, and wondered with dismay what had happened to his cute little girl. Cute, Gemma definitely was not now, with her punky hair style, dyed a different colour every week – Mark frequently pointed out to her that what she thought was groundbreaking was in fact only the style his girlfriends had adopted twenty years previously, but he was always silenced with 'Whatever, Dad. It's just different now. You wouldn't understand.'

No, of course not. To Gemma, he'd never been young.

Once Gemma had been dispatched it was on to school with Beth. An entirely different proposition. Though she was ten, Beth was still cuddly enough to remind him of what he enjoyed about fatherhood, and not yet too embarrassed to kiss him goodbye. He felt vaguely guilty about comparing his children, but it was restful to be with Beth, whose sunny disposition made a nice contrast to Gemma's spikiness.

Then he drove like a maniac to the surgery. Despite the phone call to Diana, Mark still felt stressed. He hated being late and he hoped that anyone waiting wouldn't be too grumpy – some of his patients had a tendency to think that, as their dentist, his sole function in life was to be ready and waiting for them at all times. The fact that he might have an existence, a family, a life even outside the narrow confines of his surgery seemed to be beyond them.

Mark squeezed his ageing Volvo into the one remaining parking space outside the surgery and got out to the distinctive wail of the alarm going off. Oh great. That was all he needed.

He ran into the surgery and found Maya standing looking a little helpless, while three patients sat around, pained.

'I'm so sorry,' she said. 'I was here first and there were patients waiting so I opened the door, but I had forgotten about the alarm and I don't know the code.' Mark keyed in the right number and thankfully the alarm fell silent. It wasn't Maya's fault, she'd only started working at the practise two weeks ago, and as a newly qualified dentist it shouldn't be her job to make sure the surgery was open on time. That's why they had a practise manageress. Talking of which—

'Where the bloody hell is Kerry?' said Mark.

Maya shrugged her shoulders.

'I was the first one here,' she said.

There was no sign of either of the nurses that were supposed to be working with them today. Mark sighed. It was going to be one of those days.

He apologised to the bemused patients sitting in the waiting room, answered the phone to Lorna's mum, whose defiant explanation that Lorna had a stomach ache, 'innit?' didn't fool him for a second, and called in the first of his patients.

By the time he'd seen the second, Kerry had swanned in breezily.

'Sorry, I'm late, the trains were bad.'

'But you drive,' replied Mark.

'Oh not today. I was out last night,' she leered lasciviously and bent down over the desk to reveal a rather lacy thong peeping out of a somewhat less than sexy behind. It was more then a man could take first thing in the morning.

'I think that's what you call a whale tail,' whispered Maya, who had come out to get her next patient.

Mark snorted, before insisting that Kerry went and nursed for Maya who needed the help more than he did. While he was phoning Diana, who unfortunately today was working at another surgery, to get her to find some cover for them, Sasha walked in. Sasha, their latest recruit, seemed to be the only eastern European in the country who didn't understand the value of hard work. Mark considered admonishing her, but mindful that there were still patients in the waiting room, and aware that she probably wouldn't understand him anyway, decided that, like much of his life, there really was no point.

He looked down at his day roster to see what else lay in store for him, and groaned out loud. Jasmine Symonds – a so-called celebrity who was famous for shagging on some god-awful reality TV show and, if the rumours were true, the new face of Smile, Please! – was coming in. It was one more indication that someone somewhere didn't like him. Not only had Jasmine and her ghastly mother Kayla been his patients for years, but despite her new-found fame she wouldn't go to the dentist anywhere else. Trust him to have the misfortune to have Jasmine as his most loyal patient . . .

*   *   *

Katie Caldwell stood at the school gates and watched her eldest son, George, walk mournfully away from her. It cut her heart to the quick to watch his misery and be unable to help. But what could she do when any questions about what was upsetting him were just met with a shrug? George had been in a foul mood this morning, still sore about the fact that he'd spent the previous day at football on the subs bench – again. He and Jake had both been peculiarly reticent about why George, the team's best striker, seemed to spend more time off the pitch than on it, but Katie had the deepest suspicion that there was something Jake wasn't telling her. It wouldn't be the first time.

She sighed, and kissed her younger son, Aidan, goodbye. At least she had no worries on that score. Aidan was a happy-go-lucky child who rarely cried and seemed to shrug off life's slings and arrows with an insouciance she envied, and which she longed for her older, more sensitive son.

'Jake been winding them up at football again?' Katie turned away from waving Aidan goodbye to see the tall shadow of Mandy Allwick, school gossip extraordinaire, framed in the early morning sunshine. That was all she needed.

'What do you mean?' Katie squinted up at Mandy. Why did she always feel so wrong-footed when Mandy was about?

'Oh, you know Jake,' Mandy laughed heartily. 'He's always giving that poncey coach a mouthful. And quite right too. That guy goes on and on about being fair to all the kids when it's obvious that your George is one of the best players. And your Jake is only sticking up for George.'

'How exactly is Jake sticking up for George?' Katie

had a sinking feeling in her stomach. What had Jake done now? Katie had given up going to football when Molly arrived, using the excuse that it was too cold to be out with a baby, but really it was because she couldn't stand the embarrassment anymore of listening to Jake's roars of disappointment from the touchline when George missed a sitter or succumbed to a tackle.

'Only doing what any dad should,' said Mandy. 'Shouting for George, yelling at the opposition. It's what me and Craig always do.'

I bet you do, thought Katie.

'It's that arse Jonathan who's at fault,' Mandy continued as they made their way out of the school grounds.

'How so?' asked Katie, thinking poor bloody Jonathan, someone has to stand up to the hecklers.

'Oh, you know what he's like,' said Mandy tossing her long fair mane back. 'He goes on and on about not being too competitive and not putting pressure on our kids. But the way we all see it, it's a competitive world, innit? They've got to learn sometime.'

Have they? thought Katie. *Do they* have *to learn this way?*

'So why was George put on the subs bench?' Katie asked, but deep down she knew what the answer would be.

'Jonathan said your Jake was putting the other players off, and George was taken off as a punishment.'

Katie frowned. It didn't seem at all fair to George to make him suffer for Jake's bad behaviour. But then it wasn't the first time Jonathan had warned Jake off.

But Jake would be bound to shrug it off if she raised the subject. Maybe it was time she started going to football again.

A squawk from the buggy indicated that Molly was getting fed up, so Katie made her excuses and slowly pushed her way home with a heavy heart.

*   *   *

Emily arrived into work late. She'd spent the night at Callum's flat, despite her best intentions. But weekends on her own in Thurfield were so lonely. She could have gone to see Katie but she felt she'd imposed on Katie's friendship too much of late. Besides, despite acknowledging to herself the meanness of the thought, Emily couldn't help feeling a twinge of jealousy when she spent time in Katie's perfect house with her perfect family. It only highlighted the complete and utter mess her own life had become.

The trouble was, Emily thought moodily, she was always so busy at work and her weekday social life revolved around London, so that at the weekend there was nothing for her to do at home. Or rather, there was plenty. If only she had someone to do it with, she'd be going on long walks or cycle rides round the Downs, visiting the theatre, going out for meals. Normal stuff. Like other people did.

Instead of which she was practically chained to her desk and when she wasn't there, she was out late schmoozing people she was coming to despise, or partying like there was no tomorrow with so-called friends with whom she had little in common.

When Callum deigned to let her, she was allowed

into his world, in small bite-sized pieces. He had perfected the knack of just about keeping her interested. She hated herself for giving in to him.

Take this weekend for instance. She had resolutely ignored his calls all day Friday, cried off a party that Marion was going to, claiming a headache, and crashed out in front of the TV with a pizza and a bottle of wine.

But come Saturday, after a desultory morning spent catching up on household chores, and a dull afternoon trailing round the shops in Crawley, Emily had let herself into the flat to find three messages from Callum on the answerphone. When she switched on her mobile (which she had purposely left behind), she discovered he'd inundated her with messages. In the end, she'd given in and driven over to his flat where they had made up over a bottle of wine, before dancing the night away at a local grungy club Callum and his less salubrious friends liked to frequent. He hadn't taken any drugs in her presence, which wasn't to say that he hadn't taken any at all, but it was enough for her to maintain the fiction that all was right with the world.

They had got up late on Sunday, gone for a pub lunch and though Emily had known she should really have headed back home on Sunday evening, she couldn't face the thought of a lonely night in and had been persuaded to stay another night. Hence why she was now so late.

Her nerves were jangling as she walked through the door. Luckily her boss was also late which allowed Emily enough time to get herself a latte and calm down before she started work. Emily sat down to a pile of paper-work, opened her emails to find there were still hundreds she hadn't responded to from last week, and groaned loudly. She could feel another late one coming on. It was too bad they were so short-staffed, but at least if she worked late she wouldn't have time to dwell too hard.

'Jasmine Symonds is here.' Sasha managed to display disdain in her whole body. Mark didn't approve of Jasmine much either, but she was a patient and had to be seen.

'So that tooth we root-treated last time is still giving you gip?' Mark asked once Jasmine was ensconced on his dental chair. Her crop top was hitched halfway over her stomach and her hipster jeans sagged below it. She had less of a muffin top, and more of a double choco-late gateau . . . God, it amazed him that someone so foul-mouthed, foully dressed and generally appalling as Jasmine could be deemed worthy of being in the public eye. Once upon a time people actually *did* some-thing worthwhile to be famous. Not any more.

'Too right it is,' whined Jasmine. 'It's bloody painful all the time. Those antibiotics were useless.'

'You do realise that if I can't sort it out this time, I shall have to take the tooth out,' Mark said.

'No way!' Jasmine was horrified.

'I'm sorry,' said Mark, a little nonplussed. 'I did warn you.'

'You can't mess with my teeth,' shrieked Jasmine. 'I've got a contract which says my teeth are all me own.'

'She's got a contract,' growled Jasmine's mother from the sofa. Kayla followed Jasmine everywhere and, Rottweiler-like, was always on hand to defend her daughter's interests.

'Well, if you want a second opinion . . .' This was Mark's get-out clause for all his difficult patients. Sadly, Jasmine had never yet taken him up on the offer and she wasn't about to now.

'Oh, go on then,' she said sulkily.

Mark felt his way round Jasmine's mouth. Despite her brilliant white smile, her teeth were shot to pieces. The dazzling grin covered a multitude of sins to all except her dentist. The rate Jasmine was carrying on, it wouldn't be too long before he provided her with dentures. He prodded around for a while. Jasmine responded when he poked the molar two doors down, but the tooth she was moaning about didn't evince a single response. Which meant it was dead as a door-nail.

'I'm really sorry,' he said. 'Your tooth's dead. I'm going to have to pull it out.'

'You can't!' Jasmine shrieked.

'What about her contract?' Kayla demanded. 'You must be able to do something.'

'I'm touched by your faith in me,' said Mark, knowing that sarcasm was completely wasted on these two, 'but even I can't work miracles.'

Jasmine winced dramatically as he gave her the strongest injection he could. Her pain threshold was low and this was a back tooth which would take a fair amount of work to get out. Mark toyed with asking Sasha for the right instruments but as she leant back against the sink, looking bored and playing with her nails between taking text messages (even though he had asked her hundreds of times not to), he figured in the time it would take to explain what he needed, he could have got it all himself. One day, God would take pity on him and send him a decent nurse.

'I can't lose a tooth,' Jasmine wailed. She was clearly not going to take this lying down. 'What about my contract?'

'I'm very sorry,' he said. 'But the tooth is dead, so it's got to come out. I'll make you a bridging unit, which I'll attach to the adjacent teeth. No one will ever know the difference.'

'Are you sure?' Jasmine eyed him suspiciously. 'What if someone finds out?'

'No one will find out,' said Mark. 'Your records are completely confidential.'

'You're sure about that?' the Rottweiler jumped in, looking uncertain.

'Yes,' said Mark. 'Now I have to do something about this tooth. I can't leave it like this.'

Eventually Jasmine agreed. Luckily, the tooth came out relatively easily, and Mark took some impressions for her crown.

'What if someone sees the gap?' Jasmine demanded as she got down from the chair.

'It's pretty unlikely,' said Mark, 'it's a back tooth, no one is likely to be looking. You could always try not to be photographed for a bit.'

Which was as unlikely as him getting back with Sam, he realised. Jasmine was always splashed over one tabloid or another.

'You'd better be right,' Jasmine said, 'or there'll be trouble.'

'I'll bear it in mind,' said Mark, before showing Jasmine and Kayla out to the desk where Kerry was chatting animatedly to Tony, Jasmine's third-division footballer boyfriend. Jasmine shot Kerry a dirty look, clicked her fingers at Tony and swept out imperiously, leaving Kayla to pay. Mark made a mental note to remind Kerry that it wasn't done to flirt with the patients before calling his next patient.

Great. It was Mrs O'Leary, or Granny O'Leary as the girls had christened her, an ancient crone and tooth-less wonder who clung to the ill-fitting dentures that her original butcher of a dentist had given her eons ago.

Mark reflected that he must have done something *really* bad in a previous life to deserve Jasmine and Granny O'Leary on the same day. But he couldn't for the life of him think what.

CHAPTER THREE

'Why didn't you tell me that George was on the subs bench because you were shouting so much?' Katie demanded as Jake came through the door, late from work – again. She was worn down by a hard day coping with the kids. The boys had been really naughty at bedtime and Molly had only just gone to sleep. The kitchen was still in chaos from tea, and she hadn't managed to even get into the lounge yet to tidy up. Katie admitted she was a control freak extraordinaire and always wanted everything to be perfect; Anthea Turner looked like a slut in comparison. It was hard work maintaining her standards but, by and large, until Molly had come along she had managed it. But of late she could feel those standards slipping.

'What's for tea?' Jake ignored her question. She hated it when he did that.

'Haven't got there yet,' was the short response.

Oh?' Jake evinced a pained surprise. 'You always used to have tea ready for me.'

'Well, that was before we had Molly,' snapped Katie.

'You were the one who wanted three kids,' Jake threw back at her. Bloody hell! He could always get her there. It was true, Jake hadn't been keen on a third child for precisely the reason that he had thought Katie *wouldn't* cope. She'd persuaded him she could. She wondered wistfully if Molly had been the catalyst for all their current problems and then just as quickly batted away the thought. Molly was beautiful – she wouldn't be without her for a second.

Jake had touched a nerve, damn him. In the past Katie *would* have had the house tidy and tea on the table when Jake walked in. To her that was part of the deal. She was the one at home after all, it only seemed reasonable to cook the bacon for the person who provided it.

Emily had never understood that attitude. 'It just seems so regressive,' she'd said to Katie during one of their frequent conversations about it over a glass of wine when Jake was away on business.

Katie had shrugged her shoulders.

'I don't expect you to understand,' she'd said. 'But if you knew my mum, you would. She put her career above everything: her marriage, her family. It tore our family apart. I'm never going to do that.'

Katie had had feminism shoved down her throat from an early age and was sufficiently her mother's daughter to buy into the career dream, until she'd met and fallen for Jake. The minute she knew she wanted to have children with him was the day Katie said goodbye to her career. She was not going to make the same mistakes as her mum. Her children and husband would always come first. The trouble was

504

no one had told her how hard that would be.

'Let me know when it's ready,' said Jake. 'I've just got to go online and check some deals out.'

'What, now?' Katie was dismayed. Jake's job as financial director of a rapidly expanding firm was beginning to take over their life. He seemed to be away on business more then he was home at the moment.

'Five minutes, tops,' he said, heading for the stairs.

Katie sighed. The chances were she wouldn't see him for another hour.

'What was that you were saying about George?' Jake paused halfway up the stairs.

'Nothing,' replied Katie. There was no point trying to have the conversation now when Jake wasn't the slightest bit interested. 'I'll just get on with the tea.'

'Ok,' said Jake. 'You'd better make sure it's a healthy one.'

'What's that supposed to mean?' Katie was stung into responding. She had a feeling she knew where this was going. Jake had been muttering snide comments about her weight for weeks now.

'Oh nothing,' said Jake.

'Don't do that,' retorted Katie. 'Tell me what you meant.'

Jake had the grace to look a little embarrassed. 'Well, you have to face it love, you're looking a bit more cuddly these days. I mean, after the boys you lost weight much more quickly.'

It was true, she had. In the past she had managed to shed the baby weight in a few months, but this time around it wouldn't budge.

'Are you saying I'm fat?'

'Nooo – not fat exactly, but you have to admit, babe, you are a tad on the lardy side. Nothing that a few weeks on a diet won't cure.'

The comment was delivered in a manner that was clearly intended to be light and humorous, but the result was anything but.

Katie stood open-mouthed as Jake disappeared upstairs. He thought she was lardy. Once he'd thought she was sexy. When had this changed? When she'd become the mother of his children? Could he not separate the two roles, wife and mother? Not for the first time she wondered if workload was the thing that really kept him late at the office . . .